PENDANT OF DRAGONS BOOK FOUR

THE UNCERTAIN ROAD

K. ISABELLA FROST

Printed in Australia
First Printing, 2022
ISBN: 978-0-6484104-1-6

White Light Publishing

For Kade, my real-life Guardian and first love.

Acknowledgements

Of all the books in the *Pendant of Dragons* series, none were harder to write than this one. *The Uncertain Road* truly lived up to its name as I wrote it, especially with how different a book it ultimately turned out to be while still being familiar to the series. To write as both a character I know well and a character I haven't written as before was a real challenge. I can only hope that I've captured Carden's inner core and heart as well as I could. There is nothing harder than facing the challenge of lost love than perhaps having to undergo a quest to reclaim it. So many people do that every day while in the middle of terrible circumstances. Especially at this time that I write this, I know all of us face great turmoil with the state of the world. But that is what Guardians do. They are the protectors, the ones who make their oath to do what must be done and at great personal sacrifice.

So, to start with, I want to thank all the everyday heroes like law enforcement, medical professionals and food producers for keeping us all going.

Thank you then, as always, to my parents, Lynne and Kevin, and to my siblings Patrick, Jess and David. I'm so glad to be a part of this family. To my godparents, Sandy and Charlie Ponchard, and their kids, Daniel and Sarah. Your support is always invaluable.

To my fellow creatives alike who have read sections of my work and to a few close friends who have allowed me to test my work by reading it to them. Thank you so much for your input. And a big thank you to Lauren Kelly, Julia Van Der Sluys and Karen McDermott for your faith in me and my work as well as your dedication towards helping me print, publish and release each of these novels. Without you, these books would still be simple MS Word documents sitting on my computer going unread. And to Kade Everett whose protective nature and unwavering determination inspired Carden's character.

A big thank you to the wonderful teachers, practitioners, and students of Mystical Dragon for your wonderful support and the knowledge I have gained through your courses. Especially to the lovely Jennifer Valente who has guided me with patience and kindness for so many years now. Your advice and support have kept me going in some of my darkest times, so thank you so much. And a thank you to fellow author and wonderful mystical practitioner Lucy Cavendish for her inspiring reading that helped me so much and for her shared knowledge into the magical realms. Without you and your work, I would never have come to know and understand the true nature and magic of the world and the beings within these pages.

Finally, to the readers. Thank you for opening these pages and continuing the story with the Princess and her companions. May you enjoy the journey of this darker tale of love lost and the sacrifices needed to save a soul.

- K. Isabella Frost

Contents

Preface

~ Carden ~

The choice had been offered to me, the decision mine alone. As I stood before the ancient being cloaked in the darkness of everlasting death, I felt the difficulty of my decision yet to be made.

I turned my eyes down to her, seeing her beautiful, pale features; her chest as unmoving as I had known it to be in all these months now past. Remarkable that she could be so untouched by time's passage in her death when all others would decay and fade.

Of course you would stay beautiful, my sweet, wonderful girl. You were always the purest of us.

I considered the choice before me, fearing what it would mean. She would live, but I would have to give up my life for her to do so; a thought that left my heart aching.

She will be without me as I have been without her. The Daemon was right. No matter what, we will still be apart. But at least she'll have a chance to live a normal life. How can I deny her that?

A sigh slid free as I came to my decision. For Leander I would give anything at all - my life, my body, my soul - just so she would live once again. I could never deny my soul mate, especially now that there was a chance to save her...

~ Leander ~

To enter the Realm of Death is no easy thing when it is not your time, but harder still when love is blooming in your life. I realised then as I stood in those snows that this was truer than any other truth I had known in my life. Besides that of my everlasting heart.

Because of him, my life was returning, my breath my own again and my wounds closed. And though my heart ached at leaving behind all those I had loved and lost to Azmerath's watchful care, I couldn't deny my desire to return to my love's arms.

This is right. I know it is. Carden is my soul mate, my true love... I belong with him in the Living World. That is what I want most.

I looked to my old friend, smiling softly as he gave me the same in return.

"Go to him, my girl," he said, his rough voice strangely gentle, his dark eyes softening. "You belong not in this kingdom, but in the one you should rule with him."

"I'm scared," I confessed, looking up at him and feeling a tremble fill me.

"Returning to Life's Light is always frightening," he replied gently. "Yet, you return to his embrace. Do not be afraid, Leander..."

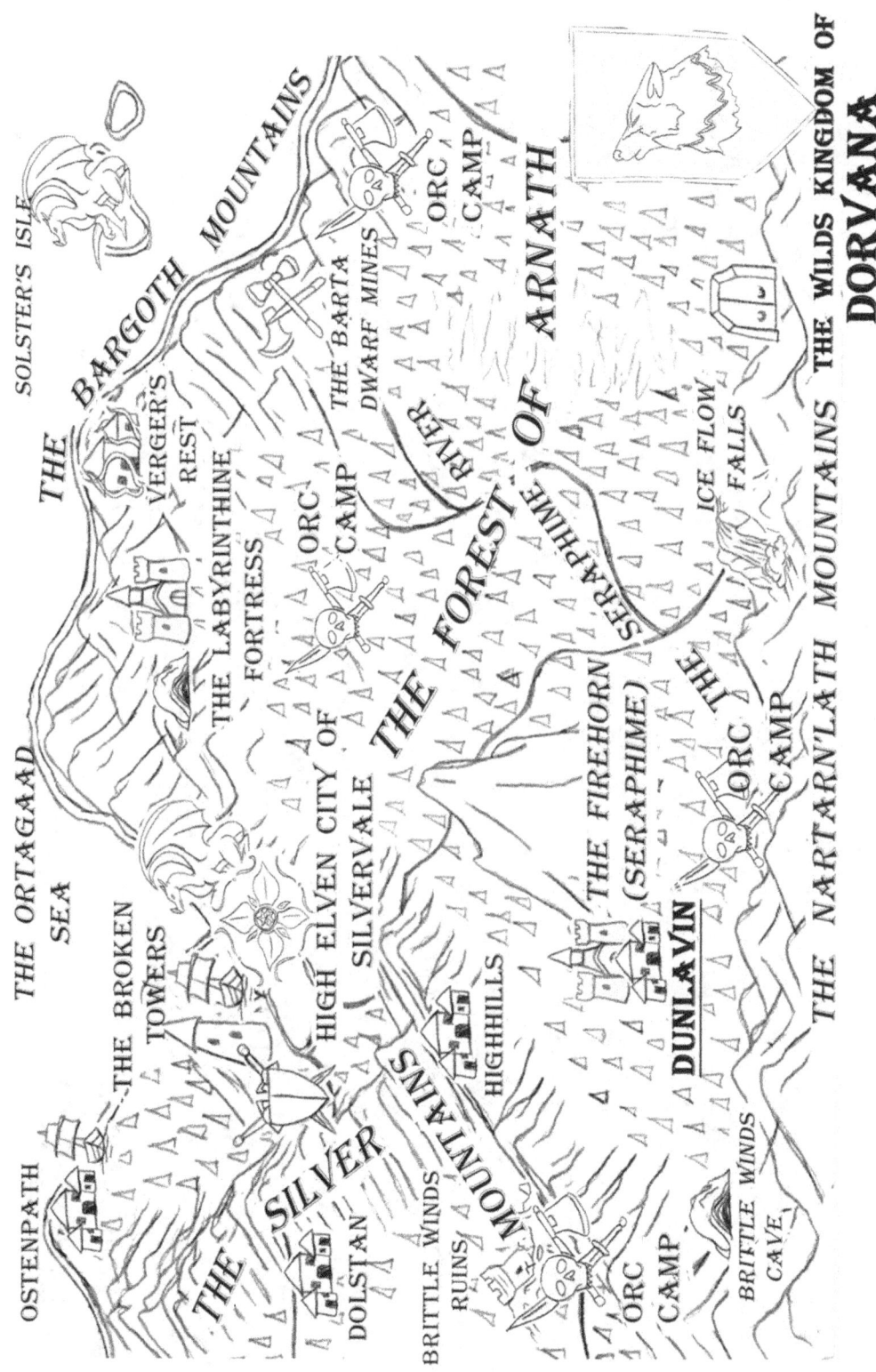

THE WILDS KINGDOM OF

DORVANA

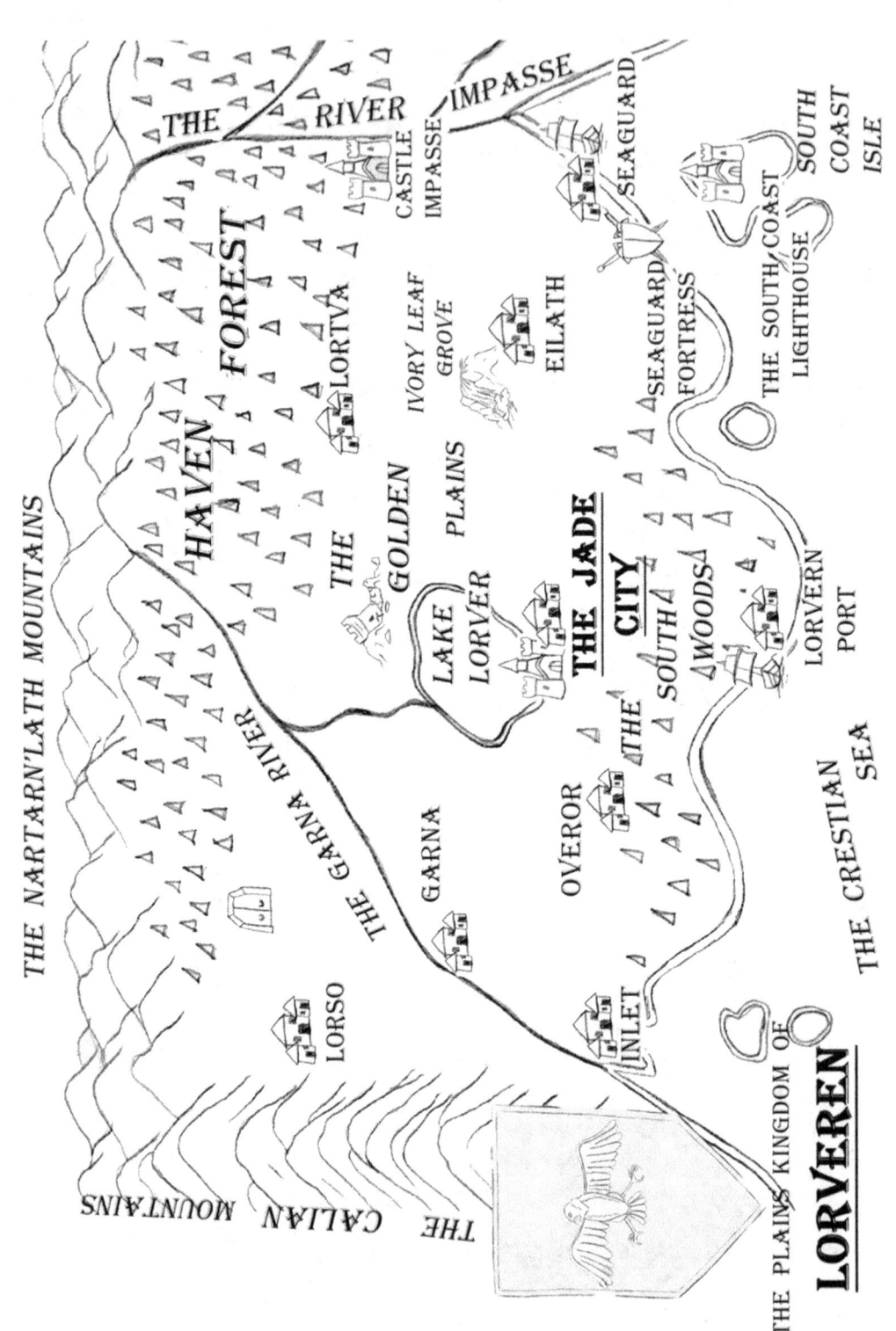

THE NARTARN'LATH MOUNTAINS

THE RIVER IMPASSE

CASTLE IMPASSE

SEAGUARD

SOUTH COAST ISLE

HAVEN FOREST

LORTVA

IVORY LEAF GROVE

EILATH

SEAGUARD FORTRESS

THE SOUTH COAST LIGHTHOUSE

THE GOLDEN PLAINS

LAKE LORVER

THE JADE CITY

SOUTH WOODS

LORVERN PORT

THE GARNA RIVER

GARNA

OVEROR

THE

LORSO

INLET

THE CALIAN MOUNTAINS

THE CRESTIAN SEA

THE PLAINS KINGDOM OF LORVEREN

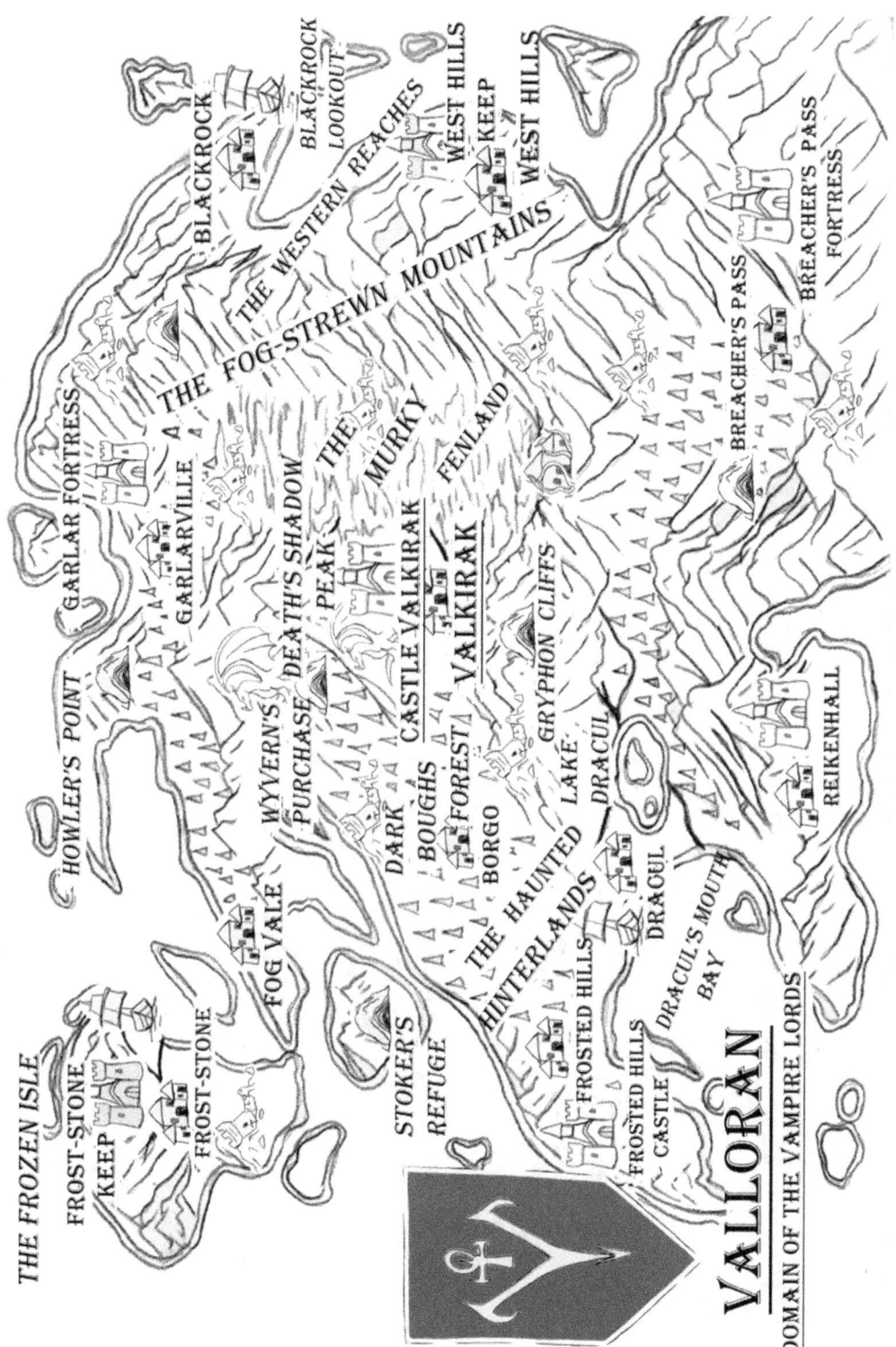

THE FROZEN ISLE

FROST-STONE KEEP

FROST-STONE

STOKER'S REFUGE

HOWLER'S POINT

GARLAR FORTRESS

GARLARVILLE

BLACKROCK

BLACKROCK LOOKOUT

THE WESTERN REACHES

THE FOG-STREWN MOUNTAINS

WEST HILLS KEEP

WEST HILLS

BREACHER'S PASS

BREACHER'S PASS FORTRESS

WYVERN'S PURCHASE

DEATH'S SHADOW PEAK

THE MURKY FENLAND

CASTLE VALKIRAK

VALKIRAK

FOG VALE

DARK BOUGHS

FOREST BORGO

GRYPHON CLIFFS

THE HAUNTED LAKE

DRACUL

REIKENHALL

HINTERLANDS

FROSTED HILLS

FROSTED HILLS CASTLE

DRACUL'S MOUTH BAY

DRACUL

VALLORAN

DOMAIN OF THE VAMPIRE LORDS

13

Chapter One
In the Kingdom of Death

~ Leander ~

The sun shone brightly from behind the clouds, the grasses smelling sweet with Spring's arrival. The bluebirds were chattering and singing as they fluttered and flitted about in their graceful dance as chipmunks scurried to and fro beneath a tree. They skittered away as I passed them by. I giggled happily, running with my dress hems in my hands, skipping over a few rocks as I turned to my sister.

"Catch me, Aislinn!" I continued to giggle.

"Leander, slow down!" Aislinn called, trying to keep up with me, her right hand clutching her dress hem, so she didn't fall. "Do not run so far ahead!"

"Catch me!" I kept running.

I ran down the small hill by the river, passing by the farms as I went. I looked back through my dark auburn hair at her, still giggling as she ran to the top of the hill and started after me.

The fields were full of wheat now, golden brown and waving gently in the warm breeze. It was always so easy for me to run and hide in there, being so much smaller than my sister.

Ducking into the crop as a farmer chuckled with his hoe over his shoulder, I hid low and watched for my sister. Aislinn came to a stop, looking around, her blue eyes searching for me, her long hair tied back to keep it from her face.

"Your Highness," the farmer nodded to her as he went about his work.

"Good farmer," she turned to him respectfully. "Please, tell me, have you seen my sister?"

"The little princess?" he asked, glancing at where I hid. "Why, I do believe I saw her pass this way, your Highness."

I pushed my way out of the wheat and jumped with my arms up, trying to roar like a dragon.

Aislinn feigned fear, swaying and laying her hand on her forehead. "Oh no! The fearsome dragon has frightened me to fainting!" she fell to the ground as the farmer laughed lightly at us.

I ran to her side and poked her shoulder. "I got you, I got you!"

"No!" she launched forward, grabbing me, and pulling me down into her arms. "I've got *you*, little dragon!"

"Aislinn!" I squealed at her fingers' rapid wiggling against my sides. "You're tickling me! Stop!"

I giggled and squirmed as she kept her furious tickle attack going, grinning widely at me. Lucky for me, my big sister was never too hard on me, and she soon eased her tickling to let me catch my breath.

"You're such a little pain, Leander," she smiled, pushing my arm so that I fell over. "But you're my favourite pain."

I crawled to my knees; my blue dress stained a little with the green of grass. I looked at her as she sat back, lounging on her arms in the grassy field, her eyes to the sky.

"Let's play another game!" I pleaded happily. "Oh please, Aislinn, please?!"

She looked to me, sighing breathlessly. "How is it that someone as tiny as you can be so energetic?"

I shrugged. "I like playing."

She rolled her eyes, brushing a few strands of her dark brown hair from her face.

"Okay," she said. "What do you want to play, little sister?"

"Hide and seek!" I exclaimed excitedly.

"Really?" she groaned, exhaustion in her eyes.

"You're so good at finding me," I told her, hoping to persuade her with my sweetness. "Please, Aislinn?"

"Oh, all right," she agreed, then pointed her finger at me. "But *no* wandering off. I don't want to have to go running back to the castle to have Ser Mithras send out a search party like last time."

"I was in the larder," I huffed, folding my arms as I narrowed my eyes at her. "You didn't look hard enough to find me."

"You strayed too far from me, little sister," she retorted, shaking her head. "While I am glad to have found you in the castle, our game started by the river."

"Okay," I agreed with a sigh. "I won't go too far. I promise."

"Good girl," she smiled. "All right, you go hide and I'll count to ten."

"To twenty!" I giggled, jumping to my feet and running from her.

"Twenty?" she frowned incredulously.

I stopped and nodded back at her. "I get more of a head start that way!"

"Oh... very well then," she covered her eyes. "One... Two... Three..."

I didn't think of my sister's warnings, even though her seventeen winters gave her more knowledge than my eight so far. All I thought of was finding the perfect place to hide myself and surprise her. But soon my giggling faded, and my excitement left me as I slowed down from my running pace. I didn't know this part of Arvon, the trees looking dark and tall, the dirt road littered with leaves as the branches reached up above me to create a green and brown ceiling over the road.

My breaths were hitching now, my chest heaving as I slowly wandered forward. *I don't know where I am... I'm lost... Oh no... I'm lost!*

I was beginning to panic, feeling like I could start to cry, but I wouldn't. I was brave, just like Mithras. That was why he had just started teaching me how to use a sword. I had to be brave if I was like him and my father.

My feet crunched the earth as I walked, coming very slowly to the end of the long road. I stared back over my shoulder at it through my long dark hair. It looked like a place where monsters would lurk in the shadows and come looking for little children like me.

I was getting ever more scared with each moment now. I just wanted my sister to find me, the game no fun anymore.

"Aislinn!" I called, holding my hands up on either side of mouth, hoping to make my voice louder. "Aislinn, where are you?! Aislinn!"

Slowly, I wandered into a clearing, pausing as I came to an old cottage. It sat there by the banks of the River Arvon, rundown and abandoned. There wasn't anyone living there, and I had never heard anyone speak of it before. I had to be outside of the town's borders, though how far exactly I wasn't sure.

I crept up onto the old porch, leaning my hand on the doorframe and peering inside.

"Hello?" I called in my small voice into the darkened house, but only the echo returned to me.

I thought about going inside to see if there was anyone there, but I knew better than to do that. My mother and father would be furious if I fell through the floor and got hurt.

Quietly, I turned away, my eyes falling on a figure standing by a tree. She was staying in the shadows of the old oak. *Maybe she can help me!*

I moved towards the woman, a little uneasy as I realised that she wore a black and deep purple dress beneath a black cloak. Her hood was up to cover her face, her hands twitching at her sides with long black nails that looked like claws.

"Why, hello there, little one," she said, her voice wispy and hoarse as if her throat were sore.

"H-hello," I murmured, tightly holding my hands together against my flat chest, feeling the soft fabric of my dress as I looked nervously up at her.

"How odd it is to see such a pretty little girl wandering alone so far from the town," she mused, looking down at me from under her hood.

"I'm... I'm not alone," I said shyly, hiding under my hair and glancing through the strands.

"Are you not?" she asked.

I shook my head. "My big sister is with me. She's seventeen."

"Really?" the woman smiled her purple painted lips at me. "And how old are you, little one?"

"I'm eight," I said, shrugging.

"Eight years old?" she pretended to be impressed. "My, you are quite the adventurer for your age. Aren't you, my little one?"

"I... I shouldn't... talk to you," I said, taking a step back.

"Why is that?" she frowned at me, her eyes just barely visible beneath her cowl.

"My... my father says I shouldn't talk to strangers," I replied.

"Your father is a very wise man," she agreed with a nod. "But I am no stranger. I have watched over you since you were but a babe."

I frowned at her curiously. "Are you a faerie?"

Her lips curled into a strange smile of amusement. "Yes, child. I am a faerie... Your faerie godmother, in fact. So, you see, I am no stranger..."

I didn't believe her, even as young as I was. Something just didn't feel right about this.

"I... I need to go home now," I said, turning and trying to move away.

Her claw-like hand closed tight around my small arm, holding me in place. I looked up at her fearfully, trying to pull my arm loose at first, but quickly holding still as I faced her.

"Do not leave, Leander," she said my name, terrifying me even more. "It is not polite to leave so soon without meeting the M- I mean, your faerie godfather."

She brushed her hood back, revealing her face to me. She was pale, beautiful, with a rounded face and a pointed chin, her hair black as night and styled in a top knot as well as braids that hung down her back and over her shoulders. Her thick lips pursed as she stared at me, vile green veins reaching from her neck and hairline as if she were sick. And her eyes! They were black as coal and without whites!

"You're not a faerie!" I cried out in panic, trying to pull away. "You're a monster! Let go of me!"

"Quiet yourself, girl," she hissed down at me, no longer trying to draw me in with her false kindness. "The Master wishes to speak with you..."

I looked up at the figure standing behind her, hidden in the darkness cast by the thick trees. He moved forward, black robes flowing, a cowl trimmed in crimson hiding his face. I saw his pale grey hands at his sides beneath his wide sleeves, his eyes green and inhuman in the shadows of his hood.

"LEANDER!" my sister shouted, and I turned to where she stood on the road.

"Aislinn!" I cried, tugging my arm free from the woman's grasp, and running a few steps as she leaped to reach me.

Aislinn hugged me close into her arms, turning her blue eyes fiercely towards the woman. My sister was nowhere near as trusting as I was.

"Who are you? Why do you come near my sister?" she demanded coldly.

The woman backed into the shadows, meeting Aislinn's gaze. "I saw her wandering and lost, so I thought I might try to help her find her way home."

"I do not believe you," Aislinn scowled at her, glaring with a fire that could have matched a dragon's.

"I meant no harm, Princess," the woman bowed her head, continuing to back away.

Then there came a call, her black eyes darting as she turned her face towards the road I had come along. I followed hers and Aislinn's gazes to see a farmer pointing, and our father approaching with Mithras and several knights.

"Father!" I cried, running towards him.

My father, Prince Ewan, scooped me up in his broad arms and hugged me as he crouched down. "Oh, Leander, my little one," he sounded so relieved. "Are you all right?"

"I'm scared, Father," I replied, crying as he hugged me, wrapping my arms tightly around his neck.

Aislinn came up at our sides. "Father, a witch stands there. She meant to steal Leander from us."

Father looked up, his blue eyes searching the trees, his bearded jaw clenching.

He shook his head. "I see no one there now, Aislinn."

Aislinn and I both looked up, seeing that the woman had vanished, along with the strange, hooded man who had stood behind her.

Where did they go?

"But... but she was right there!" Aislinn pointed at the spot, looking to Father. "She was trying to drag Leander into the woods!"

"She was!" I agreed, looking up at him. "She wanted to take me to the bad man, Father!"

"The bad man?" he frowned.

I nodded. "He... he had a black hood, and he was very scary. He was behind her."

"Aislinn?" he turned to my sister. "Was there a man that you saw?"

"No, Father," she shook her head. "I saw only the woman."

"He was there!" I insisted fervently. "I saw him, Father! I saw him!"

"Mithras," our father looked up to the dark haired and neatly bearded knight that stood beside him. "Have some of your men go and search."

"Of course, Lord Ewan," Mithras bowed his head and swiftly sent four knights to search the trees.

"They *were* there," I sniffed, crying softly as my fear refused to go away.

My father smiled and nodded. "Don't worry, Leander. They're gone now. You are safe."

"That woman," Aislinn shuddered uncomfortably. "She didn't seem... human. I truly think she was a witch."

"What reason could a witch have for approaching the Princesses?" Mithras wondered, turning his hard gaze to my father.

"I do not know," Father said, standing up and taking my hand. "But I will not allow anyone to bring harm to either of my daughters."

"Of course, Sire," Mithras bowed his head.

"Come then, my girls," Father smiled at us. "Let us go back to the castle. Perhaps it might be best if we do not tell your mother of this little adventure, Leander."

I just nodded, rubbing the tears from my eyes as I clutched his hand tightly.

As this memory faded from my mind, I realised that that day was in fact the first time I had encountered the Witch, Manth, and her master, the Shadow Lord. Had I remembered that first meeting in my childhood sooner, I think the years where I found myself haunted by them would have felt all the worse...

* * * * *

I woke slowly, feeling a strange sensation come over me. The air smelled clean and clear, feeling so gentle and cold. Light drew me from my slumber, bright, yet kind in its whiteness. I suddenly became aware of the sensation of soft silk sheets beneath and enwrapping me, a soothing, comfortable mattress holding me. My eyes carefully opened with the expectation that the light would hurt them, but it didn't. I didn't even squint as I came to take in the sights around me.

I turned my blue gaze to the room and its stone walls with wooden panelling. The balcony doors were open, the breeze from the mountains outside drifting in and lifting the white drapes to float like graceful spectres. I frowned, this place so familiar. I turned to my right as I tried to recall where I was.

A vanity table with a mirror stood there facing me, my reflection that of an eighteen-year-old girl, not a small child as I had found myself living as. I looked down at myself, my body that of my teenaged self, not my smaller childhood form like I had first thought. I frowned even harder, trying to remember how I had come to be here, but there was a cloudy haze that I couldn't break through.

At last, my mind clicked as I took in the features of this very familiar place. *My room. This is my room in Castle Arvon. I'm home...*

I smiled, sitting up and looking around at the room I had so missed. Though every book was where I had shelved them, every dress where I'd hung them in the closet, and every item I had placed had not moved, there was something different about the room. The light was softer, the air strange and floaty in its way. It was almost like reality had become a tangible, living dream where the mists of that world had blended with the clarity of the one I was from.

Slowly, with an ache in my body, I stood from the bed, finding myself dressed as I usually was, but the clothing a strange colour I had never owned. My long-sleeved dress was white, but shimmered silver, my velvet over dress a beautiful silvery blue with pale blue silk lining and trim. I found that I wore silvery slippers instead of my usual boots, my legs bare beneath my gown.

I moved to the mirror and took in my reflection. I looked the same, my hair and skin unchanged in their colour, yet the light had a softer, whiter glow against me than normal.

"Strange..." I said, turning towards the door of my room.

Maybe Father or Mother will remember how I came to be here. I can't remember what happened before I woke up. Why?

I reached for the door handle, pressing the latch with my thumb, and pulling it open. Carefully, I stepped from my room into the corridor of the family quarters, the same wooden panels and stone walls surrounding me with curving rafters high above. Again, the light seemed almost heavenly as it shone through the window by my bedroom and the one across the hall.

My feet began to walk without any real conscious effort, my mind a blank and my eyes dazed. There were no guards as I had been so accustomed to, no one there to speak with or to bow to me. There was no one. Frowning at the lack of security that should have inhabited the castle's halls, I turned to the stairs, going down by the five great windows that stood tall behind them. As I entered the main entry hall, boasting its wooden carvings of dragons flanking the grand staircase, I found not a single living being in sight.

Where is everyone? I wondered apprehensively.

My confusion only heightened as I turned towards the Great Hall, standing there upon the stairs that led down to it. I entered and looked around at the fireplaces and windows that flanked it, the room immense with no one to be seen within. The four thrones stood on the dais at the far end, silhouetted by the white light that shone through the gigantic windows and their iron designs. They were vacant and abandoned.

The chill refused to leave me as I shivered and ran my hands across my arms in an attempt to warm myself. The snapping of wood burning drew my gaze and I turned to one of the fireplaces, moving towards it and holding my hands to the flames in the hopes of getting warm. It was strange that what warmth there was in the room didn't match that of a fire that size. The Great Hall had never been so cold in all my memories of it, the four great fireplaces more than capable of heating it sufficiently.

What is going on here? Why is the castle so cold and so without life?

I looked up over my shoulder, seeing the banquet hall through the archway under the stairs, the tables cleaned and perfectly neat, their oaken surfaces aglow with the light from the windows. Yet, once again there was no sound of voices, no movement of people living, nothing but the empty room itself. I should have been able to smell the chefs working from here, but I couldn't. There were no delicious aromas wafting up from the kitchens below the stairs at all. Even the scent of the wood on the fire was dulled as if it didn't exist.

I need to find Mother and Father, I decided as I looked into the flames. *They'll know what's happening.*

I took the hem of my skirt in my hand and left the room, making my way up the stairs once again. I tried every room I could conceive of, walking through the entry hall, going past the grand staircase to the right side this time, entering the western side of the castle. I checked the library, but found it only housed the books and furniture it was meant to, no sign of my parents. I searched the training rooms and even the dungeon, but there wasn't a prisoner, guard or even a rat present. Now I was beginning to worry.

I returned to the main entry hall and pushed open one of the great doors, stepping out onto the porch that overlooked the main courtyard. The trees were without leaves, snow covering the ground. The portcullis gate was closed tight, barring me from leaving the castle and venturing into the surrounding province of Arvon. There was no point in exploring the barracks and the training courtyard through the archway to my right, my gaze already seeing that it was deserted. The servants' quarters and gardens to my left were no different.

I grasped the bars of the portcullis and rested my head there, staring at the cobblestones of the gate courtyard beyond. My heart sank as I came to realise that I was completely alone in the castle, not a single person there with me. I had never been alone here in my entire life, not even when Mother and Father left to visit Uncle Aric or another nation's rulers.

What's happened to everyone? Why I am here all alone? I don't understand.

I turned around and made my way to the stairs above the archway to the training yard. I started walking quicker, my dress swirling around my ankles and floating behind my heels, my over sleeves billowing from my elbows. I reached the walkway that crossed with this one beside the keep, turning to my left to see the Memorial Chamber, the greens of the gardens stretching far below its stone balustrades.

"Leander?" my father's voice echoed and I turned as he called again. "Leander?"

"Father," I smiled as I saw him and Mother step out from the doors at the far end of the walkway to my right. "Mother."

They turned towards me, walking quickly, and smiling brightly. Mother had her hair pulled back and her golden circlet over her forehead, her gown of vibrant blues and gold flowing with her movements. Father's greying hair was held with a tie to keep it from his face, his bearded grin so warm and welcoming.

He wore a dark blue doublet that reached his knees, his fine golden shirt worn underneath with black trousers and boots, a belt at his waist.

I moved towards them, closing the distance between us and reaching to embrace them. They suddenly passed right through me. I shuddered, staring wide eyed as I slowly turned after them. It was as if I were a ghost - or they were - passing through each other without stopping.

"There you are," my mother smiled as she and Father approached another figure.

I stared at my five-year-old self, who was wearing a blue dress with her hair left long. The small child version of me smiled with the brightest of steel blue eyes, happily running to meet my parents as my sister followed her from the Memorial Chamber.

"Mother! Father!" she cried, happily running into my father's waiting embrace. "You're back!"

"Yes, we are!" Father chuckled, hugging the little me tight, then smiling as my mother hugged the teenage version of Aislinn. "Have you been a good girl for your sister and Ser Mithras, Leander?"

"I have, Father," my younger self nodded as vigorously as children do.

"I have something for you," he smiled, holding up a blue leather wrapped book.

"A book, Father?!" she looked so excited.

"Not just any book," he said, offering it to her small hands. "This one is about dragons. A gift from your grandfather."

"I love dragons!" she exclaimed, taking the book, and looking up at Mother and Father. "Will you read it to me?! Please?!"

"Of course, my dear girl," Mother smiled, laughing softly. "We shall sit together and read it tonight."

I frowned. I remembered this day. Mother and Father had been visiting Uncle Aric and Aunt Evangeline with my grandfather, but as I recalled they didn't return alone.

"Uncle Aric!" my younger self cheered.

"Aunt Evangeline," Aislinn smiled, moving at my smaller self's side.

I felt that terrible, indescribable sensation again as my aunt and uncle walked through me. They looked just as they did before they had died, the King and Queen of Aldegaad in all their glory, though they hadn't taken those titles yet.

"Hello, my wonderful nieces," Uncle Aric smiled, his hair not yet white, but starting to grey. "It is so good to see you both again."

"It's good to see you too, Uncle Aric!" my younger self hugged his legs, smiling up at him.

What's going on? I felt myself stagger, bracing my back against the stone wall of the keep. *Am I dreaming? How can I be watching the past while I am standing right here? How can I be five and twenty-one at the same time? How?*

I looked up to see Mithras approaching from the gardens then. His armour was silvery, his surcoat a strange, softer than normal blue, the dragon emblazoned there white like pearl instead of gold. His cloak was the purest white, flowing behind him as he strode towards the scene.

Mithras never dressed like that... I thought with confusion.

"Enjoying this glimpse into your past, Princess?" he asked, and I realised that his focus was on me, not my younger self.

"W-what?" I blinked, watching as he strode through my family as if they were a smoky illusion, leaving them to continue their scene behind him.

"You look so very confused," he smiled softly at me, nodding his head. "But then, I would expect you to be, child."

"M-Mithras?" I felt disbelief wash over me as I stared at him. "You... you can see me?"

"I can see you, yes," he confirmed, his hands resting on the pommel of his sword and the edge of his belt. "Would you prefer I not be able to?"

"I... I just... I don't understand what's happening," I confessed, dazed by all of this. "My family..."

"Only echoes," he said simply, offering me an explanation. "These are but the imprints of your past, of all your days that have gone before now, playing out in front of your eyes."

"Then... they aren't real?" I looked to him, frowning.

"No," he shook his head and waved his hand, the scene fading as if made of mist as he turned back to me. "They are but shadows repeating your memories."

"I've been wandering the halls and courtyards looking for someone since I woke up..." I shook my head, feeling as if I could cry at seeing him. "But I never expected to see you again, my friend."

He smiled softly. "I am here because you need me, Leander. But, well, you have always needed me."

I felt tears come to me, and I reached out to touch him. My hand pressed to the cool steel of his armour, and I let out a loud, relieved breath. I was shaking so hard. I hugged him, sobbing with joy as he was once more before me.

"Mithras... It's been so long since I was with you," I cried. "I've missed you so much."

"And I you, child," he replied, brushing my tears away with his right thumb. "Come, sit with me. We have much to discuss."

I nodded, letting him lead me back along the walkway to the Memorial Chamber.

As we entered, I looked up at the statue of my ancestor and her dragon, her sword held in both hands before her. It was then as I saw the pendant around her neck that I reached for mine to feel nothing but my own skin. Panic filled me and I looked down at where it should have been only to see it absent from my collarbones.

"My... my pendant!" I gasped, feeling at my chest and throat with my left hand frantically. "Where is it?!"

"The Dragon Pendants cannot enter this place," Mithras answered, moving to one of the stone benches and taking a seat. "It could never have followed you here, Leander."

I looked to him, frowning. "Where *is* here? It's... it looks like Castle Arvon, but only you and I are here, no one else. And there's this strange... *glow* to everything."

"Sit down, girl," he offered me a seat at his side.

I obeyed, seating myself to his left and folding my hands into my lap as I met his gaze. He looked the way I could imagine a man who had terrible news would just before telling his loved ones.

He glanced at me and asked: "What do you remember before this place?"

I shrugged. "Um... I was... eight winters old, playing with Aislinn..."

"Before that," he urged me. "Think, girl, think."

I frowned in deep thought, trying to recall what had happened before that. But all that came was a fuzzy haze, dark shadows and blurring voices; sensations that were agonising and frightening, but unrecallable.

I shook my head. "I... I can't remember..."

"You've not been here long," he nodded in realisation, looking ahead as he rested his palms on his thighs. "Your mind is still confounded by the haze of passing."

"What is that?" I asked, the concept so strange to me. "What is the haze of passing?"

He looked to me solemnly. "It is what all spirits experience when first they arrive here in this realm."

"Spirits?" I felt my frown deepening and my confusion growing. "I'm not a spirit."

"The form you have here is that of your soul," he told me, trying to be gentle. "As is mine. Leander, I am dead. Remember? I died in my sleep in Coastwatch Keep more than two years past; slain by a wound your uncle, Fane, gave me."

I was so confused: "Then... if you're dead... how can I be with you?"

"Need you really ask?" he looked to me softly, urging me silently to find the answer.

Fear gripped me and I felt a pain in my chest. I clutched at my heart with both hands, my breathing drawing a sharpness that was beyond agonising. I gasped, shaking, and dropping from the seat to my knees. I began coughing and choking as I felt the air stealing away from my lungs.

"What's... what's happening... to me?!" I desperately gasped for much needed breaths.

Mithras crouched on one knee and set his hand to my back, trying to ease the pain. "You are feeling the how, child. The passing into this world confounds you so that you cannot feel your suffering, thus allowing you time to come to know where you are. But once that knowledge has come, you feel it all at once."

I coughed, choking, gasping, struggling to breathe as my heart felt as if it had been cleaved in two. This pain was unbearable, horrific. Nothing I had felt before was like this suffering that I now experienced.

"Just breathe," he urged me, trying to bring calm to my mind. "Take in the air as you would normally. Calm yourself."

"My... my heart!" I exclaimed, blinded by tears of pain that stung my eyes. "It feels as if it has been cleaved apart!"

"It has," he said horrifically, meaning to be gentle though he was.

I looked up at him, stunned and panicked by his words. "W-w-what?"

"That is how you have come here," he explained as gently and softly as he could. "What you feel is the cause of your death, Leander."

"My... my death?" I shook my head. "N-no! No! I... I can't be! No... I... I just... no!"

"Shh, shh, it is all right," he wrapped his arms around me, trying to soothe me as I coughed at the ground. "Just relax and let it pass. The sensation will pass quicker if you are calm. Trust me. I know."

I nodded, forcing myself to find calmness and peace, making my body ease itself. Gradually, my breathing became easier and the pain in my heart, though it didn't leave completely, lessened and faded. I took in slow, easing breaths, my hands unclenching and my eyes dripping tears as I managed to relax.

Slowly, fearfully, I turned my eyes to Mithras, trembling: "I'm... I'm... *dead*?"

He nodded solemnly. "Yes, child."

I shook my head, holding my hands to my chest as I found flashes of what had happened returning. Cold chains were on my wrists, my body lying on a stone altar, my blood being drained slowly as the Shadow Lord stood over me with a dagger... The monstrous dragon, Ragnarok, was glowing with evil black and blue flames as a battle raged on, and... Carden. He screamed for me, trying to reach me, but couldn't, frozen by Morod's dark magic. I felt the dagger plunging through my chest, screaming in agony as my bones and flesh ripped apart. My heart all but obliterated at the blade's razor-sharp passage. Then, I was in Carden's arms, looking up at him to see fear in his handsome green eyes. I had never seen him so grief stricken, his tears fighting against his usual composure, which was all but gone now.

"I...I love you, Carden," saying the much needed words sounded like a distant echo from my aching body, but he had to know what was in my heart.

"I love you, Leander," his voice had sounded so faint to my ears, his pain all too visible as I had felt him holding me and stroking my hair. "I will always love you."

That final pledge from him had given me the reassurance I had long craved after all the pain I had faced from my curse. All the uncertainty over what kind of a life I might have had then faded from me, my confession to him before these last declarations of love freeing in its way. But I could feel myself slipping, the black hooded and winged figure of the God of Death standing behind my lover, watching me. His glowing electric-violet eyes were frightening, all the stories I had heard of him nothing close to the truth.

My final words came to me: "Please, Carden... don't let me go..."

I came back to Mithras then, tears running down my cheeks as it became all too clear.

"I remember..." those two words were like the greatest agony spoken in the softest, most haunted voice I had ever produced. "So, I am... dead."

"You are," the old knight confirmed with a solemn nod of his grey-haired head. "As am I and several members of your family. Even the Guardian Mage, Aldwyn Draken, has joined us here."

"Where is here exactly?" I asked. "It looks like home, but if I am dead then..."

"You are in the Kingdom of Death," he nodded gravely, looking around at the world that surrounded us, "though this is not the paradise of the Beyond."

"It's not?" I frowned.

He shook his head, meeting my eyes. "Your death was a cursed, unnatural thing in which your very life force was robbed from you. Because of this, you cannot pass from this place into the world of the Beyond. This is... a sort of purgatory for you alone."

"I'm trapped here?!" I felt an awful sickness come over me and the urge to scream fighting in my throat.

He nodded. "Sadly, yes. That is why there are no inhabitants within the castle, why its gates are locked."

"How can you be here then, Mithras?" I asked, looking up at him again, shaking with terror. "If this purgatory is for me alone, then why are you with me?"

He explained: "Because I have been allowed to come to you and keep you company. Lord Azmerath is frightening to behold, but greatly merciful. And so he has charged me with a purpose that only a Dragon Knight is capable of carrying out, since I can freely pass between worlds."

"What is that?" I felt new tears flowing.

"To offer you hope," he said, trying to give me a tiny smile. "You are not lost to this damnation of waiting in purgatory forever, Leander. You may yet be freed."

"How?! Tell me how, please, and I'll do it!" I pleaded with him desperately, the thought of staying here agonising.

He shook his head. "There is nothing for you to do. All you may do is wait. However long that may be."

"How... how long have I been here?" I asked uneasily, settling back into my seat. "Compared to the others I left behind, how long?"

"For you it has been hours," he confessed evenly, but with a grimness to his tone, "but for them it has been minutes only since your passing."

"What?" I stared at him and looked down at the floor. "Gods... an eternity could pass for me while an hour passes for them," I felt my tears fall and an ache fill my chest where I no longer had a heart. "It will be lifetimes for me without Carden," I started to sob. "I... I may never be with him again..."

"And that, my girl, is where I offer the hope from Lord Azmerath," Mithras said, gently lifting my chin with two fingers to meet his gaze. "For you see, Leander, it is Carden who can save you from this fate."

"He... he can?" I asked, feeling a slight twinge of hope in the cavity that had taken over my chest.

He smiled softly. "He has already made his vow for you and will soon seek the way with the guidance of those who can show him the path."

I cried gratefully. *Carden... He'll save me from this. He'll pull me back from what the Shadow Lord has cast me into. Oh Gods, I love him so much...*

"For the time being, I shall remain here to keep you company," Mithras promised me, drawing my gaze to him. "And Azmerath's kindness is such that he has given you your home to reside in, allowing you distractions until the time comes for you to be freed. You may sleep, eat, and occupy yourself however you choose, all to offer some respite from the fears that cloud your mind."

"But he's coming for me?" I looked up at him, feeling the tingle of hope in me powered by love, yet needing more reassurance. "Carden *is* coming for me?"

"There is no other with the power to do so," Mithras assured me, brushing my tears from my cheeks. "Do not fear, Leander. Love is your salvation."

I nodded and rested my head on Mithras' shoulder, hugging him. The old knight gently encircled me in his arms, pulling me close. His embrace was a comfort that I had sorely missed.

"I'm glad that you're with me, Mithras," I whispered through my tears.

"I will not leave you, Leander," he said. "This I swear to you, girl."

I closed my eyes, seeing Carden in my mind. I could only imagine what it would be like to have him come for me, to see him standing there before me, offering his outstretched hand to pull me back from the brink of this deathly nightmare. Knowing that he would come to the Kingdom of Death itself for me was so far beyond my imaginings. But it gave me something to hope for.

He's coming for me. My love, my Guardian, my Carden... He never will forsake m,e and I am such a stupid girl for ever fearing he would. Gods, I love him. Please, please, please, just let him succeed. Let me be with him once again... Please...

Chapter Two
Love's Vow in Grief's Hold

~ Carden ~

I stood ready, my sword in hand, my eyes locked hard on the monster before me. He strode up those stairs, his black visage intimidating, but I would not give in. I *had* to protect her from him. I *had* to save her. He seemed surprised by my defiance, viewing me with a quizzical gaze as I readied myself.

"You won't touch her again!" I declared, gripping my sword hard.

The Shadow Lord didn't stop moving as he spoke. "You think you can stop me, boy?"

"I won't let you hurt her again!" I swung my sword, meaning to cleave the monster to the ground, but my blade was suddenly held in his grasp.

Morod yanked me forward, throwing me behind him to the ground. I rolled up into a crouching position, readying myself as he strode towards where she lay struggling. I would never let him hurt her. I would save her from him and end his blighted existence!

As I lunged, the hooded monster turned and held out his hand. I was suddenly overwhelmed, my body feeling heavy and my sword arm shaking as I tried to lift it. I couldn't even raise my blade or unfurl my fingers to drop it.

What magic is this?!

Morod turned to me, his glare hard and evil, a dark threat there that I dreaded. "I have no need to kill you, Guardian. Since you love her so very much, you shall have the honour of watching her die."

"No! No, don't!" I screamed as he turned from me, his intent locked on her. "Get away from her!"

I watched helplessly, struggling against whatever dark affliction he had laid on me as he moved to the altar to recommence his evil ceremony. I tensed my body, my muscles burning every time I tried to move against the Shadow Lord's magic.

Leander squirmed and struggled, tears flooding her beautiful blue-grey eyes, her soft, young face so full of fear and desperation. It killed me to see my beloved girl suffering so much. Taking up that cruel knife again, he stood over her with those hideous monster statues at his back. She was crying in terror, fighting to break her wrists free of the chains that held them.

Morod began chanting: "With her blood the doorway shall open. With her death the Fallen Ones shall be freed. With this dagger shall I loose her life's blood upon this altar..."

Leander screamed in agony as he began cutting her, the blade carving through her sides slowly and deliberately with the Shadow Lord's malicious attention.

No! No! I have to free myself! I have to get to her! Gods, give me strength!

I grunted and strained, feeling as if I had chains of stone laid over me, sticking me hard to the floor. I could feel the perspiration on my brow despite the cold of the room, my chest tensing and aching, my muscles feeling as if they could tear my skin apart.

"Leander!" I felt a small relief at Fawkner's shout, glancing up to see him rushing forward with a sweep of his cloak, his sword gleaming in the evil moonlight that was now turning red.

Ellora and Joran rushed with him, their weapons ready and their focus on reaching her just as mine was.

"Get away from her, vile monster!" Ellora demanded in a shrill shout, her swords swinging and singing in the air.

Morod didn't stop cutting Leander, the girl crying out with each slice he left in her skin. He held out his other hand and I watched my three allies stagger and jerk, their bodies going stiff just as mine had as they too were frozen with the same evil magic.

Leander saw it, her tear-filled eyes terrified. Her gaze fell to me for a moment, then back to the Shadow Lord.

No! Let me get free! I need to get to her!

The monster held the dagger above her, its blade coated red with her blood. She watched it fearfully as it dripped, shaking where she lay; her arms tensing above her, her legs shifting beneath her dress.

"The Dragon's Key Pendant shall be charged with her blood, her life force, the very power which frees the Destroyers," he went on with his ritual, purposefully dripping her blood like slow rain over her chest.

The Pendant around her neck began to glow with an evil magenta energy, the moons aligning above us and their light turning blood red. This was it, the ritual reaching its height along with my desperate panic for my girl.

The room shook and everyone around us staggered as the battle raged on. I looked to Fawkner and Ellora, both of them turning to me with uneasy gazes. We watched then as the dragons that were just statues suddenly came to life. They were vicious and mewling, snapping as they struggled against the chains that held them, the stone skin that covered them cracking and falling away.

"No..." I gasped, staring in horror at them.

Leander was watching them, shaking, the smell of her sweet blood strong in my nostrils. I tensed once again, trying to get to her, but the Shadow Lord's spell was still strong, despite his attention being on the beasts.

The girl looked up as Dolin and Holger ran past us, their gazes set upon Morod as he strode around the altar to face the Dragons. I hoped they would succeed, but with yet another wave of his bony hand, the Shadow Lord struck casually. The two dwarves flew backwards and slammed hard into the floor behind us.

No, he must be stopped! I can't let her die!

Morod faced the great beasts as the middle one that had to be Ragnarok looked down at him with those black fire eyes.

"Who is the one who awakens us?" the Dragon demanded coldly.

Morod bowed to him. "My Lord Ragnarok. I am Shadow Lord Morod, he who has summoned you back to this world."

The Dragon seemed interested as he hissed out his slithering tongue. "What is it that you would ask of me, Shadow Lord?"

The Shadow Lord answered: "Only that you fulfil your original intent and devour this world that I might rebuild it in my image. I beseech you to align yourself with me."

Ragnarok seemed to consider this, almost amused by the Shadow Lord's plea. He growled in response: "I am Destruction itself! I am the Devourer of Worlds, the Shadow in the Flames! I would relish the chance to destroy what my sister, Ankorect, has created here!"

Morod seemed cautiously hopeful. "Then, you will side with me?"

The Dragon nodded, glaring down at Leander. She cringed under his gaze, trembling in terror.

No... No, not her! Please, anything but her!

"Kill her!" the foul monster demanded. "Kill the girl you offer as sacrifice and drain her life force into the pendant around her neck! Kill her and I shall wreak the greatest devastation at your command, Shadow Lord! Kill her and set me free!"

No... no, no, no, no, NO!

Morod nodded lightly. "As you command," he took up the dagger again, turning to Leander as she squirmed and fought to get away, panicking.

"No! NO, DON'T!" I screamed, fighting his hold once again.

Leander looked to me fearfully, then turned her gaze back to Morod as he leaned over her, reaching his left hand towards her.

"Please, don't!" she pleaded, crying, but so quiet in her sobs. She flinched as he grasped her throat and held her down. "Don't do this! Please..."

I was moments from watching the girl I love being murdered brutally before me, feeling utterly helpless to save her.

"LEANDER! NO! GET AWAY FROM HER!" I shouted, fighting hard to reach her.

Morod raised his right hand, the dagger thirsting for her blood. He stared down at her as we all shouted - Fawkner, Ellora and I - fighting for our freedom to save her.

"Goodbye, Princess," he mewed, and she screamed as he stabbed her through the chest.

"NO! NO, LEANDER, NO!" I howled.

Morod ripped the dagger from her chest, stepping back and looking down as she whimpered in agony, her blood staining her dress' front.

"STOP HIM!" I heard Ranzel shout fearfully. "HE MUST NOT TAKE THE PENDANT FROM HER NECK!"

Fawkner, Ellora, Joran and I came free, our limbs no longer heavy as the spell that held us released. I ran forward, the Shadow Lord's hand coming up and casting the four of us backwards, our bodies hitting hard against the stone floor. Bracing my arm to the floor, I looked up, my heart sinking as he took the Pendant from her neck and held it in his hand like a hard-earned trophy.

Ellora snatched her bow from her back and began firing, but her arrows passed through him as if he were nothing more than smoke.

The Shadow Lord laughed victoriously as the Dragons broke their chains, Ragnarok outstretching his great wings and roaring into the air. Terrible black and blue flames erupted all over his gigantic body, the Dragon then launching his enormous form and flying up through the opening in the ceiling with his four brothers at his tail.

The room fell silent as the minions of the Shadow Lord all transported away under his magical command; our allies left standing amidst the dead of the fallen with no foes to fight. My eyes fell on the Shadow Lord, his laughter lingering to fade long after he had evaporated into mist.

"Leander..." I got to my feet and ran, my sword clattering as I dropped it.

I slammed my side into the altar, the pain caused by the impact to my ribs nothing as I looked down at her. Her eyes were staring blankly and wide in shock, her broken chest heaving rapidly as her blood turned her white dress crimson over her breasts.

"Help me!" I screamed, trying to tug her restraints free. "Someone! Help me!"

Ellora was at my side, trying to free her as my hands fumbled into my belt for a lock pick. I found it and as swiftly as I had been taught, I released the locks that bound her wrists and ankles. Together, Ellora and I pulled the weakening girl from the altar, my arms encircling her as I fell to sit with her in my lap.

I was shaking, fighting the tears that burned my green eyes. Aldwyn passing from us had hurt, but I couldn't endure losing Leander.

"C...Carden," she saw me, a faint smile appearing on her soft, small lips.

"It's me, Leander," I confirmed, stroking her dark hair with my right hand, my left arm cradling her shoulders. "I'm here. I've got you."

"I... I can't... breathe," she gasped, choking.

"Ranzel," I looked up to the Green Wizard standing before us as Ellora crouched behind me. "Help her. Heal her, please..."

"If only I could," the Wizard said with deepest regret. "Sadly, there is no magic, nor medicine in this world that can save her. Only the Pendant that took her life force gave us any chance of bringing her back from the brink of Azmerath's realm... and Lord Morod has taken it."

"No," I felt my throat shake as I turned to look back at Leander. "I'm... I'm not letting you go. I won't."

"Carden," she murmured, her throat visibly working to fight air down to her lungs, her eyes flickering. "I... I'm so happy I get to... to see you... again..."

"As am I to see you, my beautiful girl," I tried to smile for her, to make her feel at least some joy and give her comfort.

She reached up her left hand, her arm shaking from her life draining. Her soft, warm fingers caressed my hard cheekbone, my eyes falling shut at her gentle, feathery touch. I would gladly feel that for eternity.

"Please..." she sobbed. "Forgive me..."

"Why?" I asked, frowning at her.

"I... I was afraid," she swallowed hard as she tried to go on. "I was so scared that... that you would not want me... anymore because I was... cursed..."

"Cursed?" I frowned even harder.

She forced a small nod, slumping in my arms. "The Shadow Lord... m... made me immortal. When he... he used me to regain... his powers... he took my changing. I couldn't... grow old with you..."

"That doesn't matter," I smiled at her, now understanding her reluctance and her fearfulness when she was near me that hadn't made sense before. "None of it does. I just want to be with you, my beautiful girl. Just you."

That made her smile again, her eyes blinking as their blue-grey colour began to dull, yet still remained so gorgeously beautiful.

"I... I love you, Carden," she managed weakly, tears slipping from her eyes.

"I love you, Leander," I assured her with all of my aching heart. "I will always love you."

Her other hand clutched my shirt, tightening with all the strength she had left, her arm shaking. I could feel her life leaving her and my heart shattered inside me. I just wanted to keep her breathing, to keep her with me no matter what. And as the sky was turning black and thunder was cracking high above, I would sacrifice all that I had to give her one more breath.

"Carden..." she murmured weakly, looking up at me through her tears.

"Yes, my love?" I asked, feeling my own tears slipping free.

"I... I can see him," she whimpered, her eyes on something behind me. "He's... frightening... I never knew he would be so frightening."

"Who?" I frowned. "Who scares you?"

"Azmerath," she replied, turning her eyes to mine, sobbing. "I don't... I don't want to go with him. Please, Carden. Don't let me go..."

"No," I shook my head, tearing up. "No, Leander, stay with me. Stay with me, sweetheart, please."

Her blue eyes dulled and slowly her eyelids fell shut. Her head slumped into my shoulder and her chest fell, rising no more.

I started to cry, my heart breaking. "No... Leander, no..."

I pulled her closer, holding her so tightly, just pleading in my ruins of a heart to bring her back. But no breath came to her lips, the colour leaving her beautiful face and her eyes remaining closed. My sobs were agonising, my howling cries beyond anything I had ever known as I cradled my beloved girl in my arms. I felt like a fool, the argument we'd had, my ignorance towards her since the gardens, all of it haunting me now as I sat with her dead in my arms.

Out of the corner of my eye I could see the others. I felt Ellora's hands on my shoulders and heard her gentle sobs as she rested her forehead on my back. I felt numb to the sensation though, only Leander feeling real to me. Ranzel stood nearest us; his hat held hanging in his hand as he bowed his head. Behind him, Fawkner was on his knees, sobbing into his left hand, his sword still in his right.

There was a thump as Joran dropped to his knees, the Storvari incapable of tears, but clearly not grief. He had the look of a man who had failed. Dolin and Holger stood leaning on their tall weapons, their heads down and tears in their eyes. Behind them, Tallinn was crying, Tristan pulling her into his arms. At that moment I couldn't even hate the bastard for his actions towards my beloved Leander.

Though all the High Elves, Dragon Knights, Guardians and Wizards that watched on were surely feeling much themselves, I could go no further to notice them.

"We have failed," I heard Ranzel murmur sadly. "Gods... we have failed her."

I wept painfully, squeezing my eyes shut and kissing Leander's hair gently. I felt like my chest had been ripped by the same dagger that hers had. Gods, at that moment I wished that it had been just so I could be with her.

As I cradled her in my arms, holding her tight and refusing to let her go, I silently made a new vow, renouncing the oath I had made as a Guardian. I was no longer a defender of High-Realm, no longer a Guardian, for I had failed in that mission. No, my oath now was for her and her alone. It was now Love's Vow, no other. I would not abandon her to Death's grasp. Somehow, even as the walls around us were shaking and the world was in the throes of Armageddon, I would find a way to get her back, to free her from Azmerath's eternal kingdom. I would bring my Leander back to this world and love her for eternity.

I will find a way to get you back, Leander... I will find a way to save you. This vow I swear...

I have no idea how long I sat with her like this. In truth, I could very easily have spent the rest of my days cradling her smaller frame in my arms and never move again. My world had lost all light with her passing and I had nothing but a void in my chest where my heart once resided. I knew for sure that I loved her, for her absence had destroyed me.

I was dimly aware of the others now. They had begun pulling themselves together, the scene around us of carnage and tragedy. We had slain more than half of the force the Shadow Lord had present there, yet so many of our own had fallen. Out of the corner of my eye I watched a number of Guardians tending to Warden Alessa's body. The moment she had been slain by the Shadow Lord had perhaps marked the turning point in his victory. He had shown his insurmountable power, and yet I had still dared to face him, if only to save my beautiful princess. And failed...

There came a terrible, desperate roar suddenly and I looked up as Amethyst flew down through the ceiling opening with Gaspeite at her heels. The two dragons landed on the vast floor amidst our ranks, their glowing orange eyes scanning the room. Both looked as if they had fought a tremendous battle, likely only having survived the seven evil dragons because Morod had silently sounded his retreat.

I turned my green-eyed gaze to the two dragons, Amethyst facing me. The Dragon slowly moved towards where I sat with Leander in my arms, her face becoming ever more mournful as she approached. I swear that I could hear her very heart breaking at the sight of the lifeless girl.

A low, tearful sound came from the Dragon's lips as she lowered her long snout towards Leander's body, her eyes almost pleading. She nudged the girl's shoulder softly, moving her gently in my embrace, testing her to get a response. Sorrowfully, no response came. Amethyst made yet another mournful sound, though more ardent, pressing her horn-tipped nose to the girl's cheek, but still Leander didn't stir. The Dragon moved her head back on her long neck, her molten gaze locked on Leander's face. I caught the glimmer of a tear rolling down the Dragon's purple scaled cheek. The sound she made then was grievous and broken, the moan widening her jaws and closing her eyes. Her wings slumped down around her, pressing to the floor, her tail going limp.

Amethyst was crying in the way that dragons do, her howls of grief vibrating off the stone of the temple surrounding us. All I could do was sit there with her and grieve, gently stroking Leander's cooling cheek and jaw as I took in her beautiful features.

Slowly, quietly, Ellora pressed one delicately fingered hand to my shoulder.

"Carden," she spoke softly, trying to remain composed after having gathered herself. "I know you grieve, we all do, but we cannot linger here any longer. We must leave."

I shook my head, staring at Leander. "I'm not... I'm not leaving her. I won't leave her. I promised I wouldn't let her go."

"There is no need to leave her, Carden," Ellora told me, calling my mind back from the brink. "None of us can bare to leave her here in this dark place. But we *must* depart. The Wizards grow concerned for our safety."

I frowned, not knowing why I should care. What did my safety matter now that my love was dead? It didn't. Not as far as I was concerned.

"Carden," she used my name again, squeezing my shoulder. "Please, we must take her from this dire place of evil death so that she might rest at ease."

I sighed, nodding. "Yes... Yes, she needs to be kept safe. Where should we go?"

"Back to Silvervale," she replied softly, solemn grief still in her turquoise eyes. "We must take her and return to Silvervale with haste."

I nodded, getting to my feet slowly, balancing on one knee as I pulled Leander into my arms. I stood, holding her bridal style, tilting her head to lie against my chest as her left arm hung from her side towards the floor.

I should have carried you like this on our wedding night, my love. Not in your death.

I turned my gaze from Leander to look down at Ellora. The Elf woman nodded softly, her hand on my shoulder. There was no smile as she brushed a few strands of her fire red hair from her eyes, only a solemn air that came from centuries of age.

"Ehem, excuse me, Lady Elf, Master Guardian," Dolin cleared his throat from behind us.

I turned with Ellora and Amethyst to see Dolin and Holger standing there. Both dwarves were dishevelled and with bruises of their own, the blood of their foes smothered over them. They looked tired and exhausted, their black beards and hair knotted around their hardened faces, though their expressions were anything but hardened.

"We... uh... we found the lassie's things in the room outside this chamber," Dolin said, choking back his grief. "It... It didn't seem right to abandon them..."

I looked down at what he held. There were two piles of fabric, one of lilac linen, the other of royal blue velvet and purple silk. Leander's dress that she had been wearing in Silvervale that last afternoon before she was taken. Holger had the rest of her things; her boots and her leggings together with what Dolin carried.

"Yes," Ellora nodded coldly, dimly. "We will not leave them."

"We'll... we'll keep them safe," Dolin assured us, holding the dress close. "The lassie would want them, not that rag they made her wear."

Suddenly, the earth began to quake ever more violently, the walls fracturing around us as stone fell from the ceiling and thunder sparked above in the roiling skies. We were all staggered as the floor cracked open, fire and smoke rising through the fissures.

"What's happening?!" Tristan cried out as he tried to steady himself and Tallinn.

"The temple is collapsing!" Ranzel declared, looking around at the falling sections of ceiling.

"What has caused this?!" Fawkner questioned, stumbling to stay on his feet.

"The release of Ragnarok and his brethren!" Xzharn shouted, trying to keep his balance as he steadied himself with help from Lord Selwyn. "Their power has weakened the very foundations of this place!"

"My Lords!" a Dragon Knight rushed in from the entrance, panic in his eyes. "The Great Dragons! They have turned their destructive powers towards the temple! They belch fire and lightning upon the very earth on which we stand!"

"They mean to destroy the temple and the isle!" Ranzel realised with terror in his eyes, bracing himself to the shaking floor with his staff. "The Shadow Lord has commanded the destruction of Safferan! We must flee! Back to the ships! Quickly! Before we are buried with this temple!"

The ground shook and lurched violently, the temple coming down all around us as the moons above were blocked by the storms that had started ravaging the world.

I staggered, struggling to keep my balance and not drop Leander from my arms. Ellora steadied me, the two of us managing to slip away as a huge section of the stone ceiling came crashing down through the altar. We watched on as the stone crushed the floor and plummeted down into a cavern of fire opening beneath our feet.

Lord Selwyn was ordering the High Elves to flee, many of the dead having to be left to fall here. But I wouldn't leave Leander.

The survivors were fleeing through the archway out to the canyon from whence we came into the temple. It was beginning to cave in.

"Gaspeite! The entrance!" Ranzel pointed to the opening, shouting to his dragon.

Gaspeite snarled and flapped his wings, rushing forward to pry the archway up. He flexed his gargantuan muscles, holding the doorway and preventing the collapse. We wouldn't have long.

"Hurry!" Ranzel shouted, sweeping his hand towards the door as he beckoned the survivors of the battle through. "To the ships! Quickly! Do not linger!"

"Come, Carden!" Ellora swept her cloak behind her, heading for the door.

I followed her, pausing as I looked down at Joran. The Storvari had not moved from where he had dropped to his knees. He had his head bowed and his swords to the floor with his palms on the hilts.

"Joran!" I shouted, trying to get his attention as the Dwarves ran past to the door. "Joran, we must go!"

The Storvari shook his head. "I have failed my Sarissi. My life is now ornarikarnar: forfeit in failure."

"Joran, do not be a fool!" Fawkner shouted at him. "This whole place is coming down around us!"

"Let me be buried here with my shame," the Storvari grumbled his reply.

I shook my head. "You said that you would serve Leander no matter what, even in her death! That was your pledge, was it not?!"

He turned his violet eyes to me, nodding. "Yes, Carden Highever. It was."

"Then serve her now!" I demanded, clutching her close to my chest. "Protect her from being buried in this dark place! Help us convey her to safety!"

My words had stirred him. The Storvari got to his feet and stowed his swords in their sheaths over his shoulders. He took the lead, running forward as Amethyst charged behind us.

With a mighty roar, the purple dragon launched herself into the air and came to the opening, assisting Gaspeite in holding it for us. We were some of the last to pass under, Fawkner, Ellora, Joran, Ranzel and I rushing down the long hall as it began shaking itself apart. Tristan, Tallinn, and the Dwarves were already ahead of us with the rest of the survivors running from the temple.

Once we were through the archway, Amethyst and Gaspeite let go and took flight, barrelling up through the ceiling opening before the whole thing came crashing down.

We ran as fast as we could, the stone walls splintering all around us and the ceiling collapsing. I just had to run, to get Leander out of there safely. If she were alive, I would have done exactly the same thing. I would have carried her from this place to the safety of the grounds outside.

As we escaped the temple, I realised how unsafe the island really was. I looked up into the black storming sky to see seven great creatures beating their wings. The dragons were positioned in a ring around the island, the seven of them focused on the mountain and the land. Ragnarok and his four brothers were lashing out with continuous blasts of supernatural fire, the flaming balls glowing a sinister purplish black as they illuminated the night sky. Each strike slammed into the island with enough force to decimate an entire village. Dirt and stone erupted into the air with each blast to rain down burning to the ground. The island was fracturing around us, the earth itself splitting and belching magma from its depths. The mountain behind us was crumbling in a thunderous tidal wave of rock and snow.

Gods! They are destroying the island! I've never seen such power before!

My gaze settled on the crimson winged black dragon that flew above us. Cathal was launching his own flames down upon Safferan, roaring with evil joy at the destruction he was wreaking amongst his vicious allies. And perched on his back was the black robed and hooded figure of the Shadow Lord, surveying the destruction with a wicked smirk.

My love's killer was right there before me, and I could do nothing to avenge her. He was out of my reach, yet so close. I felt my rage burning in me and I was ready to draw him into an attack. But then I felt her in my arms, almost as if she was trying to speak to me in her deathly silence.

I can't deal with the Shadow Lord now! I need to focus on getting out of here, on keeping Leander safe! I have to save her! He can wait!

As if to illustrate the point, Tallinn suddenly shouted at me: "Carden, come on!"

I tore myself away from staring at the monster, focusing now on escaping the erupting earth and collapsing canyons. I looked over my shoulder with Ellora, Tallinn and Fawkner just in time to watch the temple crumble into rubble and be swallowed up by the burning earth. In an instant the mountain suddenly snapped and dropped in its entirety, sinking into the island.

"Move!" Fawkner barked, turning and rushing away from the devastation.

I watched as Amethyst and Gaspeite exploded from the sinking temple, bursting through the air and speeding past us above.

"YES!" the Shadow Lord's voice erupted above us in a victorious howl of pleasure. "BRING THE ISLE OF SAFFERAN TO ITS KNEES! CRUSH IT INTO DUST! SUCH WILL BE THE FATE OF ALL OF HIGH-REALM!" he began laughing maliciously, the wretched sound echoing off the collapsing rocks all around us.

Bastard!

I didn't linger, rushing down the perilously warping hillside as quickly as I could, holding Leander tight. Even if I fell, I wouldn't let go of her. My feet hit a flatter piece of ground and I skidded to the sound of the waves. I looked up, gasping as I watched the roiling sea lurching towards us, the waves starting to swallow the breaking beaches.

The island is sinking! We have to get off it now!

I sprinted as fast as I could, trying to keep from tripping, my awareness good enough that I could make these steps with ease. The ground dropped behind us, a few Guardians, High Elves and Dragon Knights who had lagged behind screaming as they plunged into the fiery depths beneath Safferan's rocky skin.

Keep moving! I told myself urgently. *Just keep going! Get her to safety! Do it!*

I was keeping stride with Ellora, the Huntress maintaining her calm despite her obvious terror. None of us could have imagined this great and terrible destruction that we were being pursued by. The thudding of the dragons' assaults was rising even louder over the roar of the collapsing mountain and the erupting lava. They had intensified the attack, determined to sink the island into the Crestian Sea along with any who yet lived. Morod was set on murdering us all.

Just keep running! Get over that hill! Get to the ships! Move it!

I reached the top of the hill at a slow sprint, planting my feet as Leander's dead weight made it a little more difficult to climb the incline. Funny, given how light the girl was, despite her height. My feet dug into the earth and I turned my eyes to the Elven ships waiting there. The survivors were boarding quickly, rushing up the planks as fast as they could. We had landed against cliffs in line with the height of the decks specifically to run fast if we had to.

Without hesitation, I ran down the sandy slope with the others, the eight of us desperate to reach the ships that were now pitching violently in the disturbed waves. In mere moments my feet were pounding the gangplank as the ship we had arrived on began pulling away swiftly. I breathed hard as I made it with my friends onto the deck, my limbs burning painfully.

Suddenly, there came a horrific cracking and screams of desperate fear. We watched on helplessly as the third ship was crushed beneath the collapse of a cliff, all those on board being dragged under into the roiling depths of the angry ocean.

"Oh gods!" Tallinn gasped in horror, covering her mouth with both hands.

The waves coming off the sinking ship hit ours, pushing it clear of the collapse.

I cradled Leander close in my arms, turning my eyes back to Safferan as our ship gained enough distance to get free of the undertow's pull. My companions, Lord Selwyn, Ser Callenhad, and the Wizards gathered with me, watching on in horror at the sight before us. We could still hear the cracking of the stones and rocks of the island, the flashes of the seven dragons still visible as they were lashing out at the ground. The entire island was falling, the mountain now gone as what remained sank into the hungry waves.

"They destroyed all of Safferan," Lord Selwyn observed with a chill of terror in his voice. "The entire island and all the living things upon its body are now decimated by the Fallen Ones' fires and swallowed by the seas."

"What power is there that can stand against such destruction?" Ser Callenhad asked with a haunted expression upon his face.

"I do not know," Ranzel shook his head gravely, watching the remnants of Safferan dip below the waves as a great black plume and red lava spewed up in its place. "We have suffered a great defeat here this dread night. We must find a way to resist, or else Lord Morod will be truly victorious."

Lord Selwyn turned and strode past us, heading for the helm. "We must return to Silvervale with haste. All of High-Realm will know what has transpired here by morning and we must prepare for what is yet to come."

My companions and I stood there as the Wizards, Guardians, Elves and Dragon Knights rushed to their duties and worries, the eight of us glued in place as we watched the plume that was Safferan. That was Aldwyn's home, where he had learned to wield magic and where he became a Guardian. Even as the best and most knowledgeable of those of us named Guardians, I doubted he would know what to do now.

"Tallinn," Fawkner turned to my Guardian sister, looking for guidance. "You are our leader now with Aldwyn's passing. What should we do?"

Tallinn shook her head, her long blonde hair flying in the wind. "I... I don't know. I truly do not know..."

"We return to Silvervale as has been decided," Ellora stated urgently, fear in her eyes. "We must seek the shelter of the city and try to come up with some means of defending against this."

Chapter Three
A Solemn Return

For nearly six days our ships battled against relentlessly turbulent waves, the sky never again lightening. Storm clouds as black as the Void choked the air and lightning cracked dryly through the heights of the world. There was no rain though, only ash spewing from the still burning wreckage that had once been Safferan.

At last, the ships pulled through the river mouth that led to Silvervale's shimmering white walls, the waters no calmer here than on the open seas. I stood on the deck of the ship as we arrived back in the city docks, my cloak around me and my hood drawn. My mood had become as dark as the skies above and I cared so very little that the air had grown thick with an unnatural cold as snow fell on the city. My heart was just as chilled without the beautiful girl who had warmed it, my days now only as darkest stormy night. Yet, I still grew concerned.

General Gailan met us at the docks with a contingent of High Elven guards, their silver armour clinking as they walked towards the ship. Even before disembarking I could see the concern on the Elf warrior's face.

As Lord Selwyn, Ser Callenhad and the Wizards strode down the gangplank, I turned to go and get Leander from the cabin I'd laid her in. I needed to take her to the Lord's House and allow her a peaceful place to lie. My eyes widened as I saw two High Elves carrying her from below deck on a stretcher.

"Carden," Tallinn seized my arm, her own black and silver hood drawn, her eyes bearing the signs of little sleep. "It's all right. Let them take her."

I conceded, though reluctantly, going with her and Fawkner down the gangplank with the rest of our group at our backs.

"My Lord Selwyn," Gailan bowed his head as we approached from the ship. "You return.... though with one less ship than when you departed."

"The battle at Safferan was a disaster, Gailan," Lord Selwyn declared as he strode onwards, removing his gloves, his own armour dirtied from the trip and fight. "Lord Morod has succeeded in his plans to awaken Ragnarok and his brethren, thus loosing them upon the world anew. In his attempts to destroy those of us who faced him, he turned the destructive powers of the Fallen Ones upon Safferan itself, burning the very isle until it broke beneath the waves."

Gailan looked shocked as he heard this. "Then the news from all over High-Realm is confirmed."

"Come, what news spreads from the other places of our world?" Lord Selwyn asked of him as we followed close.

Gailan hurried to keep up with the Elf Lord's grand stride, flustered as he spoke: "All of Aldegaad and Ivansten have been abuzz with word that the Isle of Safferan suddenly erupted six nights past like a great volcano, as if the Seraphim itself had suddenly appeared beneath the isle and destroyed it. I had thought it only rumour until your return. Tell me, my Lord, what of the Princess?"

My heart ripped a little more as he asked of her, all of us pausing our strides. Lord Selwyn looked sadly towards the two Elves who carried her on the stretcher as others brought what dead we could rescue from the temple before its collapse.

"She was slain by Lord Morod," Lord Selwyn said gravely, looking from her back to Gailan. "With the girl's death the dragons were released."

He turned and began up the white stairs from the docks, his focus shifting as he grasped the pommel of his curved elven sword. We stayed close, though my eyes did fall to Leander's small, lifeless form.

"We must convene a meeting at the Broken Towers forthwith," the Elf Lord declared. "There is much we must do if we are to hope to defend against the inevitable onslaught yet to come."

"There are arrivals seeking the attention of the Council, my Lord," Gailan informed him, almost jogging to keep up. "It seems that the fall of Safferan has been felt across all of High-Realm."

"Then we shall attend to it," he turned to us. "Masters and Mistress Guardians, you will of course join us."

"Of course," Tallinn nodded under her hood as we came to the landing.

"I must go with Leander," I insisted, looking to my girl as the guards carried her away from the docks. "I have to make sure she is safe..."

"Do not fret, Master Carden," Lord Selwyn assured me, his dark hair catching with the relentless winds that were tearing at everything around us now. "I assure you she will be well taken care of by my servants."

"She will?" I was fearful I wouldn't see her again. "She should not end up like Aldwyn."

"No, indeed not," he agreed, meeting my gaze. "Yet, I thought it prudent that she be cleansed of the horrors and taint Lord Morod inflicted upon her at Safferan. You may go to her after our conference. Please, join me."

I could feel Tallinn staring at me, knowing that my sister Guardian was silently urging me to do as I was asked as she had done so many times before. Normally, I was grateful to her for such, but at that moment I yearned only to grieve for my love.

I nodded my consent. "Of course, Lord Selwyn."

The Elf Lord nodded and continued along his path, heading up the many stairways of the city towards the Broken Towers. Not all of our party were invited, only Ellora joining the three of us that were Guardians; Tristan, Joran and the Dwarves instead making their way to the Lord's House.

I walked the long staircases and dark stone corridors of the towers with Tallinn, Fawkner and Ellora until we came to the pinnacle of the central tower, entering to find that the others were waiting for us. The room was deeply chilled with the balcony ever open to the elements, the towering high ceiling showing only the dark nightmare sky that roared and flashed above.

Once again, the five Wizards were set upon their places, their staffs in hand, Xzharn now with a replica of the one the Shadow Lord had destroyed. The five old men looked more severe than they had when we had brought Leander before them weeks earlier. I worried what she would have thought if she had been with us now.

Ser Callenhad and his second were talking just off to the side of the grand table, Lord Selwyn and Gailan standing in their place. With Warden Alessa dead there was no representative of the Guardians here in Silvervale. Or so I thought.

"Warden Riordan?" Tallinn caught sight of the figures standing off to the balcony before I did, drawing my gaze.

Riordan, leader of the Coastwatch Keep Contingent, stood with three other Guardians, one the second of Alessa. He turned to us, his greying dark hair neat and his blue eyes alighting at the sight of us.

"Tallinn Landrace, Carden Highever, Fawkner Caradoc!" he was overjoyed as he came to greet us with a grasp to each of our arms. "By the Gods, how good it is to see you all!"

"And you, Warden Riordan," Tallinn spoke for all of us as I was certainly in no mood to do so. "What brings you to the Broken Towers?"

Riordan sighed gravely, shaking his head. "Ill tidings, unfortunately."

"What has transpired?" Fawkner asked darkly, concern evident on his bearded and scarred face.

"Coastwatch Keep has fallen," Riordan replied gravely, turning to each of us in turn.

"How?" Tallinn looked both afraid and shocked as she spoke.

"Destroyed," he said simply and coldly. "By a great and terrible black dragon wreathed in flames not but five days past. It was accompanied by a contingent of Shadow Knights. Defeat was certain the moment the great beast appeared."

"Ragnarok," Fawkner uttered, glancing to the rest of us.

A chill ran down my spine at the mere mention of the foul beast. I swallowed hard, dreading to even contemplate the horrors those at the stronghold would have faced.

"How did you escape?" I asked, trying to keep myself calm even as I felt the others' fear mounting.

"He warned us," Riordan turned with a thankful smile to the balcony.

We all looked to the archway to watch in awe as a great figure lowered his head and came to enter the room, which I now realised was so tall in order to accommodate his kind. He had great wings, a body of scales coloured of brown, green and aqua, his glowing orange eyes immediately locking on those of us he recognised.

"Eamnonn," I stepped forward, amazed to see the Dragon from the Guardian Trials.

"Incredible," Fawkner smiled as he looked up at the great being we had both had the pleasure of meeting.

"Greetings Guardian Carden, Guardian Fawkner," Eamnonn said in his deep, gravelly voice. "It is so very good to see you both again after all this time."

I was actually rather glad to see the great dragon again.

Riordan was appreciative: "Eamnonn came to us early before dawn on the day the stronghold fell. He warned us of the impending threat and advised us to take all of our people at Coastwatch Keep, along with what we could carry, and flee. We are fortunate we heeded his words, for that night the great beast came and decimated the fortress."

"You knew Ragnarok was coming?" Fawkner was amazed.

Eamnonn nodded as he sat back on his hind end, his front hands to the floor. "I heard the beat of his wings on the wind and sensed the intent to destroy the keep in his thoughts. I could smell the foul odour of murder upon his scales even hours away from me, and so decided to try and save all that I could. Needless to say, he was not happy to find an empty fortress when he arrived."

"Apparently this is no isolated incident," Lord Selwyn drew our attention, gesturing for us all to take our seats, continuing on only once we had. "We have received reports from all over High-Realm, and even as far away as Harredi and Galicia of attacks by vicious monster dragons."

"Each location targeted," Gailan said gravely, "had been either of Elven military strength or a stronghold of the Guardians."

I felt a chilled dread falling into the pit of my stomach as he spoke those words. My heart became heavy and I feared what that would mean. I could feel Tallinn's terror as she sat at my right, though she did well to keep her calm.

"Even the Dragon Knights have suffered such attacks," Ser Callenhad spoke direfully, looking around at all of us gathered there. "Many of the monasteries we were using as facades to the greater populace have been burned by dragon fires and decimated, along with the brothers and sisters within their walls."

"It seems that this has been a coordinated attack against our respective orders," Samhir the Gold observed, his hands pressed together in a steeple in front of him. "Even the Tower of Mages in Harredi has been destroyed, according to the message my brothers in magic that survived the attack have managed to convey to me since our arrival here."

"And we have repelled several strikes by the Scourge against the city," Gailan added with a severe gaze. "In three days, we have defeated no less than eight attacks on Silvervale. We have bolstered the defences in response and the Mages here have increased power to the warding magic that surrounds our borders."

Tallinn shook her head, trying to comprehend the horror of all of this. "Why are they attacking such places? What is there to gain?"

"Destroying the Guardians, the Dragon Knights, the High Elves and the Magic Wielders of the world would make conquering all of Therras all the easier," Ranzel expressed with a cold dread in his eyes as he stood and began pacing, stroking his white beard in thought. "Lord Morod knows full well that these four groups are the only powers capable of uniting and standing against him without the unanimous consent of High-Realm's Seven Kingdoms."

"Indeed," Ragdobar nodded, his frail voice sounding even more so. "Without these powers to lead the charge, the Seven Kingdoms will not perceive the threat as serious, and so shall pay it no heed until it is too late."

"That's ridiculous!" Fawkner scowled, shaking his head. "Are not these very attacks themselves enough to warrant action from our nations?! Can they not see the necessity to rally together against this risen threat?!"

"In days since past, it would have been," Ranzel nodded as he paced back and forth. "But now we see the days where the kingdoms are concerned *only* with their own security, the nobles in power obsessed with finding enemies in their neighbours. Even such attacks as these will only drive them to cloister like clams."

I couldn't remain sitting now, standing and leaning against a pillar with my arms crossed. I had grown uncomfortable, needing to move somewhat as I listened. Even Fawkner stood, though he was desperate to plead a case for the union of the nations. Such idealism was admirable.

"As it is," Riordan expressed as he braced his hands against the table, "the political situation throughout High-Realm has worsened over the past three years. Mere weeks ago, Lord Fane closed all the borders of Aldegaad to any outside travellers. He has since declared martial law and plunged Aldegaad into disarray."

"Lord Fane has always been a suspicious and dangerous man," Ranzel stated, knowing the situation full well. "Such was the reason why King Aric chose to surpass him with a younger heir."

Though he didn't mention her name he still spoke of Leander and my heart ripped just a little more, driving a spike of grief and pain through my chest. I tensed my muscles, trying to fight back the agony of her loss until I could be away from them.

Riordan went on: "And since his coronation as King of Aldegaad, Fane has been pushing the nation towards reigniting the ancient war with Ivansten. Even now Aldegaadian troops amass in the Frozen Ravine gate fortress of Aldgate in response to yet more soldiers being sent to bolster the Ivanstenian lines. If the tensions between the two nations continue it will mean civil war."

"It seems the tensions between these two nations have been growing for many years," Fawkner commented gravely, his eyes hard. "For three years now, all that has happened between them has been the continual garrisoning of the Frozen Ravine. I can scarce believe either side would have soldiers enough left in other parts of their domains to protect their peoples."

"We already know that Lord Morod had a hand in the manipulation of King Fane," Ellora reminded us all. "Would it truly not surprise anyone that he would have done the same with King Dunmore in order to orchestrate this very situation?"

It didn't surprise me. After seeing the work of the Shadow Lord almost entirely firsthand, I could believe that nothing was beyond his limits. He would destroy any and all who stood against him with not even an eyelash battered in response from the kingdoms purely because they were too stupidly embroiled in these petty conflicts. I sighed. Politics always did give me a headache.

"Hardly," Lord Selwyn spoke coldly, resting his hands on the table in front of him. "Forgive me, for I mean no offence, but human rulers have always been so easily swayed by their lust of power."

"I am not offended," I said nonchalantly, completely agreeing with him.

"This lust for advancement and control makes them easy targets for the manipulations of one such as Lord Morod," Lord Selwyn went on severely. "I imagine the situation elsewhere is no more improved?"

Riordan sighed, shaking his head. "Gorvenna has dipped into civil war as the freedom fighters, the Sons of Gorven, now strike against Queen Keilantra's forces in the capital of Nargilith. And, with the stronghold of Castle Nargoth naught but burning rubble, there are no Guardians left in that nation to assist in quelling the battles."

"How many Guardian strongholds were lost?" Tallinn asked coldly, afraid to know the answer.

I didn't blame her. It was the single question that lingered in my mind, yet I refused to speak it aloud. Like her, I didn't wish to know the truth of how bad off we really were, but I couldn't turn from it either. I needed to know.

Riordan seemed drained as he answered: "We have lost Coastwatch Keep in Aldegaad, Fort Vangaad in Ivansten, Castle Nargoth in Gorvenna, Grey Stone Keep in Vorhalaas, the Fortress of Seaguard in Lorveren, and of course the Isle's Peak Tower on Safferan, and the Citadel of Dartaren. Only the Enclave in Daamenhall and the headquarters here in the Broken Towers remain."

"Have we truly lost so many?" Tallinn gasped, the shock clear on her sun kissed features.

We were all shocked, the very idea that all of the Guardian strongholds could be hit so easily in such a short time was beyond any of us. That the Citadel had fallen when it did horrified those of us who had gone there. I remembered crunching through the snow and among the dead, searching for survivors amidst the wreckage. It was Leander who had realised the threat we were under and warned the rest of us in time to flee from the Scourge that came to continue their assault. I could see her in my mind as clearly as I had that day as if it were moments ago. She looked so beautiful with the white snow behind her lifting the vibrant greens and purples of her cloak and dress, her very presence brightening that darkening place. Her blue eyes had been like cold steel in the fading light, her mahogany hair taking a reddish tint in the dusk as the strands coiled gracefully across her shoulders in the winds...

"It seems so," Riordan replied direfully, nodding to respond to Tallinn's horrified question, simultaneously bringing me back from the memory.

"If the Shadow Lord seeks to eradicate all of the Guardians and their strongholds so as not to be opposed with his invasion," Ellora spoke thoughtfully, her red hair pulled over her left shoulder with a tie to keep it neat, revealing her pointed ears, "then why exclude Silvervale and Daamenhall?"

"She's right," Fawkner agreed, looking to the Wizards and the others of the Council. "If his objective is to destroy the Order then why leave these two strongholds intact?"

"It is likely that the Enclave of Daamenhall remains because it is situated in the heart of the capital city of Balganis," Lucilius perceived, speaking in his harsh, coldly grim manner. "To destroy the Enclave would mean obliterating the City of Daamenhall *and* the Balganian Royal Family with it."

"A decidedly unwise move to make by the Shadow Lord," Samhir agreed, stroking his knotted black and grey beard.

"Why is that?" I asked, my arms folded firmly in front of my chest. "Killing us all seems to be his ultimate goal, given that he resurrected the Fallen Ones."

Samhir turned his caramel-coloured eyes to me, regarding me evenly. "Attacking a major city openly would jeopardise his plans to keep the kingdoms feuding amongst themselves. To do so, Master Carden, would mean that the Kingdoms of High-Realm would cease their squabbling and turn their attentions towards the greater threat."

"It would also mean that they would finally acknowledge the existence of a Shadow Lord when for so long now they have been content to cast such knowledge aside as conjecture and rumour," Lucilius added with a flick of his hand as if to illustrate his words as he spoke.

"It is something that Lord Morod certainly will not risk," Ranzel agreed gravelly. "As for why *this* stronghold in which we stand has not been destroyed, it is simply because they have been unable to."

"Because of your magicks?" Fawkner queried.

Ragdobar nodded loftily, seeming so old that he was barely there. "Indeed. The warding shield we have cast over the Broken Towers and Silvervale keeps all such evils at bay."

"Regardless, we are not unscathed from these attacks," Gailan spoke up, casting a hard look around at each of us. "The Scourge yet continue to make attacks on the city walls even as we speak, held at bay only by the prowess of our warriors. Mark my words, we have not gone unnoticed in the Shadow Lord's plans for destruction."

"Then... the cities... the towns..." Fawkner said, an obvious concern in his older eyes, "they are untouched by the Wyrms and their fires?"

I knew of what Fawkner meant. His concern was for his family back in Eilath, his hope that they be safe and unharmed from the nations-wide scorching of the dragons understandable.

Ranzel saw his concern as I did, nodding. "Yes. The towns and cities remain untouched by the flames of Ragnarok and his kin. At least for the moment."

Fawkner visibly relaxed, sighing a breath of relief and thanks as he held his hands in prayer, lowering his head to join them.

"Are there no Guardians left beyond those of us here and at Daamenhall?" Tallinn was now looking to Riordan again, ever the dutiful member of the Order as she was.

Riordan shrugged, shaking his head as he leaned his palms on the tabletop where he stood. "It is hard to be certain. All who remain have been sent word to take to hiding until we can find a location secure enough to gather in. I cannot say for certain that all the Guardians not at strongholds during the attacks yet live, but some might. My entire contingent remains, and so I can only hope others join us."

"You believe others will?" Ellora questioned with a raise of one sharp, dark eyebrow.

Riordan sighed, standing up straight. "At this dark time, we need all the Guardians who yet remain. To hear of Aldwyn's passing two weeks past was terrible, but to find that Warden Alessa and a number of the contingent here have fallen on Safferan during the battle that sank the island is a tragedy," he folded his arms, turning his gaze towards Tallinn, Fawkner and I, his expression pale and silently fearful. "We find ourselves once again facing the destruction of our Order at the hands of a Shadow Lord as once we did in the distant past," he shook his head grimly, looking almost hopeless. "It is just as the stories told of when the Shadow Lords eradicated the Guardians down to only one man."

"Dartaren," Ellora nodded, gaining our gazes. "The Last of the Ancient Guardians and friend to myself and Queen Leander the First."

My heart screeched as it stung again at her name. I remained composed and steely eyed, tightening the fold of my arms to keep my insides from hurting, but that didn't stop me feeling, only from showing it.

"What do we do?" Tallinn wondered, the look of a frightened woman masking her normally stoic exterior.

"Assemble what forces we can of our Orders," Lord Selwyn stated simply, "and attempt to form some sort of resistance to defend against the Shadow Lord and his Dominion."

"Defend?" Fawkner scoffed incredulously, leaning forward to gain the eyes of all those before him, his expression soured. "There is *no* defence. You speak as if we are a band of rebels seeking to strike against a corrupt king, not the formidable forces we are meant to be."

"Our forces are greatly diminished, Lord Caradoc," Lord Selwyn stated factually, meeting the man's steel coloured gaze. "What Dragon Knights remain are scattered far too few, and what Guardians are seemingly trapped between here and Balganis. The magic circles are all but obliterated and we High-Elves cannot stand alone against this threat even if we could call to the Blackfelds for reinforcement from our kin. With what forces we yet have, defence is all we can muster without the aid of the Kingdoms of High-Realm."

"What of your kind, Eamnonn?" Fawkner looked to the great Aquari Dragon for hope. "Surely the Dragons can intervene and stop Ragnarok and his brethren. They *are* dragons after all."

Eamnonn shook his head, his fire-coloured eyes dulled by his emotions. "No. I am the only Dragon willing to stand with you beyond Gaspeite and young Amethyst. The others are all cloistered away, hiding from this realm in another we call the Valley. They cannot be counted on to assist."

"Truly," Ellora looked to the great dragon, "are all of your kind hidden away there?"

Eamnonn nodded, sighing a breath that sounded like a deep rumble from his brown and aqua scaled body: "All but one other are in the Valley, but he will not stand with us."

"Of whom do you speak, Eamnonn?" Ranzel asked, leaning on his staff as he looked into the Dragon's eyes.

"Kelapas, the Ice Dragon," Eamnonn replied, turning his face to the Wizard. "You know him well, Ranzel."

"Oh, yes," Ranzel nodded with the look of a man who had just heard the name of someone he knew to be of poor reputation. "You're right. Kelapas will not aid us."

"He is too absorbed in his dominion over the Lorgath Pass and the Nartarn'lath Mountains," Eamnonn snarled, shaking his head. "Such possessiveness over a place is unbecoming of one of Dragon Blood."

"Then there is no way to stop Morod and Ragnarok?" I asked, a deep feeling of defeat in my heart.

Xzharn sat back, sighing and shaking his long white-haired head, his hands together on the table in front of him: "Not now, there isn't. Our only option to defeat Lord Morod was to do so before he could enact his plans on Safferan."

I felt a scowl rising as he spoke, dreading what I knew he was going to say.

Fawkner frowned. "There is nothing then?"

Xzharn looked around at each of us, speaking in his harsh, deep voice: "Keeping the Princess alive past the Lunar Joining was our *only* chance at defeating the Shadow Lord's plans and giving us the way to fight him head on. But we failed. We failed, and now Safferan is but smoke and magma bubbling from the ocean, Ragnarok and his brothers lay waste to our outposts and have weakened us tenfold in less than a week, and Princess Leander, descendent of High-Realm's last great champion, lies dead. All we can hope to do is stave off utter destruction and find a way to convince others to aid us in this insurmountable fight for the fate of Therras itself."

I glared at him, feeling my hands shaking as I let my arms drop to my sides, my fingers clenching angrily. He sounded accusing and I felt that his gaze was directed at us, the Guardians who had defended her.

Because we were Leander's protectors... Of course he blames us...

"We tried to save her," I defended, thinking more of Tallinn and Fawkner than myself.

"If *you*, young Guardian, had kept your feelings for her *unknown* and remained her protector," Xzharn accused me with a hard black stare, "then perhaps she would not have been so trusting of the Lost masquerading as you after your little quarrel. Perhaps she would not have been slain if she had not been seeking your attentions..."

"You accuse my relationship with her as being the reason she was murdered?!" I raged, glaring at him, feeling that side of me I tried to keep hidden deep down in the dark of my soul starting to snap and bay for blood.

"Carden, be calm," Ellora was at my side, trying to ease my anger with her gentle touch as Fawkner and Tallinn both stood from their seats.

"You dare to condemn our love as the reason Morod now wreaks havoc against this world?!" I was close to screaming at the wizard, held back only by Fawkner and Ellora.

"My Lord Xzharn," Lord Selwyn spoke up, looking to the Wizard and gesturing to me, "it is not fair to condemn this young man and his love for a woman as the cause of all that we now face. After all, we rested on our laurels in the wake of Aldwyn Draken's passing and did not bolster the city guard around the Princess' rooms. Even if we had, could we have detected the Lost coming for her with its shape changing powers? I think not."

"Lord Selwyn is right," Ranzel chimed in, standing over the White Wizard. "The Princess is dead not because of her love for this young man, but due to the actions of vile monsters whose very goal was to achieve the destruction of our world. Whether they shared this bond or not, Morod would still have found a way to reach her and enact his dark plans."

"Perhaps," Xzharn nodded darkly, gazing back at me. "However, this does not excuse the fact that such emotional bonds are dangerous for protectors to have with their charges. It is the very reason the ancient Guardians took vows of celibacy; to prevent this very incident from occurring. It is a rule modern Guardians would do well to endorse."

Tallinn threw him a glare. "Enough! This is making things worse!"

"This infighting serves no one!" Fawkner added, holding me back as I felt the urge to tear the old man's head from his spine.

"Perhaps if such ideals had been maintained to this day," Xzharn continued, clearly pushing further with this subject, "then we would not be facing the dire circumstances we now are."

I shoved away from my companions, slamming my hands so hard on the table that the section I hit bowed and splintered. I could feel the impulses of my predator deep inside me clawing to reach the surface, starting to lose my control.

I need my medicine. I'm on the edge of losing myself to it...

I narrowed my eyes at Xzharn, gritting my teeth as I felt the familiar stinging of my gums that came with the changes my body had battled most of my life.

"You are a cold and heartless old man who will never know the touch of a woman's love," I hissed viciously, but quietly at him. "And you are not deserving of it. Do *not* dishonour her like that in front of me again, for it will be the last thing you do."

There was no need to wait for a response from him or any of the others in the room. I shoved away from the table, accidentally shifting the entire thing several inches towards the Wizard as I moved.

I slipped past Fawkner, Ellora and Tallinn, storming from the chamber and rushing down the staircase towards the ground floor of the Broken Towers. As I strode past High-Elven guards, Dragon Knights and Guardians I felt my rage starting to overwhelm me and I had to just keep moving or else risk exploding.

Suddenly, there came two sets of running footfalls from behind me, but I didn't turn.

"Carden!" Tallinn called out to me. "Carden, wait!"

I stopped, turning slowly to gaze back at her and Fawkner as they jogged up to me. The two of them slowed to a walk as they travelled the last few feet, concern on their faces.

"Carden, are you all right?" she asked, her blonde hair falling around her shoulders as she came to a stop.

"That musty old bastard had no right to talk about her like that!" I erupted, fighting the angry tears that I felt. "He had no right to tarnish what we shared in such a malicious way!"

"No, you're right. He didn't," Fawkner agreed, speaking with a calmness I couldn't muster. "He's scared, Carden. They all are."

"And can you truly blame them?" Tallinn looked to me with soft eyes. "Gods, we're all scared, and we all miss her."

"No one as much as me," I growled, looking down at their feet.

"You are her lover," Fawkner granted, touching my shoulder gently. "And you were together after two years apart for only the briefest of times. Not one of us believes that to be fair. But you cannot allow what was said back there to colour your actions now."

I looked up at him sadly. "I'd say that's too late, but for the fact that I had already decided what I'm going to do back at Safferan as she died in my arms."

"What do you mean when you say "what you're going to do"?" Tallinn looked uneasy at my words.

I took a deep breath, closing my eyes. I plunged my hand into my shirt and wrenched my Guardian medallion from my neck, the chain snapping at the force of my pull. I glared down at the emblem of the shield and two swords with disdain, then looked to my two friends coldly.

"I'm done," I said icily, clutching it in my hand and squeezing it as if to break it. "I am done being a Guardian!"

Tallinn shook her head. "No, brother. You're just upset..."

"I am not your brother, Tallinn," I said firmly, staring down at her. "I am and will always be your friend, but I am no longer your fellow Guardian."

I took my sword from my belt, casting it to the floor and slid out of my black and silver Guardian over tunic and cloak.

"I rescind my oath and make a new one," I said as I dropped them, still holding the medallion. "I am a Guardian of High-Realm no longer, the oath I made when I joined the Order no longer in my heart as truth. I have but one truth: I love her, and I will do anything to get her back," with that said, I threw the medallion, hearing it clatter to the black stone floor with several resounding thuds.

"Carden..." Tallinn tried.

"I am sorry, Tallinn," I said sternly, throwing off my Guardian bracers to join my other Order apparel, "but there is no convincing me otherwise. I am through with the Guardian Order."

It hurt me to see Tallinn - my sister in oath - so wounded by my actions and decision, but my mind was made up. Being a Guardian no longer had any meaning for me.

"Why?" she asked, desperate to understand. "Why are you doing this?"

I looked back to her sadly, shrugging widely. "She's dead. It was my duty to protect her. I failed. It's as simple as that."

I turned and walked away, once again traversing the great staircase from the towers down towards Silvervale proper as the unending supernatural storm continued to rage on above. The sky seemed like a mirror for the storms that swirled and battered within my broken heart, a physical commentary on my position and emotion now. My soul was in turmoil, and I had no way to calm it without Leander, so I didn't even deem it worthy to try.

Chapter Four
Lost in the Void

I didn't regret my decision, and though I was certain that the discussion wouldn't be over between Tallinn and I, I remained confident in my choice. It no longer felt right for me to be a Guardian, so I wouldn't be one. A Guardian should be strong and wise all at once. A Guardian should have the ability to remain steadfast against all threats. But most of all, a Guardian shouldn't allow his feelings for his charge to take priority over the situation at hand. This last part was something that continued to play on my mind without remorse, battering me down with every wakeful moment.

The battle of the temple kept playing itself over and over in my mind as if I had been cursed by a sorcerer to relive my greatest failure. I kept wondering if there was something I could have done differently; if there had been some action that I could have carried out or ignored that might have spared us all of this.

Maybe if my actions were different, we would not be facing annihilation at the hands of Ragnarok and the Shadow Lord. Maybe... she would still be alive...

I sighed at this thought, walking with my eyes to the ground, my hair whipping into my face with the raging winds. The cold air was only half the strength of that which lay within the chasm where my heart had once been.

If I had done things differently, I could have saved her. Perhaps if I had just focused on the locks on her shackles and not the monster himself? That thought was wishful thinking. Given the powers the Shadow Lord possessed, it would have been easy for him to simply pull me from her with merely a thought, stopping me from freeing her. If he could freeze me to the spot as he had and still defend against the others whilst continuing that dread ritual, then this action would have been of ease to him.

I needed to see her. That was the only thing that came to me, the only want I had left. I craved neither food nor rest, only the company of my dead lost love.

Finding her seemed difficult at first as I had no idea where the High Elves had taken her. This drew a new frustration and that jealous part of me suggested that they were trying to hide her from me. I simply brushed that part of myself off my back and crushed it down into the depths where I locked all such insanities I felt.

If I give in to such insecurities and suspicious nonsense, then I am not the man my beloved cared for.

At last, I came across an Elven servant and asked him where she might be found. I realised that my way of speaking as if she yet lived was odd, but I couldn't call her departed as so many others did. It seemed harder to do so with her than it had Aldwyn and Ser Mithras. Though quizzical towards my manner of speaking of her, the Elf nodded and told me that there was a place in the Temple to Gaya in the gardens. This was where the High Elves took those of noble heart and purest innocence to rest before their final arrangements. Fitting. As I thanked him and made for the gardens, I couldn't help feeling a sense of ironic gladness at her being referred to in such a way. Though she was born of noble blood it was her way and her self that made her worthy of such a place of honour. Had I the strength to smile I might have at that thought, but I couldn't. There was still the inexorable truth that she lay dead.

The gardens were not as they were when we had been there together, the verdant greens and the blossoms now fallen under the white of snows. It seemed as if the heavens had chosen to blanket the north in such a way the day of Aldwyn's funeral and had decided to deepen it now.

A sigh escaped my lips as I looked upon this place. It was on this spot where we had argued the night Tristan had kissed her against her will.

Her words returned to me as I saw her tears upon her snow-white cheeks as clearly in my mind as if I had stepped back in time to that moment. But only one part of it all struck me like a fist of ice to my jaw.

She had been shaking, her eyes red with hurt and tears. *"YOU DIDN'T HELP ME! YOU BROKE YOUR PROMISE TO ME!"*

Those words had staggered me, making me confused. *My promise...?*

"What?" I had asked out of stupid ignorance.

"I was alone!" she sobbed, her body hunching as if her chest had grown too heavy for her to carry. *"I was scared! I wanted you to come for me, but you didn't! You didn't save me! You promised!"*

I had been so stupid, not even then realising what it was that she was saying. But as she spoke her next part I suddenly understood, and my insides were shredded with horror.

She looked at me, nearly weeping, but trying to be strong as she always did: *"Two years I waited... Two years I called your name and hoped you would come for me... But you never did..."*

"The tower?" I felt like a complete dunce as realisation suddenly struck me and my words the day I was taken from Castle Ortagaad came back to me. I *had* promised her... and I had failed to keep that promise.

"You didn't come for me," she suddenly fell to her knees as if the weight of her hurt had become all too much for her frame to hold both it and her at once. *"You... you left me there alone and they hurt me so badly..."*

I sighed as I thought of that exchange between us, of how hurt she had looked. My last act towards her before she was taken had been one of anger and blind jealousy. Though my final words to her had been of love, it could never atone for my vile accusations against her fidelity. She was innocent, I was guilty.

The day at Castle Ortagaad returned to me as I continued to walk from that spot, my mind lingering now on my promise: *"I will come back and free you! I promise! I PROMISE!"*

Those words of reassurance repeated themselves in my mind as they had every day since I had been taken from that place, and from her. Though I had made every effort to keep that promise, I had spent two years being ineffective instead of finding the solution for her. I had allowed myself to wallow in my concern and grief when I should have fought harder to return and rescue her.

And what had she done? She had endured, had languished in a cell being tortured by the Witches' powers and devices whilst being coveted by the guards who fantasised of her rape. Despite all the torment and crushing loneliness, she had still thought of me and my promise. While I had taken rest in comfort, she had shivered in the cold dark of that tower. While I had been well fed, she had been given scraps not fit for an animal. While I had found diversion in the moments where action was impossible, she had stared at blank walls and faced crushing loneliness. I should have done more.

What of her final moments? Those five days she lived as their prisoner while they prepared to murder her? How frightened must she have been? How lonely must she have felt?

That hurt more than anything else. While I sat aboard a ship chomping at the bit to reach the Isle of Safferan and save her, Leander had been locked up in that cold and terrible place; trembling, scared and alone. Every moment must have been agonising torture with nothing to do but sit there with the knowledge that she was about to die. Some great companion that knowledge must have been to her...

I should have been there...

At last, I came to a beautiful Elven temple with a silver domed roof and elegant braziers alight around it. It stood there like some timid creature's head poking up from the snow, its structure looking as if it had been grown rather than carved of white stone. There were two High Elven guards standing at the entrance with their silver and gold halberds in hand and their shields on their arms, their faces hidden beneath masked helms and charcoal-coloured hoods.

My eyes fell to the large shape that lay there beside the structure, almost half buried in the snow. Amethyst was resting on her silver underbelly, her tail wrapped around her purple, violet and blue body. Her wings lay limp around her and she rested her head on the ground, her front claws set beside her long neck.

The Dragon turned her orange eyes to me as I approached in the deepening snows, the inner light that glowed within their molten flames now dulled greatly. She looked as I was sure I must have, her already long face now more so with her grief and hurt. I didn't think it possible, but even her scales seemed to have less of their normal hue, their vibrancy faded like her fire.

For her it must be like losing a part of herself. Leander said that the bond they shared, felt as if they were in some way a part of each other, that they could feel each other. I can only relate in the fact that the woman I love is gone, but to the Dragon it must be something so profound... Gods... it must feel much the same as it does for me...

Almost as if I were afraid of what I would find, I turned from the grieving dragon and stepped towards the temple. My green eyes took in the warmly glowing light that came from within, my footfalls soft on the marble floor.

Two High Elven women in blue and white pastel gowns were slowly leaving, the ruined sacrificial gown Leander had worn, and items meant to wash one's body in their arms. I picked up the scent of her blood as it was stained into that accursed dress, feeling that darker side of me yearning to get out. I would need my medicine when I was done here.

I was hardly surprised to see Joran in the distant corner of the room as I entered. The Storvari sat in a meditative position, his hands together in front of him as he remained silent with his eyes shut. His twin swords rested on the floor beside him, his cuirass removed so that he wore his most simple garments.

So, this is Storvari grief...

Feeling as if I could begin to cry, I turned from the warrior giant to the chamber I stood in, my eyes taking in all of the details.

Unlike the exterior of white and silver, the inside of the chamber seemed more golden, its elegantly carved supports looking like some great plant had created it all from its limbs. The ceiling continued up to the dome and had no embellishments, only simple earthy designs that were so common to the High Elves. Despite the lightness of the room's colours, it was wreathed in shadows that countless candles of fine white and gold wax attempted to strip away. The candles were set into elegant golden sconces on the walls, but also in great silver candelabras that stood proud on the floor encircling the space. It was all presided over by golden-white statues of praying hooded High Elves, their faces serene and exuding a gentle love of all things.

Beautiful as it all was, my eyes found only one focus. In the middle of the room there stood a white marble altar, simplistic and stunning. It had been padded with soft white furs and dressed in silver silks with plush pillows set at the head. This is where she lay.

There was another figure with her, one I had thought I might have seen at the meeting in the Broken Towers over an hour ago.

Enchantress Illuminil stood over her, dressed in silken robes of gold and green, her dark hair pulled back to hang free, yet allow the points of her ears to be seen. Her turquoise eyes were gentle, her right hand set upon my love's forehead. She was merely standing there gazing down at the girl's face with a reverence I could never know.

She spoke then in her soft, mystical voice as if to the girl before her: "Ultuli narvil nu, Princera, ra fei narmira lorgoros. Nigh ishar hert res ne paic'ee ra mai Gaya tul'lurilish. Knir, Cherriss'un, ish irr lovirr."

I understood her words, feeling my heart ache more as I translated them in my head: *Sleep well now, Princess, and feel no more pain. Let your heart rest in peace and may Gaya watch over you. Know, Cherished One, you are loved.*

As Enchantress Illuminil gently bent and kissed her head, I half hoped she would bring her back to life. But she didn't. I think such miracles were beyond the magicks of all the Elves, Wizards and Mages that dwelt in that city combined. At least it was impossible to bring her back as her.

I wouldn't dare consider necromancy. Not on her. That would be crueller than letting her stay dead.

Enchantress Illuminil turned from the altar, moving gracefully towards me. She met my sorrowful gaze and gently nodded before departing to give me my time.

I stood there for a while like some nervous adolescent boy afraid to approach a girl he adored, just staring down at her. Slowly, almost perilously, I began to approach the altar step by step, feeling as if the slightest quick movement could turn her to dust in the breeze.

I came to the foot of the altar, standing before where she lay. She was perfect. The dishevelled gown she had been forced to wear was gone, the wounds on her thighs and sides cleaned so no blood stained her flesh. Even her hair was washed and brushed for some last shred of dignity. She had been put into a pearl white dress that sat low upon her ankles, the sleeves resting close around her arms and wrists, the shoulders gently tucked with stitching and only just exposing the soft flesh of her collarbones' outer edges. If only they had gifted her a higher neckline, this one just barely showing the ugly red and black wound in her chest where the dagger had cleaved her heart.

On her wrists and ankles there were the purplish marks left from where the cold steel shackles that held her in place for her death had touched her, the bruises a cold reminder on their own of what she had endured. But other than these marks and wounds, she looked as though she were just sleeping.

I set my green eyes upon her face, drinking in her beauteous, soft features, feeling as if I had lived a lifetime without sight of her. Her full, yet thin lips were gently parted, only the faintest white of her front teeth visible, her slender arched eyebrows like the lines of brown ink drawn by a quill on her snow-white skin. Her rounded face, subtle cheekbones and gently cleft chin made her seem like such a child in her youth, her pointed and slightly curved nose looking so delicate. Below her resting brows her eyes lay closed, the eyelids gently greyed now in her new paleness. Her mahogany hair rested behind her milky soft shoulders and neck, the dark hue of the strands seeming to make the white of her face all the more beautiful in the candlelight.

I looked to the gentle slopes of her breasts beneath her gown, hoping to see them rise with her breath. But they remained still. She drew no air into her lungs, had no beat of a living heart within her ribs, and looked as cold as the ice beyond the room she lay within.

Gods... how I must look in front of her...

I was dishevelled, my green shirt's sleeves rolled up to expose my broad forearms, my clothes hardly clean after all we had been through. I felt the grime on my forehead and the sweat on my skin, smelling the scent of my salt and efforts even now.

She smelled sweet and pure, cleansed of all the dirt and taint that must have attached to her. I couldn't imagine her ever truly being unclean, even when she hadn't bathed in weeks with all our travelling.

I took her right hand in mine as I leaned over her. Her skin was just as cold as I had imagined, no warmth left to her slender fingers. It was an alien feeling to come from her, for she was nothing but warmth and light, and so this felt wrong. She should never have been so cold to touch.

Her hands were so small compared to mine. I had large hands, tanned from my time out on the road, calloused from my manual work and use of weapons. My fingers were broad and long, my skin showing the vessels behind my coarse knuckles with the faint flecks of man hair that sparsely covered my forearms. Hers were soft, delicate and very white, her veins looking as if they had been marked by the subtle touch of an artist's brush as meagre shadows in her flesh. They looked like the hands of a musician or a writer, but such came with nobility and femininity.

I didn't know how to begin, turning my gaze to her face and studying it for a time beyond my thinking. I could have stayed with her like this forever, as long as she drew breath. Finally, I just took a breath of my own, feeling my eyes burn with grief.

"I don't know what it is I am supposed to say to you," I confessed, knowing that were she alive she would have listened without judgement. "After what has happened to you I... I doubt there is anything that is right to say."

She remained unmoving, silent in her unending sleep.

"You know... the day we met I was... beyond infatuated with you," I said, just talking for no other reason than to fill our silence, to feel as if she was more than just a lifeless body lying there. "You looked so beautiful, so captivating, standing there on the steps of the castle; dressed in blue velvet, the wind catching your dark hair, a hardcover book clutched to your chest," I smiled as I recalled that image, remembering how she had looked that day in Arvon, our first day together. "You were so young, so wilful and curious, I could hardly help my gaze. You were hardly like a noble-born girl at all; so modest, creative and kind," I went on slowly. "It was a struggle not to smile at you, not to immediately wish to speak to you and know you. But, I reminded myself of my duties, that a Guardian must show the proper decorum before a King, a Queen..." I looked at her face, my voice cracking a little, "...a Princess..."

I took my left hand and gently stroked her head, feeling the soft silken strands of her hair under my coarse palm. She didn't even flinch, though I was hardly expecting her to. The truth had all but cemented itself within me now.

"Never in my wildest dreams would I ever have thought to fall in love with a Princess," I said, fighting my grief just to hold on a little longer. "But more importantly... never did I think I would fall in love with you, Leander," I sighed, looking from her for a moment to regain some composure before once more gazing upon her still face. "I have never had many people I could truly open my heart to in this life," I spoke softly, as if to keep my words only for her. "All my life I have watched as love wilted, and so swore myself to its absence, instead pledging my life in service to protecting others, to not become as heartless as my parents," I felt my throat quiver with the threat of sobs as tears began wetting my eyes. "Then I met you... my Princess. And for the first time I found myself looking to pledge a new vow; that very one I gifted you in the grove near Eilath more than two years ago."

I shook my head, feeling my grief overtaking me and my heart cracking inside me again. This was too much to endure.

"I keep thinking of how I left things with you," I sniffed against sobs, staring at her closed eyes. "You were right about me. I should have defended you. I should have never let my jealousy rule me and instead seen when you were in need of me."

I reached into the pouch on my belt, withdrawing the silvery chain that I had kept there since the Witches had stolen her that day in the orchards. I gazed down at the silver pendant and its glimmering purple stone as it laid in my palm. It should have hung around her slender neck, not sat buried in the bag on my belt.

"I was a Guardian," I murmured, gazing at her necklace, then looking back to her sweet face. "I was charged with protecting you. And they say that my heart got in the way, that my love for you caused all of this. But regardless, I was your lover, your soul mate, and when you needed me, I wasn't there. Each time you cried out my name I didn't come to you."

I shook my head, tears falling down my face now, my hand sweeping through my hair's greasy black strands to pull it from my gaze. I watched her, hoping she could guide me, that she could comfort me as she always had.

"I promised that I would protect you," I was shaking, my tears relentless. "Gods... Leander... How can I live knowing that I failed you so terribly? How ever can I go on without you, my beautiful girl?" I couldn't hold it anymore, just letting my sobs come loose. "I failed you... and I'm so sorry, Leander... I'm so, so sorry..." I wept, dropping to my knees. "I'm so sorry... I'm sorry... I'm sorry..."

I could no longer keep my cries of grief and pain inside of me, kneeling there beside her, holding her pendant between my palms. I sobbed with my head low against my clasped hands, feeling the most hopeless and destroyed I ever had in my entire life.

"I won't ever leave you again, Leander," I promised, my heart broken into dust. "I will never abandon you again, my love. Gods... I wish I could just bring you back..."

Part of me hoped that my prayers alone would restore my Princess to life, but she remained unmoving, neither her fingers nor her bare toes even flinching an ounce to show she lived. She was just still and cold, silent and empty.

I sat with my back against the altar, my arms resting on my knees as I continued to allow my tears their mournful passage. There was nothing else I could do, no words I could give, no thoughts left that could save me from this. I was lost in the void of grief and alone without Leander by my side, though she lay just within the reach of my hand.

"I would do anything," I sighed, letting my head bow as I just gave in to the exhaustion of my grief, "just to be with you again, my love."

I closed my eyes, letting the sorrow wash over me like a tidal wave crashing over the shores of my newly darkened world. With the storms that now ravaged High-Realm's skies, it seemed that the light of the world had also vanished from my own sights, even the glow of the candles diminished.

"It wasn't Ragnarok returning that made everything so dark," I whispered, glancing to her behind me. "It was you leaving this world, Leander. Without you the sun does not rise, and the moons remain hidden. You were my light, Princess..."

I turned from her then and held my head in my hands, her pendant dangling from my right palm, its chain clinking delicately, like faerie music.

Once again I closed my eyes, trying not to lose myself fully to grief's relentless murky shadows, though it was a battle I feared I could never hope to win. The ache in my heart was as raw as it had first been during that terrible night, and while everyone with me lay their concerns upon the evil rising around us mine were only with Leander.

Both our hearts lie in ruin, though mine is not literal as hers is. Gods, maybe it would be easier for me if mine were cleaved in twain as well. I wept hard, though quietly, as the pain struck me yet again. *I would have taken her place if given the chance. Gods, if there were some way to undo what has been done to her and offer myself in her place, I would do it...*

I lay my head back, leaving my eyes shut so I could block out the world around me. The only sounds that came to me were the winds outside and my staggering, grieving breaths inside the chamber of the temple. Even the beating of my own heart seemed too loud.

Gods... Just let me have her back... Please...

* * * * *

"Carden?" her voice was soft, gentle, urging me back from the blackness I had fallen into.

It was a peaceful place, safe and quiet without the troubles that I had come to know in the Waking World. I would have stayed there, would have remained in that place. With her...

I saw her pretty lips curve into that smile I so adored, her mahogany hair sparkling with red and gold in the afternoon light as she giggled and ran before me playfully. If only such a moment had existed and not simply been a dream. We had never shared such a moment, never played so carefree and child-like together. I longed for such a moment with her.

"Carden," her voice called to me again, my brows furrowing at the sound. "Carden, wake up..."

The image of my beautiful blue-eyed princess faded from my sights into darkness and I felt coldness creeping across my flesh. The hard floor was pressed to my seat, the smooth stone of the altar against my back. An ache had come to my neck, shoulders and the small of my spine, a groan escaping my lips. A gentle clatter snapped me from my unsolicited sleep, and I opened my eyes to find myself still within that chilled, but elegant temple. I let my eyes clear as two figures crouched before me, one with golden hair like fleece, the other with strands of fire red.

Tallinn and Ellora had looks of deepest concern on their faces as they crouched before me, their eyes of hazel and turquoise studying my features worriedly. They both looked neater and free of any grime that they had collected on their skin from Safferan, their clothes clean and fresh.

"Carden," Tallinn was the one speaking, not my beloved, her voice and accent so different. "Wake up, Carden..."

I frowned, feeling bewildered that I was being awakened on the cold floor of a room, my mind scarcely clear enough to recall anything. I was in a haze from my dreams and sleep, believing that the world I had been in - though it had seemed only a moment - was the real one.

My eyes drifted to my hand, my fingers flexing as I felt the absence of her pendant's chain. That was what had clattered. I felt a thrill of panic for a moment at the thought that I may have lost this one part of her yet left to me, but it didn't last. The sparkle of silver caught my eye from between my boots and I turned my gaze to see the Pendant laying on the floor with its stone towards the ceiling and its chain coiled around it. It had slipped when my grasp on it had faltered with sleep.

I took it up again, holding it in my hand, studying the facets of its incredible stone. It was as if a fire lay within, though it didn't dance for me as it had seemed to for her.

"Are you all right, Carden?" Ellora asked of me in her oddly mature voice for such a young face.

I looked to the Elven Huntress, meeting her stare with a blink. "What... what time is it?"

"Nearly morning," she said softly, a solemn tint to her words. "Not that the sky allows us to know this anymore."

"Morning?" I frowned, confused.

Tallinn gently laid one small hand on my thick shoulder, looking deep into my eyes. "You did not join us for midday or evening meal, brother. We grew concerned but thought you to be resting in your rooms. When we went to check on you, we found that the bed had not been laid in, and that the lamps and hearth had not been lit."

"Leander!" I gasped, jumping up and looking around, towering above both women as a dizziness hit me. "Where is she?!"

"In the same place as she was when first you entered this room," Ellora replied, looking behind me.

I slowly turned to look at the altar against my back. Leander had not moved, had not changed, still laying there amidst the silver pillows and silks. She remained cold and lifeless before me, just the empty body of my beloved without her soul. Each time I looked upon her unmoving, lifeless shape I just felt worse. It was like being beaten down with cold stone and stabbed violently through the chest, only to be healed and have to go through it all over again.

I slowly took her hand in mine, her fingers barely moveable now. I dreaded the idea of seeing her beauty fade, of watching as her features were weathered away like dust coming off the stones in the wind. She had already changed so much from when I'd first met her, her shape - though still curvy - was less full with how poorly she had been fed during her captivity. Yet, her now thinned frame had only remained beautiful to me.

A hard sigh came from deep in my chest as I fought the urge to cry once more, dipping my head again to hide my face. My eyes fell shut and my grief crushed around my heart, making my chest feel tight as though I were being squeezed by a troll.

"Carden," Tallinn touched my shoulder with the lightest of fingers, her smaller form standing so close to my taller one. "Please... you need to rest... to eat..."

I shook my head, opening my eyes and letting my sight linger on Leander's deathly pale features. "No... I... I need to stay with her. I need to keep her safe..."

"The Princess *is* safe," Ellora spoke gently, looking up at me from my left. "No harm will come to her here. She is resting peacefully in the care of this place."

I tried not to think that she was right, not wanting to admit it. I had only one thought and that was to remain with my beloved girl, to watch over her in death as I had failed to do in life.

"Please, Carden," Ellora urged me, finally drawing my gaze. "She would not want you languishing in the cold by her death bed. She will still be here when you have awakened from your sleep. I promise."

Finally, conceding, I nodded, turning then to Leander. I leaned over her and looked down at her face, wishing I could stare into the dazzling blue of her steel eyes.

"I will return, my love," I assured her, feeling as if to do so would mean she knew I wasn't leaving her for long. "Rest in your eternal sleep."

I lifted her hand and gently kissed it, then leaned over and placed a second tender, careful kiss to her forehead. I stroked her hair, looking into her closed eyes one last time. My heartache was no better.

"I love you, Leander..." I pledged in a tearful whisper.

I straightened from her, laying her hand beside her hip again, then allowed Tallinn and Ellora to take me from the room. I noticed that even Joran was no longer there, the Storvari clearly having needed rest too.

Taking one final look at Leander, I tore myself from that place and left, heading back to the Lord's House.

Though they tried to convince me to take food, I simply refused Ellora and Tallinn, telling them I wished for sleep. I was grateful that they allowed me that.

The room I was given was the room Leander and I had spent the last days of her life in. To enter it was as walking into a fading, staled memory, the lamps dark and the hearth cold. With the sudden drop in the temperature of the world from the unending storms, it became an immediate necessity to light the hearth.

I piled wood into the hearth, expertly making a fire as I had been taught and had done many times before. The flames flickered and began casting their embers across the stone fireplace, the scent of burning alder wood wafting through the air.

My gaze now turned to the room around me as I took it all in. It wasn't her room, of course, this only being a place where she had stayed in the short term. It actually saddened me to know that she didn't have anywhere that she could have called home after fleeing Arvon. She had no belongings here, nothing to state the simple truth that she had existed. But for the Pendant in my hand and the dresses hanging in the closet the Elven tailor had made for her, there was nothing. She was but a ghost to the world.

My eyes drifted to the table and the piles of items that had been laid there. My Guardian armour, coat, cloak, bracers, and sword had been set there for me as if to try and tempt me to change my mind on leaving the Order. To look upon the crest marking these items now only served to fill me with disdain. Beside them were the last clothes Leander had worn, her lilac long sleeved dress folded neatly there on the table. The royal blue velvet and purple silk over-dress was folded next to it, the bodice laced merely to keep the black cord with the dress. Her dark coloured leggings were set atop her white under dress, her boots side by side on the table behind her clothes.

I reached my left hand forward, gently caressing the soft fabric that had once sat so close to her body. Like her skin, it was now cool to the touch, though nowhere as icy as her flesh had become.

My breath hitched and I felt my tears falling anew as I lifted my other hand, looking down at her necklace. In the dull flames of the fireplace, it seemed to shimmer with orange reflected silver, the stone now looking as if the only light it had was that passing through it from the flames.

The Pendant has died with her. Its spirit is now dormant, just as it was always said it would be without its holder. Then she truly is dead... I'd hoped that perhaps if the Pendant still showed signs of life that maybe she was just enchanted, not dead, but that hope was now faded.

Slowly, I coiled the slender, delicate chain and set the Pendant down on the top of her blue and purple dress, letting it sit where it once had around her neck. I turned from the table then, finding my way to the floor with my back against the bed, a bottle of ale in my hand that I had found in the bureau.

Drowning my sorrows, I thought dourly, drinking from the bottle and feeling the burning sting of the alcohol rush my throat. *I truly have fallen low.*

I had never been the sort of man to take to the drink in such times, but she was not like any other we had lost. She was mine and that made the pain worse.

If the world is ending, then let it end fast so that I no longer suffer the pain of her loss. Let me find my rest with her in the Beyond.

I had nearly finished the bottle soon enough, my wits now foggy with drunkenness, my body wavering where I sat. I felt the warmth of the fire and the carpet beneath me, but it did nothing to ease my pain and guilt.

I shouldn't be alive... I... am not worthy of living much more... Everyone feared she would be hurt because of me. How right they were... I felt the pommel of one of my throwing daggers on my belt, frowning in thought. *I belong with her, not here in this doomed world. To the Void with a peaceful passing.*

I snatched the dagger from my belt, tearing my shirt open to expose the muscles and contours of my chest. I held the blade unsteadily, studying its sheen in the firelight of the darkened room. It would be so easy to do this, so easy to simply press the blade through my own heart and match hers. Slowly, I turned the dagger and pressed the tip of the blade over my left pectoral, right where I could feel the slow beat of my heart, which steadily increased at that moment. I closed my eyes and took in a deep breath, both hands now on the hilt and pommel.

One thrust, a few moments of pain, then I'll be able to join my princess in death's embrace...

It was then, as I sat there trying to convince myself to do it, that I began to shake. My conviction broke as glass does falling to the ground. I felt my biceps weakening and my tears flowing as images of Leander flashed through my mind. I saw her looking to me with an expression of pleading fear, shaking her head as she reached for me. I imagined her soft, slender hands touching my larger ones and holding them steady as I readied myself for the pain.

Don't... that was all I heard, as if her sweet, soft voice had spoken it within my mind. *Please, don't...*

She faded from my mind's sights then and I opened my eyes, my hands shaking wildly. I dropped them to my sides, letting the dagger clatter to the floor. I couldn't do it, she wouldn't want me to.

A deep sigh filtered from my chest, and I sat there then, just watching the flames for as long as I was able, hoping to find some measure of peace when I would at last drag myself to bed.

Chapter Five
The Prophecies

I fell into a deep, dreamless sleep, my thoughts numbed to all but rest. It was a welcome relief after all the sorrow and pain these past days had brought to me. I had no desire to wake to find her still lying in a tomb, no wish to discover that she had been set to the flames and her ashes now floated over High-Realm. I wanted her to open her eyes and return to me. It was a selfish thought, my own desires all that filled me at that moment. Others would say she should be allowed her rest, that what she had been made to suffer meant she deserved peace. While I agreed with them, I wasn't so certain she was at peace. I didn't see how she could be after the horror and violence of her death.

There came a loud knocking what seemed like only moments after I had closed my eyes, my head pounding from the sound. I groaned, pulling myself from the bed, my shirt now laid on the floor after I had shredded it from my torso. I pulled open the door, looking into the hall to meet Tallinn once again. I could only try not to show my desire to be left alone, hiding the aggravation I felt at once again being confronted.

"What is it, Tallinn?" I asked softly, trying to seem kinder at least.

She looked up at me, her shoulders and neck bared, her blonde hair pulled to one side. She wore a black and silver corset with a strap around her neck and a silver top beneath that left her shoulders exposed.

"We are gathering in the dining room," she said morosely, meeting my gaze. "The others... well, you should join us, Carden."

I wanted to refuse, to tell her to leave me to my solitary confinement and not disturb me again. My heart ached so much that I wasn't sure I could face the others now... or ever again.

"Please," she urged, staring up at me with that same look of insistence I had always fallen to.

I sighed and nodded. "Just let me change."

I went and stripped out of my sodden clothing, tossing it aside for washing later, then cleansed my body as thoroughly as I could so that I was at least clean. I pulled on my small clothes, then a pair of dark pants and a dark grey shirt. I didn't bother with my weapons, fastening my belt around my hips and pulling my boots on before joining Tallinn.

She led me from the room and through the white carved corridors to the dining room of the Lord's House, making our way to the balcony beneath the eaves. I turned my eyes around the space to look at the others gathered there, noting the absence of Joran almost immediately.

Fawkner sat in a chair with his back to the arches that led into the house, his expression exhausted, his arms resting on his knees as he leaned forward. I had never seen the Lorveren Falcon Lord look so old. His bird sat upon the perch behind his seat, her golden eyes watching everything with the awareness birds of prey always possessed.

Tristan stood at the barrier of the balcony, his flask in hand as he brought the cheap booze within to his lips. He once again looked dishevelled, his ashen reddish-blonde hair looking greyer in the pale light that surrounded us. I felt the urge to hit him for what he had done to Leander, but I held back, staying my hand.

The Dwarves sat together on one of the loveseats, their sullen eyes to the pints of mead they were labouring over and the pipes they struggled to smoke. Dolin had a dark glaze over his brown eyes, looking so weak under his thick black hair and full beard. He just sat there staring at the ground as he smoked, his stein set on the table before him. Holger was staring with a lost gaze into his cup. For the few moments I glimpsed his face I saw the red of his eyes, his cheeks puffy from grief.

Lastly, Ellora leaned her back against one of the external pillars, her arms folded beneath her forest green sleeves and her brown hide and leather armour. She had one foot braced to the pillar behind her as she watched the world beyond our refuge, the flashing of red lightning illuminating her features to show her sorrow.

Just seven of us left, not including Joran and Amethyst. Our company had fallen in numbers, and it seemed such a sad sight to behold.

"Where is Joran?" I asked in an emotionless, quiet voice.

"With the Princess," Ellora stated without turning her gaze to me, her ample chest heaving with a sigh. "He said that it was commanded that he hold vigil over her body until his dying breath."

"He leaves only to eat what he needs," Fawkner added with a grief filled shake in his voice, "saying that to eat in the presence of her death bed would be dishonourable."

I nodded, moving to sit on the loveseat that was left open. This was the one I had laid with Leander on not more than a week and a half passed. I could see her there in my mind as she turned the pages of that book she had been reading. My beautiful princess was always reading some story or another, getting herself lost in the imaginings of it all. I would have smiled at that thought, but I couldn't, my face deciding only to remain sullen of its own will.

Tallinn sat in the chair to my right, seemingly leaving the seat open for Leander. I suppose such habits had been hard learned and would be harder still to break. It truly did feel that we were just waiting for her and Aldwyn to join us, but neither the Mage nor the Princess appeared.

The seven of us were silent then as we sat there, none of us certain how to break the quiet that had covered us. Our group no longer felt as it should, and I began imagining that we would seek our own paths to wait out this apocalypse.

The Dwarves would likely return to Hecturn to wait it out amidst their kin and hope to outlast the monster dragons beneath the mountains. Ellora probably would make her way back to Galvenin to be with her people, though the forest would hardly gift them any protection from the inevitable onslaught of fire from above. And of course, Fawkner would go to Eilath to await the end in the arms of his family. Tallinn would no doubt remain in Silvervale and try to do what she could to aid the remnants of the Guardian Order. She would die with them, and it hurt to think of her facing such an end.

I couldn't care what became of Tristan. He and I would never be friends, and I was still angered by all he had done. Especially after his advances on Leander. As it was, we hadn't said even a word to each other yet and I didn't see us speaking any time soon.

That left me, Joran and Amethyst. I could only guess that, like me, the Storvari and the Dragon would stay with Leander's body right until the end. In truth, none of us could look forward to a peaceful finish to our lives in that moment, but no one could be expected to when facing the End of All Things. Death was inevitable. It was now only about how we would choose to spend our time until it came for us.

At last, it was Fawkner who broke the silence, now the oldest of us men.

"So," he murmured, nodding softly as he stared at the floor, "this is what we have come to. The survivors of our company left to grieve those who have parted from us," he looked down at his hands. "It seems such a quiet thing, does it not?"

"Aye," Dolin nodded as he spoke in a mumble, "that it does."

I crossed my arms, sighing and looking at the centre of the floor before us.

"Many enemies have we faced in all our years," Holger spoke in his gruff voice, though now he sounded like a broken man, ale dripping into his beard. "But never before have I been so uncertain of victory. Never before have I felt so... defeated as I do now."

"Aye, we suffered a great defeat, brother," Dolin agreed with him, sitting there with his pipe in hand. "Though I'm not sure which part of that is worse. The great dragons now burning across the world, or that we lost the Princess," he shook his head, a tear on his cheek.

Holger nodded, his lip shaking. "Aye... Losing her... seems a greater hurt than even the destruction we are yet promised by our foe."

"We failed," Ellora rasped out, trying not to show her own sorrow as she faced the city before us. "Even in my time serving with the Princess' ancestor I never knew such defeat. Not even when the hordes of Gorth'lak ravaged the lands and victory seemed so far from our grasp."

"Already we have lost too many," Tallinn sighed, leaning her elbows on her knees, her hands together. "Ser Mithras, Aldwyn, many of the royals of Aldegaad, including the King... and now the Princess."

"It is her loss that strikes us with the hardest of blows," Dolin sighed, wiping his eyes. "Would any of us be sitting here now if not for her?"

"No," Fawkner replied gravely. "If not for Leander, none of us would have met, our paths destined away from each other. In some way, that girl was the centre of us, the one who drew us together," he shook his head as he stared thoughtfully ahead, a small smile appearing on his bearded face. "She was our commonality, our reason for coming together. Though she would say she is hardly the most important or useful of us, she was the very core of our company, the light that gave us purpose and hope. Yet, now that light is extinguished and we find ourselves as a ship without a beacon, lost in the waves of Ragnarok's return."

"She inspired us to follow her," Ellora added, turning to look at us then, "though she did so unknowingly. She was a leader, though a reluctant one, who chose to let others take charge. Such was her way."

"I'll never forget the day we first saw her," Dolin said reminiscently, smiling softly. "Aye, she was a bonnie wee thing, so unsure of herself before Lord Eilan, yet she tried to show the confidence of a ruler. And she was so grateful for anything we gifted her."

"Why did you follow her, if I may ask?" Fawkner looked to the Dwarf curiously.

Dolin smiled with tears trembling in his eyes. "Her light. Though Lord Eilan commanded we escort you to the Lorgath Pass, it was her light that made me follow her. I remember thinking that the darkness of this world could nary snuff out such a bright spark of life. That she carried a flame that could bring warmth back to this world, though I didn't know why," he turned to Fawkner then. "And you, Lord Fawkner? Why did you follow the lassie?"

Fawkner smiled softly. "She reminded me of the daughter the Shadow Lord took from me; my eldest, who was much the same age as Leander when first we met. It was when I and my men invaded Castle Arvon to take her that I saw it. At first, she seemed like any doughy little noble girl, clutching a book to her breast as if it were a shield," he chuckled as he spoke, his smile and his eyes alighting at the memory of her. "She played the part of helpless victim well," he remarked with respect. "I had scarcely the chance to duck before she hurled that book right at my head, and by the time I turned to face her she had a sword to my throat. Not that she could best me, but all the same she had the right spirit."

"Why did you beat her?" Tallinn asked, frowning in thought. "I thought she'd been trained in the art of swordsmanship since her eighth winter."

Fawkner shrugged offhandedly. "Leander had many virtues and was a kind soul, but she was flawed as any of us are. She was overconfident and a little arrogant when it came to our duel, yet also unsure of her techniques. That combination is what allowed me to overpower her."

"Was it only because of your daughter that you stayed with her?" Holger grumbled, looking as if he could slump over with the volume of mead he had ingested.

Fawkner shook his head. "No. After travelling with her and seeing the kindness she showed Joran and I, it was at first to make amends, and then... I don't know... a sense of care for the girl. As if she were my own child. It must sound daft."

"Not at all," I said quietly, shaking my head.

"I too felt a kinship with her," Ellora said softly, turning more fully towards us, her red hair catching in the breeze. "When first I saw her face, I beheld that of my old friend, and I was curious. As I looked upon her, I thought that she must truly be meant for something great to face such peril, and I felt it only right to stand with her as I had Leander the First."

"And you knew Mithras," Fawkner added, looking to her softly.

She smiled and nodded. "Yes. We were friends long before the Princess ever drew breath, and even before her parents were courting. I thought that if he stood with her then so could I, but I also chose to because she was in such need. And I yearned to see her reach her potential, to become the strong woman I knew she could be," she sighed softly then, looking down at her folded arms and shaking her head. "It seems that was not to be."

"And you two?" Dolin looked to Tallinn and I with a soft, teary eyed gaze. "Was it only because you were charged to protect her, or was there more?"

Tallinn shook her head. "In the beginning I saw her as my mission, as the one I had been sent to protect, yes. But as time went by and I grew to know her, I found... a friendship I didn't expect. Her insistence that I not call her 'Princess' or 'your Highness' grew tiresome, though I did try."

"It seems she was always determined to be our equal, not our superior," Fawkner observed quietly, now petting Farsight gently where she perched. "A rare quality among nobles these days."

"And you, lad?" Dolin urged me gently. "Was it the same as your sister Guardian?"

I shook my head, thinking about the first time I saw Leander once again. "No... I mean... I went to protect her as I was charged, thinking that I was going to stand guard over some spoilt brat's rooms while she did all that she wished without caring for anyone else. But when I first laid eyes upon her, I saw... I don't know... a humility that I didn't expect, an innocence and a pureness that I had not imagined."

"Aye," Holger nodded, drinking more of his mead. "She had all of those virtues to be certain."

I smiled sadly as I saw her in my mind: "Our eyes did meet, and I thought that I had never seen someone so pure and beautiful in my life. But I tended to my duties and focused on my task, trying not to think how much I would give just to speak with her. I never thought a princess would give me a second glance, but her gaze seemed never to leave me."

"Love at first sight," Ellora smiled knowingly.

"Which makes this all the more tragic now," Tristan mumbled, still facing away from us with his elbows over the banisters. "The world seems a cruel and unforgiving place if it can destroy such love so callously."

I wanted to strike him and knock him from his perch down into the streets and gardens beneath the balcony. But that was my other side, the darkness that I held deep down in my soul and had tried to protect Leander from. At least I had the consolation that it was not my darker half that had brought this upon my beloved princess.

"It does," I simply said, feeling tears welling in my eyes. "I cannot say that she was perfect, and certainly some of her choices were questionable," I glanced at him, then turned my gaze to the floor, shaking my head, "and... sometimes she could be too stubborn, even headstrong to the point of recklessness. But she was good, and kind, and so sweet... And... I loved her... with all my heart and soul."

I felt Tallinn's arms encircle me as best they could, though she was so much smaller than me, even a little shorter than Leander. She rested her chin on my shoulder, trying to comfort me.

"I would have married her... I would have spent my life with her," I went on, fighting back tears, "but it seems destiny was determined that it would not be. And so, here I am... lost without her..."

"It is a pity," Holger mused, swaying ever more as the drink influenced him, "that her death held no meaning. If she had died to end this blighted curse that now covers the lands, maybe we would be more celebratory in her life. But her death was an act of cruelty against an innocent girl. Nothing more."

"Yes," Ellora nodded, turning back to the storms raging above as more lightning flashed red and thunder quaked the very foundations of the city. "There was nothing honourable, or even meaningful about what happened. The Princess was simply murdered. Even Ser Mithras and Aldwyn were granted more meaning in their deaths than her. At least they died in defence of others."

"It is a dark, cold thing that was done to her," Fawkner sighed, lifting his cup to his lips. "I pray now that she be at peace in the Beyond."

"As do we all, my friend," Ellora whispered as tears streaked her pale cheeks.

I sat there, letting my arms fall to my sides. There was nothing more for any of us to say, knowing that this was all the celebration we could muster. How sadly pathetic. We had honoured Mithras and Aldwyn as heroic friends who battled valiantly and died for some cause worth giving their lives for. But Leander had been murdered. There was nothing good about that and there was no peace to be had while her killer roamed free.

We remained there for some time, just sitting in silence, the seven of us each in our own thoughts. There was no more we could do but wait.

* * * * *

The days passed without me fully comprehending them. Without the sun and the moons in the sky, and the changing of day to night it was near impossible to be sure of what time it truly was. The unending storms had blocked the world from the sight of the sky above and we were living in nothing but darkness. The only illumination that came to us was from the flashing of the lightning and what little light managed to glow against the black clouds. We turned to the time telling of clockwork to just attempt to keep in line with some sense of routine if nothing else. But that was not foolproof, many of us having to find each other when it came to meals and simply lay down when we grew tired.

The others tried to occupy themselves in whatever ways they could, attempting to find distractions to fill their time. For Tallinn and Fawkner this was mostly in the form of joining with the other Guardians in the city and trying to devise defensive measures. Silvervale had repelled two more attacks since our return, strangely small though they were. It was almost as if they were testing our fortifications. In the midst of this they both came to me at one point and tried to convince me to once again don my armour and sword, but I refused. My decision was final, and I would not turn from it now. I was no longer a Guardian, and I would never return to the Order.

When our companions did gather for meals we ate in relative silence, our hearts too heavy to speak on much. There was no joy, no revelling for us anymore. Leander's death had destroyed what happiness had lingered for us, and the threat of the monster dragons and the Shadow Lord remained hanging over our heads like the black clouds above the city. I couldn't see how anyone could make merry and smile when such darkness had come to possess the lands.

My days were simple, spent either drunk on the floor of my rooms watching the fire struggle to burn and illuminate, or staying with her by her death bed. So far nothing had been done to prepare her for the same fate as Mithras and Aldwyn. Whether that was because we hadn't the hearts to do so, or because there were many others to lay to rest after Safferan fell I do not know.

I woke from another dreamless sleep to find that I once again laid in an empty bed, reaching to where she should have been beside me. My fingers felt only cold sheets and a mattress that had not been slept on, the pillows undisturbed.

Slowly, I sat up and held my head in my hands as I set my feet to the floor, my bare chest heaving at the sight of her absence. She had laid there with me for no more than a week, and yet not having her beside me was making me feel as if she had been there so much longer.

The red flashes of lightning shredded through the sheer white drapes of the windows and terrace doors, flickering around the darkened room for a moment each time.

I took in a sigh and stood, moving to get dressed.

Once I had my shirt, trousers and boots on I left the room and wandered aimlessly through the Lord's House. I was like a wraith now, no longer weeping or moaning with the pain that had become a constant in my heart, just floating numbly. I was like one of those dissolute draugar that the Revenant of Arnath commanded, a lost soul left without purpose or thought beyond the misery I felt.

Stepping into the gardens, I barely felt the cold of the snows or the icy wind that battered against me, my body numb to all such sensations now. My only focus was on returning to the place where she lay in wait for me, to stay with my beloved as she rested in her eternal slumber.

When I arrived at the small chapel-like temple and passed through the doors, sealing them to guard against the storm, I was surprised to find the Green Wizard there.

Ranzel stood over Leander where she lay, still and perfect as she was when first I saw her there. The old man was very calmly studying her features, his right hand touched to her cheek lightly. It was akin to watching a physician with their patient, the Wizard's gaze one of thoughtful, careful examination, not grief. Yet, there was a sadness in his hazel eyes all the same.

I looked to my left to see Joran standing there with his arms firmly crossed before his broad chest. The Storvari was keeping guard over her as he had sworn, looking as impressive and intimidating as he ever had.

"Ranzel?" I frowned as I approached, curious of his intentions.

Ranzel looked up at me. "Ah. Master Carden, precisely who I was hoping to see. How are you faring?"

"How does any man fare when he has watched the woman he loves murdered before him?" I asked darkly, turning my gaze to Leander's beautiful shape.

"Oh, yes," the Wizard nodded solemnly, "I know it is something so very terrible and unimaginable. There are no words for such sorrow."

"There are not," I agreed, then turned my eyes to him. "You said you were hoping to speak with me?"

The Wizard nodded. "Yes. I have been observing the Princess for these past weeks since our return and I was wondering whether you had noticed anything... odd."

My frown deepened and I felt my jaw harden. "No..." I shook my head. "Beyond the fact that she lies dead, there is nothing odd."

I couldn't understand this man or his strange mystical ways, but I knew enough of my own heart to know that I didn't like her being stared at as if she were some experiment of magic and nature.

"Do you often watch the dead decay in their resting places?" I asked a little too harshly.

"No, no, no, it isn't like that," he tried to assure me in a constantly calm manner. "But interesting that you would use such words."

"Why?" I frowned hard, folding my arms before my chest.

"Tell me," he turned to her, his eyes flicking across her face, "what do you see when you look at her?"

I took in a slow breath to compose myself and regain my patience, then turned my green eyes towards Leander. She looked just as she had when she was first laid here, wearing that long white dress, her dark hair neat and soft, her skin pale and perfect. The only thing that seemed different about her was that she didn't look as she had when first we met. But that came from one year's maturity as she shifted from seventeen to eighteen.

I felt a tear threaten my eye and I drew in a shaking breath. "I see my beloved princess. She's beautiful and pale... and dead..."

Ranzel nodded softly. "Do you not see anything different about her?"

I nodded myself. "She has matured, what baby fat there was faded and gone as she grew older, and she is thinner from what little food she managed to eat over the two years she was imprisoned."

The Wizard folded his arms around himself, nodding thoughtfully. "Hm..."

"What are you getting at, Wizard?" I asked, looking to him.

"You see change in her, but you do not look for the changes that *should* be obvious given her state of death," he pointed out. "Observe what is *not* there that should be when beholding the dead."

I was beginning to feel a deep confusion, but I didn't argue, simply looking down at Leander and studying her.

"What do you see? What do you feel? What do you smell?" he inquired in a soft voice. "Use your very senses and find the answer that you already know. The answer that sorrow has kept you from seeing."

I did as he told me, taking in her scent as I touched her hand delicately with my own. He was right. Something was off about her. Something that shouldn't have been true was.

"I... she smells sweet, of soap and flowers," I relayed back to him. "She looks as she always did, sleeping and beautiful, and her skin is soft, but cold. That's not right, is it?"

"For someone who has been dead nearly a month, she is remarkably well preserved," Ranzel agreed, moving to her left and facing me. "Her cheeks and eyes have not sunken, her skin is not cracked or dried, her scent that of a clean, living person. There is no sign of decay, nor of any parasite attempting to devour her as it would another corpse."

"She's frozen in time?" I asked, looking up at him in complete bewilderment.

Ranzel nodded slowly. "Yes, she is. And I believe I know why. Tell me, what do you know of her curse?"

"Her curse?" I frowned deeply, trying to recall. "She... she said something as she was dying about being cursed. That it had made her fear that I wouldn't still love her. Of course, that's foolish. I can never stop loving her, even now as she lies dead before me."

"Indeed so," the Wizard responded slowly, studying the girl's still face. "She was referring to what the Shadow Lord did to her that day in Grishk'kinnar."

I scowled as I remembered. I could never forget how Tallinn and I were forced to watch on as Morod and his followers bound Leander to that altar, then forced her to participate in that vile and wicked ritual. The worst part for me was when they cut her, made her drink that foul concoction Manth had devised, and especially when Morod had pressed his evil lips upon hers.

"She told us that she was fine," I recalled. "But she wasn't, was she? She lied."

"The mental and emotional scars of what she endured notwithstanding, she was changed," Ranzel confirmed what I felt I already knew. "In restoring himself to corporeal form, Lord Morod took a piece of her into himself and away from her."

"What did he take?" I felt cold, colder than I ever had as I awaited the dreaded answer.

"Her mortality," he said simply and solemnly.

I felt a deep knot tying in my gut as I heard that, suddenly completely understanding Leander's reluctance regarding our relationship and closeness. Despite how much she seemed to want to be with me too. Now the fear I had sensed from her made perfect sense.

"He stole her mortality?" I was baffled that such a thing could be done. "So... she was... immortal?"

Ranzel nodded. "Yes. He made her immortal."

"Then how can she be dead?" I felt an anger in me then that was beyond all logic. "If she was immortal, she shouldn't have died..."

"Immortality does not mean you are excluded from dying," he explained evenly. "It only means that you do not change, or age. In the Princess' case she lost her aging, her change and her ability to bear children, but not the ability to die."

I shook my head, trying to comprehend. "So... she was grieving the loss of the future we might have had... and it made her fear that I would turn from her..."

I turned my eyes to her, looking down upon her beautiful features as I gently stroked her hair with one broad hand.

"Oh my love, I could never turn from you for such a thing," I assured her, though I knew she couldn't hear me. I looked back to the Wizard. "So, do you think the reason she is not decaying in death, the reason she is so well preserved, is this curse?"

He nodded. "Yes. The curse inflicted upon her made her body immortal, but capable of dying. However, I would say that since her physical vessel is not becoming one with the earth that she is not truly dead."

"You mean... we could bring her back?" I felt a rush of excitement fill me. "She could live again?"

"Perhaps," he said thoughtfully. "Will you come with me, Carden? I have a theory and I would greatly appreciate your point of view."

"I will guard her, Carden Highever," Joran promised, still standing there with his arms folded. His silence really did make one forget that he was there.

I hesitated, looking back at Leander's perfect white features, still stroking her soft auburn hair. I didn't want to leave her, but if there was any chance that we could bring her back then we had to follow that path and find the answers.

"I'll be back soon, Leander," I whispered to her, kissed her, then followed Ranzel.

* * * * *

The Wizard led me from the temple and through the gardens, then to the Broken Towers. Once we arrived, he guided me through to the library, inside one of the towers that the Elemental Wizards held as part of their section of the sanctuary fortress. The room was gigantic and made of the same black stone with great archways reaching high above and tall arched windows allowing light to beam into the room. Candles and candelabras lit the space as chandeliers hung high from the ceiling. There were many dozens upon dozens of bookshelves crammed to the limit with ancient tomes of knowledge and magic.

Leander would have been fascinated with this library. Though I doubt this room holds any such things as the romance and adventure stories she so adored, that allowed me a smile.

With his green and brown robes flowing as he walked, Ranzel made straight for an archive hidden in the back of the room. He seemed to search for some minutes before at last returning with a large scroll in hand.

I came to stand beside him as he unfurled the ancient scroll upon an ebony table, my eyes studying the strangely blank page.

"This is one of the Prophecy Scrolls," he told me as he set it to the table. "There are twelve, each one connected to a different line of prophecies. This is the Scroll of Champions. It chronicles every prophecy dedicated to each champion to rise in Therras throughout time and knowing."

"The page is blank," I pointed out, looking to him with confusion.

Ranzel smiled knowingly. "The page is only blank if you do not call forth the prophecy you seek, my boy. Not an easy task if you do not know how to do it."

"Then it is bound by some enchantment?" I perceived.

"Yes, indeed it is," he replied, running his hand across the page. "It contains every prophecy hidden in its magical confines. Now, what we seek is the prophecy of the Great Heroine."

"The Great Heroine?" I frowned, confused.

The Wizard suddenly waved his hand across the scroll and ancient writings appeared there. It was as if the words materialised from an ethereal world, each line seeming to be written before my very eyes. I had never seen such magic before, and it astonished me.

The title read: ***The Prophecy of the Great Heroine***.

"The Prophecy of the Great Heroine was read over twelve hundred years ago," Ranzel stated as we watched the words complete their scrolling, the etching of a beautiful female figure in armour with a great glowing sword and a dragon flanking her appearing beneath the words. "At the time it seemed that she had been discovered. However, I and some of my brothers have begun to question this claim."

"I don't understand," I looked from the page to him, frowning hard, my arms folded before me. "History tells that Leander the First, founding Queen of Aldegaad, *is* this champion."

"Is she indeed?" he questioned, turning his gaze back to the page. "Every prophecy holds within it, portents to be read. The question now is whether these portents were interpreted correctly or not."

"What do you mean?" I didn't fully understand what he was getting at.

The Wizard began trailing his hand along the lines of text as he read aloud: "In the last years of the Age of Light shall a child be born to the last royal house of Zeal: a princess, youngest of two, with hair the colour of mahogany and eyes like blue steel. As a babe she will be hunted by the Shadow, preyed upon by the Darkest of all Darkness, and doomed to lose her life givers. In her formative years she will know not what Fate hath in store yet shall face many trials in her adolescent age. She shall be known for her gentle heart, her innocence, and her connection to the Elder Ones as she carries the Heart of Purple and is bound to a fledgling of that line. This girl-child is the one to unite the fractured nations, to call the World to fight for its own salvation as she herself faces the last of the Shadow Lords in a final battle and slays him. Darkness shall cover all the lands and fire will rain from the skies to obliterate all of Therras, but this Great Heroine will stand up from Death itself to lead the people of High-Realm to save their world and end the reign of the Darkest Shadow..."

I listened intently, fascinated, and confused by the cryptic words the page portrayed.

"That... sounds strange," I confessed, rubbing my chin in thought. "What was it about this prophecy that made the Brotherhood think it was Leander the First?"

"Circumstance," he replied, running his finger across certain sections. ""A child born to the last royal house of Zeal: a princess, youngest of two..." Now, Leander the First was the *second* child of King Richard and Queen Marianne, last rulers of the ancient land of Graphtar, whose capital city was named Zeal. She had a brother, Alexander, who became the last King after his father, though only for a few years before he was slain."

I nodded thoughtfully. "I see. And the rest?"

"She was hunted from the day she was born," he went on explaining. "Lord Morod discovered this prophecy and sought to slay the child before she could reach maturity and kill him. He murdered her mother and father only days after her birth."

"Tragic, yet common knowledge," I nodded. "As is the fact that she was raised by a certain Wizard in the township of Arvon until she was of age."

"Yes. And, as a result of all that had come before, the then secret princess faced many trials until her sixteenth year when she battled Lord Morod and cast him into the Netherworlds," he said calmly. "However, slaying and imprisoning are two *very* different things, Carden."

"But the prophecy came true," I stated, pointing to the words. "She inspired High-Realm to unite and defeat the evil threatening it."

"Oh? You think so?" he met my gaze, analysing me as much as I did the page. "If she were truly the Great Heroine, then there would be no Shadow Lord currently raging across High-Realm with a coterie of vicious dragons bent on pain and destruction. And it states an age in the prophecy. The Age of Light. The very age the one we live in now was dubbed."

I could see where he was coming from, but I was uncertain. "Is there more to the prophecy? More that can help to ascertain who the Heroine is?"

He nodded, taking a second scroll and unfolding it. "Yes. Here, in the Scroll of World Fate: the scroll containing all the prophecies of the world and its perceived fates."

Again, he waved his hand across a seemingly blank page, more words appearing, but with the title: **The Prophecy of Consuming Darkness**.

Not an encouraging title. Is this prophecy about triumph or doom?

Beneath the ghost writing words there appeared an etching of two figures, one a girl in armour with a glowing sword, the other a shadowy, hooded figure with a sword of flames, battling above two vast armies that clashed violently. Two great dragons flew over them, one for each of the combatants central to the image, their flames lashing out as the central figures' swords clashed.

Once again, the Wizard read aloud whilst tracing his place on the page with one gnarled finger: "In the time when Light has returned from Shadow shall a Consuming Darkness stretch across the land with the Joining of the Three and the return of a Lord of Shadow from the Nether Reaches. So shall fire tear the Mount of Magic asunder and plunge its isle into the broiling seas, thus signalling the End of All Things. In the wake of this destruction, the Defenders of Therras will be burned by Elder Flames and the World shall stand fractured without protectors. As great wings beat in cold storms, the land of High-Realm shall be plagued by War, Famine, Pestilence and Death. Even still, those who lead will be blind to the dangers until they are shown them by a Champion of Prophecy. Then the World must decide its own fate: Stand United or burn in the fires of Apocalypse. Only then will the Bearers come forth to stand together against the evil that reigns in the Darkness, and only then will the Oldest Race return..."

I read the words myself several times, trying to find the meaning in them. This was confounding, leaving me with an aching brow and a tortured mind.

"This seems maddening and unhelpful, Ranzel," I confessed my confusion to the wise man. "What does it mean? Can you translate the intended implications?"

He nodded, proceeding to indicate with one finger: ""The time of Light has returned from Shadow" means the Age of Light. "Lord of Shadow", a Shadow Lord, and "Nether Reaches"... meaning the Netherworlds. So, Lord Morod is not mentioned by name, but by the circumstance of his return."

I nodded, understanding as he explained.

He went on: "The Mount of Magic refers to Mount Safferan, legendary as the source of the origins of the Magi."

"Then that speaks of the destruction of Safferan," I realised as a chill of terror sharply streaked down my spine and caused all of my nerves to spasm in pain.

Ranzel nodded. "Preceded by the Joining of Three, also known as the Three Moons aligning, which has just recently occurred. So, already, we can see the very real portents of this prophecy have played out before us."

"And the rest?" I urged, afraid, yet compelled to know more.

He turned his gaze back to the elegant black ink writing. "The Consuming Darkness would be the end of sunlight and the eternal night we now find ourselves facing. The Defenders of Therras are the Guardians, Dragon Knights, Mages and High Elves."

"What does *Elder Flames* refer to?" I asked, pointing to the two words.

"Dragon Fire," he responded simply. "The reported way that all the strongholds of these orders were destroyed."

The chill of terror in me grew worse and I felt truly afraid.

Ranzel continued: "War, Pestilence, Famine and Death refer to the four Dragons: Thorgeirr, Ragnar, Lothair and Amrit. Apocalypse is another name for Ragnarok. They have been named by their titles in the prophecy as key figures."

I nodded. "Then the line about those who lead would refer to the rulers of the Seven Kingdoms."

"Yes, it does indeed," he agreed with a nod of his head. "The World shall stand fractured, and the leaders are blind to the threat. This is a clear accounting of the political situation in High-Realm currently. The Seven Kingdoms are not at peace and are certainly fractured from each other. That said, we have ascertained the when, and the who of the prophecy, as well as what happens."

"And the Bearers?" I asked.

He studied that more. "Those who carry awakened Dragon Pendants. Which, as it is, we know of four Bearers."

"Two are our enemies, one is... dead... and the other is you," I reminded him, feeling that the prophecy was very misleading. "That hardly seems as encouraging as the writings here suggest."

"There are yet five Dragon Pendants unaccounted for, my boy," he replied evenly, meeting my eyes. "It is not beyond the realms of imagination that others have gained such connections as the Princess and myself. And we know Keilantra has four locked away, but no more."

I nodded, thinking all of this through. "And where is Leander in this, if you think she is actually the Great Heroine instead of her ancestor?"

"The Champion who inspires High-Realm to save itself," he tapped that section. "That is her."

I frowned, unconvinced. "The prophecy doesn't allude to the Champion's gender or any other identifying features, Ranzel."

"There is something that has been... overlooked," he stated, lining the two scrolls up. "You see, the scrolls are meant to be used in tandem, each one paired with another. The Scroll of Champions and the Scroll of World Fate are bound to each other. When the Prophecy of the Great Heroine was first read, it was read independently, not in conjunction."

"That seems a foolish mistake," I observed.

"Quite," he nodded, studying the pages. "Perhaps the error was made because in the timeline of the prophecies these two do not sit in line with one another. However, positioning is meaningless. It is the Who, What and When you must align to find the truth since dates are never given."

I half snorted. "It seems dates and names would make things simpler."

"Oh, infinitely," he said, still studying them. "But the scrolls are designed to read all of Time and show it to exist as it must. These are our guides to what may be and may not influence free will."

"So, show me why you think that the Great Heroine is in this time," I leaned over the page, getting a clear view.

"These passages here," he indicated with one hand to each scroll. ""*In the last years of the Age of Light shall a child be born to the last royal house of Zeal: a princess, youngest of two, with hair the colour of mahogany and eyes like blue steel...*"And... "*In the time when Light seems to have returned from Shadow shall a Consuming Darkness stretch across the land with the Joining of the Three, and the return of a Lord of Shadow from the Nether Reaches.*" Both speak of when these events occur, though cryptically. The Age of Light. Our current age, which, if you were to perceive it as such, has now ended."

"With an all-consuming darkness," I nodded, starting to understand. "All right. So, Lord Morod is the Shadow Lord in each prophecy as he is the last of his kind. The Age of Light is when this happens, so, now. And Leander?"

"The last Royal House of Zeal," Ranzel stated, looking to me, "which we know today as the Aldrich Royal Bloodline. A princess, youngest of two, does not refer to simply being the youngest child, but the youngest of two *daughters*."

I felt my sharp intake of breath like an icy knife in the gut. It was becoming clearer with each moment.

"And of course, a simple description of this girl having dark auburn-brown hair and bluish grey eyes, the very description of the Princess," he went on, looking suddenly enthused by his deductions, as if my seeing this had validated him somehow. "Now, if you read the rest and compare it to the Princess' life so far, she has been hunted by the Shadow Lord since she was a baby, her parents have been murdered, and she has spent her late adolescence facing tremendous trials. She also had no knowledge of the fate she would face when she was a small girl, well protected from such things inside Castle Arvon's walls."

"And what of the rest of the prophecy?" I asked.

"More description," he replied simply. "The Heart of Purple refers to the Amethian Dragon Pendant, Elder Ones means Dragons, fledgling means young dragon, and of course gentle heart and innocence are her qualities, her virtues," he turned back to the pages. "And once more a crossover is found between scrolls," he indicated. ""*A Consuming Darkness stretches across the land...*" And... "*Darkness shall cover all the lands and fire will rain from the skies to obliterate all of Therras,*" thus, indicating the event. Finally, "*this girl-child is the one to unite the fractured nations, to call the World to fight for its own salvation as she herself faces the last of the Shadow Lords in a final battle...*" And... "*Even still, those who lead will be blind to the dangers until they are shown them by a Champion of Prophecy. Then the World must decide its own fate.*" This identifies that the person referred to in the Scroll of Champions and the Scroll of World Fate is one and the same." He sighed, straightening up as he looked down at the two pages, almost seeming proud and a little relieved. "A girl of royal blood who commands the loyalty of the Amethian Pendant and its dragon, with the purity and innocence capable of breaking the bad blood between the nations so that they will unite as one."

"Then... if the prophecy says this..." I realised, staring at the pages and thinking of her laying in that tomb.

Ranzel turned his gaze to me, knowing what I was thinking: "She may yet be restored to us."

Chapter Six
Flight from the Silver City

It was difficult trying to really comprehend the emotions roiling around inside of me as I assisted the Green Wizard in his task. My heart was warmed with hope that my beautiful and innocent princess would be returned to my loving embrace and that I would see her living again. It was a wonderful feeling, though I wasn't sure exactly how that could ever be achieved. Death was not easily overcome and those that cheated it were usually punished with the appearance of angered spirits and ravenous draugar. Such was the case in the Revenant's fortress, though I was certain that the shambling dead within its crumbling dark halls were created by intention, not accident.

Ranzel called for the Council to meet again as I went to find the others. I had Ellora, Tallinn and Fawkner join us. It felt only right that they should be included in this as it would likely be us who would undertake such a task. We were the ones who had protected Leander, after all.

I was silent as I watched on, all the Wizards present as well as Master Riordan, Ser Callenhad, their seconds, Lord Selwyn, General Gailan, Enchantress Illuminil and their attendants. Including Ranzel, the Council numbered ten, the rest of us merely there for our various involvements.

They listened as Ranzel recounted all that he had told me in the library, his speech passionate and sure. I could tell just by glancing across the faces of those present who were with him, who were not, and who were undecided. Ragdobar and Samhir seemed to be sided with the Green Wizard, but Lucilius was as callow as ever. Xzharn just appeared emotionless as he listened with patience and courtesy, as if he were merely allowing his brother wizard this moment to speak. Master Riordan looked unsure, whilst Ser Callenhad seemed curious more than anything, though he hid it well. Lord Selwyn was simply hearing it all out, weighing each piece of information carefully before deciding, while Gailan looked impatient. As for Enchantress Illuminil, she held a strange air of knowing and I was certain she would side with Ranzel.

So... definitely two against, four in favour, and four undetermined. Could be worse...

I turned my gaze to my friends. Ellora was as calm as ever, though her eyes betrayed her astonishment. I could sense that she was very familiar with Ranzel's way of doing things. Meanwhile, Fawkner and Tallinn both looked as I was certain

I had when he'd explained it to me. They wore baffled expressions, their eyes seeming to glaze with all that was being explained. I didn't blame them.

"You bring before us a... compelling theory, Ranzel," Lord Selwyn spoke slowly and calmly, his hands folded together on his midriff. "And your evidence is certainly well gathered to support such claims."

"Yet, such claims must not be made lightly," Xzharn decreed with a darkness in his gaze.

"I do not make them lightly, Xzharn," Ranzel stated evenly, leaning on his staff as he paced. "I make them with careful observation and certainty."

"What you are proposing means rewriting the very established history of all of High-Realm, and indeed, all of Therras itself," the White Wizard remarked gravely.

"It also accuses he who first interpreted the Scroll of Champions over the Prophecy of the Great Heroine to be wrong," Lucilius said with ice in his voice and flames in his eyes.

I felt myself scowl, stunned that such learned men would be concerned about something as trivial as saving face over a mistake when the End of All Things was upon us.

"Is it not more important to find a way to save our world than it is to protect someone's ego, Lucilius?" Ranzel asked with a hint of surprise as he turned his hazel eyes to the Red Wizard.

"Indeed," Ragdobar nodded, speaking in his soft, old voice, "such trivialities are meaningless at this time of crisis. What is important is discerning a defence and a means to unite the peoples of High-Realm as one against the enemy."

"Especially now that our combined Orders are fewer in numbers than before," Samhir agreed, his golden robes seeming to shimmer in the light of the central brazier. "Allies are far more valuable now than ever, and such alliances may be Therras' only chance to survive the coming storms."

"This whole theory hinges on a dead girl!" Lucilius snapped, glaring at Ranzel. "How do you propose to fulfil the prophecies with its supposed figurehead laying in Death's grasp?"

My muscles began to tense at his heartless descriptions of Leander, but I managed to keep myself calm. So far, I had stopped myself from lashing out at the old men after what I had endured from them when first we returned here, but my patience was wearing thin.

"The Prophecy of the Great Heroine is clear in its details," Ranzel countered the fiery eyed wizard, reciting the words without need of the scroll before him, though both were laid on the table. "The final passage states: *Darkness shall cover all the lands and fire will rain from the skies to obliterate all of Therras, but this Great Heroine will stand up from Death itself to lead High-Realm to save itself and end the reign of the*

Darkest Shadow... We have our answer already that the girl shall be restored to life, and so will lead High-Realm to unite."

"That is no proof," Lucilius retorted with a dismissive wave to the scrolls. "The Great Heroine was already found in this girl's ancestor, who was indeed slain only to rise again."

"No," Ranzel responded, shaking his head, his tone one of simple fact. "Leander the First was brought to the very brink of death by the bite of a basilisk snake, yet saved by the spirit of Aranyal, the Great Phoenix. She did not die but was healed."

"It is all in the translation, Brother Ranzel," Lucilius argued, staring him down. "Death may mean injury, not literal death as you seem to be suggesting..."

"When has a prophecy ever been read to suggest injury is the translation of death?" Ranzel asked incredulously.

"While prophecies may be translated to mean many different things," Xzharn conceded to one Wizard, then turned to the other, "such prominent words as Fate or Death do not transfer in meaning to a lesser form as Brother Lucilius suggests. Death may mean the figurative death of one's perception of life or way of living in order to transform to another, but regardless it is a death in context."

"I do not believe this is the case here," Samhir added his voice to the conversation again. "The phrase "*Will stand up from Death itself* " sounds far more literal of the image of one returning from the Beyond. In what form, we cannot tell, but it is not merely pretty poetry to convey an ideal of life changing or of a transformation of perception."

"It is certainly written as if to convey a literal rising from death," Ragdobar agreed with a gentle nod. "And since the passage speaks of darkness covering the lands, and fire raining from the skies to obliterate the world, it is without question speaking of the time we now live in."

"This fact is true," Lord Selwyn nodded thoughtfully. "I remember the War of the Shadow and the time of Leander the First. Never at any moment did all of Therras find itself consumed so completely by darkness, nor did fire rain destruction on such a grand scale as that which we now face."

"*I* translated that scroll *myself*!" Lucilius snapped, glaring at Ranzel. "The signs were all too clear!"

"Forgive me, Brother, but clearly you have not translated the scrolls correctly," Ragdobar drew the Red Wizard's angry gaze. "The Scroll of Champions and the Scroll of World Fate work in unison with neither complete without the other. You sought only to read from the one about the Great Heroine because of Lord Morod's rumoured discovery of the prophecy. You did not complete the translation."

"We did tell you this at the time," Samhir added darkly.

Lucilius' eyes darkened as he figuratively glared molten steel and brimstone at the Blue and Gold Wizards. Now it was clear why he was so against the idea of what Ranzel was suggesting.

He is afraid he will look the fool for incorrectly translating the prophecies, so he'd rather discredit his Brother in Magic instead. Such arrogance...

"My translation," he hissed, "was... *flawless*..."

"Such matters are of little consequence," Enchantress Illuminil spoke in her misty voice, sounding distant and as if she were from a dream, her turquoise eyes surveying all of us there. "Regardless of this difference of opinion, there is still the simple fact that we face the End of All Things now that Ragnarok has been awakened."

"Enchantress Illuminil is right," Lord Selwyn stated, glancing to her, then looking to the rest of us. "The priority now is in stopping this attack that continues to rage against us. Even now the Blighted Dragons burn any who attempt to stand against them."

"We have received word of attacks by mighty dragons from villages all over High-Realm," Riordan relayed direly, folding his arms. "Small homesteads mostly, but it seems that the Shadow Lord has them driving fear into the hearts of the people."

"And apparently it is working," Ser Callenhad joined the exchange, his blue eyes locking on the Wizards and Elves. "The Seven Kingdoms have begun attempting to protect themselves instead of engaging in peace talks as they had started to."

"Then they truly mean to divide and conquer," Lord Selwyn had distress in his eyes at the thought of such a concept. "Fractured as they are from one another, the Kingdoms will be too easily defeated."

"Then it is no mere coincidence that this prophecy has come to light," Enchantress Illuminil discerned, turning her gaze to the scrolls. "It is now that the Scrolls speak of, not the past, and I urge that we listen. If a mistake was made in the translation in naming the Great Heroine, then that cannot be helped. What can be helped is not sitting by and doing nothing while the world burns."

"Do we have some plan?" Fawkner asked, his hands before him on the table, his light brown hair pulled back from his face. "Is there some method we should employ to accomplish the task at hand?"

Ser Callenhad nodded. "The Scrolls speak of the Holders of Dragon Pendants coming forth. I would suggest beginning to search for them and enlisting them to the cause."

"How can you find them?" Tallinn questioned, studying him with cool measure.

"That is simple, Mistress Guardian," the old Dragon Knight responded. "We begin by first seeking rumours of dragons sharing some strange friendship with humans. This may come in the form of legend, or gossip, or superstition, but it may be found. And we Dragon Knights have our methods of discovering the energies of an awakened pendant once we know what to look for."

"The Pendants are lost to time," Fawkner stated gravely, meeting the Dragon Knight leader's gaze. "And most are already accounted for."

"We shall seek the remaining five," Ser Callenhad replied very calmly, almost as if he had no concerns whatsoever. "At this time the search will become much easier. After all, a light shines brighter in the darkness."

"Meanwhile," Ranzel spoke up again, gaining all eyes back to him, "we shall find the way to bring Princess Leander back from the dead to the Waking World."

"And how will you do this?" Xzharn asked coldly. "Conquering death is no easy feat."

"The prophecy is clear that it must occur," Ranzel replied, staring at the White Wizard sternly. "Regardless, the Princess is cursed..."

"Cursed?" Xzharn frowned.

Ranzel nodded as all the Council members watched him with sudden curiosity: "Before her death, she had been cursed by the ritual the Shadow Lord forced her to participate in several years ago. She lost the ability to age or change. She even lost the capability of bearing children."

My heart ached as I heard those words, once again wondering how Leander had endured such a terrible truth of her own body. It was cruel.

"This curse removed all change from her," the Green Wizard went on, "and, though I am certain it was not Lord Morod's intention, it has preserved her."

"How?" Lord Selwyn asked.

Ranzel looked to him. "Though she has been dead three weeks, her body shows no signs of decay. It is as if she sleeps without breath or the beating of her heart."

"Incredible," Ser Callenhad murmured with astonishment colouring his features.

"However, such a curse means she is not at rest," Ranzel stated firmly. "The soul cannot pass completely if the body does not become one with the earth. Though she is dead it is a living death."

My heart sank.

"You believe her soul is trapped in the Netherworlds?" Ragdobar asked with great perception.

Ranzel nodded gravely. "And she will be unable to move on into the Beyond since her body remains in its entirety. That is why I believe she may be returned to it as the prophecy says."

"What the prophecy lacks is the method of *how* to restore her," Xzharn pointed out evenly. "There are too few ways to achieve such a monumental task, Ranzel. Necromancy is the most vile of magical disciplines known to the world and will not restore the girl as she was. Such magic will only bring forth another revenant, or at best a simple draugar, but not a living, breathing, thinking, feeling human being."

"Necromancy was hardly the path I intended," Ranzel clarified, leaning on his staff. "There are other methods that may be employed..."

"Beyond praying to Azmerath himself to intervene, there is no magic of resurrection with the exception of those of the Daemon Kings of the Void. That is dark magic of the worst kind, not even of balance as other such powers are," Xzharn warned grimly, keeping his black eyes locked on Ranzel's face. "And there is no guarantee that even the God of Death would hear such a plea as this that you are proposing."

"Something has to be done," I said softly, turning my gaze to the White Wizard as he looked to me. "If we do nothing, we might as well lay down and die right here."

He hesitated to speak, obviously considering the argument the two of us had had when we last spoke. He glanced at Ellora, Tallinn and Fawkner, thoughtfully stroking his white and silver beard.

"If such a quest were to be undertaken," he spoke calmly and lowly, every word delivered with purpose, "then I would ask - Tallinn Landrace, Lord Fawkner Caradoc, Ellora Snowleaf, and Carden Highever - would you four stand forward to embark on it?"

I looked to Tallinn, seeing her gaze turn to me as if she were looking for guidance. The role of lead Guardian had become somewhat of a burden it seemed, and she was unsure of what to say. I tried to reassure her with my eyes, knowing how difficult it was to speak for others.

Slowly, Tallinn turned back to the Wizard, nodding her blonde-haired head. "We would," she said simply, conviction and uncertainty strangely sharing her voice.

Xzharn nodded. "Then the Council will deliberate and consider this information. You may retire to the Lord's House for now. You will be informed of our decision."

The four of us slowly stood and bowed our heads. Ellora and Fawkner led the way out as Tallinn and I followed, the sounds of involved discussion continuing behind us.

I had no idea whether they would agree to us seeking out a way to resurrect Leander, but then again, I wasn't even sure how something like that could be done. As it was, it didn't seem that the five wizards had any concept on how that should be achieved either, which was not encouraging.

There has to be a way to bring her back. There has to be.

* * * * *

Arriving back at the Lord's House, I had the urge to go to Leander and sit with her, yet I felt that I needed to remain at hand for the decision. Had I the power of future sight I wouldn't have sat so idle in wait. The decision did not come quickly and soon it was time for evening meal. I sat with the others as we were now joined by Joran, all of us silent as we ate, though we were hardly hearty in our consumptions. It seemed that since Safferan none of us had really had a strong appetite. I know I definitely didn't.

Once again, the eight of us sat in the balcony space, passing the time wastefully with nothing to fill it. Joran was still eating since he had taken to only consuming a meal once a day. The Storvari had told me that by eating one gigantic meal each day he could devote all his time that wasn't spent bathing or sleeping guarding Leander. I had to admit that I felt much the same.

"How long does it take to make a decision?" I griped, sighing hard as I lay back in my seat with my arms crossed. "It's been *six* hours..."

"Do you not recall the Council's discussions when the Princess first arrived here?" Ellora asked as she and Fawkner were attempting to play chess. "It was days before they decided what course of action to take in regard to the Shadow Lord's plans."

"And see how well that turned out," Tristan remarked as he sat back, nursing a stein of ale.

Holger and Dolin were pacing, the two dwarves ill at ease as they waited anxiously. We had told the others what had been said and they had all shown their hopeful concern that this could be true. Even Joran seemed to be waiting around under the pretence that he was merely eating well.

"A funny lot, these Wizards," Holger grumped, pacing swiftly with his hands clasped at the small of his back and his braided black beard swaying. "They talk far too much and act far too sparingly. It is foolish..."

"Hardly, brother," Dolin replied, smoking his pipe in thought as he paced more slowly than his hot-headed twin. "They would prefer to come to be certain of the task and the way to carry it out rather than rush in. It is wisdom."

"It is cowardice!" Holger snapped, his dark brown eyes blazing with a reawakened passion. "They talk when they should act! We face the very destruction of our world, and they are busy debating the appropriate course of action in their tower instead of taking it!"

"It is foolish to rush headlong into a dire situation without first being certain you can survive," Fawkner stated, flashing his eyes from the board to the Dwarf.

"How can victory be assured with inaction and talk?!" Holger spun to him harshly.

"How can victory be enjoyed if you are dead?" Fawkner retorted evenly. "Be wise, Holger, for there can be no success if we do not live to carry it out. Caution is not cowardice, but prudence, and it is sometimes all that keeps you breathing."

"Hopefully we will have an answer soon," Dolin said, stopping his own movements and leaning his back to a white and gold pillar. "Then we will know what to do."

"I hope so," I sighed. "I grow tired of waiting, especially now that I know Leander's soul suffers wherever she is."

"A terrible fate indeed," Ellora murmured grimly, taking one of Fawkner's pieces. "We can only hope that action to correct this grievous hurt may be taken."

"I have a feeling we're about to find out," Tallinn said, staring ahead as she slowly stood up.

Holger stopped pacing beside his brother as Fawkner and Ellora turned their attention from their game to the entryway of the space. I followed their gaze and got to my feet as Joran and Tristan both looked up from their food and drink.

Lord Selwyn, Ranzel and Master Riordan approached us, the three of them moving quickly with the look of men bearing news. Whether it was good or not I couldn't tell.

"Have you come to a decision?" Tallinn asked before I could, her tone calmer than mine would have been.

Lord Selwyn nodded solemnly, his turquoise eyes flicking to each of us. "Yes... It is the decision of the Council that with the threat we currently face the necessary forces cannot be spared to seek out a means to recover the Princess' soul from the Netherworlds and resurrect her to physical life."

"What?!" I felt my rage returning and the heat of tears beating against my eyes as they screamed to be released.

Master Riordan spoke as calmly as possible: "The decision has been made to send the Dragon Knights in search of all remaining active Dragon Pendants and their holders in the hopes that such figureheads may bring hope to the people and unite High-Realm."

I turned from them, pressing my hands to the railing of the balcony as I shook hard. *They have condemned her to the Netherworlds then, to live between life and death... no... to exist! That's all she'll have! A miserable timeless existence! Trapped, scared and alone! That's worse than murdering her!*

"Does the Council truly hold no stock in the concept that the Princess is the true Great Heroine of the prophecies, Lord Selwyn?" Ellora asked softly, fearful sorrow in her eyes.

"Many of the members believe that there is such relevant proof that she is, yes," Lord Selwyn responded to the Elven woman's question. "But the simple fact is that none among us know of how to achieve the task of reviving her, nor do we know where to begin looking."

"Not to mention that Lucilius continues to stonewall all efforts towards such an end," Ranzel sighed, shaking his head. "His pride will not allow him to accept that the prophecy has yet to pass."

"He sounds a fool," Dolin remarked gruffly, puffing out rings of smoke. "Pride has been the downfall of many a mage, warrior or rogue in the past."

"Very true," Ranzel nodded. "Yet, the sad fact is that unless all of the Wizards are in concurrence about a prophecy, it will not be enacted upon. Such was the way with this same prophecy in the past with Leander the First as it is now with her descendant."

"So there is nothing to be done?" I asked coldly, turning over my shoulder to look at them. "Because of one egotistical man, she can't be saved?"

"Well," Ranzel shrugged lightly, holding his staff in both hands, "the Council and its forces will not act."

"Much as it did not in the time of Leander the First," Lord Selwyn agreed, looking to the Wizard knowingly. "Yet, still she was seen as fulfilling the prophecy in its translation at the time, was she not?"

"Oh, yes," Ranzel nodded. "She was."

I frowned, confused.

Tallinn was frowning just as deeply, but found the words I could not: "Are you saying what I'm sure we all think you are?"

Master Riordan crossed his arms, his cloak swaying as he stepped forward to meet her gaze: "Though the Council will not undertake such a task, that does not mean it cannot be undertaken by... oh... let's say... the girl's most loyal companions."

I couldn't believe what I was hearing, both encouraged and bewildered at once. I could scarcely comprehend that this Master Guardian would suggest such a thing in seeming opposition with the Council.

"You mean... have us do it?" Fawkner gave voice to my own thoughts.

"Is that even allowed?" Tallinn frowned; her arms crossed in front of her as she looked up at Riordan.

"The Council's decision is simply to not act upon this themselves," Riordan stated evenly. "But that does not mean they do not want it pursued. The only course to do so is if someone not wholly a part of their forces chooses to do it."

"Fawkner and I are Guardians," Tallinn said, uncertainty clear on her face. "Does that not technically make us part of the Council's forces?"

"Firstly, you would undertake such a quest not as Guardians, but as the Princess' companions," Riordan answered, showing us the way around such technicalities before looking at me. "Secondly, there are *three* of you who are Guardians, not two."

"Carden has renounced his oath, Master Riordan," Tallinn replied, turning her hazel eyes to me softly and sadly. "He is no longer a Guardian."

Riordan turned his gaze my way, standing at equal height before me. "Perhaps you have declared such, Carden. Yet I know that it comes from a place of grief, and it is not truly within your heart."

"Leander died and that marks my failure as a Guardian," I confessed to him. "Only if we were able to bring her back to the Waking World would I then be worthy of being a Guardian again."

He nodded softly, patting my shoulders. "Then I hope you succeed."

I nodded to him in return, watching him turn from me then as Lord Selwyn faced us.

"I would ask which of you will embark upon this quest to bring High-Realm its true Great Heroine?" the Elf Lord asked in a gentle, yet strong voice. "Though I feel I already know the answer."

"Of course," Fawkner nodded, his hands clasped behind him.

"As I followed her ancestor, so shall I do this," Ellora responded with a bow of her flaming-haired head.

"Aye, I'll go," Dolin said softly.

"As will I," Holger declared sternly.

"Sure... Why not?" Tristan wobbled as he stood, setting his drink down. "I owe the lass that much."

Joran stood and simply placed one fist to his chest as he bowed his head.

"I will go and lead as Aldwyn requested I should," Tallinn decided.

Last of all, I confirmed softly: "I will. Always."

Lord Selwyn nodded with a slight smile. "I shall arrange supplies immediately. Gather what you will and prepare the Princess, for you should take her with you."

I nodded in time with Tallinn, all of us heartened by this new hope. But before any of us could begin to move, General Gailan and two silver clad High Elven guards rushed towards us from the dining room. There was alarm on Gailan's face, his hand on the pommel of his sword as if he meant to draw it swiftly.

Something's wrong...

"My Lord!" the High Elf general rushed to Lord Selwyn, bowing his head. "My Lord, reports from the watchtowers and walls: black hooded men have appeared at the perimeter of Silvervale escorted by Shadow Knights. They look to be Shadow Disciples."

"Shadow Disciples?" Tallinn asked quickly.

Ranzel scowled. "The magic wielding human and elven followers of the Shadow Lord who hope he may choose one of them to become his apprentice. Each Shadow Lord chooses only one and that person becomes his successor. They will do anything for their dark master's favour."

"That is not all," Gailan looked truly fearful as he said the next part. "Two great winged beasts have been spotted upon the horizon flying from the direction of Arnath. Two dragons, the one of steel plates and the one of black bones."

"Thorgeirr and Amrit..." Lord Selwyn's eyes widened in terror. "The Shadow Lord has sent the Dragons of War and Death to Silvervale..."

Gailan nodded once briskly. "They will be here presently."

Lord Selwyn nodded, taking in a deep breath to regain his composure. "Very well. Sound the call to arms, all soldiers to defend the city and all power to the magical defences. Evacuate the civilians by the ports."

Gailan bowed and led the two guards away quickly to carry out the orders.

"Gather what you need swiftly, friends," Lord Selwyn stated, looking to us. "You must go at once before this attack consumes what opportunity you have."

Tallinn and I both nodded, the others up and moving quickly from the balcony. I swept past Lord Selwyn and the others with him, rushing towards my room. Joran was already leaving, and I knew he would be going to only one place.

"Carden," Tallinn seized my arm, drawing my green eyes to her hazel ones, fear set strongly beneath her blonde locks, though she tried to hide it. "Whether you would call yourself a Guardian now or not, regardless, take up your armour and weapons, my brother."

I nodded, taking my arm back and rushing through the doors into the firelight of my room. I had to move quickly, snatching a pack from the closet. I began stuffing clothing haphazardly into the bag, moving with haste to grab everything I needed. I was more cautious with my medicine bag, the last of what tinctures Aldwyn had made for me before his passing within it. With that stowed, there was only one pile of things left to me.

I carefully picked up Leander's clothing, gently wrapping it together and placing it in the bag along with her boots. Her pendant was another story as I lifted it gently from the table, placing the precious treasure of my beloved girl in my belt pouch. I would protect it for her no matter what. She would not lose that too.

Once the bag was packed, I pulled on my Guardian armour, though I really had no desire to. Once the light hardened leather was strapped around my shoulders, arms and chest, I threw on my black cloak, sheathed my weapons and took up the pack, heading for the door.

As I left the rooms and stepped out onto the main terrace of the Lord's House the night sky suddenly erupted in a hailstorm of greenish blue lights. The lights seemed to arc up from the ground all around the city where the water and mountain did not stand, striking with heavy thuds like hammers on steel against an invisible dome above. That had to be the shield that defended the city against magical attacks.

I frowned at the eerily beautiful display, lost in its majesty for but a moment before reminding myself that it was a deadly light show.

I hurried to find the others, soon joining them where they had gathered at the foot of the stairs of the Broken Towers. They were all as entranced and horrified as I was by the haunting array of green falling stars that were striking against the city's unseen defences. Even Amethyst, Gaspeite and Eamnonn were there, all three dragons watching the lights with narrowed and glowing orange eyes.

"What sorcery is this?" Fawkner asked in haunted awe as I approached, his grey eyes set upon the display.

"The Shadow Disciples have begun attempting to break the shield protecting Silvervale," Ranzel declared, holding his staff ready as he gazed at the scene from beneath the brim of his hat. "They intend to bring it down before Thorgeirr and Amrit arrive. A means to a swifter end for all of us here."

"We cannot leave via the main road," Ellora declared as she walked up from the main gates with Tristan and Tallinn, all three with their cloaks swaying around them and weapons ready. "The Shadow Knights number at least a few hundred at the gates alone."

"It is a full-scale invasion," Tallinn was perturbed, shaking her head. "I don't know how we can hope to escape this siege."

"Not all of us need take flight from the Silver City this night, Lady Guardian," Eamnonn turned his glowing fire gaze to her as he spoke in his deep and wise voice. "I will draw the dire dragons into combat to give Lord Selwyn and the others time to evacuate the city."

Fawkner looked up at the Dragon, stunned: "Are you not an old dragon yourself, Eamnonn? How do you hope to stand against the might of such vicious evil as these dragons of destruction?"

"I need only draw their gaze elsewhere whilst you make your escape, my friend," the old dragon bowed his head to the man. "If there is to be any hope for the world and its peoples, then your company must away safely."

"How?" Holger grumped, leaning on his war-hammer. "There be no path away from the city we might take that could allow us such a passage. I am all for fighting to my death, but even I would not do so in vain."

"There is a secret passage," Ranzel stated, turning to walk down a set of steps. "It will lead beneath the lines of the enemy and behind them to the cliffs to the south."

"If there is a secret passage that offers such safety then why not send all the people through it?" Dolin asked as we began to follow.

The Wizard continued to walk quickly, his staff clicking against the ground as he went. "Because it is not meant for such a passage, Master Dwarf," he explained evenly, but hurriedly. "It was designed for small groups to bypass the walls in times of need to seek help from elsewhere. A task that is no longer accomplished with so few allies remaining."

"Wait!" I looked at those with me, suddenly realising we were two short. "Where are Joran and Leander?!"

Almost in answer to my question, the Storvari appeared at the top of the stairs, his dark hair gusting around his gargantuan shoulders as he carried Leander in his arms. She looked as small as a child in comparison to the giant eight-foot-tall man, her dark hair catching over her pale white skin. He had wrapped her in part of his cloak that he wore, keeping her close to his chest. He would be of no use in a fight carrying her like that.

"Come, quickly," Ranzel commanded evenly, turning, and continuing down the stairs.

He led us swiftly along a narrow walkway above the edge of the gardens at the foot of the mountain, the marshalling forces of the High Elves rushing to positions above us. I looked up just in time to see thick lines of silver armoured Elves preparing bows with silver arrows, aiming at the sky.

The Wizard came to an edge in the cliffs that was some feet from the city's fortress walls, finding a series of runes that glowed moonlight blue as he passed his staff across them. He nodded as a door of natural rock opened to reveal the narrow passage within.

"This is the way," he confirmed.

At that moment there came two great and terrible roars from above, the sweeping black shapes of Thorgeirr and Amrit appearing in the skies to the east. The two dragons immediately began opening their mouths and launching thunderstorms of red, orange and violet fire at the city, roaring in angry hatred. Their strikes hit the invisible shield of magic, illuminating the entire city in colours of pure destruction.

"Quickly!" Ranzel shouted, gesturing urgently. "We have no more time!"

As we rushed for the doorway three more roars erupted through the night and I turned to watch Eamnonn leading Amethyst and Gaspeite into the air. The three dragons passed through the magic field as their great wings flapped and beat fiercely, their glowing eyes locked on the dire beasts attacking us.

Amethyst still had no fire, so she could only attack with physical strikes, but her companion dragons were well equipped for the battle. Jets of orange flames spewed from the maws of both Gaspeite and Eamnonn, blinding Thorgeirr and Amrit, momentarily distracting them from the city.

In a violent rage, the two apocalyptic dragons turned with red eyes towards the three defenders, beating their wings viciously and howling. The sound of the dragons fighting was like a hurricane between their roaring, the beating of their wings, the scream of their fires and the collisions of their armoured bodies thundering the air. It was truly a sight to behold, but not one any of us could at that moment afford to witness.

"Joran! Go!" Fawkner's shout drew my gaze back to the escape passage.

The others were almost all through the doorway, only Ranzel, Fawkner, Ellora and Joran left. The Huntress and Falcon Lord were ushering the Storvari through into the darkness as he carried Leander carefully, determined to protect him and her.

As they both followed, I rushed to the archway and went to pass, but Ranzel seized my arm. I looked to him with a frown, confused as to what he was doing.

"Take these with you," he handed me a leather wrapped satchel.

"The Prophecy Scrolls?" I was beyond perplexed, looking up at him as he shoved them into my hands.

"They cannot fall into Morod's hands," he insisted resolutely. "Take them with you and keep them safe. Do this, Carden."

"You're not coming with us?" I was shocked that he would stay.

"I must assist the other Wizards in holding the city's shield," he explained quickly. "We must give the evacuation every opportunity to succeed."

"That's madness!" I retorted.

"I will try to join you once we are done," he said earnestly. "There is a place in the foothills of the Silver Mountains two day's travel south-east from here. You will know it by the arch of stone that sits between two natural pillars. I will meet you there. Wait two days. If I do not come, leave. Do you understand?"

Reluctantly, I nodded, my chest heaving as I breathed heavily.

"Good. Now go. Bring the girl back from Death's Realm," he said, urging me into the opening.

I stepped into the black stone passage, looking over my shoulder in time to see him close the door. He was insane to stay, but I had to do as he asked.

I strapped the scrolls to my back with my pack and rushed to catch up to the others. In no time I was with them, finding it easy to see them in the near perfect darkness. My eyes were easily able to adjust to the kind of blackness that most humans were blinded by.

"It's too dark," Holger griped after a few minutes. "I can't see a damned thing."

"Hang on," Tristan held up something from his belt and blew a breath into it.

The orb he held illuminated the darkness and chased back the shadows with a pearlescent blue light that showed us just how narrow and close the tunnel really was. I had to admit that it was handy to have his magical abilities at our disposal, even if I did hate him.

Tallinn took charge, leading the way with Tristan at her side to light the path. It wasn't a hard route to follow since the passage only seemed to go in one direction, but it was long and with many twists, turns and slopes.

We were all hushed as we walked, only the scraping of our boots and the huffing of our stressed breathing filling the tunnel. Then, we began hearing the distant thudding booms of heavy strikes hitting ground. I dreaded to think what that sound could mean, refusing to give words even in my mind to the suspicions I had.

There was nothing any of us could do now but walk, the eight of us silent in our haunting passage from the sanctuary that had surely fallen to the fires of those beasts. I couldn't even hope for the survival of any of those we had left behind and chose not to contemplate their fate. For now, I was focused only on the next minute and the next, each one leading to our exit from the tunnel. Then, into the unknown.

At last, Tallinn and Tristan led us to a cave, slowly walking their way through and leading us amongst the crags and jagged rocks. As the light of night peeked through the opening ahead of us, Tristan extinguished the light in his hand and returned it to his belt. There was no need to attract attention to ourselves.

We slowly stepped through into the wintry chill that spread unnaturally across everything, making our way up a narrow canyon from the cave. It was very well hidden to ensure it was undiscovered. The High Elves had clearly put some great thought into the construction of this escape path. But as we came to the cliff edges it became clear that it was a passage that could bring no more to safety.

Before us lay the vale that Silvervale stood within, the mountain a black shape against the dark tremulous sky. The whole scene was lit by the flashes of crimson lightning that struck at all the lands violently, even shearing through rocks and splintering burning stone into the air in orange shards.

The city was under siege, the five dragons still fighting in the skies above, their shapes silhouetted by the flashes of the magical attacks and the storm's lightning. The Shadow Disciples were as black shapes amidst the rolling white fields of snow below, their black robes swirling around them in the winds as they hurled the haunting turquoise light at the city. Standing among them were the towering figures of the Shadow Knights, all ready to attack with swords and shields on their armoured limbs.

A great roar came as Eamnonn struck at the two evil dragons. He bellowed and Gaspeite swept to assist as Amethyst attempted to pull the dark dragons back. They seemed unable to hold the enemy dragons' attention, the two monsters turning to the city. As Eamnonn charged them one last time he was mauled by Amrit, howling in pain. The skeletal dragon hurled him away, slamming him to the ground somewhere in the distance. We could only watch him fall.

"Oh, Gods!" Tallinn gasped, covering her mouth with both hands.

Thorgeirr was trying to kill Amethyst, latching onto her back, and snapping at her. Gaspeite came to the young dragon's aid and threw her attacker off her. The green dragon grasped the smaller purple one and pulled her away as Thorgeirr turned his red eyed gaze back to Silvervale. The two good dragons could do nothing.

Amrit and Thorgeirr lashed out with their supernatural flames, breaking the shield into sections. It was easy then for the Shadow Disciples and Shadow Knights to launch their attack. Arrows flew like silver rain from the city as the High Elves fired, but they were no match for the two monster dragons.

Both beasts swept over the city, launching fiery strike after strike into Silvervale, white and silver stone scattering into the air as screams echoed in the night. The sounds of battle rose as swords clashed in a terrible cacophony from the beleaguered streets.

There was nothing to be said or done, all of us turning from the horrible scene and making our way south-east as Ranzel had instructed.

Chapter Seven
Witch Hunt

The sounds of fighting echoed in the distance for some time as we walked; the howls of the fearsome dragons ripping through the air like thunderous crashes against the very clouds themselves. Even through the tremendous tearing boom of the evil dark storms that choked the skies their monumental voices sounded as they continued their relentless onslaught against Silvervale's beleaguered walls.

As I trudged through the knee-deep snow that fell around us with my face shielded by my thick hood and my bags across my back, I could not help but envision all that was still happening back there.

If any yet survive the assault, they will be lucky to escape without drawing the attention of the Disciples, Shadow Knights or those foul, evil dragons. By the Gods... how did we ever come to this? The answer was obvious to me and panged my heart anew with relentless tearing pain. *Leander...*

I turned my eyes up through the blizzard that seemed to have swept up around us from nowhere, locking onto the shape of the Storvari walking ahead of me. I couldn't see her in his arms, her face hidden and shielded by the wrapping he had covered her in and by the mere fact that I stood behind him. His hulking torso was hiding her from my eyes. Yet, I caught the glimpse of her feet, tangled in a warm cloth to shield her skin from the bitter frosts as they dangled gracefully from his arm.

A sigh escaped my lips. All I desired was to hold her, even in her deathly condition, and just feel her in my embrace.

The way was anything but easy, the path winding through the forested foothills choked with snow. The cold was deeper than it should have been in winter, and we found ourselves struggling along the road we had chosen. I had told the others where to go, Ellora now leading us, her sharp elf eyes capable of seeing more than the rest of us.

For two days we trudged through the ever-deepening snows, soon working our way through the hip high powder with difficulty. Now the only sounds we heard on the winds were those of the never-ending storms. There were no howls of dragons, no crashing of magic against barriers, no clanging of swords meeting... no screams.

The battle must have come to its end. I don't doubt that our allies were defeated. What I do doubt is that many yet live. I don't see how anyone could survive such an onslaught as that.

"There!" Ellora shouted, her voice snapping me from my dire thoughts in order to seek her out in the darkened white.

The red-haired woman was standing upon a rise, her sage coloured cloak and hood wildly swirling and tugging around her shoulders with the wind. Her fiery locks were as a coiling flow behind her face. She was pointing with one gloved hand towards three shapes in the distance blurred by the snowy storms of the mountains' foothills.

I narrowed my eyes, straining to see. Just as the old Wizard had said, there stood two great pillars of natural formed stone, perhaps forty feet tall. Just a little beyond and between them in the cover of the sheer cliffs of the mountains was the great archway he had spoken of.

We all began to move with a greater swiftness, making for the cover of the archway as quickly and as ardently as we could manage in the deep, soft snow. Before long we were pulling ourselves up the rocky rises and hurrying into the shielding shelter of the archway. The side of the archway facing the mountains remained free of the cold harsh weather beyond its rocky shape.

To her credit, Tallinn began to take charge, focused now as she took on the role of leader. It suited her as far as I could tell.

"We must make safe this shelter," she instructed, looking then to Fawkner and Tristan. "Gather all the wood you can and get a fire going as quickly as possible. We'll not last long without the flames to warm us against this chill," she turned to the two dwarves. "Get the tarps from the supply bags and do what you can to erect more protection from this wind."

"I shall assist," Ellora declared, going with Dolin and Holger to the bags.

"I'll stand watch," I stated calmly.

I set my bag down and took the scrolls' satchel from my shoulder, standing just within the mouth of the archway. My gaze turned out back the way we had come, and I found myself longing to see some sign of the Dragons and the Wizard on the horizon. Yet, there was no sign; no beat of purple and green wings, and no figure with a staff and pointed hat emerging from the blizzard's white depths. We were alone.

"It seems eerily quiet out there," Tallinn remarked as she came to stand at my side, her arms folded in front of her ample chest. "I hear not but the winds of this unending maelstrom that colours the skies darker than night."

I nodded, frowning at the blizzard. "The sounds of the battle faded just a little under two days ago. I have tried not to think of what has happened back at Silvervale, yet my mind plagues me with the images all the same."

"As does mine," she murmured with a small sigh of unease. "Though I hope for the best and that the Silver City has survived the attack, my heart tells me that there is naught but devastation behind us."

I had nothing to say to such a remark, knowing only that she was right. There could be no survival in that city, yet I had to hope. Finding a way to restore Leander was so very dependent on having the right people with us, and to me that meant the Green Wizard. But a deep fearful dread warned me that he may be lost to us.

Tallinn looked up at me, her blonde hair flicking to her eyes only to be drawn away by the gentle hooking of her slender fingers. She studied me with those hazel orbs I knew so well, her presence strangely softened now despite the continued hardness that came from her sense of duty.

Ever the faithful Guardian...

"We will remain here for two days as Ranzel said," she told me evenly. "But if the third dawns and he does not come to us, then we must decide on what to do next."

"Of course," I replied a little emotionlessly, still watching the stormy wilds beyond our temporary haven. "It is only prudent that we not remain in one place too long."

I could tell that she once more yearned to speak on my decision, that she desired to change my mind, but I was set. I was no longer a Guardian and that would not change, despite my conditions dictated to Master Riordan. All the same, I knew the next discussion and attempt would come regardless, though, as she turned from me in that moment, I was relieved it was not to be right then.

"I will take Tristan and we shall hunt for food," Ellora spoke from behind me, her focus on Tallinn as the three moved to meet while Fawkner's attempts to light a fire began to illuminate the shelter.

"Are our supplies not enough?" Tallinn questioned, concern edging her otherwise controlled voice.

"Hardly," the Elf responded. "We were unable to effectively gather all we needed before departing the city."

"The attack saw to that," Tristan added, his voice grating on me.

"Be cautious," Tallinn warned them, permitting their quest for food. "We know not how many enemies or dangers lurk nearby in this blizzard. Return to us swiftly."

With no further words, the Huntress and the Wanderer passed me by, stepping back into the wild weather with their hoods drawn and their bows in hand. I simply watched them go until they were nothing more than moving shadows in the icy wind making their way down through the dark silhouettes of the trees.

Slowly, I turned my gaze over my shoulder as I leaned to the stone wall with my cloak around me. I began surveying the camp. Fawkner had alighted the fire and was now tending to it as diligently as any man could, determined to keep the hungry tongues licking the air. It certainly made this frozen shelter feel warmer, though the chill beyond the stone walls still managed to invade upon us with seeming ease.

Dolin and Holger had finished securing the tarpaulins over the back of the arch, the off-brown hide fabric flapping against the lines and pegs securing it. The two dwarves lumbered to take a seat by the fire, their exhaustion clear on their faces as they wrapped themselves in their fur topped cloaks. Holger took his flask from his coat and swigged back some of the ale he carried before offering it to his brother. Dolin took it gratefully, trying to combat the cold.

Tallinn was silhouetted by the glow of the flames, her arms still crossed as she stared down into the fire. I caught a glimpse of her face. The hardness she held so well in her Guardian demeanour looked cracked like a porcelain mask. Her vulnerability and uncertainty might not have been clear to everyone, but it was clear to me.

Last of all, Joran was seated with his back to the wall and his hood drawn, his eyes shut as he fell into his usual Storvari meditation trance. He remained as still as the very stone that surrounded us, never leaving her side. That was then where my eyes lingered; the small figure wrapped there in blankets laying at his side.

I could see only her face, but it still looked as beautifully white and peaceful as before. She was so innocent and sweet in her unending rest, though I could only imagine how cold she must have been at that moment. It was strange that we were in a place as inhospitably icy as this and yet she drew no shiver across her perfect skin.

At least she is spared that discomfort as well as the terror we all witnessed at Silvervale...

I remained there by the opening to the arch, on guard and watching out for any figures that might approach. Even after Tristan and Ellora returned I did not relent my position. I needed to do something and being the lookout seemed better than nothing.

I guess we'd best settle in for a long wait, I heaved out a deep sigh with that thought, watching the black storms and deepening snows beyond our shelter.

* * * * *

We had sat for nearly two days and still there was no sign of Ranzel. I had begun to truly believe that the old wizard had been killed in the attack on Silvervale, which left me disheartened.

Sitting by the fire with one arm perched on my knee and the other pressed to the ground, I let my eyes study the flicking, licking flames that danced in the rocks we had set up. It had been a cold and heartless trip to this place, and I found myself wondering what would come upon us now. All hope seemed to be fading away with each passing hour that we remained in that place.

I glanced across the fire to where Leander lay. I had purposely chosen to sit here so that I could watch over her. I hadn't yet approached her since our arrival at the camp site, still too uncertain about everything. But now, as the reality that our ally was not coming crept ever closer, I worried that I would not get her back.

She could remain trapped in the Netherworlds for eternity. Gods... what can be done without Ranzel? We needed him to save her...

Tallinn was pacing as Ellora sat with Fawkner by the fire, huddled under their cloaks, the Dwarves now on watch at the mouth of the shelter. She looked unsettled, continuously glancing to the world outside as she walked. Without the sun there was no way to be certain of the hours, our only recognition of the change from day to day coming from the darkening and lightening of the storms. Regardless, the days were black and the nights blacker still.

Finally, the young woman turned from the opening and faced us, drawing her cloak further around her as she shivered: "It has been two days and there is no sign of the Wizard. He isn't coming."

"It seems very likely now that he isn't," Fawkner agreed with a sigh, setting down the empty bowl that he had just finished his meal from.

"Aye," Tristan said, sharpening his sword. "Were he to join us he would have done so by now."

Tallinn thought for a few moments, knitting her brow as she stared down into the flames. She looked as if she were trying to discern some great puzzle that was increasingly difficult to unlock.

At last, she spoke: "We can no longer remain here. We must depart and find safe refuge."

"Without the only man who can bring Leander back to us?" I questioned coldly, turning my hard gaze to her.

"Carden, he *isn't* coming," she said firmly, trying to cement the concept that my mind knew but my heart denied. "He must surely be dead by now, along with everyone else in Silvervale."

I sighed grimly, looking across at Leander's still form again. "I know..."

There was a moment of painful silence then, only the winds of the storms raging against us sounding through the world. None of us particularly felt like talking or doing much of anything, but we all knew we had to. At last, it was Dolin who broke the quiet that had descended over our dissolute camp.

"So... uh... where should we go?" he asked softly, though his rough voice was still hard. "Is there some place that we may yet find safety?"

Tallinn shook her head, pacing again. "I am uncertain of where to go from here. With every Guardian stronghold destroyed by the dark dragons, there are too few options left to us. Silvervale was the closest safe haven we had. Now we are without allies to turn to."

"We could make for the Under Roads and back to Hecturn," Dolin suggested evenly. "Lord Eilan will have secured it, but we could always get into the city regardless..."

"Pfft! Unlikely!" Holger snorted, turning his dark gaze to his twin brother. "The cities will all be barricaded, never to open again until this threat passes. We may travel through the Under Roads, but we are without passage home, brother."

"Ah... true," Dolin conceded, nodding in grim thought.

That was when Ellora sat up, her ears twitching a little. The Elf seemed suddenly on edge as she looked to the skies, listening.

"Ellora?" I frowned, watching her. "What is it?"

"I hear a dragon on the wind," she replied softly.

Ellora leaped to her feet, the rest of us following suit as she headed for the entrance to our camp. I moved with her swiftly, turning my eyes to the storm clouds just as a black shape emerged from high above. It swooped and dived through the storms, aiming straight for us. Of course, we were all suddenly on edge as the creature moved towards us. My hand hovered by my sword, readying to draw it and fight.

I don't know how I will survive such a fight with a dragon, but I will not let it hurt Leander...

As the dragon got closer, I began to recognise her magenta wings and purple scales, her orange eyes locking onto our location. My heart lurched and I felt hope kindle in me.

Amethyst landed with a hard thud to the snowy earth, her four legs bending at the joints to cushion her touch down, and her wings folding quickly to avoid being blown away by the winds. She started towards us; her glowing gaze solemn as she approached.

The Dragon immediately growled and grunted in her language, but I could find no comprehension of what it was she was saying.

"Amethyst," I raised one hand to her, approaching her slowly. "It's all right. What's wrong?"

She continued her bleats and snaps as she spoke, looking at me with those molten orange eyes so full of desperation.

I shook my head. "I don't understand anything she says. Why does she not speak common as Eamnonn does?"

"Because she is a dragon of one of the Pendants," Ellora stated, moving to my side, her turquoise gaze locked on the Dragon's face. "Only through the

Pendant could Leander understand her words. No other could unless they can speak with the animals."

"If only there was one among us with such abilities," Tristan remarked.

Ellora nodded softly, looking to me. "I know her tongue enough to understand her."

"You do?" I was surprised by that.

She nodded. "All of the Elven Peoples can commune with all animals and dragons. It is something we share with our Fae cousins."

"What does she say?" Tallinn asked, flicking her gaze between the Dragon and the Elf.

Ellora moved forward, reaching her hands up and stroking the Dragon's snout gently. Her touch seemed to soothe her. Amethyst's urgency became calmness and she gazed back at the Huntress with gentle, though sadly concerned eyes.

"Be calm, my dragon friend," Ellora urged her in a soft voice. "Tell me what it is that causes you such angst."

Amethyst began to speak in dragon tongue, growling out her responses slowly and carefully.

"She says that she was concerned for us," Ellora relayed, still looking into the Dragon's eyes. "She left the other dragons to seek us out a day after our escape and has been seeking us ever since."

"Why did it take you so long to find us, Amethyst?" I asked gently.

Amethyst replied, looking to me as she spoke before turning to Ellora, as if to tell her to translate.

"Without the Princess' living heart to guide her to the Pendant, she had to search," Ellora explained. "She doesn't know life without the Pendant's call, but without the Princess it is sleeping and so does not call to her. She had to seek us out on her own using her sense of smell, but the storms and the battle have left her confounded," she took on a sympathetic expression then, stroking the Dragon's nose. "Oh... she is so ill at ease, so confused and overwhelmed without the Princess and the Pendant. She says that it is like she has been blinded and deafened all at once with losing her soul kindred. Her sadness is... unbearable."

I know the feeling... Though I thought the words I didn't speak them aloud.

The Dragon began to explain something to Ellora, the woman seeming to understand every grunt and growl as she nodded, listening intently. It was a difficult thing to just stand there and wait to be told the rest of the conversation instead of taking part.

"She says that she went back to Silvervale in search of us and beheld the aftermath of the battle," Ellora told us grimly. "The city is not but ruins and burnt corpses, even the Broken Towers torn asunder on the icy ground. The two terrible dragons had departed when she returned, but there were Shadow Disciples and

Shadow Knights rummaging through the wreckage. It seemed to her that very few of our allies made it out."

"What of Ser Callenhad, Enchantress Illuminil, Lord Selwyn, or any of the others?" Tallinn asked.

Ellora looked to Amethyst and sighed at the response: "She doesn't know. The dead counted high in their faceless numbers."

"What of the other dragons?" Tallinn urged, as anxious as the rest of us to know the answer.

Amethyst gave her grim response, though her tone was less dark than her previous ones.

"Eamnonn is badly wounded, and she helped Gaspeite take him to rest in the safety of the mountains," Ellora explained evenly. "He will heal, but it will take time. As for Gaspeite, he went in search of Ranzel. More than that she cannot say. She urges us to move on from here as she saw Shadow Knights searching the area."

"Then we must depart at once," Tallinn determined, turning to the camp and moving to the supply bags. "Put out the fire and pack everything up. We must stay no longer."

"Wait," I called to her, turning after her. "What about helping Leander?"

"Carden, not now," she told me, gathering things up. "We haven't the time and we must seek a new shelter."

"Tallinn, we *must* know what we are to do before we go anywhere," I insisted, moving to stand over her. "We can't just leave her like this..."

"What would you have us do?" she demanded, swinging around to face me. "What course of action would you have us take? We have no knowledge of how to help her or where to go to gather such help. Only the Green Wizard had any sort of inkling on how to seek such knowledge, and he is not with us. Unless you have another avenue which will lead us to the answer, there is nothing we can do, and we *must* move on."

I stared her down, feeling my predator stirring within me once more. It took all of my resolve to keep him in check and not unleash him upon my friend, but her words made me angry. Later I would recognise the sense and logic in them, but at that moment I didn't use my head as much as my heart. It now governed my every emotion.

"We *will* find some way to gain the knowledge we need," she said softly, trying to appease me as she could see my struggle herself. "For now, let us take her someplace safe."

"Where would you suggest?" I asked in a low, gruff voice, fighting my predator back into his cage mentally.

"Eilath," Fawkner suggested, drawing our attention with his even words as he stood from packing his bag. "You heard the reports in Silvervale. The cities and villages are as yet untouched by the wrath of these destructive dragons. For the time being we could return to my city and take refuge there."

"Perhaps we could even use the library to discern some means of restoring the Princess," Tristan added, drawing his cloak around him as he joined us.

Fawkner nodded. "The Caradoc Library holds many secrets. It is possible that the answer to bringing her back is hidden within its walls."

"Satisfied with that, Carden?" Tallinn gave me a severe look, her patience thinning.

I sighed and grumbled: "In absence of more proactive options, I suppose it will have to do. If nothing else, it will be a place where she can rest peacefully."

As we seemed agreed upon the idea of setting for Eilath, I heard Amethyst growl and snarl behind me. I turned to view her as she spoke to us, her glowing eyes flashing with the same passion I myself felt.

Though I do not understand her, I am glad to know that I am not the only one who is as passionate about finding a way to get Leander back.

Ellora frowned. "Are you certain, Amethyst?"

Amethyst nodded and grunted.

Ellora looked over her shoulder to us, still stroking the Dragon's scales in order to comfort and calm her: "She speaks of someone named Danika. She says this one would know the answer."

"Danika?" Tallinn frowned.

"The Wilds Witch the Princess and I met during our journey to Silvervale," Tristan explained, drawing our gazes as he crossed his arms. "She did seem to know a lot more than she was letting on, and even predicted the lass' death at the hands of the Shadow Lord."

"Do you think she would know how to help Leander now?" I asked, impatient and hopeful at the same time.

He shrugged. "Perhaps. But I don't see why she would help us. She made certain to continuously tell us that she had no side in the greater conflict and that she helped only when she chose to do so. All the same I do not see why we can't at least seek her out."

"It's something at least," I agreed.

Tallinn sighed, a thoughtful expression plastering her face. "I suppose then that we have a choice to make, seek out this witch of the wilds, or take the Princess to Eilath and hope the library holds the answers."

Amethyst growled something.

"Why not both?" Ellora translated for the Dragon. "Amethyst points out that it would be wiser to follow both options. Should the Witch prove unhelpful, we may still make for Eilath."

"We cannot carry a dead body through the Forests of Arnath, though," Tristan pointed out direfully. "If the creatures of that forest catch her scent, they'll descend upon us in a heartbeat. Not to mention what will happen if the Revenant should detect her."

"You're right," Tallinn nodded, meeting his gaze. "We cannot risk taking her with us..."

"Then some of us seek out the Witch while the rest make for Eilath," Fawkner said. "I will take Joran and we will bring Leander to my city to keep her safe."

"It is a very good suggestion," Dolin spoke up, moving to stand with him. "The best road to do so will be via the Under Roads. I can lead you through there while my brother remains with the witch hunting party to guide them when done."

"Very well," Tallinn nodded. "What can we expect to face from this witch?"

"Her powers are unknown to me," Tristan replied as she turned to him, "but she has a full-grown troll serving as her familiar. He's a difficult bastard to fight."

"All right," Tallinn said, completely in charge. "Then the rest of us will seek out the Witch while Fawkner, Joran and Dolin take the Princess to Eilath."

Amethyst murmured in her way to Ellora.

"Amethyst will go with them," the Elf said softly. "She must remain with the Princess and protect her."

"As will I," I said, refusing to let Leander out of my sight.

Tallinn shook her head. "I cannot have both of you go with them. Amethyst shall go to Eilath."

"Tallinn," I growled in protest.

"Carden, your skills will be more valuable dealing with this witch and her troll," she countered evenly, meeting my gaze. "Besides, you're the one who wanted to be more proactive about our actions."

I couldn't argue with her. Though I stood nearly a full foot taller than her, Tallinn had her way of pushing me back into line. Perhaps it was that she was a more dedicated Guardian than I ever was. Then again it was most likely because she knew me too well. I never did win an argument with her, and until this whole thing began, we had been almost entirely in agreement on everything.

I conceded. "As you wish."

"Can you lead us, Tristan?" she asked of the Wanderer. "Do you know how to find where she resides?"

"Aye, that I do, Lady Guardian," he confirmed with a nod, stringing his bow to his back.

"Then let us make way," Tallinn decreed.

As the others were gathering the last of our supplies and putting out the fire, I watched Joran pick Leander up in his arms again. I wanted to reach out and take her into my arms still, but I didn't. I couldn't.

"We'll take care of her," Fawkner said softly, one hand to my shoulder. "I promise you, Carden. She will be waiting for you to return."

I sighed and nodded. "I shan't keep her waiting long."

Fawkner nodded and passed me by as Joran approached. I had him pause, the Storvari eyeing me curiously as I reached under the blanket and gently stroked Leander's hair with my rough fingers.

"I'll come back to you soon, my love," I assured her gently, fighting the tears I felt trying to break my defences. "I promise."

I stepped back and Joran bowed his head to me before setting off. I just stood there then as the rest of my friends dismantled the camp, my eyes set on watching the others leave. My sight remained on them until they were nothing more than shadows in the icy winds.

It's all right, Leander. I'll find this Witch and get you back. I swear...

* * * * *

Nearly nine days after leaving Fawkner, Joran, Dolin, and Amethyst, we found ourselves climbing up the forested and snowy foothills towards the Nartarn'lath Mountains again somewhere on the border of Dorvana and Gorvenna. The thick trees of the forest had blocked much of the frozen downpour and so there was not much there for us to trudge through. But the mud was something else.

"The Witch's cave is near," Tristan said direfully as he drew his sword, his brown eyes watchful as he surveyed the forest before us. "Be on the lookout for that troll of hers. He's a wickedly angry beastie."

"I am certain we have all downed a troll before," Ellora glanced to the rest of us curiously, yet it was not a question.

"Tallinn and I have fought one before," I confirmed, my right hand by my throwing daggers, my left on the pommel of my sword. "Though I don't remember defeating it."

"We didn't," Tallinn said, walking beside me with her face hidden under her black hood. "It nearly stomped us into jelly. We survived only because of Aldwyn."

"Yes," I sighed, missing our mentor and friend. "He saved us that day."

"I've killed half a dozen of the wretched, stone-faced beasts!" Holger declared; war-hammer held at the ready in both hands. "The biggest I slew singlehandedly!"

"Really?" Ellora smirked, looking over her shoulder at him from under her hood. "Then why do you look around the forest so fearfully?"

"Trolls don't scare me, Lady Elf," he shuddered, choking back a hard swallow with a grimace. "It's groundmerks that make me fearful. Foul, poison dripping, six legged rodents... Ugh!"

"Groundmerks are easy," Tristan told him, still watching the way ahead. "Kill the biggest one and the rest scamper into hiding."

"Not the point," Holger shuddered again. "It's their nasty, pointy, clutching feet I can't stand... Ugh! The idea of them touching my flesh is enough to make me shy from a fight."

"You have a fear of groundmerks, Holger?" I asked, a little surprised.

"And what is wrong with that?" he asked harshly, anger on his features. "Can't a dwarf be afraid of something too?"

"There's nothing wrong with that," I said and confessed: "I have a fear of spiders myself."

"Ha! Easy to dispatch," he shrugged brazenly. "Just get a shoe."

"*Giant* spiders," I corrected. "The six foot or bigger ones. Though small ones unnerve me too."

"Oh... well... that's different," he said.

After a few more long, tense minutes, we emerged from the forest, stepping through the tree line into sight of the great standing shape of the Nartarn'lath Mountains before us. They seemed to rise high like a great sheer wall that spread out on both sides, the dark cloudy sky above roiling up near the peaks that were far out of our view. The pines climbed up the slopes, suddenly looking less green and more grey. Everything just seemed dark and sinister, the snow powdered ground showing the mucky earth that was wet with both rain and ice.

Before us there lay a cave with a hard wooden door that looked to have been carved from a large chunk of the bough of a great oak, a window cut out in the top. I instantly had a bad feeling as I saw it, suddenly noting the sinister carvings of ravens set into the stone doorframe around the opening.

I get the feeling this woman will not be as accommodating as any of us hoped.

Tristan led the way, crossing one foot in front of the other slowly as he walked, his brown gaze flicking to the woods that surrounded the clearing. He was diligently watchful for the troll should it try to attack us.

"It is darkly quiet," Tallinn commented, her bow in hand and ready, though she didn't string an arrow to it. "Something is not right..."

As she said that, there came a thundering roar, and the ground began to shake. We all staggered, trying to keep ourselves from falling to the hard, muddy, snowy earth, planting our feet and fighting to stay standing. The rocks on the cliff tumbled down in dribbling streams of stone with the rough quaking, but it was not an earthquake. It was the Troll.

The great beast charged out of the woods to our right, running forward with its massive knuckles pounding the ground as if its hands were a second set of feet. It skidded to a stop mere meters from us, sucking in its barrelled chest and letting out a bellowing howl so strong that it nearly knocked us from our feet.

The Troll narrowed his beady black eyes at us, anger blazing in their coal-like surfaces beneath his heavy, bald brow. He chomped his large set jaws, drool dripping from his teeth as he glared at us, the stone in his leathery hide almost seeming to get more pronounced.

"Ah! He's a mighty big one!" Holger staggered where he stood, stumbling a little as he got into a fighting stance, hammer at the ready.

Tristan and I had our swords drawn, his left hand aglow with blue flames that danced between his fingers. Tallinn and Ellora immediately snapped their bows up, arrows laced to the strings and aimed at the monster's gargantuan face. The five of us were ready, all of us expecting the thing to attack.

That was when I noticed movement out of the corner of my left eye. I glanced from the Troll to see the door to the cave open, a figure in a black hood with a tall staff striding forward in a seductively feminine nature.

The Witch...

She strode out of the shadows of her cave, her eyes flashing emerald as she took in the sight before her. She was nothing like I'd expected, despite Tristan's and Leander's telling of her. Her dark black hair had a reddish tinge to it and was pulled back from her face in a simple up-style, raven feathers laced into the strands. Her hood was attached to the neckline of the garment she wore: a magenta, close fitting dress with long sleeves beneath a corset. It seemed to have a second layer under it of lilac and deep grey, the two fabrics designed in a staggered and tattered hang around her slender legs. She wore dark leggings and black boots, her cloak swaying behind her back. Her staff was clutched in one claw-like hand, looking sinister with the bones and feathers set around its green crystal.

What I did notice about her was that if she was a Witch of Raven's Rest, she was certainly the more beautiful of the sisters. She had perfect skin that didn't possess the greenish veins Manth's had or the hardness of porcelain beauty Keilantra's had. But more than this, I noticed her power and felt her casual contempt and easy confidence as she slowly swaggered towards us. She was impressive and frightening.

"Oh, look," she said in a sardonically bored tone as she eyed us, stopping some feet away. "Five new visitors to my home in the depths of these unending storms. How... *nice...*"

Tristan looked to her as she spoke, the others flicking their gazes her way seconds later.

She smiled coldly. "Tristan the Ivanstenian Wanderer. You return to me with friends; something I never thought you would have."

"Nice to see you too," he said a little offhandedly, keeping his gaze on her. "I suppose you knew we'd be here."

She half shrugged. "Of course. Just as I know the reason you have come to seek me out, fool."

"Do us a favour then," he offered her a half smile, edging back from the Troll a little, sword still raised, "and call your troll off."

"And why would I do that?" the Witch asked almost mockingly. "Five heavily armed and armoured travellers stand on my doorstep with their weapons drawn and their intentions unknown. Only a fool would not take measures to defend their home."

"We are no threat to you," Tallinn called to her, glancing between the Witch and the Troll whilst keeping her aim on the larger. "We wish only to talk..."

"There is a lot of talk going on amongst your allies, and yet very little action," the Witch remarked oddly. "But what talk can there be if pleasantries are not to be offered? What assurance can be felt when weapons are drawn upon my familiar?"

"Call your pet off or we'll bring it down," Holger growled threateningly, glaring at the Troll.

The Troll snarled lowly at him, bringing its face closer to the ground.

"All right," I said calmly, pulling my sword back and sheathing it. "We can be civil here."

The Witch raised one sharply arched black eyebrow at me as I held my hands up slowly in an attempt to be unthreatening.

"Allow me to introduce myself," I said slowly and gently. "My name is Carden Highever. It's a pleasure to make your acquaintance, Danika of the Wilds."

She seemed quietly amused. "Hm. Princely manners along with familiarity of my name... How intriguing..."

I offered her my usual charming half smile. "As I said, we can be civil here."

"Yet, weapons are still drawn," she pointed out evenly.

I gestured to the others. "Lower your weapons."

"Carden?" Tallinn looked to me incredulously.

"We only came to talk, not fight," I reminded her. "Just lower them."

Slowly, hesitantly, Tallinn nodded to the others, and they all lowered their arms, though Holger was the least willing to do so.

"These are my friends," I said to the Witch calmly and politely, my hands still up. "Tallinn Landrace, Ellora Snowleaf and Holger Axton. You already know Tristan."

"A pleasure," Ellora bowed her head slowly to her, still watchful.

Danika seemed to be studying us, almost like she was trying to decide what to make of us. I could only hope that showing her our willingness to be accommodating to her wishes would be enough. In my mind, I kept reminding myself of why I was doing this, Leander's face flashing in front of me.

"Well, now that pleasantries are done with," she spoke evenly, moving forward as she walked her staff across the ground, "perhaps we can get to the heart of *why* you have sought me out."

"I thought you would already know," Tallinn stated as I lowered my hands to my sides. "That *is* what Tristan told us."

Danika flashed her sharp eyes to her, seeming very raven-like in her way. "I *do* know, yes. But I would prefer that we discuss this like civilised beings."

"We come to ask for your aid," I told her, cutting straight to it.

"And why would I offer it to you?" she asked coldly.

"Have you not seen what has happened to the world around you?" Tallinn asked, disbelief on her face as well as horror. "The world is in chaos and the Dominion is ravaging all of High-Realm..."

"There is no need to point out what is obvious to me," Danika stated uncaringly. "The question I asked was *why* should *I* help *you*?"

I took in a slow breath. "You helped one of us before..."

"I helped the Princess because I chose to," she said simply with a shrug, turning her gaze directly to me. "Her intentions were pure, and *I* sought her out, *not* the other way around."

"Please," I implored her calmly. "Join with us..."

"I shall tell you what I told the girl," she stated in that same uninterested tone, "my allegiances are my own. I hold no care for either the side of light or shadow, only balance."

"The balance is destroyed," I told her with an incredulous and quiet half laugh. "Lord Morod saw to that when he released Ragnarok."

"Maybe so," she said with a wave of her hand, turning back to her cave, "but I have played my part in the events to come. Go back to your war and play yours."

Tallinn stepped past me, swinging one arm out to brush aside her cloak to reveal the armour she wore. She took in a breath and locked her gaze on the Witch, taking on her well-practiced stance as a Guardian.

"We are Guardians of High-Realm and all of Therras," she declared in a strong voice, watching the Witch unflinchingly. "By the creeds and treaties that my Order holds, I demand that you aid us in this time of great need."

Danika flashed a look over her shoulder at her, standing still. "You demand?"

I knew immediately that this was going to go in a very bad direction quickly. I moved to Tallinn's side, keeping my eyes on the Witch as she slowly began to turn.

"As Guardians we have the right to call on any persons we deem necessary and able to give aid at a time such as this," Tallinn went on, never backing down. "Such is the agreements made by all the nations of Therras when our Order was founded, and so is it known by all the people across the Seven Kingdoms of High-Realm and the eleven nations of Therras. You *will* help us."

"Tallinn," I murmured, sensing the waves of contempt coming from the Witch.

But Tallinn was not going to take no for an answer and the Witch wasn't going to accept.

"It seems," Danika said, turning towards us again, brandishing her staff before her, "that we have reached an impasse in this little encounter. *I* will *not* become involved in *your* affairs. However, if it is your intent to force such an issue..." the crystal in her staff began to glow green, the air around us becoming thicker as the Troll glowered down at us and the Witch's eyes flashed with the same green flame as the crystal in her staff: "...then I will have no choice but to do what I must to destroy you."

I swallowed hard, looking to the crystal, then to her. I noticed out of the corner of my eye that my companions were now all sensing the power the Witch was summoning around us. This witch hunt had just become deadly...

Chapter Eight
Aggressive Magic

The ground was shaking, the cliffs were dropping stones down their faces, and the trees were creaking, groaning and lurching against their roots. Something incredible was happening, the Witch revealing her true power to us. There was a loud cracking of rock and earth from behind our backs, the five of us turning to watch as the forest came to life.

The trees became like great sentries, holding their limbs out to block our escape, their pine needles becoming like spears that would impale us if we tried to get too close. The earth splintered open and great vines slithered up from beneath the dirt and stone. They were like enormous serpents as wide as my body, twisting and coiling around each other with sword-like thorns jutting up from their green, leathery skins across their entire lengths. They knitted together to form a barrier, stretching in a half ring from one side of the cliffs around to the other, trapping us in the middle.

More stone broke and dirt was launched into the air to rain down in a mix of mud and snow. The gigantic thorny vines shot tangling tendrils up at the edge of the perimeter, creating yet another hazard. These grasping vines lashed and whipped at the air, viciously seeking to attack any who drew too near.

"I do not think she intends to let us leave," Ellora observed as she took up her bow, aiming between each target and waiting for one to strike.

"The time when you were able to leave freely has passed," the Witch hissed, drawing our attention as she called vines from the earth to raise her above us and set her atop her cave. "You will find no safe passage from my woods now, save that of your deaths."

"Danika!" I turned, calling to her, my hands up again. "This is unnecessary! We can resolve this peacefully!"

"There will be no peaceful resolution," she stated loudly, yet calmly. "I had already foreseen your approach to my sanctum and knew your intent before ever you did think to seek me out. I knew you would attempt to force me to do your bidding and that we would inevitably do battle as we do now. So it is that I will now destroy you."

The Troll roared, stomping in front of us and glaring with his beady eyes, gnashing his jagged teeth.

"Kill them all!" the Witch commanded him.

The Troll let out another bellowing roar, hunching his shoulders and flexing his muscles. The stone sections of his body began to extend and thicken, becoming like jagged armour over his thick, grey skin. His fists became encrusted with rock, and he punched them together with a thunderous boom that shook the very earth beneath our feet.

I drew my sword again, staring wide eyed at the mammoth beast.

"Any ideas?" Tristan asked uncertainly, his sword up in one hand, a curved dagger in the other.

"My people always said that keeping a troll talking was the key to defeating them," Tallinn recounted, her bow shaking as she took a staggering step back at my side. "They are not very smart creatures and easily fooled into doing anything."

"That thing doesn't seem like the talking type," Holger pointed out, brandishing his hammer.

"Tricking it into the sunlight will also not work," Ellora advised us, her piercing eyes locked on the thing stomping towards us. "The storms have robbed us of such an advantage."

"There must be a way to bring it down," I thought aloud, frowning as I kept my sword aimed at the enraged troll.

The Troll let out another roar and swept at us with his massive right hand. Immediately, the five of us scattered, ducking away as his fist smashed the ground. Dirt and rock shattered into the air in an explosion from his strike, raining down around us.

I landed just a few inches from a grasping vine, pulling away as it whipped at me. A swift swing of my sword cleaved its limb, causing a strange scream to sound as the rest of it retreated back into the earth. I pulled myself to my feet, turning back to the others. They had managed to move around the Troll, the women turning their bows towards its face. Arrows lanced out and struck at its eyes, hitting the softer skin of its cheeks. The Troll snarled and swept at them. Ellora grabbed Tallinn and pulled her away, the Troll just barely missing them.

"Hey! You! Get away from them, you great ugly bastard!" Tristan shouted at him and sent a ball of blue fire from his hand.

The fire lashed across the space and slammed into the Troll's eyes, making him howl as he covered them with one hand. That only seemed to make things worse, the gigantic creature staggering around now as he swept with his free hand wildly.

"Stay back!" I shouted to the others.

Ellora and Tallinn stayed low as Tristan backed away while Holger continued to circle the creature, looking for an opening.

The Troll couldn't see. This was an opportunity to try to at least to do some damage, though I wasn't exactly sure how. I had to be cautious, we all did. One lucky hit from that thing would shatter our bones at the very least, even a nudge would be enough to hurl us into the hazards the Witch had summoned around us.

The eyes are his weakness. But he'll recover. How do we take him down?

"Holger!" I shouted to the Dwarf. "I've got an idea! Just drive that thing towards me!"

"Are you insane, lad?!" Holger shouted.

Before any of us could react, the Troll recovered and roared in pain fuelled rage. It started to stomp the ground with its fists, sending shockwaves rippling through the earth. We were all thrown to the ground, the creature now in a vicious frenzy.

I rolled out of the way as it tried to crush me, landing hard on my back nearer the cave. My eyes flicked up to catch sight of Danika watching the scene with amusement. I couldn't help but be reminded of what happened three years ago in the Dwarven Under Roads when we encountered the Unseen and its experiment. The only difference then was that we had had a Storvari to help us fight and...

Leander... I'm doing this for Leander...

That thought alone was enough to drive the strength I needed into me, but I could also feel my predator deep inside. He was snapping, ripping to get out and attack the creature we now fought. It would be so easy to fight the Troll if I just gave in.

No! I can't! I must stay in control!

I turned my gaze back to the fight, watching as Tallinn and Ellora continued slinging arrows from their bows at the creature. It tried to shield its face from the arrows, scowling and glaring at them. It reached with its other hand, grasping for Tallinn. She screamed, staggering backwards as its fingers snatched at her.

"Come on, you colossal oaf!" Holger ran forward from behind it. "Face me! Not the women! Ya scared of a dwarf?! Huh?! HUH?!"

As the Dwarf started battering his hammer into the back of the Troll's leg, the creature turned its gaze towards him. It kicked behind it, tossing Holger backwards.

I watched in horror as the Dwarf flew several meters away and hit the ground hard with a loud thud and grunt. But before I could react, he was up and snatching his hammer from the ground.

"Ah! Now this is a fight!" he bellowed, charging the Troll again with enthusiasm.

The Troll howled as the Dwarf struck with an over the head downward swing of his hammer, cracking its stone and leather hide. It thrashed at him, but he just leaped back and swung from the right at its knee with a shattering strike that made it howl in pain.

Ellora and Tallinn changed their tactics then as I jumped up and hurled two throwing daggers into its back, the blades shattering against its hide. Tallinn continued to fire from her bow as Ellora took up her twin swords and leaped up the Troll's knee as Holger's strike forced it to kneel. In moments she was on top of it, twirling her blades and burying them into its back. The Troll roared and started to buck, swinging its arms up as it tried to grab her off it. Ellora just held on tight to her swords where they were wedged between the stone segments, ducking as its large hands grasped at her.

"There has to be a weakness," I frowned, watching it. "Wait... Aldwyn used fire..."

I ducked away as it stomped over me, distracted by the Elven Huntress on its back. I rolled past it and came up into a kneeling crouch, my sword in hand. I quickly sought out Tristan with my eyes, the Wanderer now near Tallinn as she continued to fire arrows at its face.

"Tristan!" I called to him. "Use your fire magic! Drive that monster towards me!"

"You have a plan?!" he questioned.

I nodded, narrowing my eyes at the beast. "We can't kill it, so we'll trap it!"

He smirked. "I'll follow your lead!"

I nodded and rushed forward to join Holger. I took a swing of my sword, slashing through the thick skin on its underbelly. The Troll howled as it snapped at me, Ellora yanking back with all her might on her swords to pull it away. As she did so, Tristan began hurling blue fire from his hands, striking the beast in the face. It howled and staggered backwards towards the cave.

"Ellora, drive it my way!" I shouted.

She nodded and jerked her blades in its back, the creature screeching as it stumbled to its right and towards me. I was going to have to time this just right.

Tallinn and Tristan continued firing arrows and fire balls, the strikes hitting the face and neck of the beast. The fire was doing the most damage, the arrows just keeping it from using its eyes by forcing them to stay shut in order to protect them.

Holger and I kept our weapons ready, both of us edging backwards towards the mess of reaching brambles and vine tendrils as we did. We would have to watch ourselves lest those limbs ensnared us.

Ironic. Using the Witch's own traps against her beast...

"Ellora! Bring it backwards!" I instructed loudly, ready with my sword.

Ellora tensed all of her muscles, straining as she planted her feet and leaned backwards. The Troll was waving its large arms now as she forced it to turn, struggling to keep its balance.

"All together! Now!" I cried out and swung my sword.

Holger attacked in time with me, our weapons cleaving into the back of the Troll's knees with loud crunches. It roared in pain, its legs starting to give. As it bent back with Ellora's pull, Tallinn fired two arrows at once as Tristan hurled a particularly large and powerful shot of fire magic. The fire slammed into its bulbous nose and beady eyes, making it scream as the arrows struck into its throat.

The Troll tumbled backwards, Ellora tugging her swords free and leaping from its back mere moments from being crushed. Flipping over from its back, she landed on her feet some distance away. Holger and I were in the shadow of its collapsing shape, the two of us darting out and away to each side of it. We landed hard on our stomachs several feet away.

There came a thundering, snapping crash as the giant creature collapsed backwards into the brambles and vines, breaking the plants with its stone body. I got into a crouch, turning to watch with the others as the beast began howling and thrashing as the Witch's vines entangled him. He tugged and slashed at the creeping lengths, trying to pull them away from his body, but it was no use.

We watched as the Troll ceased his struggles and, with a groan, lay back, closing his eyes. He turned to stone slowly, not dead, but so exhausted that he needed to rest and heal.

I let out a sigh of relief, my aching muscles relaxing.

Then, I heard a scream.

I spun around to watch as Tallinn was snatched up by twisting slender vines that came up out of the ground. She was struggling and kicking, her bow falling from her hands with the throttling of the plants.

"TALLINN!" I shouted in panic, trying to reach her.

"Hold on, lass!" Tristan reached for her with his sword ready, but before he could do anything he was suddenly grabbed by more vines.

Ellora screamed and Holger shouted, both of them slashing at more creeping vines with their weapons that slithered from the ground. Neither one could outlast them despite the damage they inflicted on the grasping tendrils, both soon overwhelmed by the snaring plants.

I didn't have a chance to do anything, all of this happening in seconds just before I felt my arms, neck and chest being bound. I struggled, trying to cut away the vines that squeezed my limbs and body, but my sword was crushed from my grip quickly, clattering to the ground out of my reach. There was nothing I could do, nothing any of us could do. We were trapped, tied up by the vines of the forest itself that were now threatening to choke the life from us. No matter the effort I put through my muscles, I couldn't break free.

My eyes turned then to the figure striding coldly towards us, her gaze hard and cruel. It seemed that where the Troll had failed to kill us, the Witch herself would succeed.

Danika regarded each of us with cold maliciousness, her eyes flaring with rage at our continued survival. Now I could see where she was like her sisters, though they never exhibited such powers as she did.

"You have all fought well," she hissed slowly, eyeing us off. "Yet, you have still failed."

"Danika," I spoke, tensing against the pain of the vines trying to strangle my torso. "It doesn't... doesn't have to be... ugh... like this..."

"Oh, but it does," she came straight up to me, staring into my eyes. "I regret that it must end with your death, Carden son of Tiernan. Especially with the future you should have had. But I will *not* be forced to face Lord Morod again."

I blinked in shock as I stared at her, her words confounding me. *How does she know who I am? I've told no one that detail beyond Aldwyn and Tallinn... How does she know? How does she know my father's name?*

She looked almost saddened as she considered me, letting out a slow sigh. "She loved you so very much. A shame..."

"Danika, no!" I exclaimed, trying to struggle free as she turned away from me.

She faced the five of us, raising her staff in hand. "Die well."

I tensed as the others struggled or looked away, each of us awaiting the crushing snap that would come from the vines constricting us to death.

Suddenly, there came a great roar and the beat of wings. At first, I thought that Amethyst had returned to us as I saw the silhouette of a dragon diving from above, but the colour said otherwise. The ground shook as Gaspeite landed, the green and brown dragon roaring out loudly and startling the Witch away from her gruesome task as she looked up at him.

"Danika! Release them!" a voice commanded strongly, my eyes turning to the Dragon's shoulders.

Ranzel sat perched upon the Dragon's back, his staff in one hand as his other braced to the beast's great scales. He was staring out from under his wide brimmed hat, his eyes narrowing as he locked his gaze on the woman.

"Ranzel?!" Danika had the haunted look of seeing someone from her deep past painted upon her face as she staggered back. "No! No, I won't go back! I won't!"

As she raised her staff, the Wizard raised his, the raw crystal in its top glowing brightly. The two began a battle of energy that lanced from their staffs, Danika taking hers in both hands as the Wizard slid from the Dragon's back. He took his staff into both hands as well, the glow of emerald energy mixing with the light of yellowish-green that came from the Witch's crystal, illuminating the whole clearing brightly.

"Gaspeite! Free them!" the Wizard commanded loudly, the Pendant around his neck glowing green at its heart.

Gaspeite turned his green scaled face and fire orange eyes towards us, lashing out with short bursts of dragon fire between us. The brambles were the source of the vines that held us, screeching like some animal in pain as the fires scorched them. The vines lost their hold and all five of us fell to the muddy, snowy ground as they slithered back into the earth.

I pushed myself up on my hands, looking to the battle before me between the Witch and the Wizard. Lightning seemed to strike from the flashing clash of energy that met in between them, the two forcing their bodies to add more power to the battle.

"You can no longer hide from Fate, Danika," Ranzel told her evenly, hardly seeming to be affected by the strain of their fight. "It is time to play your part as you foresaw."

"No! No, I will not!" she screamed, trying hard to push him back from her. "I won't be drawn into a fight with them! Not again!"

"You must," he said softly, looking to her with a gently sympathetic gaze. "I am sorry, but you must."

Danika stared back at him with fearful, wide eyes, her hands shaking. Her strength was waning, and she was struggling to hold against him. Clearly, just seeing him was enough to overwhelm her.

"I'll fight you down, old man, rather than face them again!" she shrieked with sudden rage and lashed out violently.

Ranzel took one hand from his staff and held his palm forward. The energy from his Dragon Pendant extended in a green shield just as I had seen Leander's do with hers. The difference was the Wizard didn't drain swiftly from the effort like the girl had. The shield seemed to grow in intensity, pushing Danika's magic back and allowing his to advance towards her.

Danika struggled, panic clear in her eyes. She wasn't going to win the fight and she knew it.

With one final effort, Ranzel pushed forward and was suddenly right in front of her, snatching her staff from her grasp. She looked up at him in bewilderment. He cast her staff down and hooked his arm around her as she staggered, his staff shimmering light towards her face. Danika's eyes fell shut and she collapsed into his arm, breathing but unconscious.

"I am sorry, Danika," he whispered to her. "Truly, I am."

I got to my feet and rushed to Tallinn, helping her up. "Are you alright?"

"Yes," she nodded, clearly aching as she leaned on me for help to stand. "Yes, I'm fine, Carden."

"Is she dead, Wizard?" Tristan asked, standing with us as Ellora and Holger recovered their weapons.

"No, just in a deep sleep," he said, turning his hazel gaze towards us. "She will be alright, but I suggest we bind her hands so that she doesn't try to attack us again."

I turned to him as he laid her down and crouched beside her to check her pulse: "We didn't think we would see you again, Ranzel."

"As they say," he stood, smiling at us now that he was satisfied with her vitals, "the rumours of my death have been greatly exaggerated."

"Did anyone else survive?" Tallinn asked worriedly. "Master Riordan? Lord Selwyn?"

"Others survived, but that is a conversation for our return to Eilath," the Wizard stated. "We must make haste to do so, now."

"Holger," Tallinn turned to our dwarven companion, "please, can you lead us to the Under Roads from here?"

"Aye, Lady Guardian. That I can," he said, picking up his hammer and hoisting it to his shoulder.

"Carden," Ranzel looked to me. "Have you anything to bind her?"

"Ah... yes," I turned to my pack, picking it up from where I had set it down before the battle began.

My large hands rummaged through the folds of clothes and the firmness of other items as I searched for what I needed, finally withdrawing a length of rope. I knelt over the Witch and turned her onto her stomach, lashing her wrists together expertly. I'd had to learn to be prepared for such things in the past when attending to my duties as a Guardian. On several occasions I had been called to bind a man or woman we were charged with retrieving by the Order, most commonly someone of great danger to the people.

I flashed on the thought of capturing the Shadow Lord and binding him to be dragged before the seven Kings to be tried for his crimes. *If only...*

I was done, carefully turning the woman over again and lifting her up only after I had gathered my belongings.

"Ready," I stated, holding her bridal style in my arms.

"My lady Tallinn," Ranzel deferred to my Guardian sister. "If you would lead."

She nodded and pulled her hood up again to shield her messy blonde hair. She recovered her bow and began to lead the way with Holger at her side, Tristan and Ellora ahead of me as the Wizard followed with his dragon.

I threw the Troll one final look, gladdened that it was now stone, but in a way also relieved that we hadn't slain it. A part of me believed its survival might be of importance in later days, especially with convincing Danika to aid us.

* * * * *

The rest of our trip was fairly uneventful. The path through the Under Roads opened to us only half a day from where we captured the Witch, so we were very soon within the mountains and sheltered from the raging of the apocalyptic storms. Gaspeite did not follow us, electing to meet us on the other side by flying across the peaks of the Nartarn'laths to reach Lorveren. It did occur to me, and I'm certain to everyone else, that it would have been quicker if we had flown with him. However, it was equally apparent that the Dragon would suffer under our combined weight. So, we allowed him to go off on his own, Ranzel deciding to remain with us in the tunnels weaving through the bowels of the mountains.

This journey was nothing like the one we first took through the mountains from Hecturn. We didn't come across any secret laboratories or demented loyalists of the Shadow Lord and gained no sight of goblins stalking us in the shadows. The Under Roads were remarkably devoid of life, almost as if whatever dark fiends that did lurk within the tunnels had scurried away to either hide or join the dark sorcerer in his war. In some ways this was a relief, but in others it left us uneasy. I couldn't help wondering just how much worse the state of the world above the Dwarven Roads would get if all the nightmares that lurked in the depths crawled out.

Three days into the journey, Danika finally awoke from the sleep Ranzel had put her into. She was eerily quiet, almost resigned to what was happening.

I awoke to see her sitting up, watching us with her piercing green eyes, her back to a stone wall, the firelight of our camp dancing across her hauntingly beautiful features. She just regarded us all with a cold stare that held no emotion, never once speaking a word no matter how we tried to communicate with her. She simply took what food and water we offered her, then stayed silent.

She's going to be a hard one to convince of much, I thought dourly as I watched Ellora give up on conversation after an hour of trying. *I hope the Caradoc Library yielded much richer answers to the others. Then at least we might have some chance.*

The seven of us walked through the Under Roads in silence for the rest of the journey, finally emerging at the foot of the mountains within Lorveren. The opening was in a cave in the lowest foothills, hidden away in a crevice that we had to slowly and arduously climb out of.

The air struck us and filled our senses as we exited the crevice, but it was not refreshing. The sky was sparking red amongst the black clouds still, the daylight banished from the world. The air was ashen and painful, though not unbearable, the scent of decay on the breeze. Then I detected something else: fires burning.

"Do you smell that?" I asked the others, grasping onto a rock as I climbed up onto the yellowed grasslands.

Ellora nodded as she closed in beside me, her turquoise eyes locked onto something in the distance: "I catch the odour of fires burning in great volume."

"I see no fires," Tallinn turned her gaze across the landscape, a frown on her light brow.

I nodded in agreement, surveying the way ahead. I couldn't see anything either. Not at first. Ellora was the first to spot it.

"There!" she jabbed one finger out towards a glow not too far from where we stood.

I narrowed my eyes as I followed her gaze, taking in the distant shapes. My heart sank and I felt my throat tighten as I detected a new scent. There was blood on the wind. My tongue started to burn as my mouth felt ashen. Then, my hearing picked up screams as a battle was raging by the structures. It was a small village.

"Those people are under attack!" Tallinn exclaimed, drawing her bow. "We must help them!"

"That village is some distance away," Ellora pointed out gravely, turning her gaze to the other woman. "We won't make it there in time."

"Regardless," Ranzel strode forward, his staff connecting with the ground in time with his right step as he walked, "that is the way we must go in order to reach Eilath."

"We must try to do something!" Tallinn was so passionate, more so than I had seen her in recent days. "We cannot let them be slaughtered!"

"We will do what we can," Ranzel stated evenly. "Make haste and we may yet find some people left to aid."

I turned and looked to Danika, grasping her arm as she joined me on my left. She didn't seem even the slightest bit concerned, her stare at the scene one of utter apathy. She gave the appearance of an uncaring witch very well, but I could sense her heart even then.

"Come on," I uttered, making her stride with me down the hill, Tristan and Holger at our backs.

The hurried walk we took led us to the outskirts of the village in less than an hour, our entry unbarred by the ruins that surrounded us. Fires were still burning strongly, many houses laying on the earth as ash and rubble. But we were scarcely walking into an abandoned battlefield.

Screams echoed all around us as we saw women and children running as warriors battled to defend against their attackers.

"STOP!" Tallinn shouted as a heavily armoured and gruff looking man grabbed at a screaming girl. "UNHAND HER! NOW!"

"KILL THEM!" he roared, jabbing his axe at us, the girl still screaming as he pushed her to the ground inside the entrance of a house.

None of us needed to be told what to do as multiple armed and armoured thugs rushed us. They looked much like the men who had assaulted Castle Arvon the night we fled with Leander.

"Ranzel, take Danika!" I shoved the Witch towards the Wizard and drew my sword.

Two men were rushing us as I did so, my other hand flashing with ease only to cast them both down; a throwing knife buried into each of their sternums through their inadequate armour.

"Carden! Down!" Tallinn shouted.

I ducked just as a sword swung where my head had been, turning to defend against the next blow, but it never came. An arrow whistled past me, catching my attacker in the throat, and dropping him backwards from me.

"Go help that girl!" Tallinn commanded me as she laced another arrow and cleared me a path.

I didn't hesitate, jumping up and running across the field, leaving my bags with Ranzel just as I heard the great roar of a dragon. A glance to the sky showed me that the Wizard had summoned Gaspeite, the green dragon turning his attentions towards the brigands in the centre of the village.

I drove my sword through one attacker as I passed Tristan and Holger, casting another knife to take down a second intending to strike them from behind. Holger made short work of him and dropped his next attacker with a brutal swing of his war-hammer, crushing the brigand's cuirass and throwing him to the ground. At the same moment, Tristan used his blue fire magic to set two men alight, then ran them through with his sword to silence them before facing the next opponent with an easy block.

A brigand leaped at me, but I pulled back, snatching a blade from my belt and simultaneously driving it into his jaw as I clashed my sword with his. I withdrew both blades and rushed towards the screams of the girl being assaulted as Ellora was rescuing a panicked family cornered by yet more men.

There were no thoughts in my mind as I laid a single kick to the door and burst into the house, the sound of cloth tearing mixed with her screams boiling my blood. I wouldn't allow this to go on. He was on top of her, pinning her down as his lust reeked the air. He didn't remain in that position long as I hefted him up by his collar and cast him down with an enraged roar.

The thug clambered for his sword, trying to swing it only for me to block it with my own and knock it from his hand. In one fluid movement, I twirled my sword up and buried the blade into his chest with narrowed eyes. I could feel their hue changing, snarling as I smelled his blood, growling predatorily at him.

Fear coloured his eyes as he stared into mine, his face draining of colour.

"What... what are... y-you?" he gasped before breathing his last.

I withdrew my sword from his chest, letting him drop to the floor. My own more muscular chest heaved, and my heart raced erratically, pain filling me as my throat burned with thirst. This was the worst the sensation of my beast had felt since I was an adolescent boy.

My gaze fell on a broken mirror, and I hissed, shying away from it and closing my eyes. I willed them back to being green, refusing to let that blood-coloured stare remain.

I've left my medicine too long... Damn it, Carden! Pull yourself together, man!

Gentle sobs drew my attention and I turned to the trembling figure in the corner. She was holding her tattered dress around her, her long dark hair hiding her face as tears flowed down her cheeks.

"It's all right," I said, crouching down in front of her. "Shh, he's gone. Are you hurt? Did he..." I swallowed my disgust back, "... did he touch you?"

"He... he tried," she wept, looking up at me with grey eyes bleeding tears. "He was going to..."

"I know," I hissed, glaring at the dead thug, then turning back to her. "Don't worry. You're safe now."

I brushed her hair from her face and gasped. She stared at me with soft eyes that I mistook for grey but were blue steel, her features so familiar and fair with a gentle cleft to the chin and subtle cheekbones. She pulled her ruined dress around her chest to hide her modesty, gratitude there like I had seen a thousand times before whenever I had rescued others. She said something, but I couldn't hear her, too captivated by her beauty and bewildered at seeing her.

Leander... She's Leander... How is she alive? I tried to reason with myself, letting my mind take hold over my heart. *No! It can't be her! I saw her die!* I closed my eyes and took in a breath, trying to control myself.

"Are... are you a Guardian, sir?" the girl's voice broke me out of myself and returned me to the Waking World.

I took in her features again, a deep frown creasing my brow. Her face was different, her hair a lighter brown, not auburn like I had first thought, her eyes grey, not steel blue. It wasn't Leander, this girl shorter and slighter in build. My heart ached.

"I'm sorry?" I blinked against my bewilderment.

"Are you a Guardian?" the girl asked with tears still in her eyes, too upset to notice my distraction. "You... you wear their armour..."

For her sake I just nodded: "Yes. I... I am. Here, let me help you," I brought her to her feet and wrapped her in my cloak to shield her from sight.

"Thank you," she whispered.

"Stay close to me," I advised her, taking up my sword and leading her back to the door.

I stepped back out to the destroyed village, casting my eyes around the devastation. There were so many dead innocents on the ground, the scent of their blood driving into me with maddening influence.

Clear your mind, Carden, I imagined Aldwyn was there, speaking to me. *Focus not on your darker desires, but on your oaths. You are a protector, not a beast...*

I grasped the girl's wrist with my free hand and led her quickly back to where the others were, just as another man attacked. She screamed as he lunged at me, my sword arm making quick work of him so that I could move to join Tallinn.

My sister Guardian was now resorting to her own sword as she battled two large men in dark brown armour, her quiver empty across her back. She twirled on one foot as she lashed a kick to one man and slashed with her blade at the other before spinning it back to impale the first.

"Tallinn!" I shouted as I caught sight of the third at her back. "Behind you!"

She didn't turn, her eyes on me, and for a second, I felt my breath hitch as I worried he would take her down. Tallinn twirled her sword and stabbed it back beside her waist, the brigand groaning as he was run through his midriff, abruptly halting his attack. His sword dropped from his hands, and he collapsed as she withdrew her blade.

Suddenly, upon the burning, yet cold wind there came the bellow of horns. The gallop of hooves thundered the ground and I turned in time to watch as armed men rode through the village on horseback, the green and gold standard of Lorveren flying on their lances.

The brigands tried to attack but were run down as the cavalry charged through them, swinging their swords. The green cloaked and scale armoured soldiers rode against them, their horses galloping with as much determined fervour as their riders.

In merely a few minutes the attack was ended, the Lorveren horsemen clearing the last of the assailants from the village and giving chase. They charged relentlessly, refusing to allow the brigands the chance to escape and cause more death and destruction.

My companions and I relaxed our stances, exhausted from our trip and from the effort we threw into defending these innocent people. I was just saddened that we hadn't saved more than a handful.

A rider came up to us as we gathered together with the villagers we'd saved, Gaspeite landing behind us with a whoosh of his great wings.

"Greetings, horseman," Ranzel strode forward as Tristan took Danika from his hold, nodding to the man. "I must say your timing is impeccable."

The rider removed his helm, revealing his light brown hair as it flowed down his shoulders. He regarded us with an even stare as he rested on his black mount with the quiet diligence of a dutiful man.

"My greetings to you as well," he responded, glancing at those of us from Silvervale. "I see you are not of the band of brigands who were attacking these people."

"Indeed we are not," Ranzel agreed, leaning against his staff with both hands. "We happened upon the attack and elected to lend our aid."

"Then we are most grateful. Especially if you have saved even some of our citizens," the rider said calmly, trying to hide the emotion he surely felt. "Our lookouts spotted the smoke as we patrolled the grasslands, and I commanded my men to make haste here."

"A good thing you did," Ranzel nodded.

"We have several villagers here that need attention," Tallinn reported to the man quickly, but calmly. "I am not certain how many more lay in the buildings desperate for help."

"You're a Guardian?" the man asked, looking to me with the same expression of awe as he gave her. "Both of you are?"

Tallinn nodded, sheathing her sword. "Yes... For the moment, we *both* are."

I knew that was her way of letting me know that our discussion about my decision was not yet over, but I chose not to respond. I was still holding the teenaged girl I had rescued as she had now begun to cling to me.

"My men are scouring the ruins now, Lady Guardian," the rider responded briskly. "Any we find we will take with us back to Eilath."

"We are making our way to Eilath ourselves," Ranzel stated, drawing the man's gaze. "Lord Fawkner Caradoc is expecting us."

"His Lordship returned to Eilath a week ago," the rider said quickly. "He commanded us to watch for a small group in the company of two Guardians. Though," he looked at Gaspeite with uncertainty, "I do not recall him mentioning a dragon."

"We will give you what aid we can in helping the villagers here," Tallinn told him with absolute certainty, drawing his gaze away from the Dragon, "then we will follow you to Eilath."

"As you say, Lady Guardian," the rider nodded. "Your aid is most welcome."

It only took an hour to search the wreckage of the village, the soldiers gathering the bodies of the ruffians who had attacked it, piling them up to be burned. We found a few more people hidden away, most elderly, as well as a few women and children. To describe the horrors that had been inflicted upon them was impossible and beyond my ability to stomach. I chose not to think about it as I aided the others in helping them.

A few riders had fallen, but their mounts survived, so we were able to travel together with the Lorveren horsemen and the survivors of the village. Tallinn rode with Tristan while Ellora took Holger, Ranzel choosing to carry Danika upon Gaspeite with him. The girl I rescued clung to my back as I led the horse I was given away from the ruins of the village.

I sighed as I thought once more of Leander, wishing that it was she who held so tightly to me. Then my mind turned back to that moment after I had saved this girl and had thought that she was in fact my beautiful princess.

That gave me something to puzzle over all the way to Eilath, leaving me wondering: *What sort of aggressive magic could it have been that made me imagine such a thing?*

Chapter Nine
Return to the Falcon's Nest

Our path led us over the vast and wide open spaces of Lorveren's grasslands. The once green and gold fields that had looked so vibrant and majestic now seemed pale and grim in the clouded light. It was as if the eternal darkness Ragnarok's storms had conjured had sapped not only the life from the land, but also the colours themselves. It was disheartening to say the least.

My mind was heavily occupied with what had happened in the village ruins, the presence of the girl clinging to my shoulders a constant reminder. *She was Leander. I don't mean that she looked like Leander, she **was** Leander. How? How can that be possible?*

The girl shifted her hold, her hands clutching at my armoured chest as her arms snaked around my waist. Her head was on my back, her heartbeat painfully noticeable to me.

Is it some magic the Witch cast over me before we managed to overpower her? Some means to torment me that I can't even begin to fathom? If so, why would she do such a thing? Is it to preserve her own control over at least one of us since she knew she was losing the battle?

I glanced towards the green dragon that lumbered at an even pace beside our horses. The woman was perched there on his back in front of the Green Wizard, her cold eyes glaring ahead as if she were simply watching the horizon draw nearer. Even with her hands bound, her staff taken and her magic nullified, the Witch held an arrogant posture that was beyond comprehension.

Not arrogance. She doesn't hold any such emotion as arrogance. There was desperation in her actions concealed behind a mask of confidence. Even now she is too calm and collected for a prisoner. Strange. A sigh escaped my lips, and I turned my focus ahead, clutching my horse's reigns firmly. *She was not the one who cursed my sight to see my dead beloved. That is an act of malevolence if it is done through mystical conjuring. She holds no such cruelty, unlike her vile and wretched sisters. Were it Manth or Keilantra we carry in bindings such thoughts and suspicions would be justified. But Danika... no... she's different. Still cold, but different.* It was agonising trying to comprehend this simple concept and ascertain the answer.

Once again, my passenger moved, cuddling closer to me, her chest pressing to my back. I sensed a thrill of lust from her, desire filling her every time her eyes took in my shape. She was making every effort to hide such attentions, but my...

gift revealed all she felt as a sculptor would rip away the sheet to unveil his raw, naked, and unaltered work of art.

This girl's infatuation is as fragrant and obvious as heavily spiced wine. It's simply hero worship. I've encountered it before...

My mind turned to the past, to the night we rushed the Shadow Lord at Averet. I could see Leander sitting with her back to that pillar and her wrists tied above her head. Her fear had been so potent that my *gift* had detected it a mile from her, constantly urging me to move faster and reach her before that inevitable exchange.

As I recall, she never seemed to succumb to hero worship that night, simply grateful that we had come for her. Had it not been for that moment of first sight the day Aldwyn, Tallinn and I arrived at Castle Arvon, I might have believed it to be such. But it wasn't. Leander was fettered with me from that first day, just as I was with her. Anything after that was simply appreciation...

The bellow of horns on the horizon drew me back from my ruminations, my gaze locking upon the tall stone and wood walls that now rose above us. A strident shout from the commander of the horsemen had the gates yield to our passage, but with a heightened edge to our last visit to Eilath. Armed and heavily armoured soldiers stood ready with crossbows aimed directly at us as we made for the opening in the city's defences. A hurried word of reassurance from our escort afforded us safe entry and we were soon within the boundaries of the ancient plains-city.

We were led to the city square, the Hall of the Plains standing proudly above the thatched rooves of the other buildings ahead of us. Strangely, even with the dark, stormy sky above, the ancient home of the Ranhart Kings held its majesty, offering a sense of safety none of us had felt since before Silvervale was attacked.

I dismounted, landing with the rattle of my light armour and the rush of my cloak, taking a surveying glance of everything around me. It was at this point that I noted the royal guards that flanked the gateway leading to the lordly manor; their armour of silver chain and plates, pikes in hand bearing the standard of Lorveren's falcon in gold against an emerald field.

Palace guards from the Jade City? That's odd...

The awed gasps of the people drew my attention, my gaze falling upon Gaspeite. The Dragon was lowering himself to lay upon the cobblestone street, allowing the Wizard and the Witch to slip from their mount on his back. The citizens were staring in wonderment, but there was a trepidation in their eyes and postures speaking volumes of what they were thinking at the sight of the great beast.

Clearly, they know of the dragon attacks across High-Realm. I can hardly believe no one would know by now. Especially with Silvervale's fall, Safferan's destruction, and the loss of so many strongholds.

"Sir Guardian?" a soft voice broke me from the scene as guards went to the Wizard, my eyes meeting the gentle grey of my current ward's stare. "Could... could you help me down?" she was holding a shawl around her, the marks of the attack she had suffered now only visible in the damage to her clothing.

"Of course," I reached up and took her around the waist, easily lifting her from the horse and setting her on the ground.

The girl looked up at me with an appreciative gleam in her eyes, that sense of lust and hero worship returning to me again. Her flirting was obvious, every little detail clear; the way she ran a hand through her hair, the way she let the shawl slip just slightly to allow me a glimpse of her exposed neckline and white mounds, the slight flutter of her eyelashes. All of it was meant to entice.

"Master Ranzel," a deep voice spoke, and I turned my gaze away from the flirting girl towards the Hall.

Oddvar, Fawkner's steward, approached us, his cloak pushed back, his clothing now bolstered by chain armour. Clearly, things had become much harsher in the two years since last we were within the Lorveren city.

"Oddvar," Ranzel smiled as my allies gathered behind him, nodding to the man from beneath his hat's wide brim, "it is a pleasure to see you again."

"I wish only that your return was under better circumstances," Oddvar sighed, letting his pale gaze survey each of our faces. "Lord Fawkner and King Haral await your company in the Great Hall."

"We would be happy and honoured to join them," the Wizard stated, the exhaustion well hidden in his stance and manner, though certainly there.

"We bring a prisoner with us," Ellora stated sternly, flashing her turquoise eyes with piercing accuracy at Danika. "This woman is the reason for our late return behind his Lordship. She has information of necessity to our current task."

Oddvar nodded and with a flick of a hand called two guards to him: "I will have her secured in the jail beneath the barracks of the Hall. I am certain my lord will wish to speak with her himself."

The two men took Danika by either arm, the woman remaining as calm and unspoken as she had the entire journey from Dorvana.

"She is a witch with conjuring abilities of natural things," Ellora warned them evenly. "Ensure there isn't so much as a weed or a twig she may use."

"Have the Lord's mage set up wards in her cell," Oddvar commanded the guards. "Nullify her powers and shackle her."

"Yes, Steward," one of the men nodded.

Danika was led away and up the stairs to the courtyard of the Lord's Manor. Two more men went with them, their eyes never once lifting from the Witch. I didn't doubt for a moment that she was going to be a difficult prisoner, already worrying what havoc she might employ to escape.

Oddvar turned back to us: "If you will follow me."

The others started after him, Tallinn the only one to pause with me when my hand was seized. I turned to the girl I had saved, a look of desperation in her eyes. She was as fearful now as she had been when I had pulled that marauder off her.

"Please, don't go," she pleaded softly.

"You will be safe here in the city," Tallinn stated evenly, for which I was very grateful. "Go with the healers and the others from your village. You will be well cared for."

"But... but I..." she pressed her hands to my chest, looking up at me. She was nearly as tall as Leander. "I need to thank *you* properly, sir. Were it not for you, that bandit would have robbed me of my virtue, and then my life."

"There's no need," I said a little coldly, though I was trying to remain nonchalant.

"But there is," she pushed herself closer, leaning up on her toes to bring her lips to mine. "I would give you my most intimate self..."

I stopped her, grasping her wrists, and setting her back on the flats of her feet. I had felt the urging of my predator to engage in such carnal desires, but my heart's wreckage only served to stab within me and repel it. I kept my eyes locked on hers, her confusion evident with the fall of her expression.

"What you feel for me is lust and infatuation only," I told her gently, but sternly, keeping my eyes on hers. "You seek to gift yourself to a man you hardly know, and one no more honourable than he who intended to rob you of your innocence. I will not take that part of you, nor do I want it. For my heart belongs to another; and though she is no longer a part of this world, I will not give myself to any but her."

The girl looked as if she were about to cry. She was so young, barely a woman yet by the few years marking her face. The infatuations of a young woman over a man like me were too often revealed to me, and despite my apparent youth I truly was an older soul.

"I appreciate your thanks," I told her gently, "but that is all you will be permitted to gift me, for you should find love before doing such a thing. Do you understand?"

She nodded softly.

"Go on with the healers," I urged her, releasing her hands.

"Thank you again," she murmured with longing, watching as I turned from her and joined Tallinn.

My blonde companion was watching me as we climbed the stairs, her hazel gaze showing concern, though she attempted to be a little more jovial at first. "Ever the charmer, Carden," she smiled faintly, glancing to the stairs to watch her footing. "Many a young woman has swooned upon you rescuing them."

"Infatuation with one's rescuer is a dangerous thing," I remarked grimly, never taking my eyes from the stairs ahead of me. "These girls never do know what kind of predator may lurk beneath a virtuous face, nor do they comprehend the horrors that might come of coupling with such a man as me."

"Does he awaken within you anew, brother?" she asked with quiet concern.

I nodded and let out a sigh as we reached the gateway to the hall: "I am in need of my medicine once again."

She nodded, taking her usual calm and focus whenever this task arose: "I shall craft some for you tonight. Will you manage for the time being?"

I confirmed: "For the time being."

One final nod from her ended the discussion, and we re-joined the others as we entered the main doors of the Hall of the Plains.

The familiar surrounds of the ancient mead hall was present to us as soon as we entered, everything just as it had been before our abduction two years ago.

Fawkner was obvious as he stood at a planning table off to the side of the room and away from the three long dining tables around the fire pit. He was now dressed in green finery with gold trims, his hair pulled back from his face, but left to hang freely otherwise. Beside him stood a man whose hair was a more ashen brown than Fawkner's gingery brown, his face slightly younger, though both men were surely of about the same age. He also wore clothing of emerald finery with golden detailing, but his garments were more velvet than our friend's. Behind him lingered a royal guard of Lorveren, ever watchful and prepared to defend his master to the very end.

Dolin was with the two men, immediately beaming upon the sight of us. He and Holger embraced roughly without so much as a word, the two dwarves then turning their attention to the rest of us.

"Lord Fawkner," Ranzel spoke, then bowed to the other man. "King Haral, it is an honour."

"The honour is mine, Ranzel," King Haral nodded, standing with a straightened back and his hands behind him. His eyes then turned to Tallinn and me. "And you are the young Guardians my cousin speaks so highly of."

"Cousin," Fawkner smiled faintly, turning his gaze to us, "allow me to introduce Tallinn Landrace and Carden Highever, my fellow Guardians. They have been my friends and allies for the three years past, ever since this all began."

"A pleasure, your Majesty," Tallinn bowed her head.

"I have long awaited the opportunity to meet such brave Guardians," King Haral stated with a smile, grasping Tallinn's arm in greeting, then mine. "Especially now in this darkest of times."

"With respects, your Majesty," I spoke firmly, not even thinking, "but only Tallinn and Fawkner are Guardians. I have renounced my oath."

"So I hear," the King nodded gravely. "Truly, it is a great and devastating tragedy that is required to cause a man as devoted as a Guardian to rescind such a serious pledge. I... I am most sorry that such has befallen you, Master Carden."

"My thanks, your Majesty," I replied with honest gratitude, already feeling Tallinn's gaze as she undoubtedly wanted to press the point but wouldn't in present company.

"Might I ask, your Majesty," she decided to change the subject instead, choosing a question I am sure we had all begun pondering, "why you are here in Eilath when your palace is in the Jade City?"

"In times such as these, it is Eilath that is the most defensible and vital city of my kingdom," King Haral explained with ease, ushering a couple of the group of gathered nobles out of his way as he moved alongside Fawkner, his eyes to the map on the table. "Given the state of High-Realm in these dark days, it was decided that my family and I should vacate the Jade City and come here for our own protection. But also, so that I might rally a force to combat this evil."

"Combat this evil, my Lord?" Ellora was frowning, her arms crossed in front of her chest.

"You mean that you aren't cloistering yourself like the other nations are?" Tristan questioned with surprise and a little ire.

The King shook his head: "Though we defend our boarders, especially with the tensions with our Vorhal neighbours, the darkening of the sky and the account of my most valued cousin necessitates action be taken. What good is there in battling with Vorhalaas when the Shadow Dominion rises out of the darkened mists of the past, and the Harbingers of the End Times make speed across all of Therras, dispatching all those who might defend our countries?"

"Then, you no longer war with Vorhalaas?" Tallinn asked with a hopeful tone.

King Haral shook his head. "I wish that were only true, Lady Guardian, but sadly I cannot say it is. I have been in correspondence with King Olfred since the skies grew dark and the heavenly bodies were cast into the depths of these supernatural storms, and we have come to... a compromise."

"What kind of compromise?" Ellora spoke with a hard frown of suspicion.

"That we simply cease our hostilities to each other's nations in order to defend against the enemy forces as they begin their strikes," he sighed and shook his head. "Sadly, it will not be in unison that we defend, but apart."

"Apart?" Ranzel frowned, drawing nearer as he leaned on his staff, his hat now in his other hand. "Does King Olfred not know the value or necessity in standing together against such a threat? Can he not see that to stand alone invites death and destruction at the hands of our enemy?"

"Olfred is young and impulsive still; only a man of twenty-three winters, a king at a tender age," King Haral explained evenly. "The hostilities between our two nations was ingrained into him as a small boy by his father and will not be easily shaken. Whereas I can see the benefits of our countries becoming allies."

"It is the brashness of youth and poor council which guides him," Fawkner commented with a shake of his head. "Regardless, we have more pressing issues at hand."

"Too true," King Haral agreed, turning to the map of Lorveren laid out on the table before us. "This compromise means that, for the time being, the River Impasse is secured to both sides, yet we now face threats from within our own borders."

"What kind of threats?" Tallinn asked.

"You have seen it for yourselves firsthand, Tallinn," Fawkner turned his gaze to her, leaning both hands on the table. "Reports have been coming to us for days of vagrants and bandits attacking smaller villages in the surrounding provinces. How many is it now, Oddvar?"

"Fourteen recorded attacks, milord," Oddvar responded evenly, standing at Fawkner's shoulder.

"Fourteen," Fawkner mused gravely, studying the map with a stern gaze. "It is a dire thing to have these attacks on our citizens whilst we find ourselves facing an apocalypse."

"You'd think the blighted bandits would be too busy taking shelter from the storm to be doing such vicious things," Dolin remarked grimly.

"It is the nature of the beast," Ranzel spoke with a sour tongue, eyeing off the map with distaste as he paced from Fawkner's side to move to mine. "Wherever there is chaos, you will always find those willing to take advantage. Such is the way of greedy men."

"The Shadow Lord would surely be thriving on this foul will then," Ellora scowled. "His kind were always bent on causing such harms."

"Indeed," Fawkner looked to King Haral then. "These attacks are growing in intensity, and it is clear our people are no longer safe outside the walls of our cities."

King Haral nodded thoughtfully, one hand stroking his slightly greying beard. He studied the map for a few moments, then made some indications with one finger: "The attacks have been reported in these areas. Clearly, the bandits are using the seldom used routes to carry out their cowardly strikes. Increase the number of cavalry patrols and evacuate all remaining homesteads and small villages to the cities," he commanded. "As for the other part of our preparations, send word to all the lords of the cities and tell them to send three fifths of their forces to gather here."

"Three fifths, my liege?" a Lorveren Knight-Commander asked the King with a raised eyebrow. "Whatever for?"

"We must marshal a sizable force to meet the Shadow Lord in battle when the time is right," the King explained calmly. "Begin setting up a soldiers' encampment and erect additional barricades surrounding it and Eilath. We already have more men gathered here than the city can manage. Let us find a place for them to rest."

"Yes, your Majesty," the Knight quickly left.

"I would also suggest we empty the older warehouses and create a refugee camp there," Fawkner advised, turning to another map, the one of the city. "At least then we can accommodate this inundation of civilians coming to Eilath with each day."

"Make it so, cousin," King Haral accepted.

"And what of the Witch?" I asked to the sudden stares of my companions.

"What of her?" King Haral asked.

"We brought her here with the expressed purpose of discovering all that she knows regarding... regarding our task," I couldn't bring myself to speak the full words. "It's very important that we gain this knowledge so that we might be able to defeat this evil."

The King nodded. "My cousin has told me of the prophecies. You and your companions will first be shown to quarters and allowed to rest. Once we are done here, I will leave it to Fawkner to interrogate your prisoner. You may attend if you so wish."

I nodded solemnly. "By your will, your Majesty."

"Oddvar," Fawkner called to his steward. "Please take our allies to their rooms and allow them to freshen up."

"As you wish, my Lord," Oddvar nodded and gestured for us to follow.

"I will remain here," Ranzel stated, setting his own bag down on the nearby chair. "Perhaps my counsel will be of aid?"

"It is gratefully welcomed and accepted, my friend," King Haral nodded.

As Oddvar began to lead us away, I paused and turned over my shoulder to the table again: "Fawkner. Where is she?"

He looked up at me from the map, his eyes softening: "I had her moved to the chapel near the library. Joran is with her."

I nodded my thanks. "I shall find my own way to my room."

I was glad that no one argued with me. I was in no mood for any kind of discussion, my mind and heart set only on one thing: seeing her.

With a courteous bow to Fawkner and King Haral, I turned with the sweep of one arm against my cloak and made my way from the room. I remembered the path to the library with ease, despite our absence from the city for more than two years. I was soon passing down the long corridor and approaching the twin doors.

I paused there and turned my gaze to my left, sighting the chapel. The door was open and flanked by floor standing candelabras whose flames flickered mildly in the dulled light. The scent of incense and herbs wafted from within, and I slowly made my way forward.

My boots scraped against the stone bricked floor, my eyes surveying that quiet, sanctified place. I took in all the details of the room, noting that though it held the same wood rafters and supports of the main hall it was more a place of stone and glass. The flickering of red lightning was glimpsed through the stained-glass windows, darkness coating their panes. Candles were set all around on candelabras and simple holders, the glow of the flames spreading a gentle, warm illumination around the shadowy space.

The Divine Seven were depicted in great statues that flanked the central space, their shrines each with offerings of food, gold, writings and candles as if to appease them. To my right of entering were the shrines to Isnari, Kelos and Maveria, all three goddesses depicted as beautiful feminine figures with their various symbols surrounding them in their delicate stances. To my left were Azmerath, Sungar and Thringar, the three gods exuding power and strength, each holding aloft their staff, mirror, shield, and scales. And at the head of the chapel was the statue of Ankorect, the great dragon flanked by the other six as she sat upon her hind legs, the world held in her claws as she breathed life into it.

I gazed upon the seven shrines reverently, a sense of comfort as well as unworthiness filling me. My regret returned and I sighed, looking then to the stone slab that was set at the feet of Ankorect's statue.

Leander lay there in her infinite stillness and eternally preserved youth, her body looking so small and meek in comparison to the gigantic stone dragon who watched over her. She had been laid amidst warm, soft furs and minks, an attempt to offer her comfort in her deathly sleep, her head resting on a silver silk pillow.

I approached her slowly, taking my sword from my belt and setting it to the floor out of respect for the gods and goddesses. Once again, I found myself moving as if my feet were standing atop the fragile shells of eggs, afraid to make a wrong move and cause greater destruction than that which had already been inflicted.

As I reached the altar, I took in her beautiful, silken features, pressing one hand to the fur covered stone slab. She wore the same pearl white dress as she had been clothed in by the High Elves, her long, dark auburn hair splayed out around her shoulders and away from her neck. The strands of her locks looked darker in the chapel's poor lights, but also took on a reddish tinge from the golden glow of the candles. Her soft white skin looked so like smooth snow, her rosy cheeks now pale and without hue.

My eyes flicked to her small chest, noting that her breasts still remained unmoving as her lungs lay empty of air. There was no sound from within her chest, her heart dormant. In my mind, I imagined that it had hardened and withered with the wound the knife had torn through it, my own burning with the ache of seeing it in such a way.

I started to slowly stroke her head with my left hand, feeling her soft hair and chilled skin press to my rough palm. My right hand captured hers where it lay by her hip, her fingers stiffened, but still pliable where rigor mortis should surely have set in.

Truly, she is not like the common dead, her body denied the usual decay. There can be no doubt now that she suffers some terrible curse if she is so perfectly preserved.

I gazed down at her face, locking my gaze upon her gently closed lids. The longing for her to open those beautiful steel blue eyes was overwhelming, eating at me like a groundmerk eats away at flesh on a bone.

"I came back to you, my love," I whispered to her, bringing my face close to hers as I crouched beside her death bed, afraid that any words spoken too loudly would disturb her and the gods who held vigil there. "I promised you that I would."

My heart ached and I felt my tears begin to rip from my eyes anew at her unending stillness. I looked down at her smaller hand, rubbing my thumb across her smooth knuckles as if to comfort her. I was so afraid that she was suffering and alone, that she felt no comfort or warmth where she was.

My eyes turned back to her face: "We found the Witch you spoke of Leander. That Danika who foretold your death as you sought refuge in Silvervale. She has been taken to the jails to be held until we are able to question her," I sighed and shook my head. "She was unwilling to help us find a way to restore you and forced us into a battle. We were nearly killed. Fortunately, Ranzel and Gaspeite came to us in our moment of need and freed us from her elemental clutches."

I gazed at her face, the longing in my heart getting stronger. I yearned to press my lips to hers and enact the magic of all the old fairy tales.

I shook my head, blinking away a tear. "What magic plagues you, my beautiful princess? Can you be freed by something as simple as a kiss as in the stories of old? Dare I even try?"

I studied her features, my heart aching all the worse with that thought that now burrowed its way through my mind. I considered the merits of such a thought. *Fairy tales are simply stories told from legends. Legends come from fact and life action, so... perhaps... maybe there's a chance that it could work...*

I leaned my face to hers, my forehead pressing to her cold brow, my right hand releasing her fingers to cup her cheek. A slow breath drew into my lungs in an attempt to still my rushing heartbeat, my body tense with the nervousness of even attempting such a thing.

"Please... let my love be enough to awaken her," I pleaded in the ghost of a whisper. "Isnari... Azmerath... Ankorect... please..."

My eyes drifted shut and I let my thumb tilt her face up so very slightly. My lips pressed to hers and caressed them with a slow passion while my mind continued to plead to the deities of Love, Death and Creation. The image of her waking was clear in my mind, pushing more fervour into my will and my embrace. I let my kiss slowly stroke into her still lips, my body urging her to react, but there was nothing. Only coldness and motionlessness returned for my passion.

I withdrew, pressing my lips together into a grim line, my tears slipping from my face to wet hers as I once again took in her deathly features. Still, she remained unmoving and without breath or heartbeat, her skin unwarmed and her body lying in permanent rest.

A sigh slipped from my mouth as I sat back on the edge of the altar, crestfallen and bleak. "I had a feeling it was too much to ask for that to work," I murmured grimly.

Once again, I took Leander's hand in mine, feeling her smooth, slender fingers against my palm. It wasn't the same as feeling her delicate digits with life in them, but it was at least some way to connect with her, to still feel her flesh on mine.

Footsteps drew my attention and I glanced up over my shoulder to see Joran approaching me from the shadows of the chapel. The Storvari was as solemn as ever, his dark hair pulled back from his mauve skinned features, the golden markings on the left side of his face glinting in the candlelight. He raised one thick, sharp eyebrow at me, his hands remaining at his sides.

"Carden Highever," he spoke in his monotonous voice, studying myself and my princess as he towered above us, "why do you lay your lips upon the Sarissi's? She cannot return such affections in her death."

I sighed and shook my head, looking back to Leander's face: "It was a foolish hope, Joran. Nothing more."

"A hope?" he questioned.

I nodded. "Yes. We humans tell fantasies to our young children meant to amuse and encourage. We call these fairy tales."

"And these stories encourage the kissing of the dead?" he asked with his usual emotionlessly stoic tone, though there was curiousness in his eyes when I glanced to him.

"In many of the stories, a beautiful princess is cursed by a vile sorcerer," I explained softly. "She is either slain or conjured into an unbreakable sleep by magic, never to awaken again. It is then that a prince comes to her and restores her with True Love's Kiss, thus bringing her back to life."

"And you thought that it might apply to the Sarissi," he observed.

I nodded sadly. "But it didn't work. Leander still lies in her deathly sleep without breath or the beat of her heart, despite my fervour. Perhaps I am not worthy to awaken her."

I felt one giant hand on my shoulder, turning my gaze to the large, broad, mauve knuckles and fingers before looking up into the Storvari's stern eyes. For the first time since I had met him, I saw a softness there that revealed his heart.

"We Storvari do not know of such concepts as you humans do," he told me gently, "yet I know what I see in both you and the Sarissi. You say that you are not worthy because of the blame carried in your heart regarding her demise, but this is not so."

I raised an eyebrow at him. "You speak as if you have looked within my soul, Joran."

"I have looked within both you and her," he responded evenly and reverently. "I have watched since the very start of it all and seen what lives within you when you are near each other, as well as when you are far apart. To Storvari, you and she are known as Korshil Narvar, which in your human tongue means "Two souls bound together in truest heart bond, whose spirits were always meant to be joined, and whose paths are entwined forever in perfect life union. Apart you are incomplete, your forms separate, but your spirits are woven of the same fabric. You are two as one, meant to be, and forever joined, blessed by life itself, sharing its flame." Such is what I see in both you and her, Carden Highever."

His words struck me, and I felt that I was about to weep like a heartbroken child, though I managed to hold back that flood of salt water for the time being.

"Your words speak of what we humans call Soul Mates," I expressed softly. "Two souls who are forever entwined in love and whose absence causes each other great suffering, but whose union brings blissful joy."

Joran considered this and nodded. "Soul Mates... It is perhaps the most appropriate wording for Korshil Narvar. I was not aware humans had such words in their tongue."

I nodded and turned my eyes back to Leander: "It is one of the few phrases that seem to translate with your people's meanings, my friend," then a thought occurred to me. "The words you speak when one of our companions passes, Vashabaravan Karvarn. What do they mean?"

"Vashabaravan Karvarn is a Storvari prayer for the departed," he explained reverently. "It translates as: Go now and rest, Sacred Life. It is we who grieve your passing, but you who pass shall not know pain nor grief again. Live on in the Beyond, Sacred Life. May you always know honour."

I took in a slow breath, my heart uplifted by the beauty of such words. I had always wondered the meaning of the two Storvari words he had spoken so reverently in the past, now enraptured by their translation.

"Both a beautiful and honourable prayer for those we care for," I squeezed Leander's hand as I studied her face again. "Did you speak these words over her?"

"No," he stated simply.

"Why not?" I frowned, looking up at him.

The Storvari moved up beside me, gazing down at Leander with a deeply serene and gentle stare. It was as if he were standing before the most beautiful goddess-like being he had ever known. To me, such was a true statement of her, for that was exactly how I perceived my precious princess.

"Because I offered a deeper blessing to her," he replied to my question with a gentler, murmuring voice than I had ever heard issue from his lips. "I said to her Varshira Noraana Corvark'shil."

"Which means?" my curiosity piqued.

He looked down at her with sadness in his eyes as he translated: "Beautiful soul whose light it has been my honour to walk within, be at peace now that your heart lies still in your breast and your lips no longer draw breath. You were my soul kin, my clan mate, my worthy equal, and it is with a heavy heart that I watch you depart. Though your voice shall fade from my ears, your face vanish from my eyes, and your touch no longer be upon my hand, you leave a potent mark upon my heart, and so shall never be forgotten. I wish you a peaceful forever sleep, dearest one, until we look upon each other in our soul family once more when we are all re-joined in the Beyond. Blessings of Love, forevermore."

"Even more beautiful than the other prayer, Joran," I said softly, feeling tears fall. "Do you truly see her in such high honour?"

He looked to me: "She is no longer merely a human that I pledged my service to, but a member of my clan. As are you and all of our companions. Though I am far from the deserts of my homeland and now surrounded by the cold winds of the north, I am not without my Jaaktar, for I have created a new one here with you and all our companions. We are brothers and sisters in bond forevermore, Carden Highever, and so too is Leander Aldrich."

That was the first time I had ever heard him use her actual name, always hearing him refer to her as Sarissi. It was odd and beautiful.

He went on sorrowfully: "And we have lost our clan sister in a foul death that has broken our very souls."

"We will get her back, Joran," I told him, standing and placing my hand on his shoulder. "We will find a way to restore her to life once again. Such is the vow I have made in place of my now renounced oaths."

Joran looked down to me with such sadness as I had never seen in a Storvari's eyes. Truly, it was like he had lost his most beloved little sister when Leander had been killed, not simply the girl he had a life debt to. Now I truly understood the intensity of the Storvari in a way I never thought I could before.

"That is my hope as well, Carden Highever," he said quietly.

I looked to Leander's beautiful face as I whispered the words again in certainty: "We *will* get her back. This I swear..."

Chapter Ten
Getting Blood from a Stone

I stayed there in the chapel for a long time, holding Leander's soft, cold hand in mine all the while after Joran and I had talked on the Storvari death rituals. As he returned to his meditations in the darkened corner of the room, I remained by my beloved's side, contemplating all that we had discussed. But I knew I could not stay.

I lay one soft kiss to Leander's lips, still hoping against hope and logic that to do so would awaken her, but she once again lay in complete silence. Another sigh escaped my throat as I studied her features for the last time that night, silently vowing to return the next. I didn't want her to not have my company or to be alone as she had been too often.

After I had bathed and changed, I then went to the Great Hall where I found only Tristan, Ellora, Tallinn and the two Axton brothers, all of them seated in a corner of the large table with a simple, but hearty stew. I joined them with little more than a nod and filled a cup with water, feeling oddly thirsty now.

Conversation was not attempted, nor even considered by any of us who sat there, all of us content to eat in silence. After all, there was nothing to be said and no action to be taken at this time. My mind was absent as I dipped a piece of brown bread into the stew, hardly recognising the world that surrounded me. I was trying to figure out what to do next, or even just how to cope. However, my impatience was growing and making that next to impossible.

Movement caught my attention, and I turned my emerald gaze up towards the entry from the west side of the hall. Fawkner strode through calmly, his expression a severe one. He came to stand by our seats at the table, directing his gaze to Tallinn and me.

"Tallinn, Carden, would you care to join me?" he asked.

"In doing what?" Tallinn enquired, brushing her hair across her shoulders, the blonde locks exposing the open collar of her shirt and her smooth, tanned neckline.

"I am making my way down to the jails to speak with this witch you brought to Eilath," he stated with a cold calm. "I thought that we should question her as a trinity, like the Guardians we are."

Tallinn nodded. "Very well. Carden? Have you had your fill of the meal?"

"I am less hungry for food than I am for the Witch's knowledge," I confessed, getting to my feet, and nodding to Fawkner. "Lead the way."

Tallinn slid from her chair and followed close at my side; her gaze set as hard as her jaw. We were both ready for answers, now allied in a common goal, even though we had been on opposing sides of opinion of late.

The Lorveren Lord led us through a doorway to the east side of the hall, turning to the left into a small corridor off-shooting the longer main one. Here there was a door, a guard in a green surcoat standing at alert. Fawkner simply nodded to him and passed by, opening a door that led down a set of lightly toned, wooden steps. The stairs led us into the wooden and stone bowels of the manor house, the structure only now revealing to us just how much of a fortress it truly was. We stepped onto a solid stone floor and through an archway into the guard barracks. There were quite a significant number of armoured men and women here, all of them preparing their weapons in case of a battle. The rest either slept on beds set off to one side in a partitioned section of the room or sat at large tables eating and drinking between watch changes.

Fawkner strode through without stopping, nodding in acknowledgement as he was saluted by a number of his soldiers. His focus was set on the iron gate ahead of us, swinging it open after having a guard unlock it for him.

We passed down a second set of stairs, this time into the deep stone foundations of the fortress.

The moment I set my feet to the hard stone floor, I was hit by the deep cold of the cells. My eyes took in the simplistic design of the prison. It was merely a long corridor with a guard station near the stairway to the barracks, a handful of guardsmen there working on papers under the light of candles. The only other light came from two torches set on the wall opposite the six cells, no natural light able to enter this deep down, even if there hadn't been supernatural storms blotting out the sun. Looking into the darkened cells left me perplexed. Every one was empty despite the surge in attacks on settlements. I would have expected at least someone there other than our Witch.

We reached the cell at the end, two guards watching the door with unblinking vigilance. They had been warned of what she could do and were in no way willing to fall to her hexes.

I stopped at the back of my two companions, folding my arms in front of my broad chest and setting my back to the stone wall behind me. I decided I would simply watch and wait to see what words would come from the woman's lips before making a move of my own.

Danika sat cross legged on the floor, her hands resting on her thighs, her palms down, her head bowed. Strands of her dark hair framed her face and hid her eyes, but the woman didn't lose any of her beauty. Chains were secured around her wrists and shackled to the wall opposite the cell door with length enough given for her to move around.

"So," she spoke in that sardonic voice, her eyes remaining shut, "it is at this late hour that the Lord of Eilath decides to meet me in my cold, dank cell."

"My apologies for the stark confines," Fawkner spoke diplomatically, yet honestly, "however it is necessary to keep you secured given your... prior actions."

"The cold and dark of this cell bothers me not," Danika stated evenly, shrugging under her black and magenta robes. "I make my home in a cave beneath the mountains in the Forests of Arnath. Trust me when I say that I am at my most comfortable in places such as this."

"Is there anything else I might offer you to add to your comfort?" Fawkner enquired carefully. "Extra blankets? Candles to read by? Parchment?"

"You seek to placate me," she perceived, still sitting with her eyes shut. "You offer me luxuries and creature comforts in the hopes of prising the knowledge you desire from me."

He sighed. "Well, I would much rather come to an amicable agreement through discussion and barter than to resort to..." he cleared a hard lump from his throat, "less friendly methods."

"Torture does not cause me fear," the woman remarked without concern. "It is hard to fear that which you have faced countless times in the past from those you call your own kin."

"Your sisters tortured you?" Tallinn sounded shocked, yet managed to keep her calm, her hands firmly squared on her hips.

Danika turned her face towards us, her eyes flashing open as if they were green flames suddenly sparking in the darkness. "Keilantra and Manth were always cruel. They took after our mother. She was truly wicked in her ways and was the one who made my sisters what they became; drawing Him to them like a hungry beggar to a feast."

"Him? Do you mean the Shadow Lord?" Tallinn asked evenly.

Danika nodded. "It was he who completed their corruption and drove them to become the dark beings they now are. He offered them such temptations as they could not refuse."

"But not you," I perceived.

She nodded again. "Indeed. I was tempted by nothing that he could offer by the time he came to us, my lusts only leading me to solitude in nature. I am a simplistic creature like that."

Fawkner drew closer to the cell, the Witch watching him with her sharp, predatory eyes the way a falcon watches a mouse. He leaned one shoulder to the bars of the cell, gazing in at her with a casual air.

"I am told that you are a seer of sorts," he took his time with his words, glancing to his hands as he rubbed the back of one with the other palm before facing her again. "Is it a gift your sisters share as well?"

Danika stared back at him sternly. "No. It is not held by all of us. Only Manth and I have such perceptions. Keilantra was always the more narrow sighted of our mother's daughters."

"And, pray tell, what powers do they possess?" he questioned calmly.

She snorted, getting to her feet and standing before us in the centre of her cell, her hands grasping the chains that coiled around her wrists. "Is that why you come to me, Falcon Lord? To question me about my powers and those my sisters possess?"

"No," he shook his head slightly. "To learn of your sisters' powers would be great knowledge, but it is not what drives me at this moment..."

"Yet, you show interest in my foresight," she shrugged and gestured to the glowing blue circles marked with magical runes on each of the walls. "An ability that is negated by these wards your city mages conjured upon the walls of this cell, just as all my other abilities are."

"Again, it is because you attempted to harm my companions when they approached you for aid," Fawkner stated with the same calm manner he had maintained all the way through this conversation.

"You mean when they invaded my lands?" she questioned in a hiss, drawing a few steps nearer.

"No harm or offense was intended," he attempted to reassure her.

She scoffed at his words: "You toss about words such as "harm" and "offense" as if they should mean something to me."

"If you were not offended or fearful for your safety, then why did you attack us?" Tallinn asked with a frown.

"I knew what you intended, and what you still do," Danika replied with a blatant shrug.

"Then you know it is not a harmful or selfish cause that we have," I stated, letting my hands drop as I moved to Tallinn's side. "We ask only for your aid in finding the answer to achieving this just and true end."

"Again, tossing about words as if they are of importance to a forest dweller like myself," the Witch turned her gaze up to me.

I felt like I could grow angry, but chose not to, forcing my predator back down as he began to stir within me once more. I drew in a slow breath and closed my eyes before looking to her again.

"Regardless, you know our intent and our reason if you have sight of the future," I expressed slowly and cautiously, afraid an angry word might slip from my lips. "Surely you saw what we were to speak with you about before our arrival at your dwelling?"

"I did, yes," she confirmed, leaning closer to the bars. She was a little taller than I had expected. "And I saw the outcome of such a quest as that which you intend to undertake, Carden son of Tiernan."

"Then you can tell us what we need to know," I implored her softly. "Please, give us the knowledge that leads to undoing this evil done to the world."

Danika considered us for a moment, her gaze analytical and cold. She wore the ghost of a smirk on her lips, but her expression spoke of utter boredom. Clearly she was growing disinterested. Finally, she said one single word: "No."

"No?" I frowned, anger filling me, but for the moment remaining manageable.

She shrugged and turned from us gracefully: "You gave me a request and I have given you a simple answer. And that answer is no."

"Why?!" I demanded in a snarl.

"I have many answers to that question," she stated, turning back to us as she now stood at the far side of the cell, "but I shall elect the simplest: I have merely chosen not to."

I felt myself getting enraged, my hands now on the bars of the cell and squeezing them. My throat began to burn, and I could hear the thumping of hearts from those all around me. The rhythm of those beats was like war drums in my head, driving me to frenzy.

Tallinn placed her hand to my shoulder and her other to my chest, her touch snapping me back to reality. "Do not lose control," she urged me in a whisper.

I closed my eyes momentarily and drew in another breath before calming myself. I uncurled my hands from the bars and staggered back, pressing my shoulders to the wall opposite the cell. I had to leave this to the other two or else risk losing myself to my beast.

Fawkner took control, stepping in front of me and facing Danika where I no longer could. "You have chosen not to," he repeated her words carefully, his perceptions as quick as his sword arm. "So, that means that you do indeed possess the knowledge we seek."

"I do," she confirmed calmly, confident, not arrogant.

"But you will not give it to us," he went on.

She nodded. "That is correct."

Fawkner thought for a moment, musing over her words. He was clearly trying to analyse all that the Witch had said and was now in the process of finding a path around her labyrinth of meanings and phrases. He held one arm around his middle as the other stroked his jaw in thought.

"Is there no way that we can change your mind?" he asked tactfully.

Danika remained stoic: "There is."

"Which is?" Fawkner questioned evenly.

Danika allowed herself a small smirk as she gave her condition: "You must admit the truth to me. The truth that you hide even from yourselves."

"What truth?" I asked with a hard frown.

She locked her eyes squarely on me: "That your cause is indeed a selfish one. You must admit it and understand it. Only then can you have the knowledge. Until you do, I have nothing else to say to any of you."

"But-" I leaned forward with desperation, cut off by her next words before I could take a second step.

"We are done for now," she said with disinterest. "Leave me to my meditations, please. I am in no further mood for speech."

Fawkner nodded and gestured for Tallinn and I to follow as the Witch sat back down and crossed her legs, resuming the position she had been in when we had arrived. I hesitated for but a moment, watching her through the bars of the cell before turning and hurriedly striding from the room with the others.

In only a few minutes we were back in the Great Hall.

"It's like getting blood from a stone," I scowled, shaking my head as we came to a stop before the long fire pit glowing in the middle of the room.

"Getting answers from the Witch is certainly a trial, I must admit," Fawkner sighed, nodding as he clasped his belt with both hands.

"She speaks in riddles," Tallinn observed with a puzzled frown, her arms folded in front of her chest. "Or perhaps she utters nonsense."

"Admitting and understanding that our cause is selfish?" I shook my head at the prospect. "It sounds like madness considering that we intend to undo the Shadow Lord's evil."

"Do you think she is simply toying with us?" Tallinn looked to both Fawkner and I with her question.

"I am not certain," Fawkner confessed, his hand to his chin in thought. "All that is certain is that she will not give us the answer without fulfilling her conditions."

"Strange conditions," Tallinn remarked. "They aren't likely to be fulfilled given that the truth is that we seek to end this blight the Shadow Lord has brought upon the land."

"So, where does that leave us?" I asked with a cold grimness in my tone.

"I'll confer with Ranzel about this discussion," Fawkner stated. "Perhaps he will have some insight. In the meantime, I suggest we search the library for some answer as to how to undo the dark magic cursing Leander."

"A task better suited after a night of fitful rest," Tallinn pointed out.

"Indeed," Fawkner nodded. "I shall bid you both goodnight then. I must away to my children, then the arms of my beloved Erika. I have not made time enough for them since my return and I sorely mean to."

"Goodnight," Tallinn nodded to him.

As Fawkner turned away and left, she faced me sternly.

"Come with me," she directed me. "We must make your new medicine."

"Yes," I agreed with a sigh. "You're right."

Tallinn did always like it when I had no mind to debate with her, the small smile she gave me at my response in that moment evidence of that. She turned and headed for the doorway to the guest quarters, my own feet moving at a slower pace behind her.

She directed me to take a seat in the room she had been given, then left me to gather what she would need from the keep's stores. In not but a few minutes she had returned and began setting up the glass phials and bottles with the alchemy apparatus on the table.

"Roll up your sleeve," she directed me.

I pulled my coarse shirt sleeve up my left arm to expose my defined muscular bicep and forearm, turning my gaze then to the open balcony doors. I could see how dark the lands had become with the sinister unending storms, the wind having a strange bite on the skin without chill. It was as if there was fire in the clouds, burning them black and causing such terrible destruction there alone.

A sharp pinch went into my arm, and I glanced back at Tallinn without hardly an utterance of pain. She had inserted a hollow needle into my vein with a length of tube attached, feeding it now into a bottle. My blood began to pool in the bottom of the glass container, a darker red than it should have been.

Tallinn's frown was disturbing, her eyes studying the blood with a sense of concern.

"What is it?" I asked.

"Your blood has darkened," she said softly, setting the bottle down and placing a cloth to my arm as she removed the needle.

I pinned the cloth against the crook of my arm with my right hand, watching her with a frown as she proceeded to examine the contents of the bottle. She sighed and shook her head, sitting at the table as Aldwyn once did. She began crushing herbs with a mortar and pestle.

"The affliction is progressing," she explained grimly as she worked, never once looking up as she mashed the herbs expertly. "I've never seen it as strongly embedded in your blood before tonight. When did you last take your medicine?"

I sighed and stood, still holding the cloth to my arm as I walked to gaze out the window. "I took the last of what Aldwyn mixed for me just after our return to Silvervale," I confessed in a low, soft voice. "I fear that it has not been working as effectively as it once did."

She paused and threw me a hard stare: "It isn't?"

I looked to her and simply shook my head.

She groaned and returned to her work, pressing the herbs with more fury. "Aldwyn was afraid this might happen," she stated darkly. "He told me that the affliction in your blood would eventually find a way around his treatments. I'll have to resort to his other method then," she got up and moved to her bag, rummaging through it furiously.

"What do you mean? What other method?" I asked with a frown of confusion.

"Aldwyn had created a new tincture that he believed would stave off the effects of the affliction in your blood should it overpower his current method," she explained, withdrawing a familiar leather-bound book and carrying it to the table. "He told me of it not because he *thought* it might become necessary, but because he *knew* it would."

"That's Aldwyn's book of shadows," I observed, moving to stand by her side.

She nodded as she unlocked it and flipped through the pages. "I took it for safekeeping after he passed. Now I am glad I did after seeing what is becoming of you."

"He... he never mentioned that this might be a concern to me," I sat back down.

"You were distracted," she responded softly. "Your eyes were no longer focused upon such things once you had gained the attentions of the Princess."

"Are you about to condemn me for loving her as the White Wizard did?" I asked quietly, drawing her glance.

"No," she shook her head. "No, I would never do that. If anything, I was glad to see how much improved you became once you were with her. She..." she paused, her own grief evident, "she seemed able to bring out the best in you and stave off your affliction on her own."

"I never told her," I confessed with a sigh, still holding my arm. "She knew that I have an affliction, but she didn't know what it was. I couldn't tell her. I mean, how could I?"

Tallinn nodded as she followed the steps in the book, starting to put herbs and oils into the various containers needed to mix the tinctures. "It is no easy thing to discuss," she agreed. "Especially with someone you love."

"It isn't," I said, then lifted the cloth on my arm to examine the wound. "Tallinn..."

She swung around at my call, her eyes instantly turning to my arm. There was no mark, no blood oozing from it as it had been. The only blood left was what had flowed onto my flesh before I had lifted the cloth. She immediately grasped my arm and examined it, her panic growing, though she remained calm.

"Gods!" she gasped. "You have never healed so swiftly before!"

I looked from my arm to her face. "It's happening. What Aldwyn feared since taking me as an apprentice is happening."

"I'll get the tincture ready," she swung back to her work, moving with a speed I hadn't seen before.

I sighed and closed my eyes, looking into myself. I could feel my body changing, sense it rewriting my very being. It had begun and now I wasn't certain it could be stopped. I could feel my predator stirring within me, could hear his growl as it lingered in my throat on the edge of sounding aloud.

"I nearly gave into my predator, Tallinn," I admitted, looking to her as she paused momentarily at my words. "First at the Witch's cave when we fought the Troll. I thought for a moment that if I were to let him out and surrender that I would easily be able to defeat the beast trying to crush us. But I resisted. Then, in that village, I embraced him and killed the bandit attacking that girl," shame filled me and I closed my eyes, trying to will the monster back into his cage within me. "I looked upon that innocent girl with the eyes of a predator. I felt my throat grow dry and my mouth wetting itself at the prospect of sating my thirst. And, for but a moment, I was on the edge of casting aside my humanity and draining the life from her. But I didn't. I pulled back and reminded myself of who I am."

"But you stopped yourself," she pointed out, touching my hands with hers, gaining my gaze to her hazel eyes beneath her blonde locks. "You made the choice to hold back against your beast and remain the man that you are. In all my life and in the few encounters of others with this affliction that I have had, never before have I seen a man hold against it as strongly as you, Carden."

"I fear I am losing myself," I confessed with a shaking outward breath.

"A lesser man would have succumbed much sooner than you, my brother," she encouraged, offering me a small smile as the alchemy lab bubbled and boiled behind her. "You have strength enough to outlast this illness. Perhaps it is simply the nature of your birth that gives you such strength, or the events of your life, yet I know you can endure."

"Perhaps," I agreed as she turned back to her work, leaning my elbows on my knees and letting my hands hang. "It feels as though my resolve has lessened of late. Ever since she..." I forced the words back down my throat and chose others. "Ever since the battle of Safferan I find I have but one conviction, all others lost to me now."

"Never in our years side by side as Guardians, have I seen your convictions so shaken," she said softly, a sadness hidden in her soft voice. "That you were driven to forsake your oath to the Order..."

"Tallinn, please," I stood and turned from her, facing the view of the land beyond the balcony. "Not this again."

"It is no mere thing that you do, brother..."

"Stop calling me that," I glanced back at her, clenching my hands at my sides. "I am not your brother in oath any longer; my fealty to the Guardians dissolved and my heart swayed to another vow," I sighed and turned my gaze to the floor. "Do not try to convince me otherwise. My mind is set, and my decision made. But know that I still think of you as I always did."

"Regardless of your decision," she said softly, but honestly, "no matter you renounced your oath, you are still like a brother to me, Carden. And if being a

Guardian no longer serves you, then I will abide by your decision. But do not ask me to turn from your side, for I cannot do that."

I turned my gaze back to her appreciatively: "I won't ask that of you, Tallinn. In truth, I cannot and could never ask that you leave me. Our bond is unbroken though my oath is shattered, and I will always count you as my closest ally."

She smiled faintly. "I am glad to hear that... brother."

I smiled and nodded, feeling much calmer.

Tallinn then turned back to the alchemy works, beginning to fill a blue mixture into several phials. These were smaller than I had previously used in the past, a cause for me to raise a doubting eyebrow as I wondered why they were the choice of container.

As if she knew I would ask, Tallinn explained: "The advanced tincture from Aldwyn's book requires a lesser dose, and so needs smaller containers to hold them. A benefit, given that you will need to carry these if we are to journey anywhere to achieve our goals."

"You expect a new journey once the Witch has spoken her words?" I asked as she handed me one of the phials.

She nodded solemnly. "Seldom ever is the answer on our doorstep. To restore the Princess to life will be a hard road and an uncertain one without a doubt."

"The Uncertain Road," I let out a ghost of a chuckle as I studied the phial, "is the one that leads to truth of self and purpose; the harder taken, yet it is the most worthy at the end."

"A very apt saying of your people," Tallinn agreed as she completed her work, turning back to me. "Drink that, Carden. I have made enough to last us several months."

I slugged it back, letting the liquid slide down my throat. Relief filled me and I was able to relax at last as my predator seemed to settle and slumber once again.

"The doses will have to be more frequent than what you are used to," she went on as she began to tidy the room. "One phial every two weeks should suffice, according to Aldwyn's writings. Do *not* leave it longer as you once did. Not now that the progression is as clear as it is tonight."

I assure you, Tallinn," I said honestly as I put the stopper into the empty phial and handed it to her, "that I will be ever more vigilant regarding my affliction. I have no desire to succumb to its final end for me."

She nodded and touched my shoulder. "Good. Go and get some rest. You will need to sleep so that the medicine might take full effect."

"All right. Goodnight, Tallinn."

"Goodnight, my brother," she smiled softly.

I left her to her cleaning and returned to my room, gladly shutting the door and lighting only a single candle. I stripped from my clothes and lay myself on the bed, covering my body from the hips down with the blankets. My skin felt hot now that I had taken the tincture and I yearned for relief, even if it meant sleeping unclothed.

My eyes fell shut and my chest heaved as I drew in one long breath, then released it with all of my tension. It felt good to lay down and rest in a bed after the uncomfortable nights travelling from Silvervale, the sheets a soothing luxury that helped to ease my body.

I felt movement beside me, a frown pulling at my brow. *I'm alone in this bed. No one lays with me. So why is there movement?*

A slender hand brushed across my exposed torso, the feminine fingers caressing my chest seductively. The warmth of soft, naked flesh pressed into my body, and I opened my eyes to see the figure in the candlelight. I swear that I nearly fainted dead away as I saw her, my heart leaping in my chest and my eyes widening as my breath quickened a little.

"I've been waiting for you, Carden," Leander smiled in that beautiful way she always did, so innocent despite her nudity hidden only by sheets.

"Leander...?" I breathed her name as if it were the life-giving air that I needed. "Leander, is that you?"

Her smile brought a blush of pink to her cheeks, and she shyly glanced towards my bare muscular chest before looking up at me through wayward strands of her mahogany hair.

"How?" I asked in a softly bewildered voice, reaching one large hand to caress her cheek. "How are you with me?"

She was warm and soft, just like I remembered her being, her beauty once again coloured in a creamy pink instead of the deathly snowy hue that she had taken on. Gods, she was beyond beautiful, everything about her inviting and soothing, seducing me where I lay.

She shrugged one bare shoulder as she lay her body against my chest. "It wasn't hard. I just came in, undressed and lay here to wait for you," a soft giggle escaped her perfect lips. "You didn't even notice me in your bed. You must be so tired."

"I have been," I confessed. "The journey back to Eilath and my worry for you have drained me greatly."

"There's no need to worry about me now, Carden," she spoke in her gentle voice, staring deep into my eyes with her striking steel blue ones. "Just be with me."

She placed her lips to mine and softly stroked them in a kiss so perfect and pure that I never thought I could have felt such a wonderful thing. I responded in kind, allowing my arms to enwrap her slender body, my hands pressing to her shoulders as my fingers pulled her long hair away from her neck. I just wanted to hold her like this forever, to know her in every way I could and never again let go of her.

Leander lifted her lips from mine and met my gaze, desire upon her features and lust tinting her scent. "I want you to be my first," she whispered, holding tightly to me. "I want to feel you intimately and give myself to you."

"Leander..." I wasn't sure, concern filling me for her decision.

"Please," she pleaded in earnest, longing in her gorgeous eyes and creasing her smooth white brow. "Please, Carden. I've held onto my virtue for so long now, battled to keep it against such terrible threats. I want to share myself with you, and you alone. Please?" her words were filled with such yearning. A yearning that I myself had held for her just as strongly.

I couldn't refuse her. "Of course, my love," I uttered.

Without the expected nervousness that should surely have been in her first intimate experience, Leander smiled and began to kiss my neck, positioning herself on top of my body. Her fingers curled over my shoulders as she continued her furiously passionate kissing, working her way to my chest.

A soft giggle escaped her lips. "You harden at my touch," she observed, her eyes bright as our gazes met.

I let out a breath as I felt her pressing her body closer to mine, holding my arms tightly around her. The sheets fell to her hips, our torsos exposed in the dull candlelight.

"Are you ready?" I asked her gently.

She nodded. "Yes..."

Bliss. That is all I can describe it as. Utter bliss.

She let out a soft moan at our intimate embrace, her body tensing as I pressed myself into her. I let out a grunt at the feeling, closing my eyes as I felt her tighten every muscle.

As our bodies began to move in this lustful embrace, I opened my eyes and looked up upon her stunning features. Her expression held that passion that came with such things, her hips slowly moving as my hands fell around them and held tightly. That seemed to only quicken her, and she leaned down over me, kissing me as we continued.

"Oh, gods," she gasped breathlessly. "Ugh... I've never felt anything like this before."

"Nor have I," I replied in a hoarse whisper. "I love you, Leander."

"I love you too, Carden," she responded softly, her moans beginning to grow with her breathlessness.

I felt my desire increase and began to push myself passionately, wanting to hear that incredible sound of pleasure slip from her lips with more frequency. She responded as I knew she would, her deepest core heating ever more furiously with my powerful strokes. She moaned loudly and quickly, her breaths catching with her body pressing against mine. She leaned herself back, tilting her face to the ceiling as she drew closer and closer to her release. She had never seemed more pleasured by anything I had seen since knowing her. It was intoxicating, pushing me to want more from her body.

Then, something struck me, a feeling in my own core that made my movements soften.

"Stop," I rasped out as she furiously ground her hips, my hands tightening on them. "Leander, stop!" I managed more volume.

I pulled myself from her and lifted her with my hands, turning around and dropping her onto her back on the bed. She had a look of deep indignation as I drew myself to kneel over her, my chest heaving, the sweat beading my muscular frame like dew on a leaf. The shadows took care of our modesty, the single candle hardly enough to reveal much of our bodies to each other.

"What?" she demanded breathlessly. "Why are you stopping?"

"This... this isn't right," I confessed aloud, trying to convince myself more than her.

She frowned. "What? What isn't right?"

She drew herself to her knees, exposing herself to my sights as she pulled her body against mine, her breasts pressing to my chest. She kissed my neck and brought her lips to my ear, her breath hot as it blew against my jaw.

"Having sex?" she questioned seductively, smirking into her words. "I thought that's what you wanted all along. To strip away my clothes and see me in my most natural form. To run your hands along the contours of my naked body..." her smirk deepened as her hands dropped before us and I tensed at her touch, "... to fill my womanhood with your significant length..." she went on, her hands working.

I grasped her by her wrists and yanked her hands up from my lower body, staring her down. "This isn't like you, Leander," I told her with a fury filling me, but not anger. "You are not so vulgar, and you're certainly not so practiced in pleasing a man with your body."

"There's a lot you don't know about me," she seemed to grow darker in her face, tugging her wrists free of my hold before laying back against the pillows. "Now, come on. Enter me again and drive us both to passion's summit."

"Enough!" I snapped, staring her down, leaning over her to see her face rather than the rest of her. "This is just some fevered dream. Never have you said such coarse, blatant things. You aren't her..."

"What?" she frowned.

I turned my face from hers and looked towards the floor grimly. "You aren't Leander. She lies dead in the chapel of this keep and my heart is so broken that my mind has conjured you to appease my grief."

I knew now what this was. I was asleep and this was nothing more than a strange dream in which she was alive and hungering for our intimate union. That was perhaps excuse enough for why the shadows hid her body's details from my sights and gave me only glimpses; for how could I see details that I had never beheld?

Suddenly, her hand grasped my upper arm and I tensed at the brittle dryness of her skin. I turned back to her and stared in wide eyed horror at the figure that now glared up at me from the bed.

Leander's skin had become grey and cracked, looking dead and without the softness I knew. Her eyes were sunken back into their sockets, the flesh there sallow and blackened. Her hair was still dark auburn, but without the lustre that healthy strands would have. Her muscles had thinned, her limbs like sticks as she grasped at me. Her eyes looked the same, but now held a harshness that didn't belong.

"What in the Void?!" I gasped, pulling my arm free, her dried skin flaking from her palm with the sudden movement.

She twisted her head with a sickly crack, glaring at me. "I'm only dead because of *you*, Carden," she hissed, propping herself up on the other arm, her bones groaning with the movement. "*You're* the reason the Shadow Lord killed me."

"No!" I shook my head, recoiling from her. "No! No, I tried to save you!"

Her head clicked to the side with that sickening crack, her eyes staring up at me from under her brow. It was almost like her head was now too heavy to lift with her muscles having atrophied so badly.

"You didn't try very hard," she accused, her voice now aged and rasping where once it had been so youthful and soft.

"I fought for you!" I shouted in desperation. "I tried to reach you before he could kill you!"

"You promised you'd protect me," she went on as if she were simply continuing without hearing me. "You said you loved me and that you wouldn't let anything happen to me. I gave you my heart..."

I gagged as she plunged her withered hand through her chest between her breasts, the greyed skin breaking as if it was made of porcelain. She pulled out a dusty, faded red shape and held it out towards me. Her heart looked as decayed as she now did, unnaturally clutched in her shaking, grasping, bony palm outside of her chest.

Wake up! Wake up now! Come on, let me wake up! Now! Please!

"I gave you my heart," she rasped breathlessly, staggering where she half sat and half lay," and you broke it. You broke it like every promise you ever made to me."

I shook my head, tears streaking my cheeks. "No... No, Leander... Please..."

"You broke your promise. You broke my heart," she clenched her fist and her heart turned to broken shards and dust that spilled onto the bed. "It's *all your* fault!"

My vision turned dark, and I felt myself jolt up in bed, my eyes flashing open. I was laying on my back, staring at the ceiling where I had been kneeling on the bed before that moment.

My eyes darted around the room, searching the shadows for that terrible, haunting vision of Leander, but I saw nothing. My hand yanked the sheets away, revealing nothing but my own naked body. She wasn't there, not a single sign present that she had been beside me at all. I pulled myself up to sit on the bed, looking over at where she had laid. Slowly, almost fearfully, I touched the bed with my hand. There was no warmth where a body should have laid on that side, only the heat of my own. I had been alone all that time.

I let out a sigh of relief, turning away from the bed and sitting on its edge, my feet to the floor. I rested my elbows on my knees and hung my head in my hands, closing my eyes as I tried to calm myself down.

What kind of nightmare was that? I wondered, sweat dripping down my chest and abdomen, my brow soaked with stress. *Why did I see her like that? Gods... What is happening to me?*

Chapter Eleven
The Netherworlds

~ Leander ~

Terrifying images ripped through my dreaming mind, coursing like fiery lightning across my sleeping sights. I saw such horrible things that I couldn't even describe. My vision was hazy as the events seemed to play out with no true order or sense to be had. Buildings crumbled and collapsed. People were screaming in fear and terrible agony as great sweeping black shapes beat their wings against the sky, roaring out a call of death. Blood ran in rivers. And I felt it all. It was as if I was connected to all the horror, the pain and grief all at once, my soul burning with the people that howled as they were engulfed by dragon fire.

A scream jolted me from my sleep, my eyes flying open to that strange twilight world once again. All the noise of my dreams fell into silence, my ears hurting from the din. I had never heard such painful sound in my life... or... well, now in my afterlife.

I sat up slowly, taking in my surroundings with an uneasy eye, my nightgown hanging from my shoulders as my breasts heaved beneath the silken neckline. I felt the dampness of sweat on my forehead, my body hurting as my frantic heartbeat spiked even more agony through me. My right hand clutched at my chest as I winced in pain. In all this time since I had first woken up in that otherworldly construct of Castle Arvon, the pain in my chest had never once left me. It was constant and nagging, like I was being torn through my heart and one of my lungs every time I drew a breath or felt a beat in my breast. It was an unending agony that had taken me so long now to learn to endure just so I could sleep.

I closed my eyes and drew in a deep breath, groaning out a whimpering sob as the pain sharpened. It was always worse when I had nightmares, which seemed like every time I tried to sleep lately. It was as if someone or something was cursing me and making sure that I suffered beyond my understanding. It was already bad enough that I was almost entirely alone in that ghostly castle, but the pain in my torso, cutting me mercilessly as if the knife that had slain me had struck again, was unbearable.

Calmness began to fill me, and I felt the pain lessen, though it didn't leave me. I let out a staggering breath, shuddering as I tilted my head back with the new spike of discomfort that tried dully to spear me. I pulled my knees up and hugged them to my chest, laying my head on my arms tiredly.

I was always tired now, one of the burdens of this place. It seemed that I was doomed to exist without proper rest or relief from my pains, numerous as they had become. I longed to sleep without nightmares or discomfort, longed to close my eyes and not see visions of agony or torment. I couldn't understand why it was that I was seeing such terrible things.

Isn't death supposed to be peaceful? I had wondered after the first month of this strange existence. *Aren't I supposed to rest in peace with my passed on loved ones? This seems like a place beyond all hope of such simple reprieves as unbroken sleep. Gods... Why can't I sleep?* That same question came to me now as I sat curled up on the bed, my feet tangled in the sheets. *Why can't I sleep?*

There was only one person who could even offer me some kind of an answer. Then again, there was only one other person here with me at all.

I lifted my head and unhooked my arms from my legs, decided on what I would do. Hesitation filled me as I set my feet to the floor, my eyes drifting towards the balcony and closed glass doors. The strange night was shining in through the curtains of sheer white, struggling past the gaps left by the heavy blue and gold velvet drapes. It was like countless stars glowed in chorus when night came here, the day like the whitish light of a stormy sky.

Barefoot, I made my way out into the deserted halls of my ancestral home, taking in the details of the stonework and wooden framing. There were torches lit strategically along certain walls, but no people. That was what I longed for the most. The loneliness was crushing me more than the sleepless nights or the unending pain where my heart had been cleaved during my murder.

For what felt like the millionth time since my arrival, I made my way down the beautiful wood and stone stairs of the main entryway, passing by the great window and the dragon carvings with hardly a glance. They had once been of great fascination to me, but now they seemed plain and uninteresting. Turning to my left, I passed the main doors to the forward courtyards and made my way through the archways to the Great Hall. The room felt oddly warmer now, despite the chill that always seemed to remain in this wintry place, the fires starting to do their jobs.

Once more my eyes fell upon the four thrones that stood at the end of the room, memories of sitting there with my parents and sister returning to haunt me. That was what my memories were now after so long in this empty castle; ghosts that came uninvited to invade on my unwanted solitude.

"Princess?" a voice called softly from behind me.

I turned over my shoulder to where two of the fireplaces were. Mithras was seated in an armchair he had moved by the fire for warmth, a book in his hands.

Funny thing, I never remembered seeing him move that chair into the room, nor did I see him bring in its companion that sat opposite it.

The Knight wore a blue doublet that reached to his knees, the golden dragon of my family's kingdom branded over the left breast. He had a belt at his waist, dark trousers and his boots on, his armour removed for comfort, though he had told me that he no longer craved such things since his passing.

"The hour is late to find you wandering the halls, girl," he observed, closing over his book with a thumb still on the page. "Couldn't sleep?"

"I can almost never sleep," I confessed in a tired voice, moving to stand near the arm of the second chair. "I don't think I'm allowed to have such a luxury."

"You do look tired," he said with sympathy in his dark blue eyes. "Sit down. Rest."

I did so obediently, lying back in the other chair with a soft sigh. I drew my legs up, my knees resting against the other arm. A shiver was running through me that was noticed with ease by my protector.

"You're cold," he stated, setting his book on the small table by his side, then moving to the fire. "Hold on a moment."

He cast two more logs into the hearth and stirred the flames with a steel poker, coaxing some more warmth into the room. Setting the tool back to its rack, he turned to me and crouched beside me for a moment, pulling a blanket of thick fur from behind the chair. He wrapped me in it and rubbed my shoulders.

A fatherly smile appeared sedately on his bearded face: "There. That's better, isn't it?"

I nodded. "Yes. Thank you," as he returned to his seat, I considered the blanket and its sudden appearance from thin air. "I don't understand how you seem to be able to conjure things from nothing. You weren't a mage while you were alive."

He half chuckled, his own tiredness evident, though it was from caring for me rather than from any discomfort or pain. "A trick of these sorts of worlds, my girl," he explained gently, taking his book onto his lap again. "When one has travelled through them enough, as I have, such conjuring becomes child's play. I simply will what I need into existence."

"But only things?" I asked. "Not... not people?"

He raised one thick eyebrow at me. "Yes. Only things. I cannot conjure people in the same way. People are only for Ankorect to craft and mould, not for us to make. Not really."

I nodded and huddled into the blanket, looking down at my knees solemnly.

"Is that what disturbs your sleep?" he questioned me softly, always remaining gentle and compassionate with me.

I sighed glumly. "Many things disturb my sleep, Mithras."

He studied me with a gentle gaze, his eyes seemingly unblinking as he took in the details of my forever young face. He was always so analytical in life, so it was no surprise that he still was in death, but he had seemed more so since my arrival there. Every time I turned around, I saw him watching me, his gaze careful, soft and contemplative, almost like he was seeing something that I couldn't myself.

"What things do you speak of, Princess?" he asked after a brief pause.

I took in a slow breath, staring down at my knees, following the folds of my dress as it held to my legs and waved down to my ankles where the hem bunched from my posture. I could scarcely bring the words to my mind, let alone my lips, my heart pulsing and making the pain shout at me, causing a wince to cross my face. Instinctively, my hand crossed to my breast again, my fingers passing the silken neck of my nightgown to caress my skin. I still felt no mark or wound, nothing to remind me of how I had died. There was only the cleaving pain coming to me like a wave against the shore, sharply striking the sand before washing back in the wake of my breath.

"I have... terrible pain," I confessed in a whimper, my breath hitching as the sharpness invaded my chest with my words. "Ever since I first woke up here it has never left my chest, cutting into me with every breath I draw and every beat of my heart. It is worse at night when I close my eyes and try to take myself away from the world."

"A side effect of your wound," he nodded thoughtfully, but grimly.

"Will it ever stop hurting?" I asked, looking up at him with desperate hopefulness.

"I can only speak from my own experience," he said, setting his palms to the cover of his book. "You recall my injuries, do you not?"

I nodded softly. "Yes. Uncle Fane stabbed you through the shoulder from behind during our escape from Aneuran's basilica."

"And I died from the fever that set in as a result of that wound," he said sternly, his eyes staring up from beneath his thick eyebrows.

"I remember," I murmured, sniffing back a sob as I recalled the night I had watched him die.

"When I awoke in Azmerath's kingdom," he explained, leaning his elbows on the chair's arms and clasping his hands together, "I felt such utter confusion as I had never known. I wandered through unending blizzards and vast mountain paths, lost and without any knowledge of what road to take. It was only when someone I knew came forward on this side of life's energy that I had any inkling of what was happening to me. The pain soon struck me as the knowledge that I was dead came to me, much as it did with you."

"What happened?" I asked, curious and a little afraid to hear the answer as I tilted one knee up and hugged it to my chest.

"I screamed like I never knew I could," he admitted with a sigh. "My shoulder burned with the pain of my wound as it had when it had been freshly made by Fane's traitorous hand, my chest shattering with the coursing of the infection that had ravaged my body and slain me. It was torture beyond all reckoning."

"But you were helped?" I guessed with hope.

He nodded. "Yes. My mother was the one who came to me. She calmed and soothed me, kept me here in this world in a construct of the house I grew up in. I was able to wander Arvon's streets with ease, always looking up towards this castle with the desire to come back here. But I was never permitted to do so."

I frowned. "Why not?"

"This place..." he drew in a slow breath. "It is guarded well, and Lord Azmerath keeps all new souls in a refuge of comfort whilst they heal before allowing them passage to the Beyond. Once my wound had closed and I no longer felt pain, I was permitted to depart the town and cross the bridge to Castle Arvon's gates, signalling my release into the wide expanse of infinity."

I thought about his words, considering what he was telling me. It all made perfect sense, though it was such a strange concept to contemplate at the same time.

"Then... then you don't stay here forever?" I asked with renewed hope.

He shook his head. "No. But I was alone, just as you are now, gifted only my mother as my companion until I was healed."

"So why don't I have my mother?" I turned my gaze to him with desperate longing. "Or my father? Why are they not here with me?"

He shrugged lightly, conjuring a goblet of wine from nowhere and sipping at it. That never ceased to amaze me, though I had tried and couldn't achieve such a thing myself.

"Because I was chosen to be your companion and protector here, just as I was in life," he replied evenly, setting the goblet down.

"But why?" I felt like such a petulant child, hardly grasping the simplest explanations with a longing for the more complicated ones.

"Because I, apparently, am the person you could most connect with after your passing," he responded with calm and ease as always. "It makes sense actually. You and I shared a bond unlike any I had with any other charge I took into my care. In many ways, I cared for you as if you were my own child, and I still do," then he added as if to remind himself of his place: "Princess."

"I am grateful," I said softly and honestly, laying my shoulders back into the chair, wincing as the movement caused my pain to flare for a moment. "I truly am, Mithras. I don't think I could have lasted in this world without someone at my side."

A frown pulled at my brow, and I considered what I had just said. It hadn't occurred to me until that moment that I had lost track of time there just as I had in Castle Ortagaad's prisons.

"How long have I been here?" I asked with a soft confusion in my voice. "I don't remember..."

"This place can do that," he stated with a nod, a careful edge to his words as he met my gaze. "Do not become anxious or upset, Leander. All right?"

"Why would I be upset?" I frowned at him.

"Promise," he insisted.

I nodded. "Yes. I promise."

"You have been here for eleven months," his answer shredded ice through my spine.

My blood ran cold, and my nerves screamed as if they were burning in an inferno, my entire body tensing as the truth hit me as hard as a charging troll. I felt my heart begin to tear more and I gasped, clutching my chest.

"Eleven... eleven months?" I could only rasp those two words out, nothing else drawing from my lips.

Mithras placed his hands to my shoulder as he moved from his seat, meeting my gaze with his. He held that everlasting calm without a flicker of it ever weakening, holding me tightly and yet softly as if to comfort me.

"Calm yourself. Breathe," he urged me.

I nodded, closing my eyes, and drawing in slow breaths. The pain receded, but it didn't pass, coming upon me again with each breath as it always did. I reminded myself that it was a part of me now, that the pain was natural in that place, but I also told myself that it would be all right because it would eventually fade away too. I only needed to wait it out.

"There we are," he whispered as I opened my eyes, smiling softly at me. "You're all right, girl. You're all right."

"I've... I've been here for eleven months?" I asked softly, forcing myself to remain calm.

"You need water," he turned and reached for the table, a cup suddenly appearing in his hand with fresh mountain spring water inside. "Here. Take small sips."

I clutched it in between my hands, sipping at it slowly. It was so cooling, removing the ashy heat that had formed in my throat after hearing those words.

"Better?" he asked softly.

I nodded, lowering the cup from my lips as I looked into his eyes calmly, but firmly: "You didn't answer my question, Mithras."

He sighed and nodded. "Yes. You have been here for eleven months."

I shook my head, looking down at the water in the cup: "My body must be ash on the wind or laying in a grave by now."

"No," he said, standing and moving to the fireplace, staring into the flames. "It remains untouched."

I raised an eyebrow, following him with my eyes. "What do you mean?" I murmured.

"It is your curse," he uttered, still facing the flames. "The one forced upon you by Lord Morod's dark ritual in the depths of Grishk'kinnar's black stone fortress."

I stared wide eyed at him, completely horrified and bewildered by his words.

"How do you know about that?" I gasped out my question, my breath stealing from my lungs. "How could you know? You had died before that happened to me."

He turned back to me, sadness in his eyes.

"Those of us in the spirit world can see all that happens to those we care for in the living world," he said softly. "I know the suffering you have endured, Leander. I have felt your desperate loneliness while you were trapped in that tower, your fear as you ran for your life from Queen Keilantra's soldiers, and the joy when you were reunited with Carden and the others."

Carden...

I felt tears begin to form in my eyes, sniffing a little as I set the cup down on the table. I pulled myself back into the chair, hugging into the blanket. *I miss him more than anything. Oh, how I long to see him and know that he's all right. Carden... my love...*

"I was always with you," the old knight continued gently, moving to my side, "watching over you like I always have. Even in death I uphold my duty as your knight, your protector, your mentor, and your friend. And I always shall."

I closed my eyes as my tears streamed down my cheeks, my heart shuddering in my chest and drawing the pain again. I let sobs escape now as I felt this honest truth. I had never been alone in all the times that I thought I was. I just couldn't see him with me.

"Shh, shh," he moved to my side and pulled me into his arms. "It is all right, child. I know that this is so much for you to understand, so much to be faced with when you are in so fragile a state. But fear not. I will not leave you in this place alone, or to face this challenge without someone by your side. That is why I have stayed with you all this time, and why I still remain."

I lay my head on his chest, sobbing as I let the pain be felt and the tears fall sadly from my cheeks. "Oh, Mithras..." I wept. "I hurt so badly, and I can't find any relief. And... and I miss him... I miss Carden... so much... it's killing me..."

"I know, Leander," he cooed softly, cradling me close to him. "I know."

We sat like this then for some time as he tried to reassure and calm my literally broken heart, neither of us saying another word. There was just a gentle comfort to remaining with him and being in each other's presence in silence. It was a relief to not have to try to come up with something to say to fill the void, both of us content to just be and feel. And in all honesty, that was what I truly needed at that moment.

* * * * *

The cold white of morning's light stirred me from my uneasy sleep, breaking the darkness of my rest and drawing me back to consciousness. I squinted behind my closed eyelids, a soft breath pulling into my lungs with a twinge of sharp pain, then releasing in a gentle murmur of a sigh.

Slowly, my eyes opened, testing themselves against the stream of light that broke past the velvet drapes into my room. I turned my face away, moving to rest on my right. I dragged the covers over me further to guard against the chill in the air. It seemed to never get any warmer where I was in death, always cold and without true heat to chase away the frostiness that clung to my nerves and skin.

Though I turned from the light to linger in the comfort of the shadows of the room, I didn't go back to sleep. My mind was hyper aware, seeming able to awaken in seconds in this existence, whereas it had been slow to return to consciousness before my death. My thoughts were directed towards the night before and my unsettled rest, refusing harshly to give me any kind of a reprieve from what I had felt before Mithras had put me back to bed.

Another sigh escaped my gently parted lips, the sharp pain in my chest causing me to squeeze my eyes shut and whimper. My fingers once again curled into the fabric of my dress as I held my hand to the pain, trying to will it away. It simply didn't leave, easing slightly as I managed to at least focus my mind enough to push past it and endure. It seemed that was all I ever did anymore: endure and exist.

My eyes opened and I stared blankly at the stone floor of my room, allowing myself to wander in my aimless thoughts. That was the problem with existing in that place; never having anything change or even just happen to occupy my attentions. Everything was just so static and without life.

Well... I suppose I can't just lie here all day...

Slowly, I propped myself up in bed, my limbs feeling weak and heavy now. It was likely just the tiredness of my months of restless sleep catching up to me, but it made me feel like an exhausted old woman, not an immortal teenage girl. My breathing became slow and painful as I drew my body up, everything taking that much more effort now. It was as if I had slept a month without moving.

Dragging the covers from my body and setting my feet to the floor, I got up and moved to the bathroom, intent on running myself a bath. Once again, I found myself contemplating Mithras' apparent ability to conjure things from nothing as I manually turned on spigots and heated water from the furnaces in the depths of the castle.

If only Mithras and I are here, then how come the furnaces for the hot water are running? The real Castle Arvon had a boiler staff of strong young men who stoked the fires for the furnaces needed to keep the fires burning. Without them we had no hot water or any other comforts brought to us by their work. In fact, they were the ones who built the fires in the castle's hearths as well, with the exception of the ones in the private rooms. Gods, it's so strange how I never considered such things while I was alive, but now, in this place, all I can do is wonder how things work...

More thoughts like that came to me as I lay back in the bath, gently washing my skin. Even such a basic action as that made me philosophise beyond what I normally would.

If I am dead, then why do I have skin? Why can I feel things as I did in life? Using soap and water... eating and drinking... are any of these things really so important if I am not alive? Then again, if I am dead why do I get hungry and thirsty? Why do I get tired? And where are the people who seem to be providing me everything I need? I mean, it isn't like I go and cook for myself or wash my own clothes here. Someone is obviously taking care of this place. So where are they?

I chewed on my bottom lip, lifting my hand in the bath and letting it hang just above the water. My eyes followed the droplets that fell from my fingertips to clink softly into the body of the water with tiny ripples.

The water never seems to cool here either. It is as if everything is kept so perfectly comfortable to avoid me feeling any kind of suffering at all. So strange...

After my hands had pruned and I simply tired of the infinitely and perfectly warm water, I climbed from the bath and drained it, drying myself off. With a towel wrapped around me and held to my chest by one hand, I returned to my room and considered my closet full of clothes.

All of my clothes are the same colour. They're all a silvery blue now. You'd think Azmerath would at least allow me some cobalt, teal or purple. I actually love those colours. Never mind. It's just for modesty now anyway, not to make a statement.

I randomly selected a gown and soon enough was dressed, tightening the cords at my bodice firmly. I was surprised at how slender I felt, but I knew I had lost weight in life, so it made sense.

Hunger made my stomach groan at me, and I made my way downstairs to the dining room. It was intimidating to walk into the room with its gigantic table and its thirty empty chairs. I had never been used to eating in that room without advisers, servants and guards surrounding me, my father usually at the head of the table. The shock of seeing that room without activity never did lessen.

I moved to the seat I had normally sat in. My eyes fell to the plates left there; a hot breakfast set ready for me with a glass goblet filled with exotic juice. I raised an eyebrow, looking for someone to appear, but I remained alone.

Well... thank you to my phantom chef, then... This never stops being weird.

I took my seat and set the napkin on my lap, picking up the knife and fork in silence as I began to cut the food left for me. This simple morning act felt so sombre and alienated every day I woke up now, lunch and dinner not much better. The loneliness and solitude were too far beyond description that I had finally stopped trying to find the words.

Needing distraction and having finished eating, I went to the library, pushing open the doors and walking towards one of the many large oak bookshelves. I ran my fingers along the spines of the books, seeking out something that would take my mind away from all of these nagging thoughts.

What book would I like to read? How about... A History of Galician Mages? No. No, I want a story, not historical biographies. I moved to another set of cases, scanning the titles with a narrowed gaze as I lightly chewed my bottom lip. *Hm... Let's see. Ah, this one.*

I took a book in a green cover from the shelves, turning it over to look at the title: **Of Roses and Flames**. It was a book I had read many times before; in fact it was the same romantic fiction I had been reading in Eilath before I confessed my heart to Carden that summer day years ago. It was about a handsome young knight who fell in love with a peasant girl in the middle of the war between ancient High-Realm and the Galician Empire, both of them on different sides of the war as he was with the invaders, and she was a local of High-Realm. Such stories always gave me hope that love could conquer anything, including a vicious horde that meant to tear lives apart.

A twinge of sadness touched me as I thought about Carden and I, and of how we had been torn apart from each other. I sighed, wincing as my constant pain became noticeable once again with my intake of deep breath.

I just need to distract myself. To read and forget about what I'm feeling for now.

Moving to a chair, I tried to get comfortable, but just couldn't. My body seemed determined to hurt, so I just had to make do.

I began the story with the turning of the information pages, falling at last to the first of the narrative. My eyes trailed the words swiftly, my mind conjuring the voices of the characters and the sensory details of their world to bring me the distraction I so desperately craved. At least I still had this one pleasure out of all the others I had now lost.

Three or four hours passed, and I never once moved from my seat by the fireplace, engrossed in the book. I had read about the knight's and peasant girl's first meeting, and I was now going into the part about their decision to run from their respective responsibilities. *It's so romantic how he's willing to abandon his nation's crusade to be with and protect the girl he loves*, I thought with a tiny smile.

My fingers flicked to the next page, feeling the inked words as my eyes took them in and read them in my thoughts, the scene I was on heightening. Then, a frown drew across my face. The words suddenly didn't make sense, becoming jumbled and misshapen, almost as if the printer had failed to keep the ink from running on the page.

That's strange. I must have read this copy a hundred times and it was never like that...

I flicked ahead, every page after a mess of squiggles and runes that made no coherent sense.

"What in the Void?" I wondered aloud.

My hands worked quickly, turning back to the front of the book to find that the words on those pages had changed now too. The sentences had somehow become corrupted.

"What's happening?" I whispered, staring at the altered pages with apprehension.

I have to find Mithras...

I pulled myself from my seat and started searching for him. I didn't have to go far, but I did have to go outside. He was pacing the battlements of the training courtyard, the same one that sat beside the castle's main courtyard and the gardens.

"Mithras," I called up to him as he reached the stairs into the courtyard, his silvery blue cloak swirling around him in the breeze.

"Good afternoon, Leander," he greeted me as he started down the stone steps, then frowned. "You look perturbed, girl. Is something wrong?"

"This book," I said as he reached the bottom of the steps, opening the pages in my hands and showing it to him. "I was reading it and the words suddenly turned into incomprehensible scribbles."

He raised one thick eyebrow curiously. "Did they indeed? Odd."

I nodded, handing him the book and wrapping my arms around my midriff. I was anxious and fearful of what such a thing could mean.

Mithras studied the pages with a detailed and careful eye, turning them slowly and analysing each one in turn. He then looked at the cover and glanced to me.

"It seems fine to me," he said.

I frowned. "Really?" I moved to his side and looked down at the page, shaking my head. "It's still squiggles and marks. There aren't any words."

Mithras looked perplexed, turning the cover and studying it. "Read the title."

I turned my eyes to the image on the cover and the title, ready to simply state it straight out, but I couldn't. The title looked as incomprehensible as the pages in the book.

"I... I can't. It's changed too," I murmured, frowning as I stepped back, keeping my arms folded.

"Do you remember the title?" he asked me with a suspicious tone to his voice.

"Yes, it's... it's..." I suddenly realised that the title had left me all together.

"You can't remember it. Can you?" he perceived.

I shook my head. "Why can't I remember it? What's happening to me?"

He sighed, closing the book, and turning to stare at me, searching my features as if he were looking for some answer to the cause of my abrupt amnesia. I was beginning to get frightened, trying so hard to remember the name of the book in his hands, but I just couldn't.

But I knew it only a few moments ago... Why can't I remember it?

"This shouldn't be happening," he considered, handing me the book, then turning from me as he began to pace. "You shouldn't lose your memories in this place."

"Wait! Lose my memories?!" I asked in anxious shock. "You mean I can do that here?! You never said that could happen!"

"Don't panic, Leander," he urged me calmly.

"Mithras, what's happening to me?!" I frantically pleaded, feeling like I could start to cry from the sheer stress of all of this.

He sighed, turning to face me again. "You are beginning to suffer memory loss. It is usually something those of us in spirit form experience in this place if we have not passed to the Beyond after a few hundred years in the mortal world."

"Are you saying that I've been here for hundreds of years?!" my panic only grew, my head beginning to swim as if I were close to passing out. "Is that what you meant when you told me time passes differently here to the mortal world?!"

"No," he shook his head, folding his arms in front of him. "Remember that when you first came here you felt as if you had been wandering the castle for hours, but I told you that it had been only minutes in the mortal world since you had left your body?"

I strained as I tried to recall, tears forming in my eyes as I shook my head. My chest was heaving, and I was feeling my panic rise again.

"No. No, I... I can't remember," I whimpered, close to sobbing.

He grasped my shoulders, looking me in the eyes sternly. "Concentrate, girl," he urged me firmly, his voice hard. "Focus on the memory of your arrival. Find that discussion. It is important."

I nodded, trying to steady my panicking breaths as my tears ran heavily down my cheeks. I forced my focus to that conversation, finding that there was a haze over it that didn't belong. I could see Mithras sitting with me as he met me that first day, calming me and explaining about the difference in time between the two worlds. My heart started racing and spiked with horrible stabbing pain relentlessly as I did.

"Got it?" he asked me urgently.

I nodded my head feverishly. "Uh-huh..."

"Good," he was relieved, but focused on his new task. "Time is different here than it is in the living mortal world. For us it moves much swifter than it does there. Eleven months have passed for you since your arrival, but to our companions who yet live it has been only a matter of weeks since you died. In order for you to be suffering such memory loss as you are beginning to, a hundred or more years must have passed on the *living* side of the veil, not on this side."

"If... if this is happening to me," I tried to speak calmly, though it truly was a challenge, "and it isn't what is meant to happen, then what's causing it?"

He shook his head, studying me as he tried to figure out the answer. "Have you been having any other issues since arriving here?" he asked. "Disturbing images, feelings of lethargy, a comfort in the dark that doesn't seem natural?"

I nodded, my chest still hitching with my painful breaths as I clutched at the pain in my sternum. It felt as if the Shadow Lord's knife was plunging through the bone into my heart and lung all over again.

"I've had horrible nightmares almost every night where I see people suffering and daemonic dragons laying waste to everything in sight," I confessed, trembling, tears still bleeding from my eyes. "I... I feel tired almost every second of the day and I don't want to get up or do anything, just let myself lay in the dark. I don't even open the drapes in my room most mornings now."

His eyes darkened and his mouth curled into a cold grimace as I spoke, his fingers tightening on my shoulders and upper arms with each word uttered. I knew that look on his face too well, having seen it every time something terrible was happening.

"You are being drained," he murmured in stunned and furious shock. "No... No, it can't be... It couldn't be feeding from you."

"What?" I asked fearfully, my voice little more than a whisper. "Mithras, what are you talking about? What's draining me?"

He sighed and took me by my arm forcefully, dragging me towards the main courtyard with the flow of our silvery ethereal clothes. He had never been so hostile and aggressive with me before, even when I was alive and in danger. This was something new and dark, his demeanour more like one of my captors in the fortress tower of Ortagaad rather than that of my protector.

"Mithras! Stop!" I grabbed at his hand with my other, dropping the book to the ground. "Stop it! You're... you're hurting me!"

He didn't relent, pushing his way past the archway and into the main courtyard at the foot of the keep's front doors. He led me towards the portcullis gates that opened onto the bridge from the castle and into Arvon itself.

"Mithras! Please!" I begged frantically, struggling and tugging against his steel hard grasp. "You're scaring me! Please, stop!"

His eyes widened and he slowed his pace, stopping at last, but it wasn't because of my desperate pleading. His sights were set beyond the portcullis gates, his jaw dropping and the colour draining from his face as he saw what he had obviously feared.

"No..." he gasped in his low, growling voice. "No, it can't be reaching out. Not now. It's too soon."

I hadn't fully registered his apprehension yet, still struggling against his hard grasp on my arm, but his words drew my attention. I gasped, feeling my eyes go wide as I saw what stared back at us from the other side of the smaller courtyard and the two portcullis gates before us.

On the far side of the bridge where it reached from the town side cliff to join with the castle, there stood a floating abyss. It looked like a rupture in the fabric of reality, warping and ripping more as it seemed to shriek this unholy howl into the air. Tendrils of pure darkness were beckoning across the bridge, grasping at the stones as what I can only describe as tar seemed to soak the ground beneath its gaping maw. The black ooze acted as if it were alive, squirming as it touched the stones of the bridge, moving forward slightly as if crawling towards the castle gates.

"Oh my gods!" I gasped, grabbing onto Mithras' wrist as fear clutched me tight. "What is that?!"

"The Void," he murmured grimly.

For a moment I could only stare up at him, his words sounding like some horrible impossibility. I tried to speak, but I couldn't make the words come out, fear tightening and ripping that same horrible pain through my chest as my heart sped up with my dread.

"What?" that was the only word I could hoarsely gasp out.

"That portal on the other side of the castle's bridge," he explained darkly, "is the gateway to the Void, the dark realms of the Daemon Gods. There in the twisted, hated darkness lies the most horrible and evil daemonic entities of existence, the landscape of their realm fuelled by fear and sorrow, and crafted by truly terrible nightmares. That... is where the Darkest Shadow resides..."

Even though the pain of my racing, panicked heart was beyond unbearable, I couldn't bring myself to calm down. The knowledge that I was looking into the deepest circles of the Void itself was far beyond my comprehension. Terror was no longer a fleeting thing but a constant reality. I could only stare with wide, frightened eyes as tears rushed down my cheeks and my sights remained locked on the howling, hungry gate into darkness that was begging to be fed before me.

Mithras went on slowly, dread in every word he uttered: "To be taken into the Void is to suffer eternal torment beyond the basic cruel nature of the physical tortures the living are capable of. That is a place where sleep does not come, where pain is constant and beyond agonising, and where all your fears are made flesh before your eyes. The daemonic beings grasp at the flesh of living souls who fall into that gapping maw, rending it from ethereal bones and devouring it as their victims yet live in insurmountable suffering, only to be healed and mutilated anew. And the Daemon Gods watch on from black thrones of broken bone and shattered souls, hungering for yet more suffering and visiting every torment they can devise upon their hapless victims."

I was trembling even harder, blinking tears from my eyes as I clung tighter to him, turning my gaze up to his hardened face. He was really scaring me now, but not as much as the impulse I was feeling. Despite my utter fear at all he was telling me and everything I knew myself of that evil place, I felt the urge to walk towards the portal, to surrender myself. That in itself was terrifying.

"This place is supposed to hold it back," he growled, staring with hard eyes still upon the breach floating on the path as if it were an arch built on the road to Arvon. "It isn't meant to allow it in so soon after a new soul has entered following death."

"You... you keep saying "this place" when talking about where we are," I observed, trembling, "but you never tell me anything about it. Where are we? If that... if that is the Void, then what is *this* place?"

He sighed, keeping his eyes ahead of him as he answered me. "The Netherworlds."

I stared at him blankly, my fear only growing.

"The Netherworlds?" I repeated in a small, hushed voice. "You mean... this... this is where Morod was trapped by my ancestor? This is where he was before he used me to become flesh and blood again?"

My panic was deafening, and I wanted to scream, but I couldn't. Instead, I dropped to my knees and pressed my arms to the ground. I felt myself starting to cry heavily, my heaving chest ripping as if it were being torn apart again.

"Leander," Mithras crouched beside me, placing his hands to my shoulders. "Leander, it's all right."

"How can it be all right?!" I half screamed, looking up at him as I braced my hands against the cold stone ground. "I'm trapped in the Netherworlds, just as Morod had intended to do to my ancestor! I'm stuck here and that... that... *thing*," I indicted the Void's portal with a jab of my hand before placing my palm back to the stone, "is draining me! It's feeding off me and I feel it trying to pull me in! It wants to swallow me up and make me suffer forever while I scream in pain! Tell me, Mithras, how is it all right?! How?!"

I closed my eyes and sobbed loudly, as hysterical then at the thought of eternal damnation as I had been when I was chained to that altar facing my murder. It just wasn't fair that I had already suffered so much and was now about to be dragged into the hellish dark where the Daemon Gods would make me suffer every physical, mental and emotional torture and violation that existed.

"Leander! Leander!" Mithras shouted, holding me firmly and having to lift me roughly in order to make me look into his eyes. "Leander, listen to me! I will *not* let it take you! Do you understand me, girl?! I *won't!*"

I could only cry, so frightened that I couldn't even begin to form words anymore.

Mithras stood and looked to the sky, drawing his sword and aiming it to the clouds. He was determined and angry now.

"Lord Azmerath!" he bellowed in a powerful voice unlike any I had ever heard him use. "Hear me! Help me protect this girl from the Void! Prevent it from invading this place of healing and safeguard her now!"

The clouds suddenly began to gather above us and turn dark, golden light shining amongst them. Then, with the cracking of stone and thunder, golden lightning struck from the sky and hit the stone courtyard.

Startled, I watched on as towering figures appeared, their massive bodies clad in luminescent golden armour that seemed to have been forged from light. They had enormous wings like those of great white and gold eagles, their faces hidden under enormous helms where only darkness seemed visible. They lifted their heads, their eyes glowing a powerful blue as they turned their gazes towards the portcullis gates, their gauntleted hands clenching around swords, shields and halberds of incredible otherworldly design.

I gasped, holding myself tightly, pulling back to sit as the nine-foot-tall beings stomped with heavily armoured feet and flowing cloaks of white gold light. There was a dozen of them, stepping out of the lightning and turning their attentions towards the Void gate as it hungrily howled and reached for me. Two of the great winged knights strode through the gates, passing through the bars as if they weren't even there, their sights set on the black abyss. They stood at the first arch of the castle, crossing their halberds between them, and stretching their glowing wings as they barred the way to the keep. Another two did the same at the second gate near where I sat, growling these strange, booming snarls.

"M-Mithras?" I murmured fearfully as the rest took up guarding positions all around me, lightning strikes hitting other parts of the castle as more of them arrived.

"Do not be afraid, Leander," he urged me, lowering his sword as he watched the behemoths. "They are the Angelics, the sentinels of Azmerath's realm. He has heard my call to arms and now they stand ready to defend you."

I was shaking, my tears still flowing as I looked at the Angelics in awe. They were enormous, making me feel like a small child in comparison to their gigantic forms. Just standing next to a guard tower they seemed like they would be able to easily climb it without need of a ladder. They were beautiful and terrifying all at once, but they also brought a sense of safety that relieved my painful fear.

Mithras stooped and took my arm, helping me back to my feet as the Angelics secured the castle, a glowing dome beginning to surround the grounds and glimmer in the sky above us.

"Come, girl," he pulled me to his side, supporting me as he led me away from the gates. "Let us get back into the keep. The Angelics will keep the Void from entering the castle, but you must stay within to prevent it reaching you so easily."

I was trembling, sniffing against my sobs as he took me up the steps and through the main doors, two great Angelics flanking them with their weapons at the ready.

"It will be all right," Mithras promised me, bracing me a little tighter as I felt my legs weaken. "I promise you, Leander."

I nodded and let him lead me into the keep, holding onto him as I took one final look at the gigantic Angelics now guarding my home.

Chapter Twelve
Waning Hope

~ Carden ~

I was too shaken up to go back to sleep, my mind racing with the images of what I had seen. No matter how hard I tried to close my eyes and rest I just couldn't, seeing her twisted and distorted form before me again each time. After another hour of trying to rest with no success, I dragged my body from the bed, clothed myself and left the room. I didn't bother with more than my trousers, boots and a shirt, though the air seemed to have gotten colder. Of course, the clouds blocking out the sun would account for the change in temperature.

The Lord's manor-house was quiet, almost everyone sleeping at this late hour. The heavier darkness outside told me that it had to be some time after midnight, the shadows deepening all around and making the world a blacker place. It was certainly unnerving. The only other people walking about at that time were the guards, each of them at their post or patrolling the halls with torches in some hopeful attempt to push back the dark. I could only think of how futile such acts were now that the light was gone. Now that *she* was gone.

There was only one place for me to go, all my thoughts and intents anxiously set on reaching it quickly.

The corridor appeared as I turned the corner, the doors at the other end seeming so far all of a sudden. It was like I was battling to fight my way towards the chapel, struggling down an unending hall that never got any shorter, but that was just my perception. Soon enough I was placing my broad hands to the wood grain and shoving against it gently, the door opening with a slightly rusted groan.

The chapel looked so cold, lit only with candles that seemed hardly able to illuminate even the space around their wicks, let alone hold back the darkness. It was wrong for her to lay in such a shadowy and silent place. She should have been comfortable and somewhere warm with light all around her. She deserved that at the very least.

Passing the benches, I came to the altar, my heart anxious as I yearned to see her face and be sure that I had only suffered a terrible dream. Relief filled me as I beheld her pale, beautiful, rounded features, her dark hair like a veil around her white face and neck.

My eyes flicked to her chest, taking in the small mounds beneath the pearl white of her dress, studying them for the slightest of movements. Nothing. They remained still; her chest as motionless as stone. I tried to listen for her heart, but the new medicine had done its job. My heightened senses were fading back bit by bit to human levels. At least I didn't have to worry about my predator trying to claw his way loose again for a while, but I wanted to hear the beating of her life in her chest.

A gentle hand to her slender, cold wrist produced nothing, the faint thumping of her pulse quiet and her flesh without that rhythmic flex all people have.

I turned my attention back to her closed eyes, still holding her right hand with mine as my left began to stroke her hair.

"It was just a dream," I murmured as I looked down at her, so glad to see her looking as if she were just sleeping. "I can't tell you how glad I am that it wasn't real, Leander. I couldn't stand seeing you so broken."

I sighed and let my eyes fall shut for a moment, just feeling her skin. It was a comfort to have her so untouched and without the decay of my dream. I began to miss her even more, once again yearning to dull my pain and grief with drink, and hopefully slip into unconsciousness. At least that way I wouldn't have to suffer the dreams.

As I knelt beside her, I began to recall what she had said to me in the nightmare, her accusing dead eyes haunting me. She blamed me for my failure to save her, saw that it was my fault that she was dead. She was right of course. Were it that I had simply chosen to stay my feet a little longer, to hold my position and observe, then I would have seen the truth and known her to be as chaste and devoted as she always was.

Never mind watching her prove herself. I should have acted, should have strode forward and dragged that lout, Tristan, away from her and defended her honour. That is what a man should do for the woman he loves. That's what I should have done... No wonder she thinks I failed her. Truly... I have... I shook my head, resting my arms on the altar and staring down at the fur covered stone aimlessly. *She deserves better than what I offered. I will not falter again. Not now. I will find the answer.*

After a few more moments I stood, leaning over her and looking into her silent features one more time. My palm stroked her hair as I felt tears trying to build in my green eyes once again.

"Rest, my love. I *will* find the answer to restoring you," I promised her.

Slowly, I leaned down, pressing my lips to hers with closed eyes. They were so cold and without the touch of her sweetly scented breath. Another moment of longing for her to live passed and I felt a tear slip free to touch her skin. As I withdrew from her, I saw that single bud of salt water on her left cheekbone just beneath her eye. I gently and carefully brushed it away with my thumb. For just one moment I pretended that it was hers, if only to gain the sense that she was living again. But the moment soon passed, and I softly adjusted her hair and clothes, trying to make her a little neater.

My eyes flicked to her sternum, the ugly red and black wound in her chest glimpsed beneath her white dress' neckline. It made me cringe every time I saw it and I sucked in a sharp breath, purposely locking my eyes on her face for the last time that night.

"Goodnight, Leander," I whispered, squeezing her hand one more time.

* * * * *

Days had passed in an endless, countless tide, but never had I brought up that first night in Fawkner's manor to anyone. It seemed that the burden of that deeply intimate and disturbing dream should never be shared. I was only glad that it didn't return to me again. I couldn't even begin to stomach the thought of seeing her like that, even if it was just a fabrication of my tortured, grieving mind.

The atmosphere of the city had grown ever more tense, the people trying to live their lives, but to do so under the shadows of the great storms seemed nearly impossible. It was becoming clearer and clearer that we were facing the end times, over two months now since the sun or the moons had been seen by the world. Two months since Leander had been murdered. Though the world seemed to be ending all around me, I couldn't stop thinking that mine already had the day Safferan sank beneath the waves.

I had spent half of my time with her in the chapel, watching over her with Joran at my back. The two of us hardly spoke, but there was no need. After all, what was there to be said between the Storvari and I while we sat in our constant vigil of that beautiful, deceased girl?

Needing air, I had left the room and made for the battlements of the city. That was where I witnessed the despair of the civilians as the guards were trying to keep order. It seemed now that people were growing increasingly ill from the fouled air and the wilting crops.

How long can we go on? I wondered as I watched an armed patrol of guards escorting a large shipment of crops through the gates. *Without the sun and the rains there is no life being given to the farmers' crops. How long until there is no longer food enough to support the kingdoms and riots begin? Is this what Morod has held back his armies for? Does he mean to starve all resistance from us so that when he strikes, we will be too feeble and malnourished to stop him? Gods... we have to bring Leander back. We have to. The people of High-Realm need her... I need her...*

The situation was only worsening as I made my way from the walls, a new force of men approaching behind the caravans. It was another column of Lorveren soldiers, their green cloaks swirling behind them, their scale armour clanking as they walked. By my count there had to be some two hundred arriving at Eilath's gates; women, children, elderly and wounded amongst them.

I walked the cobblestone streets, passing by the citizens as I went with a black cloak that lacked all Guardian markings around me. My eyes took in all the sights before me with a heavy heart. People were beginning to get sick, the elderly and children suffering the worst. No longer did I see children playing in the streets without worry or care, nor hear their laughter. No longer did people greet each other with smiles or speak of happy things. It was like the blackened sky had choked all the humanity from them. In fact, the sky had grown so dark that torches were lit all around the streets permanently and the lanterns were consuming more oil than could be produced.

Yet another supply to soon run dry. If this continues, we will not have any resources left.

I resolved to seek out the others, if only to silence my unending dark thoughts for a time with conversation; I knew where I would find most of them. I climbed the stone steps up to the Lord's Manor and made my way across the courtyard to the Great Hall. Here I found King Haral in deep discussions with his advisers and those of the city. It seemed the King never left the large room, always pouring over battle strategies and field reports. What little I managed to overhear seemed to suggest that things were not going well and that there were yet more attacks on Lorveren's lands. I was just waiting to hear the first reports of the Scourge and the Undead Legions making themselves known, though so far there had been nothing.

Why does Morod wait to unleash his forces when he must surely know he could simply eradicate us all with ease? Why does he wait?

I passed through that room and entered the hall to the wing the library was in. I removed my cloak from my shoulders, unbuckling the clasp as I walked, my eyes pausing on the doors to the chapel. I felt drawn to return to Leander's side, to once again sit with her and lose myself in her silent, dead company.

No... I... I can't sit in there now. If we are to find a way to free her from Death's icy grasp, then I cannot dwell by her deathbed; I must seek out the answers. As I tore myself away from that door I began wondering about the Witch in the cells. *Has she resolved herself to giving us the answers we seek yet? She's been down there for weeks now in the dark. Surely she cannot enjoy being imprisoned. Especially when her freedom is gained by simply speaking the answers we need. She is a strange woman, this Danika of the Wilds...*

The doors to the library remained open, two guards always stationed here, just as there always seemed to be at every door now. Fawkner had especially commanded that sentries be placed at both the library and the chapel a few days earlier. He, like all of us, had grown concerned that we might end up with a repeat of the invasion on the manor like that which occurred nearly three years earlier at the hands of the Revenant.

Not all of my companions were within, only a few. Ranzel was certainly present. The white-haired Wizard was sitting at the large table in the centre of the room with books piled high and lamps burning all around him in an effort to illuminate the shadows away from his sights. He hardly looked to have slept, appearing to be within this room almost every waking hour. Truly, I had not seen him present at any meal in more than a week.

Dolin and Holger were there as well, both dwarves assisting the Wizard in his tireless search. They were scouring the shelves they could reach for the books he needed, leaving the higher ones to either him or Tristan.

I locked my eyes on the Wanderer with quiet disdain as he was directed from the table to gather a few scrolls that he then brought to the Wizard. He staggered away once he had to sit by the fire as Holger did the same, both of them taking to their flasks.

I wish he would leave. That he would go "wander" someplace away from here and away from her. That traitorous bastard has no place amongst us. And see how he takes to the drink as if it is he who lost his most beloved. I suppose guilt can destroy a man, but I can't say that I know anyone more deserving. Brushing the thoughts of hatred from my mind, I walked to where Dolin and Ranzel worked.

"Is there anything?" the Dwarf was asking the Wizard, stroking his black beard in thought as he stared at the passages of ancient runes in the scroll the latter was studying. "Anything at all that can tell us what we need to know?"

Ranzel sighed and shook his head, sitting back in the chair and picking up his clay pipe as he did. "No. Nothing. Nothing at all."

"A shame," Dolin shook his head, taking his own pipe from the table, both men filling them with tobacco and lighting them.

"I take it the search continues to be fruitless?" I asked as I tossed my cloak onto a chair, folding my arms in front of my chest as I locked my green gaze on them.

Ranzel huffed a few breaths and released smoke from the pipe, nodding grimly.

"Maddeningly so," he replied with a sigh. "I had hoped that the writings of Naxxremis would have some detail about such things, but apparently I was wrong."

"Naxxremis?" I frowned. "Enlighten me?"

"The sorcerer, Dunadel Naxxremis of the Blackfelds," Ranzel replied gravely, gesturing to the ancient scroll before him. "He wrote many works on the subject of blood magic and necromancy, including restoring a deceased person with their soul and life force intact."

"The Blackfelds?" I recalled the name, studying the strange runes on the page. "That's to the far east, isn't it? Set along the border with Gorvenna and Vorhalaas?"

Ranzel nodded his confirmation, still puffing at his pipe. "Yes. It also borders the south-eastern ridges of the Black Peaks that surround Gorth'lak."

"That's Dark Elf territory," Dolin stated gruffly, taking a seat. "We Dwarves may not always get along with the High Elves and the Wood Elves, but at least they are willing to speak with us. Dark Elves are not so civil, though they do seem hauntingly beautiful to behold."

"The Blackfelds is not only home to the Dark Elves," Ranzel pointed out. "It is the origin place of all Elven Kind and home of the Three Elven Kingdoms."

"I always thought the name Dark Elf was ironic," I confessed, having met several in my time. "They hardly seem dark with their luminous skin and white hair. Were it not for their red eyes I might not think them to be so sinister."

"Like all races of Therras, the Dark Elves are not so evil, just less of them tend to be as their High Elven and Woodland cousins are," Ranzel stated knowledgably. "Dunadel Naxxremis, however, was not one I would consider to be of the fairer alignment."

"He was a necromancer," I said simply. "I can't imagine that anyone of that magical vocation is of the Light."

"He was also a very powerful Blood Mage," Ranzel added, his expression dark. "His experiments were notorious and wicked to say the least. Countless men and women of all races suffered horrific ends at his hands. Truly, there are none who so easily rival the darkness of the Shadow Lords as the Blood Sorcerer of the Blackfelds."

I half snorted and half laughed nervously, feeling my expression become incredulous. "And you sought to find the answer to bringing Leander back in this man's writings?"

"Naxxremis was the foremost researcher of the dark arts and the crafts of resurrection in all of Therras," Ranzel justified calmly, setting his pipe down as he began to study another Blackfelds scroll. "In truth, all Mages are taught about him and his methods, as he wrote about the processes of such nefarious magicks, but also warned against their misuse."

"Sounds like a bit of an undecided fellow," Dolin commented, crossing his arms as he smoked. "It is as if he chose to ally himself with both the dark and the light."

"I said that I would not consider him to be one who was of the fairer alignment," the Wizard clarified, glancing to the Dwarf, "not that he was truly evil. He did not have the want for destruction and death that many of his nature do, but neither was he against such things. I speak of his power rather than his capacity for evil."

"So, you think this Elven Blood Sorcerer might hold the knowledge to revive Leander?" I turned back to the subject at hand, though I did appreciate the academics of the discussion.

He sighed tiredly, reviewing the page again. "I had hoped so, though I am afraid that the Caradoc Library simply doesn't possess a complete record of Naxxremis' writings on the subject."

"Isn't there some other way to get what we need?" I asked.

Ranzel shook his head. "Unfortunately, I am not so well versed in such matters, just as the others of the Elemental Brotherhood are not. We are agents of Goddess Maveria, not worshippers of Azmerath and his Kingdom of the Dead. We are custodians of life and all the physical and magical world of this plain, not of the Beyond, the Netherworlds, the Void and the Nightmare Holds. Truthfully, the only most creditable authority on such things is Dunadel Naxxremis. The only other I know of who would have any inkling into his research within our immediate reach is Danika."

I frowned. "Wait. Danika studied his research?"

"Danika and both her sisters were once students of Naxxremis in centuries past," the old man explained, his voice making it clear that he didn't fully approve.

"But I thought you said all mages learn his teachings," Dolin pointed out.

Ranzel nodded. "In a sense. Mages are taught of his warnings to magic and of his more affirming techniques such as protections against the darker arts. Seldom do any seek out his methods for necromancy and blood magic. However, the Sisters of Raven's Rest did in their youth. Only Danika chose to remain upon Naxxremis' path of neutrality, guarding his teachings closely as a means of knowledge rather than practice. Manth and Keilantra, however, turned his arts towards those of the Shadow Lords' and embraced the teachings of Gorth Lavelle in a darker and more sinister combination."

He locked his hazel eyes on me, his stare becoming as hard as iron and his expression deeply serious. He leaned forward a little, though he didn't really move, his focus and presence drawing me firmly into his words.

"You have experienced this wicked melding of teachings yourself, Carden," he went on grimly. "You felt it in Castle Ortagaad when Tallinn, the Princess and you were imprisoned there on the first day. When Keilantra placed her hand to your heart."

I was stunned, grasping at my chest with one hand and letting the other drop to my side. "How do you...?" I trailed off.

"I sense it upon you," he replied, then glanced to Tristan and Holger. "Just as I sense it upon Tristan. You know the story of this forlorn wanderer, yes?"

I grimaced, glaring at the once again drunken man who was starting to drift as he stared into the fire. Had a sword or knife been on me at that moment I might have been tempted to slay him, but I stayed my hand. Nothing would have made me more satisfied than to cast him out into the world, yet I knew that to do so would upset her.

Leander was always more forgiving than me. Perhaps too forgiving...

I nodded in answer to the Wizard: "Yes. Leander did tell me of the curse which Keilantra inflicts on men. It is a truly dark and terrible fate."

"Most terrible indeed," Ranzel agreed.

I turned my gaze from Tristan and back to the old man, studying the papers before him. I couldn't discern the Dark Elven writings on the scroll, managing to make out only a few words that were similar to the other dialects of the Elven race.

"Considering how dark they are, how can the practices of this sorcerer hold the key to undoing what was done?" I couldn't say the words themselves of what had happened, already having spoken them far too often of late.

"I am uncertain, excepting that such knowledge was Naxxremis' focus. Yet, as I said, the library's documents are incomplete," Ranzel was becoming frustrated, rubbing his eyes as he rolled up the scroll and set it aside. "I am afraid that I have exhausted all such materials that describe one's soul being returned to the living world, and it is not a condition I have ever heard of before."

"What? Her condition?" I needed him to clarify.

He nodded. "Yes. Never in all my centuries of living have I encountered such a state as the one the Princess is now in. That she is without decay or rigor mortis is baffling in itself, but to know that there is an etheric tether keeping her soul bound to her body is unfathomable. I can see why the others were unwilling to put their faith in such a task being completed."

"You are not doubting your own conviction that such a thing can be done? Are you, good Wizard?" Dolin enquired with concern in his dark eyes.

Ranzel sighed. "I am unsure of where to turn for the answers," he patted the two bound scrolls he had bid me to take from Silvervale that now lay on the table beside him. "Even once more referring to the Prophecy Scrolls has yielded no more clues as to the method of her revival."

"So," Holger staggered over, bracing himself against a chair as he looked like he would collapse, "where does that leave us then?" he hiccupped.

"Unless Danika gives up her knowledge of such things or tells us what she has seen through her foresights," Ranzel shook his head grimly, folding his arms as he returned to smoking his pipe, "I am afraid that we have fewer options than are presently offered to us."

"I would consider us past such offers," a voice stated in the Lorveren man's usual calm, but gruff fashion.

I looked over my shoulder as the Wizard and the Dwarves turned their gaze to the open doors of the library. Fawkner and Tallinn were striding in, neither one of them looking particularly encouraging. Tallinn stopped on the opposite side of the table to me, her blonde hair left untied, her arms and neckline bared under her more basic clothing. She had that same tiredness all of us had, not one of us seeming capable of resting well.

Fawkner halted at the end of the table, placing his hands to its top with a sigh. His expression was grim, which left me only with a deep unease and intense anxiety rising within my chest once more.

"What makes you say such, my Lord Fawkner?" Ranzel questioned evenly.

"Tallinn and I have just come back from the jails," Fawkner explained tiredly, turning his pale eyes to each of us in turn. "Even after the many days that she has languished in that dark cell, the Witch refuses to answer us regarding our task."

"What *did* she say?" I wondered aloud, glancing between the two curiously and darkly at the same time.

Tallinn shrugged and sighed loudly, almost painfully. "She has simply repeated the same cryptic response as she ever has about admitting the truth that we keep from ourselves. That our cause is selfish. Then she simply clams up again."

"Though not before laying thin insults upon us," Fawkner shook his head, amused by the concept, but not smiling. "Never have I met a woman so maddening in all my days. It is as if she enjoys hoarding the knowledge she possesses. As if making us beg for it is amusing to her."

"She is a Witch of Raven's Rest," Dolin pointed out calmly, finishing with his pipe. "Even if she were willing to gift us the information, we could not be certain that it is the truth."

"Oh, it's truth all right," Tristan spoke up, his voice slurred.

We all looked to him, though I had to suppress my irritation at hearing him speak. His voice was like having a cheese grater go through my ears.

He went on, still staring into the fire: "She speaks only truth, which is why she is so devious. It was that which scared the Princess so deeply when we encountered her in the Forests of Arnath. If she says that she has the answers, then she truly does. The only way to get them is to give her what she wants."

"How can such a thing be done?" Tallinn demanded, bewildered by such a concept. "She doesn't simply want us to say that our intentions are selfish, but to understand that they are too."

"Which means we cannot attempt to deceive her," Dolin nodded thoughtfully. "A real dilemma."

"A test," Ranzel stated with a shake of his head. "I had thought she would have grown past such games. It appears that I was wrong."

"Unless we figure out the answer to her riddle and play her game," Fawkner said, frustration and hopelessness hinging his voice, "we are left with no means to achieve what we have set out to do."

"Then what do we do?" Tallinn looked to him, desperation in her hazel eyes, her normally cool and collected manner now broken, though only mildly. "We can't leave the world as it is. The sky is dark, and the sun is gone. A famine is beginning to plague the world and pestilence wreaks havoc upon the people. We *must* end this blight or else we will all perish."

"Our only option may be to travel to the Blackfelds then," Ranzel advised us, though he didn't sound too convinced. "If we cannot find the path ourselves through libraries or through Danika, then we will have to seek out the one person who would know such things."

"Dunadel Naxxremis?" I questioned dubiously. "You want to ask him for help?"

"He has been missing for a century," the Wizard replied, stroking his beard in thought. "Our only option would be to seek out his sanctum and his original tomes written on the subject."

"Travelling to the Blackfelds will take too long," I griped, becoming agitated. "Those lands lie on the far eastern side of High-Realm between Harredi in the south and Grotojan in the north. Even if we were to embark on such a journey, we couldn't hope to find the answer before the Shadow Lord strikes amidst this apocalypse. It's a fool's errand."

"Perhaps so, but it is all that remains to us," the Wizard countered.

I groaned and turned away, shaking my head. I didn't want to keep waiting to make a move, my desperation to bring Leander back driving through me relentlessly.

"We have little choice, Carden," Fawkner stated, agreeing with Ranzel. "We need answers if we are to even hope to quell this threat, and this seems to be one of the last remaining options beyond deciphering the Witch's meaning. We are running out of time and out of hope."

"I can see that plainly, Fawkner," I snapped quietly, squeezing my arms as I folded them again. "This whole damned situation is becoming more and more hopeless by the moment," I started to walk away.

"Where are you going?" Tallinn called.

"To speak with Ellora," I replied without pausing. "Perhaps she may have some understanding on the Witch's words."

"I'll accompany you," Fawkner said, looking to the others as I paused to wait for him by the door. "Keep at it."

Ranzel nodded, going back to his work as Fawkner followed me, the two of us stepping out into the corridors.

We were silent as we came from the library, passing back through the main hall of the house and making for the eastern porch. As soon as we exited the doors my eyes fell upon the large sycamore that stood upon the highest part of the grounds overlooking the training yard. I immediately recalled that day when I was honing my skills, exercising against straw mannequins with my sword and knives. I had glanced to that tree to see Leander sitting beneath it. She wore blue, her dark hair pulled back with a simple tie, a story of romance held in her hands. She had looked so beautiful and at peace, the quietness of such a life of ease as that which we lived in those months suiting her.

The way the sun hit her hair and painted gold amongst the brown and reds of her locks made her seem so angelic. She was beyond beautiful, the fairest woman I have ever laid eyes on. Gods, how deeply I miss her.

She was not there now, Amethyst resting under the tree without her human companion. The Dragon looked so different, drawn and tired, her violet and mauve scales seeming paler, if that were at all possible, and the flames of her orange eyes dulled with sadness. That was where we saw Ellora, the red-haired Elf sitting with the younger dragon as Gaspeite stood over them. They were obviously trying to comfort Amethyst.

"I know that you suffer," Fawkner commented as we paused at the undercover porch from the keep, "that you are ever more anxious to restore her. But you must find the balance to endure and hold your focus, Carden."

"I have focus," I responded coldly, watching the Dragons under the tree, "and I endure every day with a heavy heart, but I endure."

"You seek answers and a means to take action. As do we all," he spoke softly, his own grief clear. "Yet, you allow your pain to influence you and for impatience to grow well in your mind."

"I cannot sit by and do nothing," I grumbled, leaning my hands on the barrier of the porch and turning my eyes to the grounds below. "Not while she lies dead in that chapel, cold and alone..."

"That is why we must make our plans," Fawkner reasoned.

"The Blackfelds are leagues from here," I remarked grimly, never turning from my blank stare, "set on the far side of the continent. To seek out this blood sorcerer's writings is not practical. We can't be sure that the rest of the world will be here once we're done, nor that we will survive such a journey with the threats that now plague High-Realm. Besides, we can't be certain that the sorcerer's sanctum even contains the knowledge we seek. It could be all for naught."

"Perhaps," Fawkner agreed with a sigh, setting his own gaze to the gardens below, his arms folded on the rails. "Yet, we must do something to obtain the knowledge to save High-Realm, even at the cost of our own lives. It is our duty as Guardians, after all."

"Yours and Tallinn's duty. No longer mine," I stated in a mild growl, turning my gaze to my hands where they rested on the barrier.

"You are still a Guardian, Carden," he said, looking to me.

"Are you going to debate this with me as Tallinn does?" I asked.

"No," he shook his head. "You have renounced your oath to the Order and so too you no longer carry the crest of the Guardians. I am not intent on questioning your decision. However, you *are* still a Guardian, though now your pledge lies with Leander rather than High-Realm and all of Therras."

"Then... you understand?" I looked to him, meeting his gaze.

He nodded softly, sadness in his eyes. "Just as I know the grief you feel for her, though mine is more for a daughter than a lover."

He shook his head, looking back to the gardens. I followed his gaze to see Lady Erika with their two children. Freda had to be about eight winters by now, her hair longer and her body grown greater in height than when last I saw her. She was sitting with her mother as her younger brother wandered before them, a boy of only three or four now.

"I know what it is to love someone so deeply that to lose them causes all sense to leave one's mind," Fawkner went on, tears in his eyes as he looked upon his wife and children. "Losing Leander was like enduring the death of my eldest daughter, Brie, once more."

"Your daughter?" I frowned, never knowing he'd had one other than Freda.

"She was Leander's age," he expressed sadly, "and just as wilful. She died of a wasting disease conjured by Lord Morod after he slew my elder son when I first refused to kidnap Leander for him," he shook his head, regret on his face. "I did a terrible thing to protect Freda and Bran, to save them from their elder siblings' fates. But now, with all that plagues the world, I must face the inevitable knowledge that my family *will* die. And I am powerless unless I find the method to undo what the Shadow Lord has done to that innocent girl. It is the only way to save them."

"My family is dead," I said, understanding his worry, drawing his curious gaze.

"Your parents?" he asked.

I shook my head. "No. My family lies in the chapel of this manor house with her soul trapped somewhere. She was the one, the *only* one who I ever gained such true love from, and who I pledged such perfect love to."

I turned my gaze to the Lorveren Lord's family, feeling my eyes grow wet with tears again. I pulled in a shaking breath, my muscles tensing as I accepted that I would have to face the inevitable myself.

"I can never have what you have, Fawkner," I confessed, my voice shaking as my tears slipped free, though I didn't weep. "A family like the one you have was never really possible for me, not with my... *condition*. But it might have been when I met Leander. Then Morod stole a piece of her humanness and cost us both the joy of parenthood. If she had confessed this to me sooner, I would simply have accepted it for what it is, but she did so in her death gasps as she bled out in my arms."

My eyes took in the family one more time before turning to Fawkner again, my sights noting the figure moving to join us from the sycamore at that moment. I could see on the man's face that he felt great sorrow for me, though I wasn't sure that I deserved it.

"I lost all the family that mattered to me at Safferan," I told him sadly, managing not to cry. "If there is any chance of getting her back, then I wish to take it. If only to make a new effort, even if I fail. But the more we discuss what to do and the farther we must travel to gain the knowledge to simply make a plan of action, the swifter we run out of time."

"Indeed," Ellora spoke as she joined us, hearing the last of our conversation, her sage cloak wrapped around her and her hood back from her head. "Our time truly grows short as we now face this quickly waning hope in the wake of the Apocalypse."

"Ellora," I turned to her. "We were just coming to find you."

"As I was coming to find you," she sighed, crossing her arms before her moderate chest, her turquoise eyes full of sadness and concern. "Are we any closer to making our next move?"

Fawkner shook his head. "Not really. Our only options seem to be to travel to the Blackfelds in search of such knowledge as will aid us, or to unravel the Witch's cryptic demands."

"One completely impractical option and another frustratingly convoluted one," she sighed. "It seems that our choices are becoming fiercely limited."

"Do you have any inkling on what Danika's words mean?" I asked of her, leaning my back against the railing. "Any at all?"

She shook her head, brushing her red hair from her eyes with one delicate hand. "No. None. I cannot fathom how preventing the deaths of all the peoples of the world can be a selfish endeavour. This Witch is surely stalling. Perhaps she thinks that we will end her if we discover that she does not have the knowledge we seek."

"Not something that we would do," Fawkner stated with certainty. "We are not barbarous villains plotting a woman's demise simply because she lacks the information we need."

"Then we can only hope that she has spoken truthfully about holding such knowledge and that we can discern her riddle before our time runs out," Ellora said with finality. "As it is, we are already growing short on such a precious commodity."

"What do you mean?" I frowned, curious and concerned.

Ellora looked past me, Fawkner and I following her gaze to where the two dragons were still resting under the sycamore tree. "Amethyst's grief has grown too heavy for her to bear any longer," she explained sadly. "With the Pendant dark and the Princess dead, she has no purpose any longer."

I watched as the young dragon dragged herself to her feet, her expression forlorn and her head bowed as she padded from the tree. Gaspeite was talking to her in their tongue as she moved, the larger green dragon following her.

"What are they saying?" Fawkner asked, glancing to Ellora.

Ellora translated: "Gaspeite is trying to convince her to stay, but Amethyst says that she has made up her mind. She intends to go into the mountains to grieve the Princess and wait for death to claim her too."

"What?!" I exclaimed. "No! We have to stop her! We need her in this!"

Ellora placed a hand to my shoulder, meeting my gaze sadly. She shook her head as I tensed, her expression telling me more than her words ever could.

"There is no stopping her," she said softly. "A dragon bound to a Dragon Pendant cannot exist without their counterpart. It is a soul bond that destroys both when one dies, making the other suffer without them. I witnessed this with the Princess' ancestor when her dragon, Daroc, was slain in battle against Lord Morod's dragon, Cathal. The Queen never did recover from losing him, nor will Amethyst from losing the Princess. We shall not see her again once she leaves."

I nodded, turning back to the gardens as I heard the gusting beat of dragon wings.

Amethyst lifted into the air after a small running start, her wings flapping powerfully as she carried herself upon the gale winds tearing over Eilath. She left Gaspeite standing there to watch her retreat to the north, the Nartarn'lath Mountains' darkened visage against the black sky her obvious destination.

"Perhaps this is a sign," Fawkner grumbled, concern and hopelessness filling him. "Perhaps our last hope has now faded in the dark of this Armageddon and we can do nothing more than prepare ourselves for the end."

"Not a comforting thought," Ellora responded gravely.

"No. Indeed not," Fawkner agreed solemnly.

My eyes remained on Amethyst until the Dragon was no more than a spec in the far distance, my heart yearning to do as she did. My companions were right. The waning hope that we'd had until now was swiftly running out...

Chapter Thirteen
Confessions Made and Answers Given

I n the days since Amethyst had left Eilath the hope of the city faded quickly. If a dragon would no longer stay, then the people didn't seem convinced that there would be salvation in the coming times ahead. Most of them began to confine themselves to their homes, waiting for the end of their lives to come upon them while others took to the city's temple to pray to Azmerath for painless deaths. I suppose it was something we all yearned for, dying without suffering. Others still took to the taverns, for obvious reasons.

The discussions about the Blackfelds continued for a while, but not for too long. It was clear that the risk was too great without a guarantee of success, which left us right back where we had started, though the writings of Naxxremis had yet to be dismissed or abandoned. It was beginning to feel as if there was no way to achieve our goals and that Leander would remain dead.

I had elected to pass on having my evening meal, instead retiring to my rooms to dwell on my thoughts and on the fate that ultimately lay before me. Without the answers we needed there would be no surviving the blight that pillaged our lands, spreading from High-Realm's borders to the rest of Therras and across the world.

There's no way to bring back Leander... My mind had soured with that thought as I plied the bottle of ale to my lips where I sat in the chair by the desk, the sharp-tasting liquid burning its way down my throat. To anyone who said that drinking would dull the pain, I could only say that they were wrong. It didn't dull it, just caused a greater burn that distracted from it and let my mind wander briefly from grief.

A deep breath filled me as I withdrew the bottle, ceasing the tide of ale that had all but drowned my mouth, a sigh returning as payment to the air. I was disillusioned now more than I had been in Silvervale when first she had been laid in the temple by the Elves.

My mind kept fantasising about her opening her eyes and returning to me. I imagined her sitting up in a daze, looking around the cold chapel as a shiver touched her slender but curvy frame, fear in her eyes. She would call for me, bewildered as she sat upon that altar, her body weak from disuse, and I would come to her. I would pull my beloved girl into my arms and cradle her as she wept in relief to be alive again, my own tears mixing with hers as I promised never to leave her again. It would be a bliss in itself, but it was the how that left me scratching my head.

Getting to that moment is the hard part, I thought, staring at my hand curled around the bottle as I set its glass bottom to the table. *There must be a way that doesn't involve us travelling an inordinate number of leagues just to gain the information to do so. Ellora was right. We're running out of time. Especially with all that is happening in the world.*

I brought the bottle to my lips again, swilling down another mouthful of sharply spiced alcohol. I drew in another hissing breath through my teeth, the burn of the liquor making my whole body tense just a little. I set the bottle down and lay back in the chair, my hands in my lap as I studied the lit candles before me. The flames on the wicks danced as if they were courting each other, their glow seeming to brighten then dim, only to illuminate a little more again.

Answers must be found, but the means are beyond us. If the Blackfelds did hold such knowledge as what we seek, we would need more time to act on our designs than would be given to us if we traversed High-Realm to receive such answers. But, if someone else could discover the secrets on our behalf, someone closer who possesses the right contacts...

My mind was suddenly alert as I came to a conclusion that I hadn't before. I had lived a life before this one that made me many contacts in Gorvenna, some of whom would be too happy to gather what we needed. For a price, of course.

I took a quill and a piece of parchment from the desk, decided on writing to the one person who I knew could help. As I dipped the pen and set writing to the page, I could only hope that my letter would be received by him alone and not by an agent or our enemy.

Varel, my friend and mentor.

I trust you are doing well and still living in Nargilith. As I am sure you know, the world is in peril and the Guardians are all but eradicated. Things are growing worse than I could ever have imagined. The girl I told you of in my last letter is dead and my heart is heavy with her loss. To add to this, I have also renounced my pledge as a Guardian because of this loss, yet I remain with my companions, determined to somehow help in this fight. And also, to grieve her.

I am not merely writing to you because of my care for you as a son for a father, but also to ask for your help. You have contacts within the Guild that may be able to recover certain documents that one of my companions seeks. He searches for the complete works of the Elven Blood Sorcerer, Dunadel Naxxremis, specifically the volumes relating to all methods of bringing a person back from the dead without them becoming a lost soul, a draugar or a shambling zombie.

I know I ask for a lot, Varel, but I truly need this knowledge to save a young girl from eternal damnation, and to rescue High-Realm from the doom that we now find ourselves facing. Leander is the only one who can fulfil the prophecy that ends this blight, and to do that she must first be resurrected from Azmerath's realm. In addition, any news on the Shadow Lord and the wicked Queen Keilantra would also be useful, as would my old armour. Please send it all to Eilath in the usual ways. Secrecy is more important now than ever before. I will owe you a hundred sovereigns for this and shall give them to you when next I am in your city.

My thanks, my friend.

Carden Highever

I set the quill down and waved my hand across the page, encouraging the ink to dry before taking the letter in my fingers and running my eyes along the scrawling text. I read the words over and over, ensuring that they were correct before folding the page and sealing it with candle wax.

With any luck it will reach him before things grow any worse.

Donning my hood and cloak, I took the letter and left the Lord's house, the guards hardly batting an eyelash at my passing. It wouldn't take long for me to complete my task, knowing who to approach after my last visit to Eilath. I had taken a tour of the city when we had first arrived there after fleeing Aldegaad, though I had done so without telling Leander. She might not have understood, and it was better that she didn't know what I was doing, but I need to be prepared. Besides, I always sought out the Guild's messengers when first I entered a city I meant to stay in for any length of time. I had done the same thing in Arvon as well. It was just a habit Varel had taught me since I was young.

The tavern was where I found the messenger, a man in a black hood and leather armour over black and grey clothes, his face hidden in the shadows of his cowl. Fortunately, I had already met him several times before and knew him to be trustworthy.

We traded some mild banter, though only enough for courtesy sake, then I gave him my instructions, handed him the note and paid him thirty sovereigns, my pockets always fairly well stocked since I had joined the Guardians. If nothing else, I could ensure with my gold that the messenger would remain reliable, though the mention of who the letter was for made sure it would be delivered.

I went to the bar then and had a drink, waiting for the messenger to depart. Once he had and I finished my drink, I left, stepping back into Eilath's streets. Only minutes later I was back inside the Lord's house and retiring to my room, undressing and laying down to sleep.

Maybe now we will get somewhere...

I closed my eyes and allowed myself to disappear from the world, the drink weighing on me enough that I could at least avoid my dreams. Or so I thought.

Once again, I felt that I was not alone, opening my eyes and half expecting to have her in bed with me as before, but this time she wasn't. Leander stood by the window, dressed in a gown of sheer silvery blue. She had tears on her cheeks, her soft voice sobbing as if she meant not to wake me.

"Leander?" I frowned, sitting up in bed.

She looked over her shoulder at me, startled by my call to her. "Carden... ugh..." she immediately started to wipe her tears from her eyes.

I stood from the bed and moved to her, placing my hands on her bare arms with all the gentleness I had in me. I could feel her sadness, though it was strange to see her standing there at all.

"Don't..." she whispered, turning her face down as I tried to look at her. "I don't want you to see me cry."

"I've seen you cry before," I told her softly, trying to be reassuring. "There is nothing to be ashamed of, my beautiful girl."

"I'm... I'm not ashamed," she murmured, keeping her eyes down as she rubbed her arms with her hands, crossing her forearms in front of her.

"Then what's wrong?" I probed softly.

She looked up at me, her eyes so full of fear and hurt, but also longing and love. They were tinged with the waters of her sadness, her thin lips parting just a little as she drew in her breath, which seemed pained.

"I'm afraid," she confessed softly.

"Of what?" I frowned.

She placed her hands to my bare chest, studying her fingers as they traced the shapes of my pectorals. Her touch was so gentle, and I felt my yearning for her grow as my desire began to call forward that familiar hardening. I tried to suppress it, simply looking deep into her eyes with all the understanding and love that I had.

"Leander?" I tilted her chin with two fingers, making her meet my gaze. "Please, tell me, my beautiful girl. What are you afraid of?"

She was trembling, her lips quivering as more tears slipped from her eyes. "Being damned," she murmured. "Even now the Void reaches for me, trying to drag me into it. But I want to be with you, to have you hold me in your arms... to... to feel you intimately."

"But you're dead," I was aware enough this time, knowing that what stood before me was not her. "This is only a dream..."

She shrugged. "Then, for now be with me in this dream, and when you wake, please... please save me."

She was almost crying as she said those last three words, the desperate pain so clear in her soft, alto voice. There was no way that this wasn't Leander. The version of her that had haunted me in the other dream was so much more aggressive and experienced sexually, but also accusing and sinister in her way. This girl before me was much more like the innocent one I knew so well.

I nodded and pulled her to my chest, holding her tight. She felt so warm to my touch, her body against mine a comfort I so desperately longed to have again.

"I *will* save you, Leander," I told her gently. "I promise. I'm searching for the way even now, as are the others."

"You're the one who can save me," she murmured, looking up at me as she pulled back just enough to see my face. "I love you."

"I love you too," I murmured, stroking her hair.

She reached up and gently kissed me, her arms encircling my shoulders as she did so. It was passion, but uncertain just as it should have been with her, yet neither of us resisted as we gave in.

"I will keep you safe," I whispered as I kissed her, working my way down her chin and jaw. "I will protect you."

"I know," she replied in breathy gasps.

Cloth tore as I tugged her free of her dress' collar, kissing my way down her neck. She let out a soft moan of pleasure as I caressed her throat with my lips, pulling her closer as I gripped her tight. Then, she cried out and I felt myself losing all control, her hands bracing against my strong, muscular upper arms.

"Carden... s-stop!" she gasped.

I couldn't, my hunger for her relentless as sweet ruby droplets stained her snow-white flesh. The girl whimpered, closing her eyes as she lost all of her remaining strength.

"Carden... C-Carden..." she whimpered out my name as I lay her back in my arms. "Please..."

I drew my face back, breathing in a deep gust of air as I tasted her sweetness on my lips. This was beyond ecstasy, my yearning for her only intensifying. My gaze flicked down to her and I felt myself snarl as she looked up at me with wide, terrified eyes.

I struck again, biting deep as she screamed...

A scream of my own woke me from the nightmare and I sat up in bed, trembling. I felt my predator rising again, my focus pushing to its limits to hold him back down. But after a few moments I had succeeded and was left to my distress.

I looked around the darkened room, hoping to see nothing until a glancing gaze caught sight of her standing by the window with a black hood over her head, her eyes an unnatural green. That was a shock that caused me to immediately light a lamp and spread the flame's glow through the room. My eyes flashed back to that corner, but there was nothing there, no figure at all, only bare walls and an empty space by the window.

Bewildered from my nightmare and confounded from seeing her standing there one minute, then not in another, I set the lamp on the bedside table and lay back, trying to settle myself down.

Relax. It's just another nightmare. Nothing more. Somehow though I couldn't really convince myself of such a statement.

* * * * *

More countless days with no clear sign of measurement passed, the skies only seeming darker now as the clouds of supernatural shadow thickened. The city was growing ever more tense, and the guards were struggling to maintain their own calm, let alone that of the people. It wouldn't be long before revolts began, and riots flooded the streets.

All eyes were upon the Hall of the Plains and the leaders of the nation within, the people expectant that they would come up with some solution that would save them from this doom. A lot was now riding on the shoulders of King Haral and Lord Fawkner, the two men having been in conference for hours as I stood upon the balcony looking out over the city.

Once again, there had been a flood of refugees as new attacks raged across Lorveren, this time reports of Scourge forces coming to us. I knew it wouldn't be long before they appeared, and so they had. We were almost out of time.

I waited for some sign of a messenger from Nargilith, hopeful that the man who had raised me from a child had found some means to assist. So far there was nothing and I was growing fearful.

I hope the message reached him. If it fell into the hands of Lord Morod or any of his allies it could stop us. I sighed, looking down at my hand as I knuckled the rail of the balcony. *Nearly nine weeks have passed since we arrived at Eilath and still we have discovered nothing to bring Leander back, nor have we discerned any other means to battle Ragnarok and Morod. Surely there must be something to be done.* It was maddening and I had only one desire left to me. I wanted to be with her.

"Carden?" the familiar voice of my friend and ex-sister Guardian drew me from my silent musing as she approached from the doorway.

Tallinn had grown haggard, her lack of fitful sleep as clear around her eyes as her fleecy yellow hair that flicked in the wind around her shoulders. She looked harder now too, like she had endured a horrific amount of suffering that changed her. It was her tireless duties that had done that, the young woman having spent *every* waking moment coordinating with the city's guardsmen on protecting the citizens.

Always a Guardian no matter her grief. Aldwyn would be proud.

"Are you alright?" she asked, coming to my side, both our cloaks swirling around us in the chilled wind. "You look exhausted."

"You should say so of yourself," I pointed out, blinking against the strands of black hair that flicked over my eyes.

She half laughed and half grimaced, leaning her arms on the rails. "I find that sleep eludes me. My mind is awash with concerns for the safety of the city, as well as the task we've yet to even embark upon."

"As does mine," I confessed, turning my green gaze back to the storms. "I doubt any of us have slept well since the sky grew dark."

"Very true," she nodded, glancing to me as she brushed her blonde locks from her eyes. "I... I have heard you at night, Carden."

I raised an eyebrow as I turned my gaze to her. "What have you heard?" I asked guardedly.

"Your cries of anguish," she admitted with a slight shrug, still leaning her arms on the rail, "your murmurs of grief, the moans as you sleep."

I sighed and turned from her, watching as crimson lightning flashed across the sky to hit somewhere in the distance. The strikes were growing more frequent, almost as if the storms were building to something greater.

"You can tell me anything," Tallinn urged me softly.

"My sleep is broken by horrific nightmares," I confessed quietly, shaking my head as my gaze drifted towards the gardens below us.

"What sorts of nightmares?" she questioned with the raising of one slender, sharp eyebrow.

"About Leander," I hesitated, feeling myself tensing already. "They are... often lustful and terrifying."

I couldn't believe I was telling Tallinn this, that I was speaking of my nightmares aloud. I had sworn to myself that I would lock them away from the sights of my companions, never to reveal them again. But Tallinn was always the one I could talk to, always the one who could draw a secret from my lips. It was just in our bond and always had been.

"Lustful?" she asked with a deepening frown. "Do you mean...?"

I sighed in aggravation and exhaustion, turning to face her. "They were sexual, yes."

She didn't speak, nor did she judge, simply nodding her head in response to my words. Her unquestioning acceptance of such things was one of her better qualities.

I went on: "The first I had the night you gave me the new medicine for my affliction. I had thought I was still awake, but I wasn't. I... I found myself laying with her, both of us... naked and in the throes of our passionate embrace. But when I realised that I was dreaming and I pushed her from me, she became... insistent."

"Insistent?" she asked.

I nodded, glancing at her. "Touching vulgarly... Speaking in a way unlike her... It wasn't her and I could see that. When I turned from her, she grasped my arm and drew me back to her. I saw a vision of a living draugar before me, Leander yet not Leander. She pulled her desiccated heart from her chest and crushed it into powder as she accused me of letting her die..."

"Oh, gods. Carden," Tallinn was touching my arm then, sympathy in her eyes. "It sounds horrific."

"It was only the first," I confessed, turning my eyes to the mountains in the distance to keep myself from breaking. I needed the focus to go on: "Since that night I have had many dreams, some as pale and faint as mists, others as vivid and real as you are standing beside me now. For the last week or more I have endured one where she begs me to save her, sobbing as she stands by a window."

Images flashed through my mind, and I closed my eyes. I felt my tears trying to break through the barriers of my eyelids to wet my cheeks, fighting to hold them back and not cry like I wanted to.

"I took her in my arms," I explained in a shaky, snarling voice, "held her to my chest, told her I loved her... then I ripped her throat out with my teeth."

Out of the corner of my eye I could see Tallinn's expression twist into one of shock and mild horror. I didn't blame her. She knew the danger that lurked inside me, sensed the violence and hunger that dwelled in my heart. I was dangerous, a monster of fairy tales and legends. Now, with Aldwyn gone, the truth of what I was lay only with her.

"These dreams," she was careful as she spoke, choosing her words with caution, "are just dreams. They are the grief and guilt you feel over the Princess' death, something I'm sure we all feel..."

"I enjoyed it," I whispered, feeling both disgusted and invigorated by the image of the girl's blood on my hands and across her neck. "It was... euphoric, like the bliss that comes from deep, unbridled sexual climax."

"Euphoric?" she staggered a little. "Carden... have you had your medicine?"

I nodded, turning to her fully. "Yes. Yesterday. That is what scares me, Tallinn."

She nodded, though she didn't speak, her eyes showing her own fear at my words as I turned away to gaze back at the darkened fields.

"I wonder if it is the darkness that pervades the world," I mused grimly, studying the shadows that made the land seem as if it were drenched in night while it was day. "Do you think it could be affecting me, making me more prone to my predator?"

"I'm not sure," she admitted uneasily. "Do you feel such desires now?"

I shook my head. "No. I have only felt it in those dreams, and each time I wake in terror. I... I don't want to hurt her. Gods..." I nearly sobbed as I tensed and closed my eyes again, the image of Leander standing in the shadows of my room invading my mind, "I must be going insane. I keep seeing her everywhere I look."

"It is grief," Tallinn reasoned, drawing nearer to me again now that she was certain that I was no danger, "compounded by the frustration that you surely feel."

"Frustration?" I looked to her curiously.

She nodded knowingly. "I have known you for many years, lived with you as if you were my brother, not merely a fellow Guardian. I know that you are frustrated that we have not taken any action to bring her back to the living world. I can see it so plainly."

"Frustrated doesn't cover how I feel," I replied with more harshness than I had intended. "Leander still lays dead in the chapel of this house while we have spent nearly three months trying to discern a means to restoring her. Our efforts are now spread between a tight-lipped witch who withholds the answer and the works of an Elven Blood Sorcerer that we lack access to. And in order to stop the violent apocalypse that plagues all of High-Realm we have to obtain the knowledge of at least *one* of these two sources so as to resurrect her. Meanwhile, we are no closer to any more answers than we were the day Morod murdered her."

It felt good to say all of that aloud, to actually articulate it properly rather than just simply letting small bursts out at any given time. I drew in a slower breath, feeling relieved.

"We've made some progress on the task of obtaining the Dark Elf's writings at least," Tallinn informed me. "King Haral sent word to the capital and was able to locate one of Naxxremis' books. Ranzel was reading through it when I left him."

"Was he hopeful?" I asked coldly.

She sighed and shook her head. "Since it was an abridged edition, he didn't think it would have all that he wanted. But it might at least allow him to glean some means to survive all of this."

I half snorted, shaking my head. "Survive all of this? To be honest, Tallinn, with all the havoc, destruction, war, death, pestilence and famine Ragnarok has unleashed on Therras, I'm not so certain that surviving is enough anymore."

"I believe you may be right," she agreed, leaning forward on the barrier again, her golden hair catching in the breeze.

We were silent then, neither of us moving even as guards patrolled past us, and the increasing winds whipped our hair and clothes. I had no thoughts in my mind, my whole body numb as I stood there trying to come up with something that could make all of this seem better. Sadly, the truth was that there was nothing.

How can the world seem better when the one thing that ever made my life feel right is lying dead?

Tallinn smirked suddenly, then chuckled softly, drawing my gaze as she kept her eyes forward to the gardens below.

"What is it?" I asked.

"I was just recalling something Aldwyn said when we were beginning our training with him," she said, smiling as she giggled a little. "Remember when he talked about survival, and I said that it wasn't always enough to simply survive?"

I nodded, recalling the day when we were training at the Citadel. Aldwyn had been preparing us for a five day stay in the woods with minimal supplies meant to teach us the skills to survive, which Tallinn was, of course, the best at already.

"I remember," I said.

"He said to us: Tallinn, Carden, you must understand the very nature of survival before you can truly master it," she repeated the words that our old mentor had told us that day. "Survival by its definition is a discomforting and coarse state that no one yearns to exist in. Life is not meant to be a struggle to survive, but survival breeds a will to live when there otherwise isn't the likelihood of doing so. It is the fight to live, not merely exist, and it demonstrates the selfishness of human beings in one of the better lights that the more self-serving natures can be seen in."

"Wise words from a wise man," I said, then considered them. "Wait..."

Tallinn's smile faded as she looked to me, her eyebrow raising again. "What is it?"

"Selfishness," I tested the word, my mind clicking together all the pieces of the puzzle that had been plaguing me for months. "The Witch said that she would only tell us what we wanted to know when we admitted our selfishness."

"Yes, which is absurd because she wanted us to confess that our intentions relating to such answers are selfish, which they aren't," she reminded me.

I didn't argue, knowing that I couldn't stand to wait any longer to draw out this answer. I had finally grasped it and knew what I needed to do.

"We need to get Fawkner now," I told her, moving swiftly for the door.

"What?" Tallinn rushed after me, her face plastered with confusion. "Why?"

"I've figured it out!" I said with a hint of excitement and a lot of urgency. "I know what the Witch's riddle means!"

* * * * *

The Witch was silent, sitting cross-legged in a meditative stance as she perched on her cot, her eyes shut and her expression peaceful.

I moved to the bars, stopping there suddenly as I tried to calm my racing heart and restrain my excitement at having figured it all out. "I know what it is that you meant when you spoke of our selfishness," I told her, watching her through the bars.

Danika opened her eyes as Fawkner and Tallinn joined me, the two still looking perplexed since I hadn't yet confessed my revelation.

"Do you now?" the Witch asked with a cold smirk, glancing at me without turning her head.

I nodded. "You said that our intentions are selfish, that this is the truth we hide from ourselves. Our intention is to end Lord Morod's blight upon the land and save all of High-Realm."

"Wait, I don't understand," Fawkner was frowning, deeply puzzled. "How is preventing an apocalypse selfish?"

"Because," I watched the woman as I spoke, seeing her react to my words with calm and quiet pleasure, "saving the world means saving ourselves."

Tallinn gasped and nodded, half smiling at me. "Survival is self-serving, yet not evil. I understand."

"Yes," I exchanged a glance with her before turning back to Danika. "We act selfishly because though our intentions are noble it means that our own lives do not end."

Danika smiled victoriously, getting to her feet with a swish of her black and red robes, her eyes burning with delight. She strode to the bars, pausing a couple feet from them as she met my gaze.

"Yes, very good," she prided us. "That is precisely what I wanted you to understand. Though as Guardians you intend to stop a dark and sinister evil from destroying all those innocents who dwell within the world, you also save yourselves and your way of life by doing so."

"Because no one wants their way of life to end," Tallinn perceived, nodding her understanding as she folded her arms before her.

"And so, your intentions are both noble, yet selfish, just as I had said," Danika was pleased, smiling at us. "I had faith that you would discern my meaning."

Relief flooded me and I felt as if I could scream joy to the heavens as I almost wept with a newfound ease. The confession had been made and the riddle solved, the barrier to what we sought now removed.

We can do it! We can finally save her!

"Then you'll give us the answers we need," I assumed.

"No. Not just yet," she turned her eyes to me, my joy instantly crushed as my expression fell.

"Why not?" I frowned. "We answered your riddle and confessed what you wanted us to. We understand your meaning..."

"Not *all* of it," she said cryptically, her eyes locked squarely on me. "While the vast majority of your companions serve this intention purely, you, Carden son of Tiernan, do not."

"Yes, I do," I was baffled by her words. "I serve it as much as any other member of our company. And I admit that I selfishly wish to survive this."

"But that is not your primary reason for embarking on such a quest as the one that lies before you," the Witch went on, folding her arms before her and studying me with her penetrating gaze. "Your true intention is born of that which cripples you; the one emotion that should uplift, according to the bards, yet can be more devastating than any weapon forged by men."

"You speak of love," Fawkner discerned as I felt utterly confounded by her words. "That is what you mean."

"You feel it too, Lord Fawkner," Danika flicked her eyes to him. "And while love certainly plays a part in this for you with the wife and children you seek to defend, your intent remains the survival of all the world as well as yourself and of your family," she turned her fiery emerald gaze back to me. "But you, Carden, are not holding the same intention."

"You're saying that love is selfish," I scowled, trying to keep my calm. "There is *nothing* selfish about love. It is the most noble of emotions."

"Is it indeed?" she questioned me, beginning to pace slowly. "The bards certainly paint love in such a bright pink light, do they not? They sing frequently about the bliss and nobility of love, but what of the darker side of it?"

"What darker side?" Tallinn asked, seeming just as puzzled as I was.

"The pain," Danika pointed out, "the misery, the heartache, the yearning and the desire to have love. People clutch at it as if it is a possession, longing to hold it within their hands as if it is some tangible thing," her eyes locked on me, and she came straight to the bars. "And when the one person who invokes that most powerfully from your heart dies and departs from this world, you reach and claw to hold onto it, wishing and begging to keep them close so as not to feel love's absence."

"Love is selfish," I murmured as understanding struck me.

Danika nodded, withdrawing from the bars to get a better look at my whole face. "Yet, it is noble. Love truly *is* the most powerful of emotions, for it is the only one that is vague in its extremity, yet extreme in its vagueness. So, it is both noble and selfish."

I looked down at my feet, my hands clutching the bars of the cell as if I were the one trapped behind them. I felt like a fool, suddenly knowing that all the pain and frustration that I had felt over trying to get the answers to save Leander were in fact the means to do so.

"Do you understand now, Carden *Highever*?" she spoke my last name obviously.

She knows the truth about everything else. It isn't a surprise that she knows the truth about my name.

I drew in a slow breath and nodded. "Yes. I understand," I hesitated just a little, steeling myself for my confession as if it would be my last and my worst.

"While the others seek the answers you have in order to save all of Therras from the Shadow Lord's reign of terror, I seek them to restore Leander to life."

"And *why* do you seek to do that?" she asked simply, already knowing the answer and obviously just wanting to make me say it.

I sighed, letting my gaze stay on the floor, shame filling me: "Because she is part of a prophecy and part of the means to save High-Realm."

"And the truth?" she urged.

I knew I was trying to forestall, but I couldn't any longer, tears slipping from my eyes as I looked to her and confessed: "Because I love her and I miss her. Because... because I let her die and I just want her back."

Danika smiled softly, nodding her head as she was finally satisfied with my answer.

I pleaded softly as I sniffed back the sobs that I had tried to keep from spilling out in front of everyone for so long: "Please, Danika? Will you help us bring her back and save High-Realm? Will you tell us what we need to know? Please?"

The Witch reached out her hand to me, touching my rough cheek with her soft palm, her thumb wiping a tear from my face. She held a sympathy that I had never imagined could exist in her eyes, the strange woman of the wilds seeming gentle now.

"We all forestall when faced with something we do not wish to endure," she told me softly. "That is the only reason I refused your request before, but no longer. I will help you in this quest."

I nodded and met her gaze. "Thank you. Truly."

She smiled and gave me a single nod before stepping back, looking to the others. "I will aid you willingly now and offer my foresights, though I would prefer to remain neutral. However, we all must do what we would sooner avoid."

Fawkner turned to the soldiers at the end of the hallway. "Guards. Release the prisoner."

As the guard unlocked the door, Tallinn drew me aside and looked up at me, wiping tears from my cheeks with her thumbs. Her sisterly concern was comforting.

"Are you alright?" she asked me softly.

I nodded. "Yes. It... it needed to be said."

"It did," she agreed. "There is no shame in it."

"It is why I can no longer be a Guardian," I said softly and honestly.

"I see that now," she sighed and nodded. "It is no longer your path."

The guard left us as Danika stepped from her cell, Tallinn and I turning to her as she stretched with a loud groan.

"Oh, it feels good to be free of that cell," she expressed gladly, lowering her arms from their outward stretch. "Though I am accustomed to dank and cold stone rooms, I prefer to know I can leave them at any time I so wish."

"Provided that you are in earnest about your willingness to aid us," Fawkner told her, his hands clasped behind his back, "I will return your effects to you, and you will be free to walk the house and city at your leisure."

"And once your task is complete and your goals achieved, will I be permitted to return to my sanctum?" she questioned him coldly.

Fawkner nodded. "Of course."

"Very well," Danika nodded, turning on her heel and heading for the door up to the house. "Let us gather your companions then. Your confessions have been made and so, as promised, my answers will be given."

Chapter Fourteen
The Quest for the Doorway

It didn't take us long to gather the others, minus Joran of course, though considering the proximity of the chapel to the library he could probably hear us. Ranzel was still within the library studying the tome King Haral's men had managed to procure for him when we arrived, his expression one of quiet expectation as he laid eyes on the Witch.

"Ah, Danika," he offered her a gentle smile, leaning back in his seat as he flicked the book closed with one hand. "Finally, you join us."

"An outcome you surely expected, Ranzel," the Witch responded, folding her arms as she stood before the end of the table opposite him, her black and magenta clothes swaying to a slow stand still. "Though there is a part of me that is glad to see you, I would much rather we not do battle again."

"Quite right," the Wizard agreed. "The last one was rather disconcerting as it was. I never have liked confronting my students, least of all you."

"Well, I was *always* your favourite," she smiled knowingly.

"Student?" Tallinn raised an eyebrow, looking between the two magic wielders as we both came to stand to the side of the table between them. "You two were mentor and student?"

"Ranzel also considered me his protégé," Danika stated, her eyes still focused on the old man. "It was certainly high praise from one so ancient and powerful as a member of the Elemental Brotherhood."

"A truth not to be forgotten," Ranzel said with a smile, adoration in his eyes as he studied her. "You were the only one of the three who did not break my heart."

"I'm assuming that you refer to Manth and Keilantra," I guessed, folding my arms.

"You assume correctly," Danika said, glancing to me for a moment as Fawkner moved to stand at Ranzel's side. "All three of us were students of Ranzel long ago, though that was before we sought out Dunadel Naxxremis, and my sisters discovered the teachings of Gorth Lavelle."

"The first Shadow Lord," Tallinn had an edge of dread to her voice, her comment more to herself.

"Yet, you took what you had meant to from Naxxremis and returned to High-Realm with a different intent than that of your sisters," Ranzel sounded a little proud of her. "I always knew you were the one to resist the lure of power."

Danika nodded. "I have always held to that which you taught me, my old friend. Good and evil are but concepts used by mortals to describe ideals and the forces of the world. By choosing to remain outside the sphere of such definition, we magic wielders can remain objective and clear."

"Not in all cases," Ranzel sighed. "We all have our intentions and desires, Danika. Which was perhaps the point of your little test."

She smirked. "You knew yet chose not to say anything to the others."

Ranzel smiled knowingly, getting to his feet, his green and brown robes slowly unfolding to hang around his tall frame. He nodded his head once, his eyes twinkling above his long white beard and beneath the strands of his silvery hair.

"Lessons must be learned by oneself, not by simply being given the answer," he responded wisely. "And of all the lessons that stand of importance at this time, it is the lessons of truth and humility that will get us through to the promised end."

"Wait," Tallinn was just as shocked as I was. "Do you mean to say that you knew how to have her cooperate all this time and did nothing?"

"Ranzel," I shook my head, feeling my tension returning, "you could have ended this so much sooner."

"Understanding was important," the Wizard stated, turning to us, "and it cannot be given, but discovered. You had to come to the conclusions yourselves in order to understand the meaning behind them, or else you would not have learned."

I knew that what he was saying was wise, that he never spoke without purpose and never acted needlessly, but at that moment I couldn't help feeling enraged. Had I not been so determined to find the answers that we so sorely sought, I might have erupted at both of them. However, I remained cool and collected.

Damned Witches and Wizards. Nothing is ever simple.

"It makes sense I suppose," Fawkner granted thoughtfully. "Yet, it was truly a riddle that stumped us."

"Yes, well, I certainly feel stupid," Tallinn sighed, her hands now on her hips as she shook her head.

"An unfortunate symptom caused by the enigmatic ways of wizards and witches," Ellora said as she walked through the doors, her fiery hair swirling behind her shoulders and the lengths of her leather armour swinging with her movement. "They bring much wisdom when they come to us, yet they do have a tendency towards making one's head sore."

"That's saying it in a mild way," Holger grumped as he and Dolin followed her, both of them dressed in their blue tunics and hide jackets. "All academics give me a headache."

"Because you are no academic," Dolin replied, looking over his shoulder at his twin. "As it is, the very word academic is impressive for you."

"Aye, that it is," Holger admitted, stroking the three twisted plaits that hung from his chin. "I'm more of an... *active* learner than a reader. If you get my meaning."

"Oh, we surely do, Holger," Ellora smirked, looking down at the Dwarf now that she had moved to Ranzel's side opposite Fawkner.

I caught a flicker of movement out of the corner of my eye, turning my gaze towards the door. That was when I saw Tristan. The reddish-blonde-haired man looked very dishevelled as he somehow staggered into the room. He wobbled, bracing his shoulder into the doorframe with a mild grunt, his eyes bloodshot and his clothes mussed.

I can't believe that this man once tricked us into a trap set by my mother and a group of Gathlorks. Either we were utterly disadvantaged to make his job easier, or since then he has gotten worse.

"Still curled up at the bottom of a bottle of ale, Tristan?" Tallinn remarked tersely, her disdain for the Wanderer mirroring my own.

"Uncurled and nursing one hell of a hangover," he responded, straightening himself up where he stood. "Argh! My head feels like a troll stepped on it."

"We can only fantasise," Tallinn commented sourly, turning from him.

Danika flashed her gaze at Tristan as he wobbled his way into the room, narrowing her emerald eyes. It was clear that she didn't trust him, or that she at least didn't approve of his behaviour. Truthfully, I didn't know a single one of us that did.

"Still the fool, I see," she observed as he leaned his palms on the table opposite Tallinn and me. "Then again, I always knew you would take to the drink when things got rough."

"Do you intend to insult me, Witch?" Tristan asked her with little to no interest, still a little groggy. "My skin is tougher than the barbs on your tongue."

"Interesting," Danika mused. "It seems that you were only courteous because you were in the Princess' company. Perhaps you were trying to entice her towards your bed?"

He snorted. "You don't know the first thing about me, or what went on between the lass and I."

No, but I did, I thought coldly, glaring at him across the table. For a moment I considered snatching the solid silver candelabra from the table and beating him down with it as the image of him pushing Leander into a forceful kiss flashed through my mind. It would have been so easy and deeply satisfying to do so, but I resisted. After all, Leander wouldn't have wanted me to do that.

"You forget, Tristan," Danika eyed him off, leaning towards him with her own palms placed to the table now, her dark hair framing her pale white face, "that I have the ability to see all that is, was, can be and will be. So, I know *everything* about what happened between you and the Princess. Remember that."

Tristan swallowed back, his eyes widening a little. He nodded, seeming to have awoken enough from his drunken stupor to face her.

"And perhaps it would behove you to cease your consumption of ale so that you may be of some use to this company," Danika went on in a mocking tone, almost chastising him like one would a child. "If for no other reason than to add another sturdy sword, steady bow or accurate spell caster to the mix when we are met in battle, then at least do so for decency's sake."

Tristan nodded. "Aye. That I will."

He started to straighten up his appearance, pouring a cup of water from the jug that was on the table and gulping it down swiftly. To watch him try to sober up was almost amusing, but not enough that I would forget his actions.

"You said you would give us answers," I said in an effort to change the subject, turning my attention wholly on the Witch.

"And so I shall," Danika confirmed with a nod.

"What answers do you have, if I may ask?" Fawkner spoke up, clasping his hands behind him. "Knowledge from your teacher in the Blackfelds? Some rumour in passing?"

"The knowledge I carry comes not from books, though it can certainly be found in them," the woman responded, standing up straight and folding her arms before her moderate chest, "but from the sight that flows from my inner eye as its gaze pierces the veil of time."

"What are you saying?" Ellora raised a curious eyebrow at her. "That you have looked into the future for the answer?"

"Yet another reason for my little test," Danika responded glibly. "Though I had foreseen your company seeking me out to aid in your quest, I had not yet seen the means to success. I have since come upon such knowledge."

"Through your foresight?!" Holger scoffed and snorted obnoxiously. "Oh please! There is no such thing!"

"You think so, do you, Dwarf?" Danika turned her penetrating gaze to him calmly.

"This'll be good," I murmured to Tallinn with a smirk, drawing a slight chuckle and an amused glance from her.

"Seeing the future is a parlour trick," Holger stated like any sceptic would. "It is the same as speaking to spirits and divining the road ahead in tea leaves. It is all trickery and falsehoods, nothing more."

"Really?" Danika questioned in her usual mocking tone. "So, you do not believe that a person like me could, oh, for example, look into your past and see what you know but I could not?"

"If you could truly do that," Holger challenged her gruffly, stepping a little closer and glaring up at her, "then not only would I accept these so-called arts as real, but I would also tar and feather myself before acting as a chicken scratching in the yard."

Tallinn and I exchanged a look, trying not to laugh as we both knew what was coming.

Danika smirked and casually said: "The incident with the milk pail, the cow bell and laced apron is certainly an amusing, yet unsettling event to see from your past."

Holger's eyes widened and his face paled. "H-how... Uh... What are you...?"

The woman went on, amused and a little wicked in her own way: "I am impressed that you were able to aim so high given that you were on all fours. That you chose to drink from said pail is also quite astonishing, though not for the same reasons."

Silence filled the room, all of us staring at Holger with wide and shocked expressions. I doubt any of us could believe what we were hearing, and I knew most of us had no desire to gain further details. To know what he had done in its entirety would be mentally scarring since hearing this much was horrifying enough.

"Is that proof enough of my abilities?" the Witch asked, still smirking down at him.

Holger went bright red in the face, his beard nowhere near as thick as his brother's and so unable to shield him as readily.

He stuttered and coughed, bewildered and embarrassed all at once. "I... I..." he tried to find the words, "I was young! It... it was on a dare! And how did... Why... Uh... Oh!"

"I think you're about to imitate poultry, brother," Dolin remarked, patting Holger on the shoulder.

We all started to laugh as the Dwarf turned away, hanging his head and muttering coarsely: "Blasted witch!"

"That never grows tedious," Danika chuckled as she turned from him and back to the table. "It seems that there is an abundance of fools looking to be humiliated."

"Very good," Ranzel chuckled, regaining the seriousness that had previously hung over the room. "Now that there is no longer a question about your sight, perhaps we could discuss what we had come here to."

"But of course," Danika nodded, bowing her head to Ranzel. "As I said, I had needed to look into the future in order to discern precisely what was needed to answer your requests, and so I have found it."

"You know how to resurrect Leander?" I was hopeful and desperate, my excitement rising in me as I found myself trying to hold my calm.

"Resurrect is *not* the right word," the Witch replied. "But yes, I have seen the means to bring her back to the world of the living."

"And how do we do that, my lady witch?" Dolin asked, showing her the utmost respect for fear of ending up with the humiliation his brother had.

"We must seek out Azmerath's Doorway," Danika said simply.

Silence once again filled the room, all of us staring at her with astonished and confused expressions. The mere mention of the words was confounding and unfamiliar. The only thing I knew for certain being that the doorway had to belong to the God of Death himself.

"I have never heard of such a thing," Ellora broke the silence, frowning at the woman.

"So few people have," Danika looked to Ranzel. "Even you would not know of it as more than legend, teacher."

Ranzel nodded vaguely. "That is true."

"Then you have heard of it?" I asked.

Ranzel folded his arms, one hand stroking his beard in thought. He turned from the table and moved to stare into the fireplace, for a moment lost in his own thoughts.

"Azmerath's Doorway is an ancient legend from a time long before the Dragon Pendants, the Guardians, the Dragon Knights and even the Elemental Brotherhood," the Wizard explained slowly, wonder held within a grim tone in his voice. "Because it is legend upon legend from aeons before the recorded histories of High-Realm, I didn't consider it to be an option worth approaching. Apparently, I was wrong."

"Never a good omen," Tristan commented darkly, "when a wizard says he is wrong."

"What do you know of the doorway?" I enquired, trying to keep myself even toned and of a steady mind.

"It is a doorway carved of black obsidian," Ranzel described as he studied the flames, "set into an arch of stone with silver engravings; an ancient and forgotten language that legend states were written by the Divines. According to the myth, the doorway opens a portal into Azmerath's realm that allows the living to step into the World of the Dead."

"Such a thing cannot be possible," Tallinn sounded uneasy by the mere thought of the doorway, her arms folding around her as if to protect herself. "The living can't follow where the dead walk."

"That isn't strictly true," Ellora spoke up softly, a haunted expression in her eyes. "My people's Keepers of History tell stories of men and women setting foot in the realms of the Dead King in search of those who have passed before their time. It is said that they step through a doorway between worlds as if stepping between two rooms and come to face Lord Azmerath upon his obsidian throne in the mists of the Beyond. There, they plead with him for the return of their loved one and offer tribute that he might grant their request."

"It is the same as the legend of which I speak," Ranzel turned back to us. "Azmerath's Doorway is the only way to restore a person from death without resorting to necromancy. I had hoped for another way to restore the girl to life to become apparent, but clearly the author of our destinies has other designs."

I felt a cold shudder go through me as I thought of what the quest to find this door would mean. I could only imagine what stepping through it to meet Azmerath himself would be like, a deep fear filling me. Then I thought of Leander. *She must have seen him already. Gods, she had said as much as she was dying...* I closed my eyes for a moment, remembering her fear and feeling it as if it were my own.

"We are certain that there is no other way?" Tallinn asked.

Danika shrugged. "You wanted me to provide you with the answers you seek and so I have. To restore the girl without making her a draugar, we must travel to Azmerath's Doorway and beseech the King of Death for his blessing so that he may return her soul to her body."

"Which can only be done because she does not decay like a normal corpse," Ranzel noted thoughtfully.

"Where is it?" I asked the one question no one had deemed to yet, turning my green gaze to Danika's face. "Where does the doorway lie?"

Danika's expression darkened as she looked to me, her eyes filling with a sympathy I didn't expect. I knew what she was about to say would chill me, but I didn't care.

No matter what, I will seek out the doorway and bring her back. I must.

"The Doorway," she spoke slowly, almost hesitantly, "is hidden in the far north-east at the heart of the dark land of Valloran."

I gasped and my eyes widened, my heart sinking in my chest. No matter how much I had prepared myself for her words, I had not expected those ones to come from her lips. I was numb, my hands dropping to my sides as I felt a cold sweat break down my back and through my shirt, every muscle immediately hurting.

"Valloran?" Ellora asked in murmured horror. "It cannot be."

"The Realm of the Vampire Lords," Fawkner shuddered as he uttered the words, his legs shaking as he sat down. "This quest is now the stuff of nightmares."

"Is there truly no other way?" Tristan asked uneasily, bracing his hands to the table.

Danika shook her head. "The path to Azmerath's Doorway leads to Valloran's dark forests and snowy earth."

I felt as if I would collapse, my head swimming with the stress of such news. *Not there... Gods, why does it have to be there?*

Tallinn was suddenly grasping my arm as I felt myself drawing closer to passing out, her eyes staring up at me with deep dread and silent understanding.

We both knew what it meant to go to Valloran, and we both feared what would happen if we did.

"That black land is many leagues away," Dolin commented, trying to appear strong, though the lack of colour in his cheeks and his wide eyes betrayed him. "It is even farther than the Blackfelds. To get there we would have to travel east from Lorveren, through Balganis and into Gorvenna, a place that does not welcome us. After that, we would step into the Blackfelds and make our way north only to journey through Grotojan."

"And there is no guarantee that the Orcs have not sided with the Shadow Lord," Holger added grimly, his arms folded in front of him. "If they have, they will surely kill us on sight ere we reach the northern border of Grotojan and the frosty lands of Valloran."

"Even if we did," Dolin sighed darkly, shaking his head as he set his hands to the table's edge, "the Vampire Lords would not be welcoming."

"There are but two options," Danika stated, simply, delivering the news as calmly as if it were about an unusual swell in the tides by the shores. "We either make our way to Valloran and seek out the doorway, or we remain here and await our inevitable and gruesome deaths."

"That's not an option," I sucked in a breath, trying to compose myself. "We can't give up. Not now that the answer has been given to us. As much as it pains me to say it... we *must* go to Valloran."

Tallinn sighed and shook her head. "We have been seeking the answer and this is it. Regardless of how dark and terrifying it is, we must follow it."

"That still leaves us with a great distance to follow," Dolin reminded us calmly.

"Then we go by ship," Ranzel stated, drawing all eyes back to him. "We make our way to Valloran by the seas and avoid entanglement with our enemies, whilst also cutting out the time it will take to travel."

"It is certainly a better option, and the odds are much improved given the winds that blow upon the world with these storms," Ellora agreed.

"I will summon a ship to Seaguard in Lorveren's southernmost reaches," Fawkner declared, considering everything carefully. "As for dealing with the Vampire Lords, I believe approaching it diplomatically will be more appropriate. I will arrange an escort of soldiers to accompany us as an honour guard, but also to give us more safety."

"A very good plan, Lord Fawkner," Ranzel nodded approvingly, turning to the man. "However, I would ask that you allow me to secure passage. I feel that a civilian ship will get us further than one of your nation, and it will most certainly draw less attention."

"Very well," Fawkner nodded. "Then we depart tomorrow morning. I will also have Joran prepare Leander's body for transport. It is better that we keep her close."

"Agreed," the Wizard nodded.

"There is still one more thing needed," Danika added, stopping everyone from moving. "We will need the pages written by Dunadel Naxxremis accounting for the method to open the doorway."

"You tell us this now?" Tristan flashed his hard gaze to her. "What game do you play, woman?"

"I am merely ensuring our success," Danika responded evenly. "Though the Vampire Lords may know the method to open the doorway, I believe it better to be prepared ourselves. Just in case."

"So, how are we supposed to get these pages?" I asked, folding my arms as I faced her.

She smiled and turned over her shoulder to me, a knowing gleam in her eye. "That is not a concern that will last more than a few more hours."

"What do you mean?" Tallinn frowned at her, agitation on her soft features.

"Your companion," Danika noted me with a point of her finger, "has made efforts to procure whatever may assist in this quest. Fortunately, the delivery he had hoped for shall be made before dawn breaks. With it comes the pages we need, so fret not, my friends."

"You have?" Tallinn raised an eyebrow at me.

I nodded. "We'll discuss it later."

"Indeed, for we have much to do now," Fawkner directed us calmly. "So, let us attend to our tasks."

* * * * *

I returned to my room after the last evening meal we had partaken of in Eilath, my mind a swirl of emotions. I still had much to do in regard to packing my things for the trip and I yearned for time to myself to prepare. I was just hoping that I could sleep with ease.

Entering the lamp lit room, I closed the door, then turned to face the bed, pausing as I noted the wrapped-up package that sat on the covers. It was large, about the size of a big cushion, a hide cloth the covering for what lay within. Slowly, I crossed the room and studied it, catching sight of a note that lay on top of the package. Flipping it open revealed to me some very familiar handwriting and made me recognise the validity of all of Danika's claims.

The smile that tugged at my lips at seeing the writing of my friend and adoptive parent was unstoppable.

I knew he'd come through for me. Varel always does.

I pulled open the package, the familiar hardened black leather armour I had once worn now revealed to me. It felt good, like greeting an old friend I hadn't seen in a long time. My right palm ran across the smooth cuirass, and I felt a comforting relief fill me.

It's good to have this back.

My eyes flicked then to the small envelope that had been tucked into the collar of the cuirass, the edge just poking out. I slipped it free with two fingers, opening it and studying the pages. It would undoubtedly need translating in many parts, most of it written in the Dark Elven language. But the map needed no explanation; a perfect layout of the lands of Valloran.

As I studied the map, my eyes fell to a central fortress that stood out above all the others. *Castle Valkirak... Gods, I never wanted to go near that place again for as long as I live.*

I sighed and took the pages, wrapping them in the envelope again with the map. As I stowed it into my pack, I knew that I would have to face what I didn't want to, but I also couldn't turn from it.

It's all for Leander.

"Carden?" that soft voice murmured, making me pause.

Immediately, I began worrying that I had fallen asleep and that I would once again be drawn into a nightmare of death and horror. But I had to turn. I needed to. Moving over my right shoulder, I faced the bed and gasped. Leander looked up at me, sitting on the edge of the bed, her slender yet curvy frame clad in a blue velvet dress, her long dark hair hanging freely around her face. She was so beautiful, but sad, her eyes tired while still bright. Just the sight of her made my heart flutter.

"Leander..." I gasped out, bracing my hands to the desk behind me. "Am... am I dreaming?"

She looked confused, shaking her head. "You're not dreaming. No."

I moved towards her hesitantly. "Are you real?"

She shrugged one shoulder softly, never taking her eyes off my face. "Yes... I am. I'm here, but... but I'm not."

"What do you mean?" I frowned, moving to stand over her, wanting nothing more than to touch her.

She looked up at me with those steely blue eyes, her lips parting a little as she tried to form her explanation. She looked perfect and so like the girl I remembered her to be.

"I'm dead," she said softly. "So... I'm not *really* here. I'm... like how the Shadow Lord was when we first met him."

"Incorporeal?" I asked.

She nodded and shrugged her shoulder towards me. "See for yourself."

Slowly, hesitantly, I extended my left hand towards her right shoulder, expecting to touch her smooth, soft, warm skin. My fingers, then my knuckles, and finally my whole hand passed through her, a strange tingling sensation caressing my flesh. I withdrew it slowly as she closed her eyes at the unusual touch, her eyelids flicking open as she faced me again.

"Are you a ghost?" I wondered, frowning.

She shrugged. "I'm not sure what I am," she turned her gaze towards the bed and my armour, then to my pack. "What are you doing? Are you going somewhere?"

I nodded, deciding that if this were just a dream that I would play it out with the same nature that I would a normal wakeful conversation. "Our company is leaving tomorrow," I said evenly, gathering up my old armour. "I was just getting packed."

"That's not Guardian armour," she observed.

"No," I agreed, setting it on the table, choosing not to turn to her just yet. "I am no longer a Guardian."

"Why not?" I could almost hear the frown in her voice.

I turned to her, seeing the look of dismay on her beautiful, youthful face. "Because of you," I said honestly. "Your death changed me, and I want nothing more to do with the Guardians. I made a new vow; one I intend to keep."

"What vow?" she asked, watching me as she leaned one hand to the mattress and lay the other across her lap.

"That I would find a way to undo your death," I told her softly, moving to sit on the bed and bringing myself down to her eye level. "That I would give you life again and save you from whatever suffering you endure."

"Carden," she sighed, looking deeply into my eyes, longing and sadness clear in hers. "Oh, Carden. I want that, I truly do... but I *am* dead. I've passed on and I'm just here to wait for you."

"Wait for me?" I raised an eyebrow at her.

Leander nodded. "Morod has won. He's destroying the world slowly and painfully, planning to starve the people into weakness for his ultimate attack. I just... I wanted to come and be with you in whatever way I can until we are together again."

I frowned. "But... we're coming to get you, to help you come back to life and fulfil the prophecies."

"The prophecies are false," she whispered sadly, earnestly staring into my eyes. "They were about her, not me. My ancestor was the Great Heroine. I'm just dead. But it's all right," she smiled softly, reaching out her hand to simulate touching my cheek. "We'll be together soon, and we won't ever suffer or be kept apart again."

"You're right," I agreed, sighing softly. "We won't be apart, Leander," I stood and turned to gaze down at her. "We leave Eilath in the morning to board a ship at Seaguard. From there we sail to Valloran where we will bring you back to life."

She stood up, desperation in her eyes. It was as if she was hopelessly determined to convince me against this path I was taking.

"Carden, I'm dead!" she exclaimed. "I can't return to my body! I... I want to, but I can't! I've tried!"

"You just need help," I tried to be reassuring, smiling at her. "We'll get you back and undo all of this. I promise you, Leander."

"Are you taking me with you?" she asked.

I nodded, turning back to my pack, starting to stash the medicine I had into it. I knew I would need it.

"Yes. You will come with us so that we can keep you safe," I explained without turning. "I won't leave you trapped in spirit when your body refuses to return to the earth. The pain must be terrible for you."

"It is," she half sobbed. "But please, Carden, it will be all right. I won't hurt once you're with me again."

"A few weeks and we will be together again," I murmured my oath. "I promise you, Leander."

She sighed and I saw her look down at her hands out of the corner of my eye. "I... I just hope that you don't regret this."

Those words drew a new frown to my brow, and I turned over my shoulder as she looked up at me. She tried to smile, but it was just a saddened grimace. She began to evaporate, the colours of her form becoming like wispy shadows that disappeared into the darkness of the room. She was gone and I suddenly felt her absence all the more.

"I hope I don't either," I murmured, turning back to my work.

Chapter Fifteen
Sailing Upon Turbulent Seas

The next morning, under heavy escort, our company set out. Ranzel's dragon would be accompanying us on the trip to the port. A trip that would take a few days. We each had a horse, Joran going with several guardsmen in a cart pulled by a stout workhorse. He was guarding Leander's body as always, the girl resting there in the safety of the rocking wagon. Admittedly, I never took my eyes off her, always riding my steed at the rear of the cart for that reason. Thankfully, it was an uneventful trip.

Our considerable troop was not far from the edge of Seaguard when Tallinn at last turned her attention to me. She had been contemplative for the last day or so and I was just waiting to hear the words that would surely tumble from her lips.

"You contacted the Guild," she stated without tact, gaining my gaze back from watching the cart ahead of us as I guided my horse forward.

I frowned at her. "What?"

"The Guild," she turned her eyes to me with a severity I hardly saw from her anymore, maintaining her grasp on her own mount's reins. "That is how you came to possess the pages from Naxxremis' works Danika claimed you would receive."

"I have not shown you anything," I pointed out, keeping my eyes ahead in the unending, smoky darkness that was alleviated only by the flashes of lightning.

"You have not needed to," she responded evenly. "The armour you wear is proof enough."

I could see that she would not relent with her assertion, nodding my head briefly. "I wrote to Varel," I stated calmly, trying to show my resolve rather than the utter panic that had spawned such an action. "I simply told him of everything and asked if he had any means to assist us."

"Contacting Varel *means* contacting the Guild," she insisted firmly.

"He is my family," I defended, throwing her a hard stare through the loose strands of raven black that flicked across my brow. "Would you tell me that I am not to speak to my adoptive father when the world is tearing itself apart?"

"No. I didn't mean that," she shook her head, seeing my frustration. "I only meant to ascertain the means by which you have obtained the last of what is required for our journey."

"Yes, well, you are right then," I conceded, turning my eyes ahead again, laying them upon Leander's unmoving shape buried in the furs in the cart.

"You will owe them now," she said after a moment, flashing her eyes towards me again. "You know that, right?"

"A hundred gold as I have promised," I nodded.

"It will be more than that," she sighed. "The Guild are... well... you know what they say about honour among their kind."

"That will be my concern, not yours," I advised her calmly. "For now, let us just focus on the task at hand."

"It is certainly dire enough as it is," she agreed with a nod from under her hood. "You never know. We might all be killed, and they will be unable to collect their payment from you."

I chuckled lightly. "Ah... Always the optimist, Tallinn. You are a woman of great irony."

She laughed softly, smiling to me. "As are you, Carden."

I smirked. "Huh... Then I am a very homely looking woman at the very least, if I am one at all."

She realised her mistake and laughed more. "That's not what I meant! Gods, you are as infuriating as any little brother!"

"If you were my sister by blood, I would be proud to be your annoying little brother," I confessed.

That drew a gentle smile from her, and she nodded her head softly. That smile didn't last as she then turned her eyes ahead and frowned. "Something is wrong," she coaxed her horse forward, heading for the front of the column.

I took after her, trusting Leander's safety to the Dwarves, Joran and the soldiers that surrounded her. As my horse galloped at a steady and easy pace up the hillside, I came alongside Tallinn, our attentions falling to where Ranzel, Danika, Ellora, Tristan, Fawkner and Oddvar had brought their horses to a halt.

"What is wrong?" Tallinn called, slowing her mare as my steed followed suit.

"Fawkner's falcon has sighted something," Ellora replied, her hood covering her red hair from the speckling of rain we could feel falling from the clouds.

Fawkner was staring off into the sky as if to view something just out of sight, his expression dark. It was the magical sight he shared with his bird causing him to have such a stare, the graceful falcon's gaze shown to him as if he were the one witnessing all that she did.

"Seaguard is under siege," he uttered darkly, frowning as his bearded jaw clenched. "The garrison is trying to hold the lines long enough for the townspeople to flee, but they are overwhelmed."

"More bandits?" Tallinn asked.

He shook his head, returning from his sight and back to us: "No... It's the Scourge."

I tensed as I heard his words, knowing what was likely laying ahead of us. Those monsters were at last making their presence felt and assaulting a town full of innocents.

"This can be no coincidence," Ranzel mused grimly, steadying his horse.

"We may have a spy amongst us," Danika hissed, glancing back towards the column of soldiers riding behind us.

"No matter," Fawkner said, shaking his head and turning his horse towards the road to the town. "We must still make our way to Seaguard and to our waiting ship. We cannot simply abandon our quest because the Shadow Lord has sent his forces to counter us. Oddvar, summon the men forward."

"Yes, milord," Oddvar turned his head to the soldiers. "Charge forth upon Seaguard! Draw your swords and slay all foes who stand in our way!"

Through the unending darkness, our horses charged, their hooves thundering like a storm onto themselves. Dust kicked up from the dried land as the rain now began to come, flowing from the heavens like bitter tears from the deities as if the scene of turmoil and mindless violence that waited in Seaguard had broken their hearts. Even then as we drew nearer at what should have been the height of noon, we heard the screams of innocents and the roars of beasts. The fires that alit the town glowed brightly, causing an orange haze to mar the ever-nearing horizon.

The three-dozen strong cavalry that surrounded my companions and I charged up the hill and straight over it without stopping, horns bellowing as they sounded their arrival to the beleaguered town. They didn't stop, speeding into the town without faltering, their swords unsheathed as bolts shot from crossbows into the stalking shapes of the monsters that were assailing the townspeople.

My black horse leaped over rubble and burning ruins without fear, my own sword drawn in my right hand as I guided him forward. Tallinn and her horse were right behind us, the two of us moving without hesitation to engage the Scourge.

In the briefest moment that I had before my fight began, I took in the scene before me. The close streets were overrun with Gathlorks, Hurgarks, Orcs and Gymphs, several Erks even visible, crushing Lorveren soldiers who had been defending the people. There were bodies strewn about of both Lorveren people, and Scourge beasts alike, blood washing the street like a river in the increasing rainfall.

Screams drew my gaze as I saw several women running down an alleyway with children clutched to their chests, soldiers from the town with them. As Hurgarks rushed them with their arms waving jagged looking weapons, the soldiers struck with swords, axes and maces. They easily dropped the four-foot beasts and moved to engage their larger counterparts.

The roar of Gathlorks drew my gaze as fire consumed a house. Three of the large dark-skinned creatures were rushing me with their swords raised. I kicked my heels and coaxed my horse to trample them, sweeping my sword to take the head off another that attempted to attack the fleeing civilians.

The Shadow Lord's war has truly begun...

Fawkner galloped through on his dark brown stallion, swinging his sword into the fray with two soldiers flanking him, all of them downing enemies as they went. The defenders who had been in the town before our arrival sighted the Lord of Eilath, rushing to him as more of their number battled the horde that rampaged through the streets.

As I slew another Gathlork, I turned my eyes to the darkness at the edge of the town. I was greatly relieved to see the others riding through with Joran guiding the cart under escort. My momentary panic was fading fast.

An arrow whizzed past my shoulder, striking a Gymph that had leaped in the air with intent to slay me. It shrieked and dropped to the ground, Ellora's eye turning then to another as she strung her bow swiftly, killing it before it could strike.

"My Lord!" a soldier rushed to Fawkner under escort of several others.

"Soldier," Fawkner turned his horse towards the man as our companions gathered, the riders with us clearing the street swiftly. "Report."

"Seaguard is overrun, my Lord," the soldier on foot reported diligently, his bloodied sword at his side, his chest heaving with breathlessness. "We have been attempting to evacuate the civilians, but the Scourge forces come in an unending tide. We are not sure from where."

"It's as if a magic portal has been opened to spill them forth and ravage the town," a second man added hurriedly, panic in his eyes.

"That may very well be," Ranzel stated darkly. "The Shadow Lords were known for opening portals to allow their forces to access parts of High-Realm when they warred against us in the distant past."

"How would they do such a thing?" Tallinn asked, trying to calm her horse.

"A disciple would be nearby," Danika answered, turning her sharp eyes from the scene around us. "One of the Shadow Lord's acolytes with a mind to become his successor. It will be a man in black robes, a human, concealing himself somewhere nearby in the town. Killing him will close the portal."

"How far would he be from the portal?" Tallinn turned her eyes to the Witch, her blonde hair flicking in the wind.

"Not far," Ellora spoke up. "He would have to remain in sight of it to maintain it."

"Indeed," Danika agreed. "Such magic requires great concentration and power."

"The portal is at the western edge of the town," the commanding soldier explained. "But we do not see a way to it."

Fawkner concentrated. "Farsight. Seek the portal and find a way through to it," he instructed the bird, though she was not with him.

Her call went out and we sighted her flying above us. It only took a moment for Fawkner to get us the information we needed.

"There is a way through the marketplace," he relayed what he was seeing. "The Scourge do not see it. And I see the Acolyte... He stands upon a rooftop overlooking the market where the portal lies."

"I say we kill the bastard!" Holger growled, spoiling for a fight.

"And so we shall," Fawkner said firmly, turning his eyes to us. "Ellora, Danika, you both have knowledge of these acolytes. Go with Carden and slay that dark disciple."

"Very well," Ellora nodded, turning her horse.

"We'll meet you at the docks," I told him as Danika joined us.

"You had best hurry," the soldier advised us. "The Scourge are trying to burn the ships as well."

"Then they do mean to stop us," Tallinn seethed, drawing her sword. "Go on, you three. We'll clear a path to the docks and stop the Scourge from destroying our ship."

"I'll lend a hand," Tristan followed the three of us. "Might as well make myself useful."

I didn't bother arguing, though I didn't want his treacherous help. I simply nodded and charged my horse after Danika and Ellora, the four of us galloping down the cobblestones. But we didn't get far, the roars of two gigantic Erks causing us to skid our horses as they slammed their massive fists to the ground and turned their beady eyes our way. Fortune favoured us, however, as a second, louder roar ripped through the air and flames lashed down upon the two beasts. Gaspeite struck with his claws from the sky, his green wings creating a gust that knocked the two creatures to the ground, clearing our path.

It was all too easy for us to find our way to the market, the four of us dismounting from our horses and hurrying through the backstreets to where we could see an eerie glow. We peered out of the cover of the alley to see a terrifying, rippling portal edged with the same eerie green energy the Shadow Lord so commonly used. In the middle of it was a rip in the air that led to some dark and sinister place where the Scourge were pouring from like a plague.

"The Fortress of Grishk'kinnar..." I exhaled painfully, staring at the black towers and grey wastelands on the other side of the portal.

"Then the Shadow Lord *is* aware of our plans," Ellora surmised, turning her turquoise gaze to the rooftops. "We must find the Acolyte before this swarm of beasts cannot be quashed," she studied the scene for a few moments, then jabbed her finger towards a figure standing up on a terrace. "There."

Tristan spotted him at the same time I did, nodding with a scowl. "Let's go end that bastard."

"First, perhaps a distraction," Danika raised her staff, the crystal glowing a dark green in its top.

The street suddenly erupted as the roots of trees stretched up like tendrils, striking at the Scourge that marched through the portal. The beasts roared and slashed as the Witch cast her spell to halt them and allow us our passage.

We didn't waste time, the four of us rushing forward into the area where Lorveren soldiers were engaging the Scourge that had made it past the reaching roots. Our swords clashed with those of our enemies as we cut our way through to where the Acolyte was holding the portal.

The Acolyte turned his human gaze to us, snarling. He was heavily protected by Gathlorks, the beasts charging as Tristan and I rushed to draw their gaze. It looked like an unwinnable battle, but we were fortunate again as Gaspeite swooped overhead and loosed a column of fire down over the Scourge forces still emerging from the portal.

Taking full advantage of the Dragon's assault, Ellora drew her bowstring and fired. The Acolyte was distracted by the sudden attack of the majestic being. He cried out a grunt of pain as the Elven Huntress' arrow lodged in his chest, staggering briefly before a second ended him. The portal sputtered and sparked, its magic failing with his death just as more Scourge were starting their crossing. They screamed as the portal collapsed on them, ending them and blocking any more from coming through.

I downed another Gathlork and turned to the others as I withdrew my sword. "That should stop them."

"Yes, but the Scourge still swarm the city," Ellora pointed out, firing another arrow as she walked, dropping a charging Hurgark.

"We can hold!" a soldier shouted as she struck down the Orc that had charged her. "That Dragon has done a mighty job of clearing the beasts!"

"Then let us make for the port," Danika lowered the magic of her strike, the roots settling back into the earth. "We have little time to waste."

In minutes we were riding through the town at a gallop, the soldiers starting to get the upper hand now that the portal had been closed. Some of our escorts joined us as we made our way towards the docks where ships were burning in the waters.

I sighted the others defending the cart, Joran on the street now with his twin blades cleaving the air and cutting down our foes as the Dwarves stood upon the cart with their weapons ready. The Storvari had a pile of Scourge at his feet, his muscles and size making him a greater match than any of us for the beasts.

As we neared, I sighted the single ship that was under the heaviest siege; a black hulled brig that looked very familiar. The *Black Asp* was hurriedly making ready to depart as the Harredi pirates that crewed her were repelling boarders, their silvery scimitars slicing through enemies with ease and violent fury.

"Move aboard with haste!" Ranzel shouted, his sword in one hand, his staff aglow in the other. "We run short on time!"

I leaped from my horse and ran to the cart, scooping Leander up in my arms since Joran was otherwise busy. The Axton brothers rushed with me as I hurried to the gangplank, no time left to ponder the Wizard's arrangement for our passage to Valloran.

The rest of my companions ran up the plank as the pirates began casting off, Oddvar and Fawkner following with the soldiers they were leading. We reached the main deck just as Kororsh, the captain's loyal Storvari first mate, was downing several Gathlorks with a sweep of his great sword.

Captain Karrer swung her elegant blade as she kneed a Gathlork in the ribs and threw him from the ship, the last of our escorts and her crew joining us. The dark-skinned woman strode to the helm, her onyx hair swirling in its braids, her ragged clothes of silks and linen rippling around her corseted chest.

"Nice to see you all again," she commented briskly as she passed us. "Make for the mouth of the inlet! Full sail! Get us ahead of this attack!"

As she took the helm, her crew pushed the *Black Asp* from the docks. The ship turned with a groan of its timbers and made its way through the darkened waters with ease.

"I must say," Tallinn spoke to the captain as she moved to the stairs, pausing there, "that we are all surprised to see you, Captain Karrer."

"As I am certain you are, Guardian Tallinn," the Harredi woman said a little breathlessly. "We will get down to business very shortly, but first we must escape the bay so that the Scourge cannot pursue us."

* * * * *

A few hours later, we had broken away from the bay and were sailing along the southern coast of Lorveren, heading west. Of course, there was a shortage of places to keep all the soldiers we brought with us, and space would be cramped, but it was what it was and none of us would dare to argue. We had more dire things to concern ourselves with at that moment anyway.

I left Leander in Joran's care, going with Tallinn, Ranzel, Fawkner, Danika and Ellora to the captain's cabin to deliberate on the plan. We had relayed the story to Captain Karrer with all the detail we could, expressing our urgency and our need as we stood around the lamp lit table with the waves thrashing against the windows.

"Travelling to Valloran in order to seek out Lord Azmerath and his kingdom of death," Captain Karrer shook her head, her hands pressed to the table before her. "Never before have I heard such dangerous intentions laid out before me."

"I understand your scepticism, Captain," Tallinn said, mirroring the woman's pose, "but we have no alternative."

"There are always alternatives," Captain Karrer said coldly, eyeing her off. "That little skirmish in Seaguard was a clear indicator that this is a foolish and needlessly dangerous endeavour."

"It is not needless," I insisted, leaning over the table and staring into her hazelnut-coloured eyes. "You have seen the battle at Seaguard, so you know that the war looming on the horizon will be terrible."

"War is always terrible, Master Highever," she retorted, folding her arms before her bulging chest. "That is the very nature of war."

"The Shadow Lord has made the sky black," Ellora declared sternly, never once removing her gaze from the woman's face. "He has unleashed the monstrous Fallen Ones of myth upon the world to wreak terrible havoc. Already they have laid waste to all of High-Realm's Guardian strongholds, the Mage's College of Safferan, the sanctuaries of the Dragon Knights *and* the city of Silvervale. There are next to no defenders left in Therras capable of facing this onslaught. Fewer still in High-Realm."

"And so your only recourse is to follow the guidance of a wizard and a handful of prophecies," the Harredi woman sighed, shaking her head. "I mean you no disrespect, Ranzel, for you have been well regarded amongst my people for generations. Yet, I cannot see how this path will undo the chaos that plagues us now."

"As I explained," Ranzel stepped forward, his staff moving in time with his right step, "the prophecies reveal that Princess Leander is the Great Heroine of High-Realm who must unite all the fractured nations to stand against the Shadow Lord and this enduring Armageddon. In order for her to be able to do so she must first be restored to life, and our means to do that lies within the borders of the northern land of Valloran."

"A long and perilous journey," Kororsh stated in that same monotonous way that Joran did, his massive arms folded.

"Very true, Kororsh," Captain Karrer agreed with him, turning her gaze back to us. "Under the best of circumstances, we would find ourselves sailing on turbulent seas to make such a trip from here. But now, with this endless darkness and violent infinite storm, the passage is next to impossible. You ask for a miracle where none may exist."

"Only fear makes a woman as hardened as you make such assessments, Captain," Danika stated in her usual manner, her own staff held in both hands.

"Yet, the way remains open to us even though the waves do crash violently, and the sun does not light our course. Passage *is* possible."

"Possible, yes," the captain agreed, sighing as she took a moment to stare down at the table, the light of the lamp moving as the sea rocked the ship. "But it is dangerous enough just travelling such a course. Have you considered what you will face upon landing on those haunted frozen shores?"

"The alternative is complacency," Ellora remarked, folding her arms as she looked sideways at the woman through her dampened red hair.

"Ellora speaks truthfully," Fawkner muttered, pacing a little, his bird watching him on the nearby cabinet. "Our only other recourse is to find a place to wait for our ends, be it by the hands of the Scourge, the Undead Legions, the fires of those dire dragons, or by starvation and disease."

"We do not ask you to go with us on this journey to Death's Throne," Tallinn looked to Karrer pleadingly, yet calmly. "We only ask that you transport us to the lands where we may make such a pilgrimage ourselves."

"You will be well compensated, of course," Danika added enticingly.

Captain Karrer sighed and shook her head, turning from the table to the large windows. She watched the lashing waves and the flashing lightning in the relentless darkness with a grim expression, her shoulders tense under her off-white shirt.

At last, she nodded. "Your quest is uneasy enough. I will not add to your troubles," she turned to face us. "But we must decide our course swiftly."

"Any suggestions would be greatly appreciated," Ranzel nodded.

Captain Karrer gestured to Kororsh, the Storvari stooping his head beneath the rafters of the cabin as he moved through the room to a cabinet. He rummaged there for a short time before at last returning with a chart that showed the currents and flows of the ocean surrounding High-Realm. The giant laid this out on the table and allowed his captain to examine it.

"We are here," she pointed to our position on the map, "a few miles outside the western edge of the bay in which Seaguard is located. We have two possibilities open to us regarding this passage. We can head east and curve our way around the coast of Harredi before turning north. That will bring us up the eastern edges of both the Blackfelds and Grotojan, bringing us to land on the south-eastern point of Valloran... here," her honey brown finger jabbed the place on the map.

"That looks like a long journey," I commented as I surveyed the map apprehensively.

"Twice as long as going to the west. And the vast collection of small islands all along the far eastern coast could prove devastating in these storms," Captain Karrer agreed, turning her attention back to the map as she traced her finger from our position again. "We could continue westward on the Crestian Sea to the far shores of Aldegaad and Ivansten, then turn north to the Ortagaad Sea. We then cross through those frozen ice fields and head directly to the north-east, which would bring us to this port in Valloran's south-western reaches," she once more tapped the map.

"A path yet wrought with perils of its own," Ellora noted, her turquoise eyes set on the trail.

Captain Karrer nodded. "The darkness means that passing Aldegaad and Ivansten will be easier done without drawing their navy. However, we would have to pass the remains of the Isle of Safferan."

"Which is still alight with the burning rock of its destruction at the hands of the Shadow Lord and Ragnarok," Fawkner stated, leaning on the table.

"And the Ortagaad Sea is under the watch of Queen Keilantra's forces," Tallinn sighed, shaking her head. "Not to mention its proximity to the western edge of Gorth'lak."

"However, the eastern route brings us dangerously close to two nations that hold ties with the Dominion, despite one being that of my people," Ellora added thoughtfully, weighing our choices, "whereas the western passage leads only to one as Gorth'lak cannot launch ships at all."

"You will have to make a decision," the captain said evenly, looking up from the maps at us.

I thought about it, pulling the papers I had received from Varel out of my belt. I swiftly found and unfolded the map, laying it out on the table before us.

"This decision must be made with thought lent to practicality," I considered as I studied the smaller map. "Azmerath's Doorway lies here, within the walls of Castle Valkirak, the fortress home of the Vampire King. In order to reach it, we will have to traverse the Haunted Hinterlands from the south-west and up through the Dark Boughs Forest that spreads throughout the entire centre of the nation."

"Certainly viable," Ranzel nodded, "though not without its dangers."

I continued, trailing my finger from the eastern port then: "However, to travel from the east would leave us traversing the Fog-Strewn Mountains; a labyrinth of confusing mountain trails where thick mists blind the eyes and disorient the mind. The paths are treacherous, and it would be too easy to fall to our deaths from such narrow ledges. Then, even if we managed to navigate our way through the path before any number of creatures get to us, we must still pass through the Murky Fenland; a domain of foggy quagmires that was once the place of an ancient battle between the Vampire Lords and the Werewolf Chieftains. Countless graves lay there in that boggy place and the dead are known to wander freely amidst the sunken tombs."

"Clearly, you have studied this place well," Fawkner observed, glancing at me.

I sighed and nodded. "I travelled there once."

"With Aldwyn and I," Tallinn added softly. "Valloran is not a pleasant place."

"That is to say nothing of the Vampire Lords themselves," I sighed grimly, knowing what those creatures were like. "Imagine every deceitful noble of every nation in High-Realm, then give them near invulnerability, eternal youth and immortality."

"A disturbing thought," Danika commented with distaste.

"So, what would you suggest then, Carden?" Ellora asked me calmly, yet quietly.

"The western route is the safest and the quickest," I advised, tapping my finger on the port town at that edge of the Valloran map. "There are only two towns to pass through before Valkirak and the castle that resides above it on Death's Shadow Peak."

The irony of the peak's name that Castle Valkirak was built into was not lost on me. In fact, knowing what I now did, it seemed to me that the name of the peak was perfectly appropriate, given what was guarded there.

"It sounds like the right path to take," Fawkner agreed.

"I'll have my helmsman chart our course to High-Realm's west and round the cape off Aldegaad," Captain Karrer decreed, standing up from her position leaning over the table. "Fortunately, we have excellent winds to take us where we want to go. Unfortunately, the waves will batter us fiercely and slow our progress."

"How long will the trip take?" I enquired of her with as much calm as I could manage.

"Several weeks," she responded. "We have enough supplies to last the passage. Let us just hope that we don't draw the attention of our enemy too soon," she started for the door as she added: "You will have to share quarters, three to each. I hope that will not be a concern."

"Hardly," Fawkner said casually, studying the map. "See my man Oddvar for your payment, Captain."

She nodded and left the room, Kororsh following her.

I took the rest of the pages that I had received from my belt, handing them to Ranzel. "These should be of use to us when we arrive in Valloran," I said with hope. "I can't read them, though I am sure you and Danika will certainly be able to."

"They will take time to decipher," the Wizard analysed as he studied the pages, "but we now have the time to do it. Ellora, perhaps you would be so kind as to assist?"

The Elven Huntress nodded. "Of course. I should be able to translate the Dark Elvish into my own tongue before converting it to Common."

"I will go and attend to my men," Fawkner sighed as he headed for the door. "I only pray that we do not have any incidents with these pirates."

I stood and turned to go, but Ranzel took my shoulder lightly. "Carden, perhaps it is best that you hold onto the map," he advised me, holding the map up to me. "You were the one who received it, after all."

I nodded, taking it and leaving the room without another word. There was only one thing on my mind. I had to make sure that she was all right and see to it that she was comfortable.

As I walked the narrow wooden halls of the rocking ship, I was overcome with a sense of dread. Something suddenly felt wrong, and I had the need to move quickly, though silently. It was as if someone was urging me to witness something that was being done in secret; like I was being warned.

I edged my way around the corner of the corridor, my eyes locking on the open door of the cabin where Joran and I had placed Leander after our arrival onboard. My muscles tensed in moments at the sight of the man that sat at my beloved's bedside, his filthy hand cupping her smaller, tender one.

I wanted to rush forward and smash Tristan's head into the wall, to cave his skull in and render him useless before casting his corpse into the swelling ocean, but I resisted. She wouldn't want me to do that. Instead, I stood there and listened carefully.

Tristan was once again drinking from his flask, the small leather container held in his free hand with the stopper removed. He tilted it to his lips and took a swig, the scent of cheap ale permeating the air and mixing with the salt water that was invading the ship's wood. The Wanderer then turned his eyes down to the Princess' pale face, a sense of longing lurking beneath them.

"Don't worry, lass," he was saying to her softly, still rubbing her hand with his thumb. "The way to restore you is set and we make our path towards it even now," he swigged back and chuckled a little before looking to her again. "I suppose you'll be back on your feet and giving me trouble again in no time. Just like in the forests."

I narrowed my eyes, my gaze flicking to her silent and unmoving expression of sleeping death before flashing back to him.

"You... were *too* trusting," he accused her softly. "It's a little funny actually, but I suppose that's just part of your charm. You try to see the good in everyone," he sighed and looked at his flask. "Even a useless, treacherous drunk like me."

He swallowed back his drink, then put the stopper in, releasing her hand and slumping back a little against the wall. He started stroking her hair and face, almost as if he loved her. That provoked my ire, my predator beginning to claw its way up from deep inside me again. Somehow, I managed to maintain my control.

"I know you don't think of me the way I do of you," he went on to her, speaking in the hushed way one whispers to a lover. "No... your mind is filled with that princely Guardian who denies himself. It doesn't mean he loves you, though."

I balled my fists at my sides, slowly taking my first step towards the room.

Oblivious to my approach, Tristan went on, still caressing her as if she were his: "You don't like lies. I know that now. And... I'm sorry, Princess. Truly I am. I never should have done what I did to you. I hope that you forgive me," he sighed, looking down at her with longing. "I suppose I'll find out when you awaken. Who knows? Maybe death has changed the way you feel."

I was at the door now, tense and glaring at him as he laid his lips upon hers. I was seeing red, though I kept myself from tearing him from the room.

"Rest well, Princess," he whispered to her. "May my love for you help to bring you back."

"Tristan," I murmured his name with a scowl.

He turned swiftly, looking up at me with bewilderment. It was clear that he hadn't expected me to come upon him touching her, his hand immediately going to the knife at his belt.

I tensed and gritted my teeth at his action. *Big mistake, traitor...*

"Carden... I... I was just paying my respects," he excused, standing up swiftly.

"Is that what you were doing?" I asked coldly, stepping into the small room while keeping my hard stare locked on his face, noting his hand at his knife.

"Aye. Nothing more," he nodded, moving to go past me. "I'll be off..."

I braced my hand to his chest, preventing him from going anywhere. I could feel my strength changing, growing stronger as my muscles coiled like some great cat preparing to strike.

"I know what you're doing," I uttered, looking him in the eye, the two of us close to the same height.

"Do you now?" he asked with less concern and more threat to his voice. "You didn't seem to know much back in Eilath the first time. Or in Silvervale."

I narrowed my eyes at him. "Get out. Now."

He scoffed: "Is the great Guardian succumbing to petty jealousy? Do you think her to be yours?"

"We made our pledges to each other," I said evenly and lowly. "You know this."

"The pledges of a young girl are fickle and passing," he commented with an attempt to appear wise. "She was drawn to me..."

"No, she wasn't," I shook my head, snarling at him silently with my eyes.

"She *was* drawn to me," he repeated more firmly. "That is why she kept me close, even after all that had happened between us."

"You misunderstand her compassion for being in love with you?" I asked incredulously. "Are you truly so thick?"

"What? Do you think you're fooling anyone with your brooding orphan routine?" he lashed his tongue, spilling his venomous words. "You're no more an orphan than she was the day you met her."

"Is that what you think?" I maintained my calm.

"It's what I know," he responded, trying to intimidate me by standing over me. "Remember, I've met your mother. And so has the Princess."

"A traitor who has sided with Morod..." I started, but he cut me off.

"Aye, a traitor to her king and her husband," he nodded, staring me down. "Just as you run from your birthright, so too does she run from her wedding vows. How like your mother you are, boy."

"You know *nothing* about me," I growled.

"I know more than you would like me to know," he went on with an equal snarl to mine. "Do you think I was so drunk that I could not see your expression when the Witch mentioned travelling to Valloran? It was brief, mind you, but it was that of a man getting ready to flee."

"I have been to Valloran with Aldwyn and Tallinn," I tried to keep my calm, though my heart was racing, and my breathing was growing heavy. "I know what those lands are like..."

"I know you've been there," Tristan said with an arrogant smirk, "just as I know that Vallorans and Gorvens share heritage and physical attributes like olive skin, green eyes and black hair. Makes it easy for one to pass for the other, doesn't it?"

I frowned, narrowing my eyes. "Balganians and Dorvans have such similarities to each other. That proves nothing, Tristan."

"No use denying it," he shook his head, jabbing a finger to my armoured cuirass. "I can see it as readily as I can see the armour you wear now. Armour that you wore when you were but fifteen... Strange that it should still fit so well..."

"You don't know anything," I hissed, shoving past him to reach Leander.

"I know you lied to that girl about everything," he countered, grabbing my arm. "You did it because you were afraid she wouldn't accept you for *what* you *really* are."

"Walk away, Tristan," I warned him, feeling my blood boil and my predator rising.

"Come on then. Let's have a go," he tried to provoke me. "Just you and me, nothing but fist right here. Winner takes her."

"She is not some trophy to be won," I snarled, glaring over my shoulder at him. "You have no respect for her."

"More than you," he replied coarsely. "At least I had the decency to tell her the truth about *my* past. Then again, I'll bet that playing the tragic, brooding hero has made many a young girl wet her eyes... and other lesser seen places."

I snarled, letting loose a roar and grabbing him by the throat. He was pinned to the wall a moment later, my hand crushing around his neck and trying to shatter his windpipe. He choked and sputtered, struggling to breathe as he grabbed at my wrist. His eyes widened as he looked upon my features, the feeling of the colour in my eyes shifting as obvious to me as their hue was to him.

Stop! I have to stop! I'm falling into his trap! He's baiting me!

I let go, releasing my fingers from his neck and stepping back.

"So..." he coughed, rubbing his throat with one hand, bracing his shoulders to the wall. "It's true... You are a..."

"Do *not* mention it to *anyone*," I warned him harshly, baring my teeth.

He nodded, straightening himself up. "Aye. I won't. I just had to be sure that I was right. But a little word of advice: once we reach Valloran there will be no hiding the truth from the others anymore. Especially not the Princess after we revive her."

I nodded, stepping into the cabin, my hand on the door. "Noted," I turned my gaze to him. "And don't you *ever* lay a hand on her again. Regardless of my feelings, you have no right after what you did. Am I clear?"

"Crystal," he nodded.

"I'm glad we've come to an understanding then, Tristan," I said calmly.

"As am I, Carden," he agreed, dropping his hand from his throat. "We sorely needed to clear the air between us."

"That we did," I confirmed.

We said nothing else to each other, Tristan turning away as I closed the door over.

I knew he wouldn't tell anyone what he had deduced about me, my little demonstration ensuring his silence. I had been holding back all this time, relying on my medicine to keep me from crossing the line between man and monster. But now I was beginning to see that line blur more and more, dread filling me at the knowledge that it would soon be gone.

I slumped to the floor beside Leander's bed, looking to her uncertainly. She was completely undisturbed by the row the two of us had had right in front of her, her features perfectly still as she slumbered endlessly.

A sigh slipped from my lips, and I rested my arms on my knees, bowing my head as I closed my eyes. *I can't deny that he's right. The closer we get to Valloran, the closer we come to my secrets being revealed. I will just have to cross that bridge when it comes to it, but telling Leander... gods... I should have told her from the start... Now I don't know what will happen...*

I sat listening to the groaning of the hull and the washing of the waves around me, just trying to silence my nagging thoughts. My only hope was that when she awoke Leander would be accepting of the truth... *and* forgiving...

Chapter Sixteen
A Storm of Serpents and Swords

For almost two weeks, the *Black Asp* battled its way across the tides and straits that ran along the south and west of High-Realm's shores. The winds were worse upon the open waters than they were on land, the waves trying to crush the brig against the rocks with every heave. There was no denying just how foolishly dangerous this whole venture was, but we had no choice. To travel to Valloran on foot was suicide, and to pass the eastern shores of Therras was far too deadly. The western to northern passage was our best bet.

The ship rounded the edge of Aldegaad's south-western cape, turning north at the captain's command. I was on deck to see this, my eyes focusing on the distant shape of ships in the north. The flags that flew were not familiar to me, a red and gold design flickering wildly in the breeze.

Fawkner came to my side with Ellora, the three of us turning to each other only to nod our silent greeting before facing the ships again.

"Those ships," Ellora commented softly, narrowing her eyes at them. "I have never seen their standard before. Are they from a foreign nation we have not yet heard of?"

Fawkner was frowning as he studied the flag: "The flag seems to bear a hound in gold upon a field of red and black. It is not a heraldry I have yet seen before."

"It is certainly not one of High-Realm or of Therras," Ellora agreed, leaning her slender hands on the railing of the ship. "Such heraldry does not exist among any of the eleven nations."

"It's Aldegaad," I said dourly, feeling my face darken at the realisation.

"Aldegaad?" Fawkner looked to me incredulously, his hood dripping with the heavy spray that came up from the sea.

"Impossible," Ellora shook her own sage hooded head. "The heraldry of Aldegaad is a golden dragon upon a royal blue field. It is the only nation to carry a dragon."

I seethed as I saw the truth of it all before me, the ship coming into view of Aneuran's ports. That same flag of a golden hound backed by red and black hung over every balcony and fluttered on every flagpole in the city. There was no sign of the blue and gold that belonged to Aldegaad, all of it replaced now by these darker colours.

"Fane has changed the heraldry now that he is King," I surmised, glaring at the white palace sitting atop the bridge across the natural stone arch into the bay. "He has done away with the original standard just as he has done away with King Aric and the royal family."

"A hound is a creature of loyalty," Ellora remarked coldly, venom in her voice. "There is no such virtue in that vile man's black heart."

"Indeed not," Fawkner agreed with repulsion at the very notion. "Perhaps the new standard isn't meant to suggest his loyalty, but instead demands the loyalty of his subjects."

"Subjects certainly seems the right word," the woman hissed with distaste, clenching her fist on the wooden barrier before her. "I see nothing of the old Aldegaad here, only a dark kingdom where subjugation of the people allows a tyrant to rule."

I sighed, shaking my head and looking down at where my hands rested on the barrier. "I am just glad that Leander isn't alive to see this. It would break her heart."

"It surely would," Ellora agreed, gazing past Fawkner to look upon me.

I thought of my beloved girl and of the expression seeing her homeland so darkly changed would bring to her soft features. It was too terrible in itself to view, my heart aching at the pain it would cause her to see the Aldrich legacy so crassly destroyed by her uncle. If she had been standing beside me, I would have pulled her into my embrace and tried all I could to comfort her, knowing it to be a futile practice, despite my intent.

None of the Aldegaadian ships made from the bay to pursue us, their sails remaining furled away and their anchors staying locked to the sea floor. We all knew Fane would not risk his fleet just to chase one passing ship with no colours flying. It wouldn't be practical.

* * * * *

The next two days brought us along the Sapphire Straits, so named because of their normally blue gem colouring, though they were darkened now. The straits passed between Aldegaad and Ivansten at the border where the Nartarn'lath Mountains' most western edge met the sea. Several miles west from there we could see the ominous orange glow of the fires that had consumed the Isle of Safferan still boiling in the darkness.

The central mountain should have been visible from here. It should be standing tall and silhouetted by the darkening sky, a sigh escaped my lips as I stared at it from my place on the portside of the ship near the helm where Captain Karrer and Kororsh were working to navigate the swells. *That there is now only the volcanic glow of the fires that destroyed it is a tragedy in itself. But the tragedy I witnessed there... well... losing her... I...* Another sigh escaped as the thought fled from my raw mind. I had no desire to revisit that night again, not after all the times I had in the past.

"The destruction of Safferan has caused great turmoil upon the seas," Captain Karrer was explaining to Tallinn and Fawkner as they stood nearby, the Axton twins joining them after climbing the stairs from the main deck. "The isle's sinking has disrupted the tides and the continuing eruptions cause great waves that make this passage harder to endure."

"But we will make the passage. Will we not?" Tallinn sounded uncertain, though I didn't turn to watch the scene unfolding behind me.

"The *Black Asp* is a sturdy vessel, Lady Guardian," Captain Karrer replied with confidence. "We made the trip through the far volcanic south of the Storvari nation while two mountains erupted from the seas."

"It was no easy task," Vamdrim sounded cocky as he added his own words, standing beside his captain with his arms folded in front of him, "but we traversed the dire straits all the same. Even made some good profit in South Storvarkar."

"That was where I met Kororsh," the captain sounded proud as she spoke. "I saved him when he was nearly devoured by a great serpent of the deep. He has been at my side ever since."

"As I always will be, my Sarissi," Kororsh spoke with that same reverence that Joran always used when referring to Leander.

My heart panged and I yearned for her company. I pulled away from the barrier overlooking the destruction, making my way towards the stairs.

"How long until we head east?" Fawkner was asking as I started down past the Dwarves.

"Another two days," Captain Karrer answered. "It would normally be a swifter passage had we a clear sky and normal weather to sail amidst. We shall reach the Ortagaad Sea very soon."

The Ortagaad Sea, I half snorted at the thought as I opened the door to the next deck and made my way down. *Another wretched place that caused my princess horrific pain and misery. I should have been with her, or I should at least have rescued her. I let her down...*

Reaching the room where Leander lay, I stepped in and took my place on the floor beside her bed. I had set up a bedroll here and had been sleeping with her to keep her company. Joran was always at the door, never leaving and hardly speaking. He and I understood each other without words now, both of us upholding our vow to protect her, even in death.

Anyone else would be too squeamish to even attempt to sleep beside a corpse. But not me. After all, she isn't really a corpse. She's Leander still, though she doesn't draw breath. As I sat with my back to the wall and my arms balancing on my knees, I half smiled at that thought. *I must truly love her then if such a handicap as death doesn't stop me wanting to be with her.*

I found myself studying her porcelain features in the light of the lantern swaying on the wall. My eyes travelled the shapes of her face, tracing each structure of bone that lay beneath her white skin. Her youth was perhaps what made her death so much more a tragedy than the mere event had been.

She was too young to die...

A sigh slipped free of my throat, and I reached to my belt pocket, tugging loose the silvery chain that I had kept there. Raising my hand, I opened my palm and studied Leander's silvery pendant where it lay in my hand. The fire of the lantern danced through the facets of the dark purple stone, shimmering as if the flames lingered within it rather than in the lantern. Had I known better, I'd have thought the Pendant was awake. But it wasn't, the heart of the crystal dulled almost to black.

Ser Mithras once told us that the Dragon Pendants are alive. Now I see what he meant. Leander, Amethyst, the Pendant... they were a trinity, united together as one. But without Leander, the Pendant slumbers and Amethyst has fled into grief. Maybe that is where the power of the Pendants truly lies then; not in the wards and charms of the necklace, or in the strength of the dragon that comes to it, but in the heart of the human who carries it.

Realisation came to me, and I felt even sadder, lowering my hand clutching the Pendant as I turned my eyes to the silent princess again.

Leander's heart was the source of the Pendant's power, the catalyst that let it function. Without her, it is darkened and just like any other ordinary piece of jewellery. She's dead, and so now it too is...

* * * * *

I didn't leave that room after that, choosing instead to remain by my Princess' side until we reached Valloran. I spoke to her where I could, trying to offer words of comfort, though she did not react. It just helped to act as if she were alive and trapped in some cursed sleep.

Rest came to me as little as it ever did, my mind racing with the dark images of her murder at the hands of the Shadow Lord. I attributed that to being so near to where she had died, knowing as well as any mage that such places held powerful energy after such a traumatic event. That didn't assuage my rattling heart and mind however, the images of Leander in that deathly form that came to me in dreams still haunting me.

"I don't know why you're so determined to make this trip," her voice startled me, and I sat up from my bedroll, looking to her bed.

Leander was sitting up with her hands placed to the mattress, the white gown she wore hanging from her shoulders daintily, looking as if a single movement could make it slip free. Her dark hair framed her face as her steel blue eyes focused on me with sadness.

"This is all for nothing, Carden," she whispered softly, that pleading expression painting her soft features. "Can't you see that?"

"You sound as if you don't want to live again," I managed to mutter as I sat up more fully, turning my gaze to meet hers.

"I do. Really, I do," she sighed, looking down at her knees as she shook her head. "I just know that what you're trying to do won't work, and I don't want you to suffer the heartbreak that will come because of that."

"My heart broke the day yours was cleaved in two, Leander," I said in a small murmur, turning my gaze from her for a moment. "I can no longer suffer such a thing as heartbreak. Not when it has become part of my every waking moment, and even my sleeping mind."

I could feel her staring at me, her desire to touch me as strong as my own. That meant that my ability to sense her emotions was strengthening and that my predator would start awakening more fully very soon.

I'll have to take my medicine...

"I never wanted to hurt you," I whispered, glancing back to her. "I only wanted to keep you safe."

She shrugged one shoulder softly. "Well, I couldn't be safer than I am now."

"You're dead," I argued quietly.

She nodded. "Yes. But I am protected by Lord Azmerath. Morod, Ragnarok, even the Darkest Shadow, they can't hurt me anymore."

"I will not give up this quest," I said firmly, keeping my eyes locked on hers. "I cannot just leave you in Death's grasp when there is a way to restore you."

"You don't have a choice," she murmured, a frown creasing her perfectly smooth brow, the thin arches of her dark brown eyebrows bending with the movement.

"There is always a choice, my love," I told her, leaning closer to her, taking her pendant in my hand and showing it to her. "Always."

She flicked her gaze to the Pendant in my open palm, her eyes studying the faceted gem at its heart with the same discernment and wonder I had always seen in her. She then looked to me, a fearful expression flashing through her eyes and across her face, though only briefly.

"I am making the choice not to give up on you," I said, holding her gaze with certainty. "I can't. I won't. I love you with all my heart and soul, Leander."

She smiled softly at my words, tears slipping down her cheeks. But before she could utter another syllable, the pounding of a fist on wood woke me from my slumber.

I groaned, jolting up where I lay on the floor, panic filling me as I sought her out. She was still beside me, laying on the bed, her hair and dress undisturbed as if she hadn't moved at all. I grimaced as I realised, I had been dreaming.

The pounding on the door came again.

"What is it?" I called, frustration in my voice.

The door opened and Tallinn poked her head in, her chest heaving from exertion. She looked panicked; her eyes wide with worry.

"Carden, you have to come now," she said hurriedly, still holding the door handle.

"Why? What is it?" I asked, still groggy.

"We've made it to the Ortagaad Sea and we're passing Gorvenna," she told me.

I was surprised. "That was quicker than I expected."

"Me too," she agreed as I got to my feet. "But things have taken a turn for the worse. Please, come quickly."

Hearing the urgency in her voice, I nodded and grabbed my cloak, passing by Joran as I followed Tallinn from the cabin. We both rushed up the stairs and out of the hatch onto the deck, the cold, wet air that swirled up from the sea hitting us in the face as our breath appeared before us in vapour clouds. We had entered a scene of chaos. The Harredi pirates and the Lorveren soldiers were manning battle stations, large crossbows quickly being mounted to the railings at the sides of the *Black Asp*.

"This way," Tallinn led me swiftly through the mess of soldiers and crew, making for the helm deck where the rest of our companions were gathering.

"What's going on?" I asked, my dark hair catching in the wind as my cloak flapped from my shoulder.

"The lookouts have spotted ships cutting their way up from Travarna," Fawkner explained quickly, the urgency of it all too clear. "Their course and speed show them heading to intercept us."

"How many ships?" I asked, looking to the starboard side of the *Black Asp* in some attempt to see them.

Ellora was perched over the edge of the railing on one foot, the other pressed to the rope ladder that reached up the mast, her right hand clutching it tightly. Her left hand already held her bow at the ready, her sharp elven eyes better suited for long sight than any of ours.

"Five ships," she called to us as she relayed what she could see. "Two frigates and three brigs. They fly the colours of Gorvenna, but I see the banners of Gorth'lak mixed amongst the figures on deck," she gasped and turned her eyes back to us frantically. "They carry a force of Gathlorks!"

"Any other Scourge?" Tallinn requested, her own unease clear.

Ellora looked back to the ships and shook her head. "No. Just Keilantra's human soldiers and Morod's Gathlorks."

"The *Black Asp* will not last against five vessels as well as a force of trained soldiers and vicious Gathlorks!" Captain Karrer shouted from the helm. "Our only mercy is that the summer months have thinned the ice fields enough for us to make this passage easier!"

"Then we'll have to defeat them," Fawkner declared, moving along the deck.

"Oh yes!" Dolin said, leaning on his axe. "And how precisely do you propose we do that?!"

"I say let them come!" Holger lifted his hammer into both hands, spoiling for a fight.

"Leave it to me," Danika said, taking her staff in hand and striding towards the ship's bow, her cloak swirling around her.

"You have a plan, then?" Tristan asked her as he drew his own bow.

She nodded. "I shall summon the means to defeat our pursuers from the natural world. The rest of you need only repel our boarders long enough for me to succeed."

"I shall keep Danika protected," Ranzel declared as the Witch began casting her spell, the crystal in her staff aglow. "Keep the enemy back. I will summon Gaspeite to aid you."

Fawkner nodded and began directing his men as Ellora leaped back to the deck, rushing with Tristan to the aft where the captain was still working the helm.

Now I could see the five ships streaming through the relentless waves towards us, the howls of Gathlorks carrying on the wind.

The clouds seemed to darken and thicken, thunder cracking as lightning flashed blue now instead of red. I knew immediately that it was Danika who was conjuring the storm right as rain tumbled down upon us without pity, soaking our already damp clothes.

Tallinn grabbed my shoulder as one of the brigs started to make its attack run on us, its occupants waving their swords as the Harredi pirates manned the javelin launchers. I faced her as the rain drenched her hair, the woman staring at me with uncertainty in her hazel eyes.

"Are you with us, Carden?" she asked me softly.

Knowing she was referring to my distant mood of late, I nodded: "Yes. I'm with you," I drew my sword in my right hand and a dagger in my left.

Satisfied with my answer, Tallinn took up her own sword instead of her bow, standing with me as Dolin and Holger took to my right, weapons at the ready. Fawkner and Oddvar had their swords unsheathed now too as the Lorveren soldiers and Harredi pirates prepared for the battle.

We braced ourselves as the brig drew close, hooks flying from the deck to latch onto the *Black Asp*. The ropes tied to them began being pulled by soldiers on the enemy ship to draw us close within moments. A second brig was getting nearer as one of the frigates came up on our portside, the crew readying the javelin launchers to fire.

A roar and a flash of flame caused me to glance over my shoulder as screams followed amidst the thunder of the storm. Gaspeite swooped past the frigate, belching flame across the starboard side and alighting the enemy launchers. The green dragon roared and set loose three fireballs at the sails, burning the wet canvas and creating great rips that slowed the ship down.

It's good to have a dragon on our side.

I turned back to the brig boarding us as Gorvennan soldiers in black and gold rushed across the planks they had laid, Gathlorks storming onto our deck with monstrous howls behind them. They had hardly stepped across the gap between the two ships before the Lorveren soldiers gave up a mighty shout and charged forward with their swords, axes and shields. They immediately began driving against the Gorvennan soldiers, the swirling mess of green and gold mixing with black and gold like a maelstrom on the deck. The Harredi pirates were in the fray moments later, swiftly becoming a mass of reds and browns swinging scimitars to cleave down our enemies.

Tallinn and I moved with the precision we both carried from our Guardian training, the two of us acting as if we were one. Our blades cut the air and clanged against those of Gathlorks that meant to slay us, my free hand launching the first throwing dagger into the throat of a Gorvennan soldier.

Tallinn dispatched her foe, kicking him backwards into two others, the three Gathlorks plunging into the wildly whipping icy seas with screams of monstrous panic. She turned her attention then to a Gorvennan soldier and started to fight him back as Holger joined me in battling a group mixed of Gathlorks and Gorvennans, the two of us striking hard. Dolin swung his twin axes into the fray, carving down a Gathlork that struck for Tallinn before he could hurt her. The four of us rallied together to hold the line.

Out of the corners of my eye, I glimpsed the others; Fawkner and Oddvar leading the troops with singing swords as they beat back the Gathlorks. Fire flashed behind them as one of the brigs erupted into flames. Gaspeite swooped to blast his dragon fire upon the helm and the aft, sending panicked soldiers screaming as they plunged into the water to douse their burning clothes. They were trying to take down the Dragon with javelins, but he was too swift, ripping a launcher from its position on the deck before hurling it into the other frigate. It landed with the shattering of wood and the screams of soldiers as the Dragon belched another column of flame against the brig that was trying to close on us from the other side.

I swung my sword around and cleaved a Gathlork's head from its dark brown and purple shoulders, the burly beast crumpling as I turned to the next. A flash of my left hand loosed another throwing dagger, the next Gathlork staggering enough that I could run him through and shove him over the side before moving back to the middle of the deck.

The whistle of an arrow surprised me as it passed by my left shoulder, a Gathlork yelping behind me as he was struck. He fell away and I turned my eyes to the helm deck to see Ellora loosing arrow after arrow with expert accuracy, her sage cloak rushing around her as the rain slicked her leather armour to make it shine in the lightning flashes.

I didn't waste time acknowledging her aid, turning onto the next foe as a Gorvennan soldier rushed me. A few quick slashes of my blade and an elbow to the face dropped him to the deck. My sword came up in a swift arc to cut down two more Gathlorks, my left hand hurling a knife into the chest of another that tried to board us.

A powerful crash drew my attention as a green flash caught in my sights. Ranzel was fighting back enemies with his sword and staff, the crystal in the staff blasting enemies back with magic. The old wizard was moving surprisingly fast for a man of his age, casting down enemies indiscriminately. He stomped the base of his staff, a ripple throwing four Gathlorks and three soldiers away as he continued to defend Danika.

I slew another Gathlork just in time to watch the Witch raise her own staff, the crystal glowing with a seaweed-coloured light. That was when a mighty roar came from the depths, and I stared in horror at what rose from the seas.

A great body slithered beneath the waves, scales of dark green shimmering under the water. Fins like webbed spikes cut the surface as the creature bowed its body and circled below our ship. Another two beasts began to break the water, their snarling fish-like faces hissing loud roars as their bulging eyes stared unblinkingly at the ships.

"Sea serpents!" Tallinn exclaimed beside me as she saw them, the rain and thunder making shouting necessary amidst the fighting.

"I have summoned them!" Danika declared, angling her staff towards the enemy ships. "Hold the line!"

The two of us turned our attentions back to the fight just as we heard the tremendous roar of one of the great serpents. It reared like a snake, standing some one hundred feet tall out of the water. I shuddered to think how much of it still lingered beneath the waves.

Its gaze locked on the frigate that was lagging beside the *Black Asp*, opening its mouth in a vicious roar as it plunged into its attack. Fire erupted from the stores within the ship as the serpent broke its hull, shattering its midsection in two. The soldiers and Gathlorks were now trying to escape in panic as the serpent squeezed and crushed the frigate, tearing it apart. The screams of those in the water only increased as the black skinned, double-finned Culler Sharks of the sea joined in, feeding in a frenzy on all who fell into the surf.

The third brig suddenly exploded as one of the other serpents began destroying it, the sharks sweeping across its hull in search of prey. There was no denying that this was a massacre, but none of us could argue with the Witch's magic. This was our only choice.

I turned my attention back to the battle as a third enemy ship was obliterated by the serpents, the last of the frigates now taking on water as it veered off into an ice shelf. It crashed with the thunderous breaking of wood on ice as I brought my blade to meet another Gathlork, pushing him back into his allies.

The Harredi pirates had managed to loose the boarding lines from the enemy ship and Captain Karrer was pulling the *Black Asp* hard to port as it staggered in the waves. One of the serpents came up on the other ship's right and closed its jaws around it, crushing the deck and splintering the hull to pieces. Now we had only to repel those who were still onboard the *Black Asp*. Gaspeite flew past and set fire to the last brig as it attempted to limp back to the port of Travarna, all but securing our victory.

Tallinn and I were back-to-back, swinging our blades with whirling fury, carving through any enemies that got too close. All around us, the Lorveren soldiers were making the deck clear with aid from the Harredi pirates, the Gorvennan soldiers mostly attempting to flee now that they were losing the battle. The Gathlorks, however, were not as timid and kept coming.

Fawkner joined us as the Dwarves shoved two more men overboard, his sword twirling over his shoulder to impale a Gathlork that rushed him.

"We've all but won this battle!" he cheered, his face and beard soaked with the rainwater, his hair sticking to his forehead and jaw.

"Those blighters will surely have a hard time gaining on us now!" Dolin agreed, roaring as he cut down a Gathlork with his twin axes, then head butted a second straight into Holger's swinging strike.

"Especially if that lady witch can continue guarding us with sea serpents!" Holger bellowed and struck with his hammer, propelling a Gathlork off the side of the ship and into the crashing waves.

I stabbed my sword down into the chest of one of the beasts that I had downed, crouching over him as his black blood coated my blade. We had all but cleared the deck now, the last of our enemies either diving into the sea of their own volition or being cast over the side by Fawkner's soldiers.

"Gods," I heard Tallinn gasp, swinging my gaze up over my shoulder to see her wide-eyed stare and her paling face. "That's... that's not possible."

I frowned and followed her line of sight to the hatch that led below deck. My heart felt as if it had stopped in my chest, my eyes widening as I saw *her*.

Leander stood on the deck of the ship, her long hair soaked as it caught in the wind, her white dress sticking to her body with the rain. She looked bewildered, though her eyes locked onto me the second I saw her.

"It cannot be," Dolin gasped at my side, pausing with his axes in hand. "The lassie is dead! How?!"

"Leander..." I dragged myself to my feet, moving towards her, my sword hand loosening around the hilt of my weapon, which clattered to the deck a moment later.

She was shivering, looking up at me pleadingly. She was right there before me, standing bare foot on the drenched deck of the ship, the wind driving against her white clothing and pulling it to reveal the shape of her body.

"Carden," she whispered, a small smile spreading on her thin lips.

"Carden! Carden, no!" a voice was shouting, Ellora's by the sound of it. "Carden!"

It was like I was under some kind of spell, my hands reaching out to take her in my embrace. I felt her hips in my palms, my muscles tensing enough to pull her to me. She smiled more as I did, her left hand touching my face as her right lingered by her side.

"You're here," I was close to tears as I looked into those beautiful blue steel eyes. "Gods... Leander..."

"I love you, Carden," she uttered softly, drawing closer to me.

Those words made everything around me feel as if it had all slowed down. I could only feel Leander, my sights taking in her alone as the images of the violent waves and the bucking ship faded from my mind. *She* was my sole focus, even as I heard the panicked voices of my companions calling as if from across some vast distance. Nothing mattered. Not now that my beloved was in my arms again.

Something was tugging at my mind as she reached up on her toes, her lips pressing to mine. An impulse was screaming in me, yelling for me to open my eyes immediately. But I couldn't bring myself to do so, not wanting to let her go or lose her as she kissed me.

Open your eyes! it was a thought in my head, but it sounded like Leander's voice. *Carden, open your eyes! Now!*

I allowed my eyes to peek open just in time to see the silvery flicker of a dagger rising up above Leander's shoulder. Her slender fingers were curled around the hilt, her smile now one of malice as she angled it towards me.

She's going to kill you! the voice in my head screamed the way Leander would have. *Carden! Stop her!*

I didn't think, time speeding up and returning to its normal pace. I simply reacted, my left hand snapping up as Leander brought the blade down towards my shoulder. My fingers crushed around her slender wrist, and I jerked my body away from her, thrusting her hand forward in an arc back towards her.

Leander grunted and gasped, her eyes going wide, her breath hitching as her chest heaved beneath her soaking white dress. She stared at me, the rainwater dripping from her eyelashes as she still clutched at the dagger.

My eyes widened and my gaze flicked to my hand, which still clutched around her smaller wrist. Blood was covering the blade and staining her dress, a pool oozing across her midriff around the knife.

No! No, no, no! I screamed inside where I couldn't outside, watching as she slipped from my hold and crumpled to the deck...

Chapter Seventeen
The Haunted North Hinterlands

My hands were trembling, my wide and terrified gaze locked on her slender shape as it fell. She landed hard to the deck, her head lulling to her left shoulder as her wet hair splayed out under her and across her face. Her chest heaved its last as her blood pooled around her, washing from the fresh wound as the rain and surf continued to beat across the ship.

A strangled scream tore from my throat, and I threw myself to my knees, grabbing for the dagger that I had plunged through her midriff just beneath her sternum.

"No! No, Leander!" I cried out in panic, tears blinding me as I frantically tried to save her. "Leander, I'm so sorry!"

A rattling breath slipped out of her lips as they remained parted. Her heart stopped beating and she was once again dead in front of me.

"NO! GODS, NO!" I howled to the sky. "LEANDER! PLEASE, DON'T GO! NOT AGAIN!"

"Carden!" Tallinn was suddenly pulling at my shoulders as I started to reach for Leander's body. "Carden, stop!"

Fawkner was on me as well a moment later, trying to drag me back with his arms pinning mine. I struggled and thrashed, battling to free myself from them and reach her.

"UNHAND ME!" I roared at them, snarling like an animal. "I HAVE TO GO TO HER!"

"IT'S NOT HER!" Fawkner shouted at an equal level to my own, holding firm as two of his soldiers rushed to aid him. "IT'S NOT HER, CARDEN!"

I didn't really hear him, squirming as hard as my muscles would allow, my strength beginning to increase as the thought of what I had done plagued me.

"I KILLED HER! I KILLED HER! OH, GODS!" I was screaming in my grief.

"No, Carden, it isn't her!" Tallinn tried to insist as the rest of our companions rushed to where we knelt over the dead girl.

"It is!" my voice was becoming raw from screaming, my body slumping as I saw her blood on my hands. "I killed her..."

"No," Danika strode into view, her staff clicking against the deck loudly. "You have been fooled by the same illusion that deceived the girl at Silvervale."

I heard her words, but it took me a moment to register them as Ranzel knelt beside Leander's body, checking for a pulse. I turned my teary gaze to Danika, then frowned as I looked back to Leander.

"Illusion?" I murmured, confused by the word.

Suddenly, the deck was full of gasps as Leander's features began to melt away. She looked as if her skin was liquefying in the rain, her dress tightening and turning into closer fitting black garments. Her hair retreated into her scalp as her skin warped into a hideous pallid colour, her nose receding to become two nostril slits in a mound of flesh. The eyes were the last to change, shifting from those soft steel blue ones to some kind of horrendous black without whites.

I recognised the creature before me with dread, having seen it before during the ritual in Grishk'kinnar when Morod had stolen Leander's changing. It was one of the Shadow Lord's chief disciples; the shapeshifter that had infiltrated Silvervale with Manth and Keilantra. It had posed as me to deceive Leander and lure her into a trap so that they could force her to face her own murder. And now, it had done the same to me.

"It is the Lost," Danika confirmed as she stood over the creature's corpse, "the Shadow Lord's skin-walker. You did not kill the girl, Carden, but instead the very creature that stole her from you for its master's bidding in the first place."

"The Lost..." I was bewildered, relaxing my muscles and slumping to the deck. "Then it was trying..."

"Trying to kill you, yes," the Witch nodded, jabbing the dead thing with her staff. "It chose to emulate the Princess specifically to confound you, as is its nature."

"Well, I suppose that answers the question of who the spy amongst us was," Dolin regarded the creature with disgust. "The foul wretch must have been with us all the way from Eilath..."

As he said that, I felt a sudden shard of panic flash through me. *If the Lost has been on board all this time, then it was likely hiding its true form. It came from below deck, so it could have... Oh gods! Leander!*

I threw myself to my feet, ignoring the startled reactions of my companions as I charged below deck, drawing a knife from my belt. I didn't even think to go back for my sword, rushing along the narrow wooden hall quickly with a desperate need to reach her. That need only intensified as I heard the sound of bodies being slammed against walls and of Joran growling.

I sprinted into view of the cabin, skidding to a stop just as the Storvari stepped on the last of four leather-bound Gymphs he had been fighting. The other three were already dead with their greenish black blood sprayed across the walls. Joran twirled both of his curved blades and buried them into the shrieking creature, destroying it once and for all.

"Joran?" I was breathless, terror clear on my face as I saw the scene of carnage the Storvari had created.

Joran turned his violet eyes to me, his greyish-mauve features hard and stern. He withdrew his blades from the dead Gymph with a sloshing grind, standing upright as he faced me.

"Carden Highever," he bowed his head lightly to me. "These foul Hessiik attempted to access my Sarissi's deathbed. It was necessary for me to end their existences."

"Is she...? Did they...?" I couldn't form the words.

He shook his head. "No. She remains untouched."

Deep relief filled me as I sheathed my dagger, stepping over the bodies to the door. The Storvari simply returned to his duties as I looked upon Leander. She was still there, her white dress dry and clean of any stains, her hair falling around her face and shoulders in mahogany waves that caught the gold of the candlelight.

I dropped to my knees before her, sobbing as my relief became overwhelming. She wasn't alive, but at least she wasn't harmed any further than she had been. She was safe, still lying in her bed as if nothing had happened to her.

Ranzel, Tallinn and Fawkner entered the cabin a few moments later, the three of them surveying Joran's handiwork with stunned expressions. I didn't bother to look up at them, glad that they didn't try to stop me from my tears.

"Gymphs..." Tallinn murmured, staring at the monsters laying there.

"The Princess was their target, without a doubt," Ranzel nodded thoughtfully, leaning on his staff, his hat and robes dripping water onto the floor. "It is clear now that the Shadow Lord is aware of our intentions."

"Then he will try to stop us again," Fawkner stated with a relentless knowing. "How has he not discovered our location yet, or come to harm us himself?"

"Like the Princess, I carry a Dragon Pendant," Ranzel indicated his necklace of emerald mounted in gold. "It nullifies his omniscience and so he is unable to view us. It may be our only advantage now to complete this quest before he comes after us anew."

"I will tell the captain to make all haste to Valloran's shores," Fawkner said, turning and striding from the door.

Tallinn stepped into the room as Ranzel watched over me, her footsteps slow and tentative. She dropped to her knees at my side, my sword in her hand. She had retrieved it from the deck for me.

"Is she alright?" she asked softly.

I nodded, my voice hoarse and barely more than a whisper: "Joran guarded her well. It's obvious that they meant to... to..."

I couldn't say the words, not wanting to think of my beloved being dismembered by those foul Gymphs. I just closed my eyes as Tallinn wrapped her arms around me, trying to calm me as the ship rocked in the stormy seas surrounding us.

* * * * *

The rest of the passage north through the frozen ice fields of the Ortagaad Sea would only take three days, and while they were silently uneventful, they were anything but peaceful. An unease had fallen over the ship, its crew attending to their duties with heavily watchful eyes while Fawkner's soldiers patrolled the decks like they would guard the city of Eilath. They were constantly seeking out the next threat, which we all knew would come sooner rather than later. It was only a matter of what form that threat would take on.

Ranzel, Danika and Ellora had confined themselves to the captain's quarters to work on the translation of the pages I had given them, their careful study having already yielded them much. That was what I heard in passing, though I didn't go above deck again for the rest of the trip.

I sat on the floor of the cabin I shared with Leander, watching her lie there in her breathless sleep, hoping still to see the flicker of movement under her closed eyes or at least hear the creak of the bed. No such sounds or sights came to me, however, and I resigned myself to sitting in silence, staring at her pendant. Lately I had come to be drawn to the necklace more and more, studying every curling leaf-like design, observing every refraction of light through the facets of its crystal, gauging every texture of its form in my hand. I had come to know it well, but it was only serving as a reminder that she was not with me.

A sigh slipped softly through my closed lips, and I bowed my head, my arms resting over my knees, my hands held together with the Pendant hanging from one. I had stripped away my armour, the front of my jacket left open to allow for some measure of comfort. I was feeling unwashed and tired, my sleep disturbed at the slightest of noises with the hope that Leander might open her eyes and sit up.

But she's not going to, I thought hopelessly, staring at the grains of the floor beneath my boots. *Not without help from Azmerath. I just pray it hasn't been too long for her to come back to us.*

A gentle knock came to the door, and I lifted my head as it opened. Tallinn stepped through, dressed in her armour and cloak, her hair pulled back neatly to leave only a few coils of golden fleece-like strands framing her narrow face.

"How are you faring, Carden?" she asked.

Her concern for me since the battle three days ago had been welcome. It was the only warmth that I had been feeling as we travelled farther north, and the weather became colder. She knew I was still living on frayed nerves after the Lost had been killed and its illusion had broken.

"I've been better," I let out a sigh, shaking my head as I let my gaze fall to the floor again.

"I'm sure you have," she nodded, folding her arms as she leaned against the doorframe. "Is it what happened on deck that troubles you?"

"In part," I confirmed, staring at Leander's pendant again with longing. "Feeling her die in my hands again was... was..." I sighed had. "There are no words for what it was."

"It wasn't her though," she pointed out softly.

I nodded. "I know. It was just another of the Shadow Lord's cruel tricks. But that isn't all that vexes me."

"I know," she sighed and shook her head. "It's about Valloran."

"I swore I would never return to those dark lands," I murmured, keeping my eyes to the floor as I lowered my arms and sat back. "Now I am about to set foot upon those shores again and face *him*."

Tallinn didn't need any explanation. She knew who I was talking about, though I didn't want to so much as think his name, let alone utter it aloud.

"Everything about my life will be revealed to our friends," I grimaced at the idea, feeling my body tense, "and I have no idea how many already know, or how those who don't will react."

"They will react how they react," she said with more wisdom than her youth would lead one to expect. "All that you can do is focus on what must be done. The rest can be attended to later."

I nodded my agreement, looking then to Leander's body. "That's true. It still seems like payment for what we are trying to do. Maybe that is right in itself."

"You think you are being made to pay in order to bring her back?" she asked with an incredulous frown.

I shrugged, looking back to her. "Why not? These things always have a cost, after all. Maybe the cost will be me losing her anyway."

"I doubt that" she responded as if the very notion was ridiculous. "Leander is not a judgemental woman."

"Yet, there remains a nagging in my mind that will not abate," I said softly, turning my gaze back to Leander and reaching out to gently stroke her cheek with one finger. "I feel as if something comes now with the intention to tear us apart, even once we have conquered Death's grasp."

"The whole of Therras is at war," Tallinn pointed out grimly. "That is no strange feeling."

A shout from above drew our gazes, the words "Land, ho!" sounding distant through the wood over our heads. I felt myself tense at the call. But I had no time to be uneasy.

"I will get my armour on and help Joran prepare Leander to travel," I said, getting to my feet. "I'll see you on deck."

Tallinn nodded and turned, leaving me to my work.

In mere minutes, I was stepping out onto the deck of the ship with Joran following, Leander wrapped up in his arms like a swaddled infant. The sudden glare hurt my eyes and I held my hand up before my face to cast shadows over my sights until I could see. My vision cleared and I stared up at the dark grey sky, the cloudy rain cover like that of a normal day.

"I did not think to see daylight again," I heard Ellora saying as the others were gathering by the side of the ship. "Even grey rainy daylight. It is a relief."

"Clearly the darkness is yet to spread this far north," Ranzel assessed as he studied the sky from beneath his hat. "Though it has certainly begun to."

"Utterly astounding," Dolin breathed a deep intake, releasing it with a smile beneath his thick black beard. "Drink in that crisp northern air."

"Aye. There is nothing like it," Holger agreed, looking then to Ellora. "Is there, she-elf?"

"Certainly not," Ellora nodded, smiling as the Harredi crew were beginning to cast moorings to the dock.

"Let us not linger," Ranzel said, turning and starting for the gangplank. "We still have quite a trip ahead of us."

"You know that we will follow you no further," Captain Karrer stated as she walked beside him, Kororsh already on the docks seeing to the tying up of the *Black Asp*. "Our agreement was only to take you to Valloran."

"Of course, Captain Karrer," Ranzel agreed, one hand to his sheathed sword, the other clutching his staff. "But I would ask that you remain for our return journey."

"And if you should not return to us?" she asked as he reached the docks, Joran, Tallinn and I following behind Fawkner.

The Wizard turned to her with a knowing look: "Then do as you will, but I will send word to you within the week."

She nodded and bowed her head, one arm to her chest. "As you will, Ranzel."

As the captain returned to her ship and the Lorveren soldiers began to disembark, we all gathered with the Wizard.

"Is there a plan from here?" Ellora asked, looking around at the port town that surrounded us. "Or do we just head along the paths according to the map?"

"First, we must announce ourselves to the Lords of Valloran," Ranzel explained, beginning to lead us from the ship. "It is a courtesy that must be upheld."

"I shall need to do that, I assume," Fawkner stated as he walked beside the old man.

"Oh, yes. Very much so," Ranzel agreed with a nod, his eyes hidden in the shadow of his hat. "A visiting lord would be the most appropriate candidate, of course."

"Very well," Fawkner nodded, shrugging deeper into his furred coat in an effort to guard against the cold. "How shall we go about doing that?"

Ranzel slowed his pace, his eyes towards the snowy road and grey town that lay ahead of us. "I believe we tell this individual."

I turned my gaze to where he was looking, keeping my hood drawn against the chilled winds. Immediately, I tensed, my hand grasping my sword in readiness to fight.

There was a man there sitting atop a black horse with glowing red eyes. He was dressed in obsidian armour with a black cloak pulled around him, his hands shielded in heavy gloves. His face was hidden beneath a cowl and a cloth mask, only his inhuman golden eyes visible in the small amount of porcelain flesh that could be seen. At his hip was a sword and across the breast of his chest piece was branded the insignia of the House of Valerian.

"Is he a vampire?" Tristan asked with a twinge of anxiety in his voice as he tightened his brown coat and cloak around him.

"A messenger from the Vampire King and Lord of the House of Valerian," Ranzel confirmed grimly, looking then to Fawkner. "We must tread carefully."

Fawkner nodded, taking a step forward as he followed the Wizard with Ellora at his back. Two green cloaked soldiers passed us to flank their lord as he approached the masked and cowled vampire, the rest of us trailing behind them in silence. I made certain to keep my face hidden, glad that Joran had elected to draw a hood over Leander's as well. I did not want them to see her yet.

"Hail and well met, visitors to Valloran," the vampire messenger spoke in a deep voice thick with a Valloran accent. "My master demands you announce yourselves and your intentions here in our lands."

"I am Fawkner Caradoc," Fawkner introduced himself, nodding to the messenger, "Lord of Eilath, cousin to King Haral of Lorveren. We come here seeking to make our way to Castle Valkirak."

"I am certain you do," the messenger responded, studying each of us with his golden eyes. "My lord demands you attend the castle as his guests."

"Your master knew of our arrival?" Fawkner asked, frowning.

The messenger nodded. "He did. For whatever aid you seek in our lands, you must first go before his Lordship and inform him of your intentions. Considering that you say you are planning to make for his castle of your own designs, I would say that delaying would not be wise."

Fawkner nodded. "Of course. We shall make haste to his castle at once."

The messenger turned and jabbed one finger towards the edge of the squalid looking town, indicating vast snow-covered grasslands with a deep forest in the distance. There was a winding road of dark stone leading towards the forest and the great peak that stood out before all the other mountains in the distance.

That was the mountain known as Death's Shadow Peak and the place where Castle Valkirak awaited.

"Follow the Borgo Road to the town of Valkirak at the foot of Death's Shadow Peak," the messenger instructed, turning his hard stare back to us. "I will ride on ahead and alert my master to your approach."

"Our thanks," Fawkner said with a slight bow of his head.

"Be warned," the messenger said direfully, narrowing his eyes at us. "The road has become more dangerous of late, and you have a considerable number with you. There are not horses enough for you all. Go with caution and do not stay in the forests after nightfall. It will be your doom."

Before any of us could say another word, the messenger reared his horse, the animal neighing like some kind of possessed creature. He turned the reins and the horse charged away at a heavy speed, the rider's cloak swirling behind him as he made for the road he had indicated.

"Humph," Dolin remarked sarcastically, narrowing his eyes at the rider from beneath his blue hood. "Friendly fellow."

"Aye," Holger agreed gruffly, hefting his hammer over his shoulder. "All that was missing was the part where he goes "leave this place or ye will die!" Overdramatic fear monger."

"Regardless of this reception, we have our path laid out before us," Ranzel directed, starting forward and away from the docks. "I suggest we make for the next town along the road before the sun begins to sink. Carden, your map would be of great aid."

"Of course," I withdrew the folded map from my belt as I walked towards him.

"Why do you think he warned us not to wander the forests at night?" Tristan asked as we started to make our way, the heavy footfalls and clanking armour of the soldiers with us like a chorus at our backs. "If he was a vampire, why warn us against his own kind?"

"Vampires do not burn in the daylight as many people think," Danika advised him, following behind the Dwarves. "That is a myth that they appropriated themselves. More likely the messenger was referring to other more ferocious creatures that lurk in the dark places of this land at night."

I chose to say nothing as Ranzel took the map, glancing towards Tallinn. She and I knew all too well what things prowled the Haunted Hinterlands, neither of us willing to openly speak of such things.

"The people seem afraid," Oddvar noted as we passed through the town, the townspeople rushing into the cover of their homes quickly. "Is the Vampire King a tyrant?"

"Not a tyrant," I explained evenly, "just fearsome. None wish to enrage him, and strangers are rare to Valloran."

"Especially hailing from High-Realm," Tallinn added, drawing her hood closer and swinging her bow from her shoulder in case she would need it. "More so now that the skies above High-Realm are covered by darkness."

"Understandable then," Tristan nodded, drawing his own hood.

We started on the road through the hinterlands, the sky seeming to grow heavier with clouds as snow began to fall. Soon enough, we were walking through a blizzard, though there was no heavy wind. The air was so cold that we were shivering hard and struggling several hours into our trip.

"It's bloody freezing here!" Holger complained loudly, trying to shield his hands under his coats even though he wore gloves. "Even the Nartarn'lath Mountains were not as cold as this frozen place!"

"We do not have the luxury of complaining, Holger," Ranzel called back to us as we climbed a hill, the forests slowly coming into view in the distance. "We must move swiftly if we are to find safe lodgings in the next town and move equally quickly to the one after that tomorrow. It is a three-day journey to Castle Valkirak, and we cannot risk travelling at night."

We made the next village before sunset, but only just, the soldiers escorting us looking uneasy as we heard the howling of wolves in the distance. Our only options were to buy out the local inn and the boarding house so that our company had space to rest. Several soldiers took to standing as lookouts. They would change over after a few hours as those of us in our smaller company rested as best as we could.

The next day was the same as the first, the Borgo Road taking us through the Dark Boughs Forest just as the map had shown. I left the navigation to Ranzel, though the road was well paved and didn't deviate much aside from a few minor turns to go elsewhere in the kingdom. The Wizard kept us on track, and before nightfall we had made it to the next town, once again renting out all the rooms that we could.

The third day was harder, however, the air crisper and foggier now as a great storm had begun to blow across the landscape. The forest was so thick that the sunlight that did manage to pass the heavy cloud cover was soon blocked by the limbs of the twisted black trees.

As the sun was beginning to sink, Fawkner had his men surround us and take up their arms just to be safe. I stayed by Joran's side, wary of the forests and worrying for Leander's safety. I threw a quick glance to her only to see her still resting in the giant's arms like a sleeping baby.

"How much farther to Valkirak?" Fawkner asked in a hushed voice, looking to Ranzel.

Ranzel was becoming anxious himself, frowning as he lit the stone in the top of his staff to shed a luminous white glow across the road.

"I am uncertain," he murmured. "I am afraid that we may have left the last town a little later than we had intended."

"It certainly seems darker than it should be," Danika observed, her own staff alight with the same glow as the Wizard's.

"The sun is setting," I said coldly, feeling it in my bones. "I can sense it."

"Have you taken your medicine?" Tallinn asked me in a hushed voice.

I shook my head. "Not yet. I'll take it when we reach the next town."

Something was moving nearby, one of the soldiers jumping at the rustling of the bushes. It was getting too dark now to see and the men were beginning to light torches in the hopes of leading our way with more illumination.

"My Lord," one of the men called to Fawkner. "Something is out there."

"Most likely just an animal," Oddvar called, his hand to his sword all the same.

A howl went up in the distance, causing us all to pause where we stood. I tensed as I recognised that tone, swallowing hard.

No... Not now...

"A mere wolf," Holger snorted. "It is nothing to be concerned about."

"That is no mere wolf," Ellora murmured, her eyes searching the shadows of the trees nervously.

More howls went up across the land, deep and foreboding in the darkness. Moments later, we could hear the frantic rustling of the trees as something came running along the hidden trails. Everyone began searching for some sign of what creature was charging towards us, a soldier suddenly shouting at the back of the column.

"A large beast!" he cried. "It just leaped across the road!"

"Where is it?!" Fawkner called, drawing his sword as he searched for some sign of the creature.

"There!" another soldier pointed towards the right side of the road.

I flashed my gaze to where he was pointing just in time to see the burly back and tail of some large, furry creature slip into the shadows of the boughs. I didn't need any further evidence to know what it was, drawing my sword just as a soldier at the head of the column screamed. We all looked to where he had cried as something massive pulled him into the forest with a gurgling shriek that ended abruptly.

"Werewolves!" I shouted, snatching a dagger from my belt.

"Close ranks!" Fawkner commanded as we started to tighten our lines. "All of you! Close ranks!"

The soldiers did as commanded, two more screaming as massive, clawed hands ripped them from the road and into the woods. The glowing eyes of the monsters appeared all around us as they howled, their footfalls heavy.

"Danika! Light!" Ranzel shouted, stomping his staff to the stone ground.

Danika did the same, her staff brightening the illumination spell coming from its crystal in time with his. The whole space glowed with white light and revealed our quarry for a brief moment. Three enormous, seven-foot-tall werewolves shielded their snarling faces, their black fur looking almost blue in the magical light. They were up on their hind legs, their bushy tails swaying viciously as they flexed their clawed fingers. They snarled and roared at us, darting backwards into the forest.

"Damn it!" Holger snapped, brandishing his hammer at the ready. "This reminds me of the night the Shade Seekers attacked us in Hecturn!"

"I would prefer Shade Seekers to these monsters!" Dolin scowled, his battle-axe loosed from his back and held up at the ready.

"Joran," I turned to the Storvari. "We will need your strength. Give Leander to me."

The Storvari didn't argue, just laying the girl in my arms before unsheathing his twin blades and roaring into the darkness. I crouched as I held the girl close, keeping my sword up in an effort to protect her.

We can't travel with them surrounding us. Gods... I doubt that we will last to sunrise...

The werewolves began attacking, rushing forward as the soldiers tried to block them. More men were yanked from the ground, their screams echoing in the forest as they were killed, their blood looking black in the night as it splashed onto the stone ground.

Ranzel touched his pendant, the green glow and roar from above alerting us to Gaspeite's arrival. The Dragon was flapping his wings as he searched for a way to bypass the thick trees without harming us. He snapped a few branches away and managed to blast flames down into the breach, two werewolves silhouetted as they tried to flee.

One of the large creatures rushed us, but was slain instantly by Joran's powerful, swinging arms. He cleaved it down, dropping its enormous body to the road a few feet from us. Arrows whistled past my head then as Tallinn, Ellora and Tristan opened fire with their bows, trying to discourage the creatures.

"It's an enormous pack!" I called to the others, having now observed at least a dozen werewolves. "We have to move somehow!"

"Carden's right!" Tallinn cried, firing an arrow and scoring a strike on a werewolf, making it whimper like a dog. "We will not last if we remain here!"

"Agreed!" Fawkner swung his sword, slashing the hand off one of the creatures as it reached for him, a soldier then crying out as it mauled him instead. "My men are rapidly falling to these creatures! They are not trained for combating such beasts!"

A werewolf suddenly appeared before me, picking up a soldier and throwing him backwards into the shadows where two more werewolves proceeded to rip him apart. The creature snarled as it stalked towards me, blood and saliva dripping from its jowls. I could only stare back, waiting for it to make its move. As it roared and launched itself at me, I heard the whistling of a crossbow bolt. The shimmer of silver struck through the darkness and lodged in the monster's neck, forcing it to reel in pain.

More bolts glimmered as they shot through the shadows and struck into the beasts surrounding us, their howls of pain accented then by the galloping of hooves.

I turned my gaze to the road ahead just as black horses charged into view. The riders wore the same armour and hooded cloaks as the messenger we had met by the docks, their silver swords unsheathed.

"Vampires!" Ellora declared, her eyes wide.

I had never thought that I would be glad to see the knights from Valkirak in all my life, but in that moment I truly was grateful.

The vampires twirled their blades, cutting through the werewolves, their horses faster and hardier than any we had in High-Realm. They began to dismount, one of them dropping down in front of me, her golden eyes taking in my appearance before she swung her sword and slew the werewolf that had been attempting to attack me.

She reached one gauntleted hand to her neck where a golden pendant with a red stone hung, the glow of magical energy shimmering as she touched it.

"Feldspar, come to me!" she commanded.

In response to her words, we heard the roaring of another great beast as the vampires surrounded our beleaguered position. A gigantic red and silver dragon landed with a thunderous crushing through the trees. He had four great twisted horns rising from his skull, two more on his nose. He roared as he turned his glowing orange eyes towards the trees, snapping up three werewolves and crushing them in his jaws.

The vampires managed to repel the last of the beasts with the aid of the red dragon just as Gaspeite landed and took out one of the werewolves with a snap of his tail. Now that I could see them, I was stunned that there was only a dozen of the black clad knights to defend us. As the werewolves scampered away, the knights eased their stance and the red dragon calmed himself, turning his fiery gaze towards us.

The ground was littered with dead Lorveren soldiers, nearly half of our escort eradicated by the werewolves. Several of the great beasts also lay dead on the ground, their bodies cracking as they began to change and become human again.

Joran crouched beside me as he stowed his swords, taking Leander back into his arms as I got to my feet. Reluctantly, I gave her back to her protector.

The leader of the knights strode towards us, her pendant glimmering in the light of the Wizard's and Witch's staffs. "Lord Fawkner?" she looked for him over the top of her mask.

Fawkner nodded and stepped forward as he sheathed his sword. "I am Lord Fawkner."

"It is good that you are alive," the knight said evenly, returning her own sword to her hip. "The King wanted us to ensure you arrived at Castle Valkirak safely after our messenger returned. It appears that we arrived right in time, though not swiftly enough to save all of your men."

"Regardless of the losses, you have my thanks," Fawkner placed a hand to his chest and bowed his head to her.

She nodded to him, then turned her gaze to each of us in turn as a large, burly man came to stand by her side. He was dressed exactly the same and had identical golden eyes staring at us from under his cowl.

"You have a unique gathering of races with you, my Lord," the woman observed, her penetrating gaze softening as she locked them on me. "His Majesty will be very interested to meet you all. But *you* will certainly draw his gaze."

I folded my arms, staring her down as she approached me. She was not much shorter than me, standing about three inches taller above Leander's five-foot-eight stature. I detected the ghost of a smile as she studied me, then removed her hood and mask. She had long hair as dark as the obsidian armour she wore, her features as familiar as her mother's.

"Carden," she smiled at me warmly, her fangs now visible with the parting of her lips when she spoke. "It's been too long."

"It has, Syrena," I agreed with a vague nod.

"I'm sorry," Tristan drew our gaze, his frown shared by the rest of our group, barring a few who already knew everything. "I don't mean to be rude, but who exactly are you?"

The girl before me smiled and nodded. "Of course. I forgot that you are foreign to our lands. I am Syrena Valerian, commander of the Valkirak Blood Knights and Princess of Valloran."

"Your Highness," Fawkner nodded respectfully. "It is an honour to meet a member of your esteemed family."

"An honour you clearly have already had the privilege to know," Syrena turned her gaze back to me, "given who you travel with."

"What does she mean?" Dolin looked up at me. "Do you know this strange lass, boy?"

I nodded, studying Syrena's beautiful, young and very familiar features. "I actually know her very well," I turned to look back at the others. "She is my elder sister."

The looks on my companions' faces said it all. They were dumbfounded by the news, only Ranzel, Danika and Tallinn not showing any surprise. Even Joran raised a curious eyebrow at me as he clutched Leander close to his chest.

"Your sister?" Ellora murmured in disbelief.

I turned front on to them, letting my hands drop to my side as I stood beside Syrena: "My name is not Highever. I took that name in Gorvenna where I had spent many years living. My real name is Carden Valerian, Prince of Valloran and son of King Tiernan."

"You're a... a..." Holger stuttered.

"A prince?" Dolin quickly finished his brother's question.

I nodded with a pained sigh. "Yes. I figured that since it is my sister that has come for us that there is no point in hiding the truth any longer."

"And further explanations will have to wait until we have arrived within the walls of Castle Valkirak," Syrena stated, summoning her horse to her side. "The werewolves are only startled and will return soon in larger numbers, and with a blood lust greater than before. As well as a taste for vengeance. We haven't got far to go, and I suggest we move swiftly."

"And our fallen?" Fawkner asked.

Syrena looked to him apologetically. "I am sorry, but we cannot carry the dead with us. Though, from the body the giant carries, I can see that you have done so for quite some time already."

"She's... she's important, Syrena," I told my sister firmly, but quietly.

"Then I know why you're here, little brother," she said with a soft sigh. "Only her body may be carried, no others."

I nodded and looked to my companions as she mounted her horse again. I knew they were feeling betrayed, the shock still evident in their eyes. Tristan's was not born from the same place as the others, his instead from seeing my sister before him. His suspicions were now confirmed.

"We will escort you," Syrena declared to our group. "Stay close to us," she looked to her red dragon. "Feldspar, lead the way."

The Dragon nodded and turned, starting along the road with his wings close to his sides so as not to bring the boughs of the trees down upon us.

As we began walking, Tallinn came to my side. "You've admitted the truth now," she whispered.

"Only part of it," I sighed, "though I am certain the fact that I am a vampire is self-explanatory."

"It surely is," she agreed. "Though, if my memory serves, you have more to your heritage than simply being of vampire blood alone. Your other aspects may yet be revealed to our companions."

"No matter," I decided, pulling my cloak further around me. "All that matters now is that we will be able to complete our task."

She just nodded her agreement as we fell into silence.

I started considering what lay at the end of this road, knowing that my reunion with my sister was joyous next to the one to come with my father. Oh, how I dreaded it.

There's nothing for it now, I considered grimly. *Time to return home...*

Chapter Eighteen
Hall of the Blood Kindred

U nder the escort of the two dragons and my father's Blood Knights, our group continued through the forest in complete silence. The revelation of my true identity had surely left my companions to ponder the nature of my being, something that I would have to attend to when we had time to settle at the castle. As for myself, the prospect of returning to my ancestral home was not an easy one.

I left for a reason, after all. So did Syrena. We both intended on such different lives, yet it seems that our father's will comes to pass no matter what. Well, at least I know one thing: he would never side with the Shadow Lord. He is too proud, unlike my mother.

The thought of Adriana made me cringe and I pushed her from my mind swiftly. The last time I had seen her was during the battle at Safferan and I didn't long to lay eyes on her again any time soon. Having to see Tiernan was going to be difficult enough as it was.

After another hour, we broke through the lines of the forest and came upon the sight we had all been searching for. The town of Valkirak looked like any other; walled off and protected by armed soldiers, the human guardsmen loyal to my father. The houses were quiet with candles lit in the windows, the citizenry uneasy enough under the best of circumstances, but more so when werewolves howl in the night and Blood Knights charge through town to hunt them.

My eyes drifted up to Castle Valkirak, the Hall of the Blood Kindred itself. It stood high up on the cliffs of the pointed mountain, Death's Shadow Peak. It was built like some ancient fortress of old; towering spires and battlements reaching high, but none as high as the keep tower in the centre of the structure. Gigantic stained-glass windows were visible even from this distance, the many additional sections reaching out all around it like a maze of rooms. The castle could be accessed only by a long bridge across a chasm in the cliffs, via a road leading through the town and up to its intimidating grand gates. There were shadows mulling about the towers; great winged forms that swooped and let out howls into the night. They unnerved my companions, but I found them comforting.

"What foul beasties be those?!" Holger exclaimed.

"I've not seen their like before," Fawkner concurred with an uneasy glance skyward.

"They are Castle Valkirak's protectors, beyond our soldiers," Syrena explained.

"Winged protectors of a mysterious nature?" Ellora queried. "What are they?"

"Gargoyles," I answered. "Great warrior beasts that defend their charges by night and by day are as unmoving stone. Don't worry. They won't attack us."

"Well, that's comforting," Holger remarked.

"Feldspar," Syrena looked to her dragon as she brought her horse to a stop. "Take the other dragon to the caves in the castle. I'll come to you later."

Feldspar growled his confirmation of her orders, then spoke in dragon tongue to Gaspeite. The green dragon looked to Ranzel for direction, but once the Wizard had nodded his approval, he took flight with the red dragon. Both of them flew up towards the castle as we began our short trek to the town.

Soon enough, we were crossing the bridge over the chasm and passing through the gargantuan gates, the presence of more black clad Blood Knights making everyone uneasy. It had been a very long time since I had last set foot within the walls of the ancient castle of my grandfathers, every single brick and tile looking the same. The castle actually seemed like the perfect comment on its own about its immortal inhabitants.

Maybe they're all made of stone too...

We came to the main stairs that led to the tower keep, two sets of enormous ebony doors placed into huge stone archways the key feature. A gigantic round window of stained glass was constructed into the wall above the doors, its shards the hues of reds and burgundies to represent our clan's heritage. The blood was life, after all. It also boasted a large V shape set into the glass tinted in shades of silver, grey and blue, the single letter both standing for our family name and for our race.

Syrena slipped from the saddle of her dark horse, a Nightmare, one of the most graceful of its supernatural breed. It was essentially a horse blessed and enchanted with the blood of our kind. My sister turned to us as a human servant took her horse and that of her husband, Caedmon, the large, burly Blood Knight who had stood at her side. I knew him well, his father the Vampire Lord Hargreaves.

"My father is expecting us," Syrena turned her golden eyes towards Fawkner and Ranzel as Tallinn stayed at my side. "We will go directly to the throne room, though I must warn you that he had been in a bit of a bad mood when I did depart."

"When is he not?" I asked with a sly smirk.

Syrena nodded, smiling faintly. "I know what you mean, brother. He seems like he rarely smiles anymore."

"Given the state of the world, I can hardly blame him," Ranzel said evenly, leaning on his staff.

Syrena nodded. "Regardless, just be warned. He will wish to question you - *all* of you - about your purpose here. He is very thorough and severe with such interrogations."

"Does he know about me?" I drew closer to her, my hands balled up at my sides as my unease forced more tension through my already stressed body.

She looked to me with a stare that already gave her answer, though she spoke anyway: "The messenger who rode ahead of you saw your face and recognised you immediately. He has told father of your presence here," she shrugged and tried to smile. "On the bright side, maybe seeing you will lift the foul cloud that looms over him."

"Let's hope so," I sighed.

"Follow me," Syrena turned, striding up the dark stone steps beside Caedmon, their black cloaks shimmering as they trailed behind them, their obsidian armour taking on a crimson tint in the torchlight.

Our party started after them, passing by six Blood Knights who stood at alert flanking the stairway with sharp and sinister halberds in hand. At the doors were four more, two to each set, armed with the same halberds and shields, their inhuman golden eyes staring out at the darkened courtyard before them. They allowed us to pass without incident, briefly bowing their heads as I walked by them, my hood now cast back.

The perks of being a prince... Is it any wonder I left Valloran for High-Realm. At least there I am unrecognised. Now I know how Leander felt...

We stepped into the grand hall of the castle, a three-storey high enormous room with a fountain set in the centre. Black marble columns rose up from the floor to the ceiling high above us, the stonework arches curving to meet in the centre where the middle line of the castle ran the length of the hall. Two grand staircases encircled the far end of the massive space above a large stone archway that was flanked by the black, red and silver banners of the kingdom. The standard of Valloran was a black V with a sharp Ankh above it set against a dark crimson background with black and silver detailing forming a cross with rounded edges surrounding it.

"So... uh..." Dolin cleared his throat as we passed through the mammoth hall, our steps echoing all around us, "what do we know of this King Tiernan? What is his reputation like?"

I had the answers to the Dwarf's question, knowing my father better than anyone there. Aside from my sister and her mate. But I had no desire to discuss him until after we had met with him.

It's better the others see for themselves, I thought.

Thankfully, Ranzel took the lead in answering.

"Well, for starters," the Wizard said, removing his hat with one hand as he walked with his staff in the other, "King Tiernan is one of the oldest living beings in all of Therras. He is nearly five thousand years old."

"That is mighty old," Holger commented, looking to his brother. "Older than the halls of Hecturn or even the Silver Steel City of Morthenhas."

"His age may allow us to garner his support," Ranzel continued on as we drew near the fountain in the middle of the room. "He is old enough to remember the days when the Dominion first rose to power under the leadership of Shadow Lord Gorth Lavelle, and the day when the Defenders of Therras imprisoned Ragnarok and his wretched brethren in the redoubt on Safferan."

"And his opinion on such events?" Ellora asked with a raised eyebrow, her unease understandable.

"The Valerian Royal Family are well known for opposing the Shadow Lords," Ranzel stated calmly, "and King Tiernan is no different. He is an ardent royalist and traditionalist, which can make him rather difficult to convince of the validity of more modern methods."

"He is set in his ways," Fawkner noted with a nod, glancing to Oddvar.

"A peril that comes with living such a long and unending life," the Wizard nodded, reaching the fountain and passing it. "Immortality can harden the gentlest of hearts if they are secluded and disconnected from the world. It is why I have chosen to be the Green Wizard and walk alongside the people of the earth."

"Gods almighty!" Tristan coughed, staggering as he stared at the fountain. "What is that foul liquid spouting from this thing?!"

I threw a cursory glance to the fountain and the oozing dark red liquid that flowed heated from its spouts. The scent of copper and salt was overwhelming now that we were so near it. I felt my throat burn and I immediately pushed my mind towards the task at hand. I would have to get my medicine later, mentally reminding myself to do so.

"Is it not obvious?" Danika asked of the retching wanderer, her steel hard gaze turning from him to the fountain. "It is a blood font conjured by magic to ensure a fresh supply of whatever blood his Majesty desires. They most likely keep it as decoration, or drink from it at grand parties."

"Ugh... It gives me the creeps," Tristan shuddered, pushing away from it as the rest of us continued under the balcony the two staircases led to.

Syrena pushed open the large ebony double doors, clearing the way into the castle's throne room. It was a little smaller than the hall, though not by a lot, the same black marble columns and blood red running carpet decorating the otherwise darkly hued room. There were tables running the length of the room off to the sides, several noble vampires standing there in red and black finery. They watched our party with hunger in their eyes, some of them having gold irises while others had shifted their pigment to the crimson scale.

The Lorveren soldiers who had survived the attack by the werewolves looked nervous as they now faced a room full of blood thirsty immortals, each man glancing around him like a deer being stalked. It was perhaps a very true and accurate analogy of the situation, though my father's command protected them, as did mine.

At the far end of the room stood the dais, which was raised up several steps to look down over the room in two tiers. On the first tier nearest the floor with only three steps to climb were two thrones, one to each side. Another five steps up and central of the two lesser thrones was that of the King; a high backed and darkly designed seat of wood dressed in black and crimson velvet.

At last, my eyes fell to the figure I had been trying for decades to avoid seeing again. My father sat upon his throne dressed in a long over robe coloured in deep crimson with black detailing and silver trims, his long doublet tunic made of black velvet with gold trim. Around his neck was a golden chain encrusted with dark red jewels and a large V hanging from the throat, his hands adorned with brassy golden rings that boasted the same gems. On his head he wore an ornate but slender golden crown with a single red blood ruby set above the brow. Beneath it, his deep midnight black hair was pulled back in a clasp to hang across his shoulders and away from his youthful face. To look at him anyone would think he and I were brothers rather than father and son, for we were so alike.

Father eyed our arrival with cold and callous crimson eyes, his foul mood all too clear by the more vicious hue and the way he rested one cheek mildly into his hand. His elbow pinned the cushioned arm of the throne on his left as his right hand tapped the wooden edge of the other armrest with one impatient finger.

Syrena stopped before the throne and bowed her head, hands at her sides as one foot crossed over the other in her fluid movement.

"My Lord Father," she addressed him in an official manner, standing upright to lock her gaze on him. "We have brought to you the visitors from High-Realm."

"There are considerably *less* men present than my messenger reported were to arrive," he observed in his usual cold tone, the echo of the room carrying his words even though he barely raised his voice.

"They suffered casualties on the Borgo Road just outside Valkirak when werewolves ambushed them," Syrena made a point of explaining things briefly, trying not to exasperate his already foul mood.

"Did the beasts slay anyone of importance?" my father asked nonchalantly.

I threw a glance to Syrena as I caught the others tensing out of the corner of my eye. Ranzel held a hand to them as Fawkner scowled but remained calm for the sake of diplomacy. My sister flicked her eyes to me, her own dislike for his way of speaking all too clear to me as she turned her attention back to Tiernan.

"*No*, Father," she responded, trying to hide her distaste for his indifference to lost human life. "Only *soldiers* perished."

"Is that contempt I sense in your tone, girl?" he narrowed his crimson eyes at her.

Syrena bowed her gaze from him to the floor, blinking nervously as she shook her head swiftly: "Of... of course not, Father."

"Good," Tiernan eyed her coldly, then turned his attentions with a flick of his crimson eyes to our party.

He studied the faces there with less than interest, still tapping his right finger as he sat up straighter. Syrena was now moving to stand before her lesser throne, her hands held before her as Caedmon stood at her side, his hard eyes locking on us as much as his master's.

"Which of you is the Lord from Lorveren?" Tiernan demanded in a clear and commanding voice that rang off the walls and columns of the room, his lips flashing his fangs as they moved to twist out his words.

"I am, Sire," Fawkner stepped forward, brushing aside his cloak with one hand before bowing his head respectfully. "I am Fawkner Caradoc, Lord of Eilath and cousin to King Haral of Lorveren."

Tiernan smiled darkly, settling his shoulders back into his throne. "We seldom receive visitors from so far south of our borders. Especially those of noble heritage, my Lord Fawkner."

"I am honoured to be granted an audience with you, Sire," Fawkner played the diplomat, offering a mild nod to the King. "The reputation of your Majesty and this legendary castle proceed you and can scarce live up to the reality which I now behold."

Tiernan smirked a low chuckle. "You speak with a silver tongue, my Lord. Had I not been informed of your lord-hood, I might have thought you to be a common warrior, given your attire," he mused for a moment as he studied him. "You wear the armour of a Guardian as well as the garments of a noble."

Fawkner nodded. "I am both a Lord of my country and a Guardian, Sire."

"And I see that you are not the only one of your Order," Tiernan's gaze fell to Tallinn. "It is an unexpected surprise to see you in my halls again, Tallinn Landrace."

"It is an honour as always, King Tiernan," she bowed her head swiftly.

"I do not see Aldwyn with you," my father observed, briefly scanning the gathering of High-Realmians once more.

"Aldwyn was slain this past year," Tallinn replied in a strong voice that masked her pain, "before the darkening of the sky above High-Realm."

"Ah. Yes," Tiernan considered with a cold and knowing smile. "The portents of doom that have surely directed you to my far-off kingdom with such a vast variety of peoples," he scoured our company with curiosity and a hint of hunger.

"You have quite an entourage assembled here; two Dwarves, an Elven Huntress, an Ivanstenian, many Lorveren men, a Witch from Raven's Rest and even a Storvari of the far south where the land is almost nothing but deserts."

I decided to stay silent no longer, my nerves on edge enough as it was. But it was my father's frown that stayed my feet only for a moment as he locked his narrowing gaze on Joran.

"And even more intriguing," he said slowly as he settled on the small figure in the giant's grasp, "is the dead Aldegaadian girl in the southern warrior's arms. Utterly fascinating."

"My Lord Tiernan," Ranzel moved before I could, his staff held up only to gain my father's gaze. "Your perceptions are unsurpassed for certain and your knowledge of the peoples of Therras impressive. However, there is a rather pressing need at hand and our presence here comes at a time of great peril."

"Oh, I am *very* aware of the peril of which you speak, Ranzel Earth-Guard," Tiernan recognised the Wizard immediately, still looking as confident and arrogant as ever. "It seems that when a wizard appears in a king's court that there most always must be some great catastrophe at hand. Such seems to be the case with you, my old counsel."

"Yes, well," Ranzel smiled mildly and nodded to the Vampire King as he stood from his throne, "such is the life of a Wizard. We never stay in one place or another for too long."

"So very true," my father agreed, striding down the dais and setting foot to the carpet with his robes flowing around him. "I suppose I should not feign insult when I am certain that you work upon other rulers as you do with me."

Ranzel and Tiernan stared each other down, the power between them like electricity crackling through the cooled air of the brazier lit room. They lingered in their locked gaze for a few moments before my father turned his eyes to Joran and Leander once again.

"Your intentions seem well advertised, given the girl your Storvari companion clutches to his chest," Tiernan remarked as he took a few steps forward. "I can only assume that you have come for the one thing that is accessible *only* via *this* castle."

I stepped out from behind Joran where I had made sure to linger when we had entered the room, immediately gaining my father's stare. "As always, your assumptions are correct, Father," I said evenly, one hand to my sword's hilt.

My father's eyes immediately softened and began to change the moment he saw my face and heard my voice. The crimson hue of his irises retreated beneath his black pupils and turned a warm amber gold as he stopped suddenly in his tracks.

"Carden," he spoke in a gentler voice, his surprise giving way to reserved joy. "My son... So, the messenger was telling the truth."

I nodded as he approached me. "It has been a long time, Father."

"Too long," he smiled, placing his hands to my shoulders. "I can hardly believe my own eyes."

"Believe them," I replied, glancing to Leander's body, then back to him. "You know why we're here and I must ask for your aid where I believe you might be less generous to my companions."

Tiernan withdrew his hands as a shadow crossed his eyes at my comment, but he didn't lash out. He simply nodded and clasped his hands behind his back firmly.

"Of course," he said evenly, the harsh king returning once more. "You seek aid, and I shall give it, but only because it is *you* who asks. I will arrange rooms for you and your companions, Carden. It is late, but I will also have the chefs prepare a light meal for your party."

"Our thanks, my lord," Ranzel held his hand to his chest and bowed his head. "I am certain that you will need explanation about our intentions here."

"Not at all, Ranzel," Tiernan turned from me, moving back to meet the Wizard's gaze. "The darkened sky over High-Realm and the destruction of Safferan can only mean one thing: Ragnarok has returned."

"You know of the fate of Safferan, Sire?" Fawkner asked with surprise.

Tiernan nodded. "News has travelled far since the Isle of Magic sank into the ocean in a blaze of fire, as have stories of the destruction being wrought by the foul dragons of Ragnarok. Tidings of the Shadow Lord rallying the Dominion has also reached me, and that is something the House of Valerian has never tolerated," he turned his eyes back to Leander's lifeless shape. "I can only assume that this dead girl has something to do with ending this terrible blight, which is why you seek Azmerath's Doorway."

"It is, my Lord Tiernan," Ranzel confirmed.

"Syrena," Father called and my sister came to his side. "Please show our guests to their rooms."

"As you wish, Father," she bowed her head obediently.

Father simply nodded his head, turning and making his way back up the steps to his throne as my sister traversed down them to join us. Without too much discussion, she took us from the room, leading us back the way we came.

I threw one look over my shoulder as my father returned to his throne and sat back, an adviser in dark red coming to his side to speak on some other subject.

Well... he hasn't changed...

* * * * *

A few hours had passed since our arrival at Castle Valkirak, and we had found ourselves settled in the west wing of the tower keep. Syrena had led us through the dark stone halls to each of the rooms, though she had done this only with our close party, the soldiers directed to the human guardsmen barracks. She and I both agreed that it would be better than lumping them into the Blood Knight quarters where they might become a tempting meal for some of the more vicious members of the castle's elite warriors.

I had been given my old room, nothing in it looking to have changed in my absence. A set of Blood Knight armour was placed on the mannequin in the corner of the room, along with my royal sword mounted on the wall and my sharper silver throwing daggers. The closet was full of fine clothes of deep crimson, black and silver, black boots resting beside the dresser in the corner. The banner of Valloran hung on the wall opposite the four-poster bed which was dressed in crimson and black with crimson velvet drapes surrounding it. Even the books were still set upon the shelves, a few laid out on the desk where I had left them after my last visit.

I stepped from the bathroom, drying my hair, fresh black pants on while my athletically defined torso remained bare. My eyes locked onto the room for the umpteenth time since arriving in it.

Father has clearly kept everything neat and just as I left it. I must admit that is a surprise, though not a pleasant one.

I flicked my eyes to the large window as I started to dab the water from my chest with the towel. I could see the great balcony of the west wing stretching out over the enormous chasm beneath the castle. There was mist below the balcony, darkness consuming the view beyond. The flicker of natural lightning came, and rain began to patter at the window as I broke myself from the panes. I turned to the shirt I had laid out on the bed from my own bag, reaching for it.

A knock came to the door as I took it up and began to pull it on over my muscular arms. "Come in," I called without concern for my modesty.

Syrena pushed the heavy, thick wood door open, stepping into the room. She had bathed since showing us to our rooms and now wore a gown of dark crimson with silver details over a black linen long sleeved dress. The bodice was laced in silver and her hair was brushed long to hang almost to her hips, pinned back only by her slender and delicate golden circlet. Now she looked more like a princess.

"How are you settling in, little brother?" she asked me as I started doing up my shirt.

"Well enough," I responded with a nod. "The room seems as it was when I last visited."

She nodded, looking around at everything with a faint smile. "Father would never admit it, but he is rather sentimental when it comes to the two of us. I returned to find my room in much the same state."

"Who knew that he actually cared?" I remarked as I started to rummage through my pack.

Syrena sighed, her look of sadness clear, even out of my periphery. "Mother's betrayal hurt him. It made him more callous than he was when we were children."

"His five thousand years of age may have had a hand in that too," I pointed out, withdrawing the phials of medicine Tallinn had made for me before sitting in the chair at the desk.

"Age can make us cold," she agreed with a sigh, folding her arms around her before she glanced at me. "Had I not known any better, I would think that you were suffering such affects yourself, little brother."

I sighed and stared at the floor. "Loss can do that too."

"It's the girl, isn't it?" she asked, my green eyes flicking to her golden ones as she spoke softly. "The one you brought with you?"

I nodded grimly. "Yes. She was murdered right before my eyes," I seethed as I growled the next words: "By the Shadow Lord."

"You loved her," Syrena perceived.

"I still do," I said, my expression softening at that single thought. "That is why I am doing all of this."

She smiled and laughed faintly. "Oh, my brother, how very little you have changed," she placed her hands on my shoulders. "The world is on fire as dragons and monsters rampage across the face of Therras, and you come home seeking to bring the girl you love back to life. You're still a romantic."

I nodded, half smirking, half grimacing as I set the last few items I needed on the desk, studying the phials of medicine before me.

"My reasons are not wholly selfish," I said softly, then looked to her. "Where have you put her? Not in a crypt, I hope."

Syrena shook her head, running a slender hand through her raven locks and casting the strands over her shoulder: "No, of course not. Your intentions to use the Doorway made it clear that she should not be confined to the crypts. I had the Storvari lay her in a room down the hall at the far end. I thought you'd like her to be on a bed."

"She should be comfortable," I nodded softly, taking one of the phials and loosing its cork stopper. "It is the least she deserves after all she has been through."

Syrena nodded softly, clasping her hands before her waist as I drank my medicine.

"That stuff looks like it tastes foul," she observed with a worried expression as I took water from a pitcher to wash it down.

"It does," I confirmed as I took in a breath after my mouthful went down. "But it keeps me in control of myself."

"You know what Father will say to that," she murmured, touching her neck softly.

I turned my eyes back to her, seeing the faint, but unmistakable scars of a vampire bite on her throat. The two pinpoint scars looked raised amidst the rest of her skin, her hand gently grazing them with an edge of sadness.

"Did he do that?" I asked softly.

She shook her head. "It was Mother. She found me in Nargilith and forced the change on me to accelerate my vampirism," there were tears in her golden eyes, which were now dulling with her sadness. "It was why I returned here to Valloran and why Father hates her so much."

"I can understand," I stood, looking down at her as I took her hand from her neck and wiped her tears away with my thumb. "Father was always so protective of you."

"He wanted us to change naturally," she said, looking deep into my eyes, "not by the violent rape that Mother chose to carry out. She was just impatient and trying to recruit me for her new master."

"How did you escape her?" I asked softly, afraid to know now that she had mentioned violation, though I wasn't sure if it was just because of how her change was initiated or if it was about her intimacy as well. Either way, I felt hatred in me for the woman who birthed us both.

"Caedmon," she whispered, looking down at her hands as she touched them to my shirt, absentmindedly playing with the fabric. "Remember how the three of us had fled after Mother's and Father's feud became too much? While you stayed with Varel in Nargilith, I travelled with Caedmon. He discovered what Mother was doing and broke into the den where I was being held. He was too late to prevent the change, but he at least ended the carnal assaults of the men serving Adriana," she half snorted. "It was all designed to break me down for her master. To make me his servant, like her."

That confirmed my worst fears and I felt deeper sympathy for my sister. I pulled her close and held her tight, stroking her hair and back gently.

"I'm sorry I wasn't there to stop them, Syrena," I apologised with all my heart. "It seems that I am just incapable of defending the women in my life with any real success."

"Don't say that Carden," she looked up at me, stroking my cheek gently. "You're a wonderful brother to me and always have been. And I am certain you are a wonderful mate to that girl too."

"I... I should go and see her," I said softly, looking to the door. "I just need to make sure she's all right."

Syrena nodded. "Of course. I'll accompany you."

We unhooked from our sibling's embrace and left the room, Syrena leading me with the clicking of her soft boots and the swaying of her trailing gown to the end of the hallway. Joran was standing at the door like he always did, his arms folded before his enormous chest, his eight feet of height intimidating even to the vampires that patrolled the castle.

The Storvari nodded his head to me, and I opened the door, stepping into the room with my sister at my back. A sharp intake of air filled my lungs as I took in the candlelit confines of the room. It was a gentler feeling guest room than others in the castle, the walls lined with mahogany boards, the bed clothed in a dark green rather than the reds and blacks of the royal house.

My eyes drifted to Leander where she lay on the bed, her head and shoulders resting in the plump white pillows, her hands by her hips. Her white dress was a little ruffled and I moved to smooth it out, making sure it was neater and sitting comfortable on her lithe frame. I didn't think it was possible, but her body had started to look thinner. Concern filled me that she might not last much longer.

"She's very beautiful," Syrena stated in a hushed voice, almost as if she was trying not to awaken her. "She looks like a princess."

"She is," I said softly, staring at the girl's still and silent face as I stroked her dark auburn hair. "This is Princess Leander Aldrich the Second, heir to the throne of Aldegaad."

"The descendant of the Great Heroine?" Syrena was stunned.

I nodded. "Yes. Though I think of her as the woman whom I gifted my heart to," I sighed, my chest aching. "I feel so empty without her, Syrena."

"I know," she said in a quiet tone. "I can hear your thoughts, brother. I can see the day you pledged your love to each other. Did you really not tell her that you're a prince?"

I shook my head, still studying Leander's face. "It just didn't seem important. Besides, I had no intention of returning here, so it didn't really matter."

"Do you still feel the emotions of others around you?" she asked.

I nodded. "Yes, though I try to resist it. The only person whose feelings I long to sense is Leander."

"Then she truly is your mate," she sounded contemplative. "Carden, I will- "

She was cut off as a human servant came into the room, drawing our attention to him. He looked nervous, but it wasn't because of what we were. He was uncertain about me as he had never dealt with me before.

"Uh... excuse me Princess, Prince," he said with fearful respect, "I do not mean to intrude but your father has requested that you join him in the private study."

"Can it wait?" I asked a little harshly, not wanting to leave Leander.

He shook his head. "No, your Highness. He is rather insistent."

I sighed, throwing him a glare. "Very well. Tell him that we will be with him momentarily."

"Yes, Prince Carden," the servant nodded and left the room swiftly.

I sighed, grimacing as he spoke. I didn't need to turn to know that Syrena was smirking at me, sensing her amusement even with my back facing her.

"You really don't like being called "*Prince*". Do you, little brother?" she said with quiet amusement.

"Not really," I replied evenly. "It never sat right with me," then a thought occurred to me, and I recalled what Leander had said to me when we danced in Arvon: "Though it seems I wasn't alone in that dislike. Leander never liked being referred to as "*Princess*" by everyone that she met all the time either."

"Perhaps you two had a lot more in common than you both thought," Syrena suggested sympathetically.

"Perhaps so," I agreed.

Syrena sighed and turned to the door, pausing to look back at me. "Anyway, we had better go and meet with father before he becomes impatient."

I nodded softly. "Yes... I suppose we should," I leaned down to Leander, whispering to her: "I will be back soon, Leander. Rest well, my love."

I laid a soft kiss to her cold lips, pausing only to study her features one more time before I stood.

Reluctantly, I left her lying there and followed my sister into the dark grey corridor, walking briskly as we made our way to meet with our father.

Chapter Nineteen
The House of Valerian

yrena and I were not in any real hurry to join our father in the private dining room, but we also knew that to keep him waiting was not wise. I considered him in comparison to King Aric and Prince Ewan when I had first met them, finding that Leander's uncle and father had been of a far softer nature than my father. When either of them summoned her, it seemed as if she were allowed the time to come to them without urgency, her presence welcomed with gentle smiles even *if* she took a little longer to reach them. Tiernan was not so allowing. He always acted as if every summons was of dire circumstance and scowled if we were to dawdle.

His demanding nature is not something I missed, I thought dourly, glancing at Syrena.

I forced all sour thoughts from my mind as we reached the dining hall, pausing before the doors only for Syrena to knock loudly. She threw a nervous look my way before we heard Father's voice.

"Come," he called clearly, but without sounding as if he was shouting.

I opened one of the doors and we stepped into the room, looking upon the scene before us.

The room was long, the wall opposite the doors lined with the same immense green stain glass windows as the rest of the castle, night's light shining through coldly. It had been a long time since I had seen moonlight and it felt reassuring despite the chill of our dark northern surroundings. There was a long table of black ebony set there running the length of the room, the ends of the table pointed to the walls. A fireplace was lit at one end, a small cluster of dark red velvet armchairs gathered around it. Candles burned on the mantelpiece while tall candelabras illuminated the rest of the room. It looked liked some dark scene out of a horror story, though I didn't feel like some hapless young woman who had been lured to her doom by the sinister Count.

Father was standing by the fireplace with his hands clasped behind his back, his golden eyes studying the flames. He no longer wore the heavier robes and adornments of a king, his head clear of his crown. He now just wore the long doublet, his hands the only parts of him still bejewelled.

"Father," Syrena spoke as we came to stand before him, her tone uneasy despite the strength she pushed into it. "You wanted to see us?"

"Yes, Syrena," he turned, smiling as he locked his eyes on me, "Carden. It's time we did a little catching up."

I folded my arms in front of me. "You didn't strike me as all that familial earlier, Father," I remarked coldly.

Tiernan nodded and moved towards us, his demeanour much calmer now that we were alone. "All a part of my throne room persona," he explained, though he still wasn't the warmest of men to be around. "Recent events have forced a sense of severity to be required when dealing with the people. We've had to declare martial law with the increase in werewolf attacks since the sinking of Safferan."

"So, Valloran *is* being affected by the Shadow Lord's actions as much as High-Realm," I said, a little satisfied to know that he couldn't just ignore the situation.

"The darkening of the sky and the release of Ragnarok is certainly of dire concern to me, my son," he said firmly, narrowing his gaze as he moved to the table. "The danger does not lie solely upon High-Realm, but on the rest of the world too. Even now the Shadow Lord's influence is spreading across the sea in search of a foothold on our shores. We are but weeks from losing our skies now that reports from the border show that Grotojan has all but lost theirs."

He gestured to us, Syrena and I taking a seat side by side with our backs to the doors as he seated himself at the head of the table. The hearth silhouetted him, and he looked a little more impressive and intimidating.

"Have there been any signs of Scourge or Undead Legions in our lands?" I asked, genuinely concerned, though I stayed calm.

"Not as of yet," Father responded, hands in front of him, "but I have seen fit to increase the patrols of our borders just to be certain."

"Surely you can see the importance of why we have come if these are your concerns," I started turning my attention towards our task. "Reaching Azmerath's Doorway..."

"Can wait for the moment," Tiernan said, cutting me off as he rang a bell by pulling a velvet rope that hung by the table. "We must catch up, as I said."

"Father, this is important..."

"Maybe so," he turned his gaze to me fiercely, "however, you have an obligation to your bloodline that you *must* fulfil."

"I have only one obligation..." I disagreed, cut off again.

"You are not a Guardian anymore, Carden," Tiernan stated, eyeing me coldly, his palms on the table. "It is all too clear to me that you have turned from that path now. A path, I might add, that I was not wholly in favour of my *only* son following in the first place."

"Are we really going to do this?" I asked him, snarling under my breath and staring him down with the same hard gaze. "Do you *really* want to have an argument with me, Father?"

For a moment, I felt as if we were both trying to burn each other down with our fiery stares, my body tensing as I got myself ready for a fight. But a fight never came as my father leaned back in his chair calmly.

He smirked a little at my reaction, nodding: "You can still hold your own. Good. I had worried that your fighter's instinct had lessened with the sacrifice of your Guardian oath."

"If anything, I am more dangerous and determined than I was before," I responded as a pair of girls and a man entered the room. "I will fight when I have to."

"Good," Father prided, turning his attention to the humans that had joined us. "Now, we must dine."

I turned my eyes up to the humans, noting the scant clothing that revealed the man's muscular torso and the small skirts and the wraps around the chests that left the girls otherwise exposed. They were slaves, the steel collars on their necks making that clear to me.

The man knelt beside Syrena and offered his arm, my sister baring her fangs as she took in his scent. She immediately buried her fangs into his forearm and started to drink, the scent of blood filling the air.

The two girls came to my father's side, his arm encircling the blonde while he pressed his hand to the bare back of the brunette.

"I chose this one specially for you," he smirked, shoving her into my lap before pulling the other girl close and biting into her shoulder.

The girl looked up at me with a nervous stare as she balanced on my lap, her eyes like sapphires and her hair like dark red wood. She was of Aldegaadian heritage, this much was obvious to me. The scent of her blood began tempting me through her flesh as the mixed aroma of her arousal at my touch and her blood's fragrance began reaching to me like a delicate hand.

My hands were around her hips to hold her steady and for a moment I saw Leander staring up at me in her place, the bite marks that littered her soft white skin looking recent.

"No!" I pushed her from my lap and stood from my seat. My mind cleared and I saw the real girl as the image of my love faded away. "Get away from me!"

"M-Master?" she looked fearfully to my father.

Tiernan lifted his head from the shoulder of the other girl, her moans resembling pleasure as blood dripped from the fresh bite in her olive skin.

Father narrowed his gaze at me, frowning. "Is she not to your liking, son?" he asked as Syrena stopped feeding and turned her attention to us.

"I do not drink blood," I told him firmly. "I am still human for the most part and eat as humans do."

He rolled his eyes at me, shoving the girl in his lap to the floor, then scowled at the brunette as she dropped to her knees and bowed her head. Their subjugation left a bitterness in my throat, and I could only tense at the notion of their enslavement while living in Castle Valkirak.

"Do you ever stop denying what you are?" Father scowled, standing from his chair and staring me down as the two girls cowered at our feet. "You deny your heritage as a prince and you refuse your blood as a vampire, perhaps even the blood of the dragon and the elven line within you as well. And why? All to be like *them*!" he jabbed an accusing finger at the frightened girls as they started to sob quietly. "*They* are *weak*! *All* humans are weak, Carden!"

"Does that give you any right to enslave them?!" I demanded angrily as Syrena stood up to my left, the male dropping by her feet. "Our kind may be the stronger but remember that humans can be sired by our blood and our bite in unison, and so can become just as strong!"

"A gift *we* give!" Tiernan snapped back at me. "It is not something that *they* can decide! The blood of the vampire runs in *our* veins, *our* bloodline the first of the immortals!"

"That doesn't mean we can enslave humans," I argued firmly.

"You speak as if we have some ultimate grand scheme to subjugate humanity," he scoffed incredulously at me. "That is *not* the purpose of our race. *These* humans are indentured slaves who work off their debts or those of their parents to one day be freed. And half of them end up choosing to remain."

"Carden, we don't make them suffer," Syrena put her hand on my shoulder, trying to calm me. "You know that feeding from a human can be pleasurable for them if done right."

"I've never fed from a human," I said firmly, glancing from her to my father, "so I wouldn't know."

"Then do not be so quick to judge, my son," Tiernan looked to the humans then. "Get up. Go eat, rest and take care of yourselves."

"Master?" the brunette girl murmured, still on her knees as the others stood. "Have... have I done something wrong?"

To my surprise, Tiernan leaned down and lifted her to her feet before gently stroking her hair out of her teary eyes.

"You have done nothing, girl," he assured her, glaring at me. "The prince simply refuses to accept himself," he looked to her again and gestured to the doors at the other end of the room. "Go on. Go."

"Yes, Master," she bowed her head and left the room as the man and the other girl followed.

"I care for my subjects, Carden," Tiernan stated as he moved to the sideboard by the windows, taking up goblets and a bottle of dark red liquid. "Many of these slaves have come to us after Orc raiding parties made the mistake of crossing into our borders. *They* use the women for unspeakable acts of carnal violence while we *only* ask for their blood."

"The appearance they present seems less altruistic than you expect me to perceive," I said lowly, folding my arms in front of my chest.

There was a knock at the door as Father began pouring the bottle out into six steel goblets, silver the single metal that would not be found in the castle except when forged into weapons.

"As they say, appearances can be deceiving," he turned and called: "Come."

I was relieved to see Ranzel and Fawkner as they entered the room under escort of Caedmon. Caedmon had exchanged his armour for more comfortable black, red and grey finery, much like my father and sister, moving instantly to stand with Syrena. He just nodded lightly to me, not really a big speaker. I was feeling like I had fallen into a different and darker world to the one I belonged.

"Ah, Ranzel, Lord Fawkner," my father welcomed them into the room. "I am glad that you could join us."

"Your invitation was most welcome," Fawkner bowed his head and offered a friendly expression, hands clasped at the small of his back.

"Indeed," the old man agreed with the Lorveren Lord's sentiment, turning to my father as he paused there with us. "And we do have a good many things to discuss, Sire."

Fawkner was dressed now only in his green finery, his Guardian armour stashed away in his room. He had even cleaned and neatened his hair and beard. Ranzel was much the same, his cloak and hat now removed, and his silvery white hair and beard combed out. He still carried his staff, though he didn't have his sword with him.

"That we do," Tiernan turned and offered me the first goblet he had poured.

I shook my head, gaining his exasperated stare.

"It is not but wine, my son," he stated firmly, shaking his head as I reluctantly took it. "Honestly, you and your sensibilities."

"I just don't want to be tricked into drinking blood," I responded coarsely, still distrusting him though the liquid certainly smelled like wine.

"I would not pour blood for mortals," he offered the next to Fawkner, then the third to Ranzel, studying him briefly. "Nor for immortals who are not of our kind."

Syrena took the fourth from him and sipped at it as Fawkner sampled it, swishing it in his mouth to test it. He nodded thoughtfully as he analysed the bouquet of the wine, his frown one of musing rather than perplexity.

"Hm," he nodded, then swallowed. "A very interesting flavour. I detect northern grapes mixed with... juniper and... something else... a spice of some kind."

Tiernan smiled as he gave the last to Caedmon then drank a mouthful of his own, savouring it before swallowing to answer: "Northern Spiced Wine from Galicia, one of the finest vintages to be had. This bottle is a thousand years old. I thought it appropriate given the status of my guests."

"A thousand years?" Fawkner nearly coughed, stunned as he managed to maintain his composure. "My Lord, that is quite generous of you. It must surely be a rarity."

"Perhaps so, though not one of my rarer vintages," Tiernan said smoothly. "I have quite a wine cellar full of various bottles from all over Therras. You know, I do believe I even have some Fortified Kelvar Tosh Wine from the land of the Storvari. Heavy stuff to be sure, but worth it. One must not try more than a thimble's worth if one is not of the Storvari constitution. Or ours, of course."

"Perhaps you could show me your collection during my visit, Sire," Fawkner suggested, carrying out the usual pleasantries.

"Indeed," Father agreed, taking his seat again and offering both the Wizard and the Lord a seat on the opposite side of the table to my sister, her husband and me. "Now, to the business at hand. You have come to my shores seeking my aid and that of my country. I would ask that you tell me of the situation in High-Realm."

Ranzel nodded, sipping at his wine before setting it down: "Though the hour at which we speak on such matters is late, my Lord, the dire situation at hand necessitates such discussions. The Shadow Dominion has returned from Gorth'lak's Grey Wastes and is once more encroaching upon the world. Up until the fall of Safferan, their efforts were secretive as the Shadow Lord manipulated the world from behind the scenes. But now we face open war."

I sat back, glancing at Syrena as I took a mouthful of the tangy, berry flavoured wine. She was fascinated and hard, her demeanour not as I remembered, though that was most certainly due to what she had been forced to endure in the last quarter of a century. She looked upon the discussion with a warrior's eye, every movement she made as careful and tactical as if she were on the battlefield.

My eyes flicked to Father's as he listened to the Wizard, deep thoughtfulness playing across his features. He was both knowing and curious as the old man explained what was happening in the south, maintaining that arrogant calm he always seemed to possess.

"Do you know the identity of this Shadow Lord?" Father questioned with a dark gaze.

Ranzel took in an uneasy breath and nodded, purposefully locking his eyes on Tiernan's: "Yes, Sire. It is Lord Morod."

"Morod?" my father actually looked horrified, an expression I didn't expect to ever see on his face. "Are you certain that *this* Shadow Lord is that same vile monster?"

"Unequivocally, Sire," Ranzel nodded grimly, resting his hands together on the table. "He was identified through research in the Caradoc Library in Eilath, and via the Dragon Pendant he carries around his neck," he smiled and looked to Syrena. "Something that I see you yourself know the touch of Princess."

Syrena touched one alabaster hand to the necklace at her décolletage, her fingers caressing the crimson stone at its core as it hung gracefully beneath her collarbones. "Yes, I have held this pendant since I was old enough to appreciate such things," she was taken aback by the Wizard's observation. "You know of it?"

He indicated his own pendant with a gentle tap of one finger to its stone: "I myself am a holder. Given the dragon that you can summon and the colouring of the heartstone in the Pendant's core, you possess the Ruberian Dragon Pendant."

"Are there more holders like us?" she asked curiously, fascinated by the Wizard's words.

I couldn't help but smile. This was so familiar now, the memory of sitting in Hintana after we had fled Unlarta returning to me. I recalled how Leander had possessed that same curiosity and fascination when Ser Mithras had told her of the Amethian Pendant. A fondness for those innocent days lingered in my heart.

She was so gentle and filled with wonder. Gods, how I miss seeing the joy she gained when she learned something new.

Ranzel nodded in answer to my sister's question: "There are others, though not all of the Dragon Pendants have been accounted for. As of today, we know of *five* active Dragon Pendants, each with a holder and a dragon, as well as four inactive ones. That leaves four unaccounted for."

"You say that you have located nine of the thirteen?" Tiernan asked with curiosity and scepticism, studying Ranzel curiously.

Ranzel nodded. "Yes. Your daughter and I carry one each while the four inactive ones and the Topazian Pendant are in the possession of Queen Keilantra of Gorvenna."

"How has she acquired five pendants?" Syrena asked with a perplexed frown. "I thought the legends of the Pendants made it clear that only a direct descendant of the original holder of each could command them."

"That is true," Ranzel agreed, an awkward expression on his face. "However, Keilantra only commands the Topazian Pendant. The others she has collected to keep from finding their true holders and becoming active."

"Foul witch," Tiernan hissed distastefully. "And the others?"

Ranzel sighed. "The Obsidian Pendant is in Lord Morod's possession, much as it was twelve hundred years ago. I believe that his passage into the Netherworlds in physical form may have had an ill effect upon it, unfortunately."

"That's terrible," Syrena murmured, shaking her head. "That a talisman of good should become so corrupted is a horrible thing."

"Indeed, your Highness," the old man agreed.

Caedmon regarded him with a studious frown, his mind working as he spoke in his bass voice for the first time since our arrival: "you said that nine are accounted for, yet you have spoken of only eight. What of this fifth one that you say is active?"

"Well," Ranzel cleared his throat, a hint of sadness upon his face, "active is perhaps inaccurate at this time."

Fawkner took in a slow breath before adding in gravely: "The Amethian Pendant is the fifth Ranzel speaks of, and we have seen it work its wards on several occasions firsthand..."

"But?" Tiernan urged with a downward glance as he tilted his head back.

Fawkner sighed, looking to his hands with the same dejected expression as a grieving father. "It has fallen dormant when its holder was killed."

I turned my gaze to the table, feeling the familiar stinging wetness of tears filling my eyes. Just hearing the words made my heart swell with pain even though they hadn't mentioned her name.

I can't cry. Not in front of my father. He isn't a heart reader or a mind reader so he wouldn't understand.

"I see," he nodded grimly, studying the goblet in front of him. "Who possessed the Amethian Pendant?"

"Princess Leander Aldrich of Aldegaad," I said her name as strongly as I could manage, gaining his gaze as I forced myself to meet his eye. "She was the one to carry the Amethian Pendant and had a dragon as her protector. She was... she was murdered by Lord Morod."

"Really?" he frowned deeply.

I sighed and made myself go on: "She was... kidnapped from Silvervale eight months ago by Keilantra and Manth, the sisters of Raven's Rest. We pursued them to Safferan and to Ragnarok's Redoubt with a force consisting of Dragon Knights, High Elves and Guardians. But we..." I tensed, the words getting too hard to speak, "we were unable to free her. Lord Morod was too powerful and killed her to raise Ragnarok."

"Then he has possession of the Dragon's Key Pendant?" my father looked to Ranzel and Fawkner, concern deep in his eyes and straining his features.

Ranzel nodded. "He controls the Apocalyptic Dragons with it even now. He has been turning them upon the strongholds of all who stand as defenders of Therras and eradicating any who could fight against his tyranny. And with the turmoil between the Seven Kingdoms at this time, rallying the combined forces of High-Realm looks to be unlikely."

"I assume you have some plan devised to combat this threat?" Tiernan asked them evenly, placing his hands together in a steeple, his elbows against the chair's arms.

"The Prophecy of the Great Heroine," the Wizard answered with quiet certainty, his hazel eyes full of conviction. "It holds the answer to ending this blight and saving all of Therras."

"The Great Heroine has been dead for more than a thousand years," Tiernan pointed out, standing up and sweeping from his seat with a rush of his robes as he moved to the fireplace again. "She defeated Morod during the War of the Shadow and saved all the world from the Darkest Shadow's evil. I was gladdened to see their reign end when she proved victorious over them."

"I don't recall our people ever taking part in that war, Father," Syrena said softly.

"There were vampires in the war," I confirmed grimly, looking to her. "They sided with the Darkest Shadow against High-Realm."

"No," Tiernan turned over his shoulder to regard us, his eyes as heated as the hearth. "*Our* people were *not* a part of that war. I elected to keep us out of such matters while two lords chose to go against my ruling."

"They did?" Syrena frowned, leaning her hands on the table as I sat back with folded arms.

Tiernan stared into the fire as he spoke, almost as if he were looking into the distant past: "You are both so young, my children, barely decades into your lives. I am not surprised that this is unfamiliar. The Lords of Valloran were divided after Lord Morod made his presence felt on behalf of the Darkest Shadow. Most of us were unwilling to side with him and instead chose to fight should the Dominion attempt an assault on our lands, while those who hungered for domination and power cast away their loyalty to the kingdom. They marched under the banner of their traitorous lords and allied themselves with the Dominion only to be destroyed in the final battle that swept through High-Realm's northern reaches. Those that fled back here were tried for their war crimes and met the Final Death. The rest that survived went into hiding throughout Therras."

Father turned around to face us, folding his arms before him, his expression hard and unforgiving. He had seen so much in his years. More than my sister and I could ever imagine.

"The House of Valerian has stood against the Shadow Lords and their Dominion since Gorth Lavelle first rose to power four thousand years ago," he stated firmly and with unrelenting conviction. "Where we lead, the other Vampire Houses follow, for we are the oldest of the clans and the ones created by Lord Azmerath to steward the world and the mortals under our care. Such is the nature of our being. Where the High Elves are the Immortals of Light, we are the Immortals of Shadow, both races holding the balance necessary for the world to exist in harmony."

"Yet, the Shadow Lords represent evil," I pointed out darkly. "They use the qualifier of shadow."

Tiernan snorted. "They are darkness of the most severe and primordial evil. They are not the natural shadow of the world but a perversion of it. *We* are the ones who maintain the balance and undo the wickedness of their deeds. That is the purpose gifted to us by Lord Azmerath when he forged our immortal bones. Do you understand now, my son?"

I nodded softly, finally getting it. "I do, Father."

"Then, you will join us?" Fawkner asked hopefully, gaining my father's attention. "You will rally with us against the Shadow Lord?"

"I will have to convene the Council of Lords to come to that decision, but I will give all the aid I can," he confirmed, looking then to Ranzel. "Provided that your solution is viable."

Ranzel nodded. "Yes. Well, it is in these times that the world needs a figure of importance. A Champion."

"Thus, your citing of the Great Heroine and her legend," Tiernan returned to the old man's original discussion. "A noble sentiment, but with one flaw: she is *dead*."

"That statement, my Lord Tiernan, is both correct and inaccurate," Ranzel smiled knowingly.

"Is it now?" Father waved his hand, sitting back down in his seat. "Then, by all means, enlighten me."

"You refer to Leander the First as the Great Heroine, however, the prophecies were misread," Ranzel explained evenly, clasping his hands together before him. "Careful review of the Prophecy Scrolls has revealed that we are now in the age when the Great Heroine must arise and unite the fractured nations of High-Realm in order to inspire them to save themselves. Then she will face Morod in a final battle. That heroine currently lies in this castle, drawing neither breath nor heartbeat."

"The girl..." Father realised. "*She* is the one you speak of."

"Princess Leander the Second is the Great Heroine of the prophecies," Ranzel confirmed with a nod. "She was slain by Lord Morod to bring about the end of the world. However, she may save it again, provided that we restore her to life."

"Which is why we have come here," I told Father, locking my eyes on his. "Her death wasn't a natural one and so she is cursed, her body left without decay, which gives us the chance we need. Azmerath's Doorway is the only way we can resurrect her," I sighed softly. "We need your help."

Father partook of his wine, savouring it again before setting the goblet down. He was not a man to make a decision lightly, but he was also quick witted and able to make that decision whilst listening to the relevant conversations.

"I will help however I can, of course," he said, turning his eyes to the three of us. "However, I feel it is important to point out that the time with which to accomplish this task is heavily limited."

"How so, my Lord?" Fawkner set his own goblet down, mashing his lips together against the sweet taste.

Father shrugged lightly, resting his arms on his chair. "I assume you have the written works that may aid in such explanations."

Ranzel nodded, taking the papers I had given him from his robes. "Yes. We have these pages from a tome written by the Dark Elven sorcerer, Dunadel Naxxremis."

Father shook his head. "No. That won't do. Syrena, my darling, please fetch *The Compendium of Death God Rituals* for me."

"Yes, Father," Syrena got up and swiftly left the room for the briefest of moments, darting away so fast that she was no more than a flickering blur of colours.

We waited only a few moments before she suddenly appeared at Father's side as if she had popped out of thin air, an enormous black book in her slender hands. She laid it on the table, standing over his shoulder as he proceeded to search the book's contents before turning the large parchment pages to his desired portion.

"Undoubtedly, the pages that Naxxremis wrote speak a good deal about the Doorway, though I doubt it holds *every* detail," Father assumed as he ran his finger along the page.

Ranzel nodded. "Yes, we needed to translate the Dark Elven before we could discern it, and while it proved to be a wealth of knowledge regarding the myth of Azmerath's Doorway it certainly held no information on the practicalities of it."

"Meaning the Dark Elf didn't have any idea on how to actually open it," Caedmon said sourly, leaning back in his chair with his arms folded in front of his bulky chest.

"Which is where *The Compendium of Death God Rituals* is more complete," Father stated as he analysed the pages before him. "Unfortunately, I must study this briefly to ascertain the method as I have not seen the Doorway open in my lifetime."

"Really?" Fawkner was surprised. "I would assume that over five thousand years your castle must have played host to many an adventurer wishing to gain access to it."

"We entertain such guests every few years," Caedmon responded evenly, turning his golden eyes to my friend, "but none have ever opened the doorway. The trials to do so are difficult and have proven fatal."

"What trials?" I asked curiously, the prospect of facing a dangerous death hardly making me flinch.

"In order to open the Doorway and go before Lord Azmerath in his realm, you must gather a tribute to prove your worthiness," Father explained as he studied the book. "We have known that the trials were important in such demonstrations, though the purpose was not discerned until reading this book more closely."

"What kind of tribute does the God of Death demand for an audience?" I spoke coldly.

"In order to gain an audience with Lord Azmerath and open his Doorway, one must prove they have the three attributes of the God of Death," Father read aloud, running his finger along the page with the words. "The first attribute is that of Grace, represented by the feather of a Gryphon. The second is Protection, as embodied by the shell of an egg stolen from a Wyvern's nest. The third and final attribute is Compassion, found only through a Phoenix gifting the pilgrim its tears. If the pilgrim's heart and intent is pure for the one whom they appeal to the Lord of Death to restore, then these gifts shall be acquired without failure under the gaze of three witnesses chosen. Only then will Azmerath's Doorway open upon the night of the dark lunar trinity."

"A Gryphon's feather, Wyvern's egg and Phoenix's tears?" Fawkner contemplated the words as he sipped at his wine again. "Such creatures would certainly be difficult to find."

"Especially in such a short amount of time," Ranzel agreed grimly, flicking his eyes to me. "The passage states that Azmerath's Doorway will only open upon the night of the Dark Moons. Incidentally, that is a week from now."

"We have to gather the tribute within a week?!" I exclaimed in disbelief. "How?! How are we to do this?!"

"It is easier than you would think, little brother," Syrena spoke up, standing straight as she held her hands before her hips. "There is a rookery of Gryphons a few hours south of the castle, and a cave where a Wyvern nests a few hours more to the north. We could easily acquire the feathers and the egg shell in two days."

"The Phoenix tears are harder," Caedmon added, looking to me from where he sat with Syrena's vacated seat between us. "The only way to get those is to leave an offering beside the deathbed of the one you seek to resurrect and wait for one to accept. Then you must plead with it."

"Then I'll have to gather the items and pray I am successful," I sighed, set in my decision.

Father looked up at me with a scowling frown. "You? No, no, my son. *You* are *not* doing any such thing."

"*I* am *not* arguing about this, Father," I said firmly, meeting his hard gaze.

"You have allies who can take up the challenge," he attempted to argue anyway. "Let them attend to this task while you attend to your duties as a prince."

I shook my head. "No, Father, I will do this..."

"What reason do you have for throwing your life away for a mortal?" he hissed.

"I made a vow," I responded, narrowing my eyes his way and speaking with all the conviction I had left to me. "A vow that broke all others I ever pledged the day Leander was murdered. I swore that I would find a way to bring her back from Death's Kingdom and undo what that bastard Shadow Lord did to her. I intend to keep that vow, and so I am the one to gather the tribute and seek an audience with Lord Azmerath to plead for her."

Father nodded with a cold eye. "It is love then. You have chosen a mortal girl."

"I have," I confirmed.

He shrugged. "I suppose there is nothing more I can say to convince you not to proceed. Very well, my son. You will have to choose *three* of your companions to go with you into this task. They will have to represent the attributes of Grace, Protection and Compassion if you hope to succeed."

I nodded, feeling a sense of relief at his words. "I will choose the three that are most suitable then."

"I hope for your sake that you survive," Father took up his goblet again, "though I suggest that you do not dally, for you will have but *one* chance to open the Doorway. If you have not gathered *all* three items of tribute before the Dark Moons, you will not have a second chance. For the darkness that spreads across the skies will have overwhelmed Valloran as it has High-Realm within a few weeks and will blot out the moons, dispelling their affects, thus rendering the Doorway useless."

I tensed as I heard his words. *One chance? That's all I'll have to save her? Gods... As if this wasn't hard enough....*

Gathering my composure, I nodded and stood up, pushing my chair back with the scraping of wood against the marble floor.

"Well then," I said evenly, looking to my father with a calm gaze, "I had best get started."

* * * * *

The sun had risen across the land with a gentle gold as morning broke over the castle. I hadn't wasted any time, immediately seeking out the others to discuss who would be best suited to join me in gathering the tribute for Lord Azmerath. It hadn't been easy to decide who would accompany me into the Realm of the Dead, let alone gather the items required to do so, but I had done it, despite one choice that didn't suit me as well as I wanted.

I can't believe I had to take him, I scowled mentally as I glanced at Tristan over my shoulder, trudging my way along the trails towards the gryphon rookeries. *I would have much rather Fawkner to accompany me along this road, given his compassion and care when it comes to Leander. But I suppose I have no choice...* I shook my mind away from those thoughts, turning my gaze to the dirt and stones that led up the craggy cliffs before me. *My focus has to be on the task at hand and on saving Leander's soul. Who knows what horrors she's enduring on the other side.*

There were six of us in our small gathering. Ellora and Tallinn were the ones I had chosen first to join me in this challenge, Tristan only coming along once I realised that none of the others could fulfil the role - and after Danika told me that these three were who she saw accompanying me in success. I didn't even bother asking Joran, knowing that the Storvari had his duty to attend to and that Leander needed him to guard her. I still didn't like the idea of leaving her with my father, but I had no other choice.

I considered the two women as they walked with me, their bows over their backs, their cloaks swirling with the wind that tugged at our bodies. Tallinn had fashioned her hair into a single tied back plait for the time being while Ellora had kept hers with the same free flowing style she always did.

As I pondered them, I knew I had chosen the right companions for the task. *None are as graceful as Ellora. Were she not a huntress I believe she would make the greatest and most beautiful dancer in Therras, that grace evident in all her movements. Perhaps such is the way of the Elves. And Tallinn... I have never known anyone to be more protective than her. As a Guardian she is the most recognisable image of a protector in all of Therras. They are both right for this.*

My green eyes flicked to the two black armoured and cloaked figures ahead of me. I couldn't help my smirk as I stepped up my pace to catch up with my sister and her mate, chuckling lightly.

"Father must have been furious when you said you would guide us, Syrena," I said to her, amused.

She laughed softly, nodding as she threw me a glance over her shoulder, the sunlight making her seem even paler. "He was so enraged I thought his head would burst. I half expected him to lock me in my rooms just to stop me, but he didn't."

"He knows it doesn't work after all the times he has done so, and you have found a way out," Caedmon smirked adoringly at her.

"He knows it is just easier to let me do as I will," Syrena agreed, turning her eyes ahead of her again.

"My ma was much the same," Tristan chimed into the conversation from the back of the group. "She eventually gave up on trying to stop me from doing such things. She just figured it was easier to let me make my own mistakes and learn from them than to try to prevent me getting hurt."

"She sounds as if she were a very wise woman," Ellora observed, pulling her cloak closer as the chill from the snowy air bit at her skin.

"Didn't mean she didn't worry," Tristan added, sucking in a loud breath of the bracing air. "All parents worry for their children, of course, but she just decided to be more practical."

"A sentiment our father doesn't share, despite his insistence that we be warriors," I commented without turning, letting my eyes wander the high cliffs that we were beginning to climb. "He would do well to learn from your mother, Tristan."

"Aye, that he could," the Wanderer agreed, this being the most civilised we had been with each other ever.

"How much farther to the rookery?" Tallinn called; her hood drawn to guard her ears against the cold.

"Not much farther," Syrena responded, stepping over the natural steps that led up the foothills and crags, her hand on her sword's hilt. "We will be there once we climb the cliffs here."

We continued up for a little bit longer in silence, the way seeming more difficult than we had all first thought. I felt as if I was struggling with my breath as I climbed, a concept that was not logical given my athleticism. I could run for two hours without losing my breath.

"The air is getting rather thin, is it not?" Ellora asked as she braced her hands to the rocks, climbing up slowly.

"Aye. It is getting harder to breathe," Tristan nodded, pulling himself up with a hand to a boulder, his sword unsheathed to serve as a means to latch onto the harder earth.

"Gryphons roost high up cliffs such as these to discourage predators and to protect their hatchlings," Caedmon explained, easily leaping up the next three rocky steps without any effort. "It is natural for winged creatures to choose high perches for their nests, after all. Just look at eagles."

I nodded, turning my gaze back to the way we had come. The valley we had passed through lay below us surrounded by miniature peaks of rock and stone, Death's Shadow Peak visible behind us in the distance. It was almost noon already, the midday sun shining through breaks in the cold clouds that hung above us in their wispy grey and white forms. The light showed the drop beneath us clearly, a fall from there sure to be fatal. At least to a human. I wasn't so certain how I would fare given that I was an unturned vampire, but I couldn't imagine I would do well.

"You two don't seem exerted at all," I observed, calling up to my sister and Caedmon.

"We are fully fledged vampires," Syrena reminded me, confirming my own suspicions. "Our bodies handle activities as strenuous as this with ease and our lungs take in smaller amounts of air to survive than humans. Thinner air is hardly an issue for us."

"Most fortunate for you then," Ellora remarked breathlessly. "It must be the thin air that slows us because clearly none of us are unfit."

"True," Tristan agreed, pulling himself up the next ledge as we all dragged ourselves higher along the craggy slopes. "So... we need to gather... a feather from a Gryphon... tears from a Phoenix, and... and the shells of a Wyvern egg to bring the lass back to life."

"So my father says," I confirmed, managing to step up the next rise a little easier than the last, my black cloak gusting around me.

"Such quests are never simple, are they?" the Wanderer asked breathlessly, side stepping a narrower ledge. "You never just find the place you need to and do the thing you set out to. There's always a little bit extra."

"Ancient artefacts and doorways have a lot of safeguards to unlock," Tallinn pointed out, reaching up as I offered her my hand and lifted her to where I stood. "Thank you, Carden," she went on: "These sorts of tasks are designed to ensure that the people attempting to use or gain access to such powers are both worthy of doing so and are responsible enough to be gifted such honours. It is just the way ancient builders and craftsmen work."

We reached a less craggy place where there were leafless trees growing in twisted shapes beside a few with thin foliage, the plateau wider before another sharp peak.

"It seems like a wise method, if I'm being honest," I confessed, taking in a deep breath as Syrena and Caedmon led us through a narrow gap in the rock walls. "There are far too many individuals who would use those powers for evil."

"Now, that is very true," Tristan agreed, the last to step through the gap.

We entered a deep undercover area where trees had grown up thinly and sunlight shone down through the large openings in the rocks. There were enormous nests set up in various areas, one laying before us as we carefully navigated our way amidst the boulders and rocky outcroppings that littered the area.

I let out a slow breath of awe as I looked upon the creature that lay upon its nest before us. It had silvery and golden feathers all over its body, its enormous wings resting at its side tinted with white at their tips. It had the head of an eagle, its sharp bird eyes studying us the instant we stepped into view, its front legs like an eagle's talons while its back ones were the paws of a lion. It had to be twice the size of a horse with a quizzical demeanour that I never thought its kind could ever possess. It was truly beautiful to behold, my heart warming at the sight of it.

I have never seen a gryphon before. It is one of the most majestically incredible sights I have ever beheld... a pang of sadness filled my heart and I sighed softly. *I wish Leander could have been here with me to see it. She would have loved this beautiful creature.*

"It really is a gryphon," Tallinn breathed out her wonderstruck words, her face lighting up. "I've always wished to see one with my own eyes."

"As have I," Tristan agreed, staying in the cover of the boulders we had come to stand behind. "Never in all my wildest dreams did I ever think I would behold one. What about you, Ellora?"

"I have seen these wondrous beings before," she smiled, her turquoise eyes alight with her admiration of the creature, "but not frequently. They are a rarity to the lands of High-Realm now."

Syrena touched my shoulder, drawing my gaze to her. "You have to approach her and see if she will give up her feathers to you."

"Me?" I was a little surprised.

She nodded. "You're the one who has taken on the task of seeking an audience, so it is your hand that must gather the tribute. Go forward and approach the gryphon."

"Do so carefully," Ellora advised me, meeting my gaze with hers. "Gryphons can become flighty if threatened."

"Then I'll be sure to be unthreatening," I said, moving around the boulder and starting towards the gryphon.

"I will accompany you," Ellora stated, following me as the others remained behind.

Slowly, the Elven Huntress and I made our way across the flat stone ground towards the gryphon and her nest. The gryphon was watching us curiously, cocking her head the way an inquisitive bird would. I felt like I should have been fearful, yet I was anything but afraid.

Instinctively, as I drew nearer, I held out my hands in a nonthreatening way, lowering myself to one knee just within her reach. Ellora crouched lowly behind me, studying the gryphon with wise eyes. She had her hands out to her sides both in preparation to snatch up her bow if she had to and in a gesture of peacefulness.

"Hello beautiful," I spoke softly to the gryphon as she watched me with those dazzling eyes. "I am not here to threaten you or your eggs. I just want some of your feathers, if you'll permit me."

The gryphon made a kind of clucking sound as she watched me, tilting her head to me.

I held out my hand to her the way I would a dog, hoping to gain her trust. "Shh... It's okay. See?"

She lowered her head, studying my hand and sniffing my scent, the sudden tugging gust of her breath pulling at my skin for a moment. She clucked again and chirped, seeming to brighten up as I drew a little closer. That was when she lowered her head and allowed me to gently caress her feathers.

A smile pulled across my lips and I nodded as I petted her gently. "Yes... That's right. Good girl. You really are a beautiful creature, aren't you?"

She seemed to like me petting her, a pleasured clucking sound coming from deep down in her craw. I let my other hand reach out and stroke her chest feathers, feeling their silkiness and the large thud of her heart beneath her breast.

"I would never cause you any harm, beautiful," I assured her. "If she were able to, I know a girl who would love to see you."

The gryphon seemed rather pleased with my compliments, her beak opening almost as if she were smiling.

I just smiled gently back and continued to pet her for a moment longer until she tilted her head away from me. I frowned as I withdrew my hands, watching as she began grooming herself. Slowly, the gryphon turned her face back to me, three silvery and gold feathers pinned in her beak. She offered them to me gently, waiting until I held up my left hand before releasing them into my palm. I smiled down at the feathers, then petted her cheek again with my right hand, giving her a thankful nod.

"Thank you," I said, petting her for a little longer before turning and leaving her to herself.

"You got them," Ellora smiled at me as we both stood up tall again.

I nodded, relieved as I looked at the feathers in my hand. "I hope the rest of the items will be as easy to get."

Chapter Twenty
Gathering Death's Tribute

A tremendous roar ripped through the cave's stone walls as a column of angry fire erupted out of the smoky shadows, scorching everything in its way. We ran as fast as we could, our legs pumping hard as our cries filled the air. The light of day ahead drew our gazes and we forced ourselves to go faster, the heat of the inferno closing in on us. Tallinn and Tristan were out of the tunnel first, both of them screaming as they leaped from the ledge and ducked beneath it just as Ellora and I followed. The two of us just barely made it down the sloping hill as the fireball struck the icy air, melting the snowflakes wafting down from the sky.

I landed hard, coming up in a roll to crouch, turning my gaze back to the cave as the fire swiftly evaporated. My chest was heaving, my clothes and armour singed by the flames that had nearly devoured us. Ellora knelt beside me, her eyes widening as we both watched the enormous creature emerge from the mouth of the cave. I swear, the Elf looked as if she were about to run screaming, though she didn't.

The Wyvern stormed out of the cave using the clawed knuckles of its wings as front limbs to walk on, its glowing orange eyes reminiscent of the dragons I had seen, though far less sympathetic. There was only rage there beneath the ridged, scaly, brown and cream coloured face that snapped an elongated snout furiously at the air, baring lines of pointed teeth, each one as long as a steel dagger. Its six horned crown scratched at the top of the cave opening, causing dust and pebbles to tumble from the cliffs as it snarled viciously, stepping fully into view. Its tail snapped and whipped violently, the arrowhead end cracking against the stone walls of the cliffs as its large feet crushed the skulls and bones of others who had been foolish enough to try to get near its lair.

The Wyvern reared up, preparing for another strike.

"MOVE!" I shouted, ripping myself away and running for the nearest large rock.

Tallinn leaped over it with me just in time as the Wyvern launched a second tremendous, sustained blast of flames after us, the heat of it forcing us to sink our bodies low to the ground. I closed my eyes and turned my face towards my shoulder, my knees up as the fire tore at the air and burned the side of the rock facing the enraged beast. I could actually feel the hot air of its deadly breath across my knees, my skin feeling as if it could crackle and flake away if the beast didn't stop soon.

At last, the fire attack ceased as the Wyvern roared, stomping around before the mouth of the cave fiercely.

I opened my eyes, propping my arms behind me and looking to the others. Tallinn was snug up against my side as she had tried to make herself as small as possible, soot on her cheeks and forehead from the fiery blast that had nearly claimed us. Tristan was standing with his back to a much larger boulder that stood about nine feet high, his expression and exasperation making him seem as if he wouldn't stand much longer. The side of the boulder facing the Wyvern was black now, superheated from the attack with embers burning in the stone crevices and smoke curling from the newly ashen surface. It was then that Ellora looked up from where she crouched beside Tristan, lowering her hands from her red-haired head as she peered fearfully back towards the beast.

None of us wore our cloaks, having given them to Syrena and Caedmon so as not to get set on fire, as Caedmon had jokingly remarked. I had simply thrown him an incredulous look when he had made his comment, but now I could see the sense in it. They were out of range of the cave and nowhere near the angered Wyvern's sights.

I shook my head, reminding myself of my words the day before: "Okay... Not as easy as the gryphon!"

"That's an understatement!" Tallinn said in a rush, her chest heaving beneath her corset and shirt. "That thing's set to kill us!"

"Yeah, we really pissed it off!" I agreed, looking back up and ducking down behind the boulder as a furious roar ripped the air.

Another scorching column of flames stroked across the top of our cover, burning the air and the stone relentlessly, though it only lasted a few seconds. We both released a little tension as the heat died away and smoke choked us. We covered our mouths in some attempt to protect our burning sinuses and throats. We recovered as the smoke cleared, sweat beading our brows from the embers that cooked the rock we hid behind as ash drifted down over us amidst the snowflakes.

"How the Void are we supposed to get near that thing's nest?" I wondered aloud, breathing hard and letting out another cough.

"Preferably without getting charbroiled," Tristan remarked, ducking away as the Wyvern roared and sent a fireball past where he hid.

"There must be a way," I considered our options, glancing around the edge of the boulder. "We need that eggshell."

I let my emerald gaze take in the layout before me. The Wyvern was stomping in a dangerous pacing motion before the mouth of the cave, the cliffs above it rising too steeply to climb. There didn't appear to be any other openings visible to lead back inside the cave, which meant that the only way in was to go via the mouth it was guarding. That was going to be easier said than done. The area around the opening into the cavern was barren except for a few scorched and blackened trees, everything there just bare rock covered in snow.

Nothing helpful, my eyes fell on the broken bones of the past adventurers grimly. *None of them stood a chance against this beast. It looks hopeless, but we **have** to succeed. We **have** to! Leander is counting on us. She's counting on **me**...*

"Dying for an eggshell," Tristan laughed darkly, fear in his tone as he lay his head back against the rock. "That's gotta be the funniest reason to end your life ever."

"Hold firm, Tristan," Ellora patted his shoulder as she too gazed around her hiding place, searching for an answer to overcome this challenge. "We will not die. Victory lies within our grasps; we need only find the path to reach it."

"Why? Because the Witch says so?" he snorted, chuckling coldly as he glanced over his shoulder at the Wyvern. "Has it occurred to anyone that maybe she's just trying to kill us off like her sisters would? Sending us to a wyvern seems like a fine way to end us without getting her hands dirty."

"Danika isn't trying to kill us," I retorted, turning to crouch on my knees, my hands to the boulder as I continued to analyse our options. "There would be nothing for her to gain. Now, we need to figure this out."

"Why don't we just get your sister to bring her dragon down on this thing and kill it for us?" the Wanderer suggested.

Ellora slapped his arm, glaring at him. "We cannot kill this creature simply because it is in our way. That is wrong."

"And it killing us is okay, is it?" he responded curtly.

"It is just protecting its nest," Tallinn turned to check out the cave entrance, her shoulders against the rock. "It probably thinks we mean its hatchlings harm."

"I *did* try to approach it peacefully," I reminded her as I glanced her way.

She glanced up at me in turn and nodded. "Yes, but wyverns aren't like gryphons. Gryphons are majestic and approachable; wyverns are heavily territorial."

"If only we had an expert on dragon-kind with us," I sighed, turning my gaze back to the wyvern as it now scratched at the ground and roared viciously in an attempt to draw us out.

"I wish Mithras were here," Ellora murmured with a hint of sadness in her otherwise stoic demeanour. "His knowledge of these creatures would be invaluable."

"We'd be a might better off if we had the Princess too," Tristan added, getting his sword ready. "She could summon her dragon to fight that thing."

"Yes, well, neither of them is with us," I said coldly, the pang of pain in my heart worsening with this conversation. "We just have to find the solution ourselves."

"Any thoughts, Carden?" Tallinn asked me softly, putting her hand to mine.

I frowned, narrowing my eyes as I took in the surroundings of the cave again. The lack of vegetation made sneaking up difficult, the openness of the area leaving us with no cover to try an approach. We weren't even that far from the opening, ironically, so that meant that getting there would be easy enough. *If* we didn't have the massive obstacle of a fire-breathing wyvern set on tearing us apart.

A ledge off to my left caught my attention, a large boulder hanging there right in the path of the Wyvern. It would take some serious force to dislodge it and drive the Wyvern away from the entrance, but it would give me time enough to get inside. The only issue then would be keeping the creature distracted until I could secure the shell and escape.

"Tristan, can you conjure some magic to knock that boulder from that ledge over there?" I asked, indicating the ledge with a nod.

The Wanderer turned over his shoulder to get a look, his brown eyes analysing the boulder and ledge swiftly. He nodded, his jaw twisting under his dark reddish blonde beard as he wiped his sooty forehead with his hand.

"Aye, that I could," he confirmed. "But I'd have to get behind it."

"All right," I took charge, looking to my three companions seriously as I explained, "here's the plan. Tristan will go up behind that boulder and, using his magic, will force it to fall into the path of the Wyvern, making it try to evade it. Ellora, Tallinn, that is when you both go to the opposite side and start drawing its gaze."

Ellora nodded thoughtfully. "Firing our arrows won't cause it any harm, given the solid plates of its scales, but they will irritate it enough to hold its gaze."

"We'll just have to dodge the flames and tail," Tallinn stated, not wholly convinced this would work.

"Then Tristan will use magic to keep it confused," I continued with my planning. "If the three of you keep hitting it from three sides at random it should become too bewildered to know where to strike. Meanwhile, I'll get the eggshell and once I'm out we'll just run for it. Agreed?"

"Agreed," Tallinn and Ellora said together, both nodding.

"Why not?" Tristan shrugged, getting ready to move. "It's better than waiting for it to kill us."

I looked towards the Wyvern, waiting for it to turn its gaze away. It didn't seem to be willing to, so I grabbed a rock and hurled it as hard as I could in the opposite direction of our planned path. The Wyvern heard the rock collide with the cliffs, spinning and roaring in anger as it started to think that someone was going for the cave. It stomped towards the sound, releasing a blast of fire amidst an enraged roar in the direction I had thrown the stone.

"Go!" I pulled myself up and ran behind the cover of rocks with Tristan on my heels, the women moving to get into position in the opposite direction.

The two of us circled around the rocks as the Wyvern returned to where it had been standing, its nostrils flaring and its eyes blazing as it hunted for us. We were very close to the boulder in question now, the Wyvern only a dozen feet from us. I tensed as I crouched low, nodding for Tristan to get into position.

"I'll not drop it on you," he said as he clambered up the cliff.

"I appreciate that," I muttered, staying low and watching the beast.

The sound of Tristan scrambling up the rocks drew the Wyvern's flaming eyes, the creature snarling in its throat as it narrowed its gaze in our direction. It stalked forward, its wings clawing across the ground keeping its front half low. It was getting a little too close for my liking and I was certain it would see me as I drew my sword.

My sword isn't going to do much against those jaws or that flame breath... a cold sweat touched me at that thought and I swallowed hard.

There came a loud flashing bang, and the cracking of stone drew the Wyvern's eyes up away from me. It roared and leaped backwards, flapping its wings as it partially took off, staying only a few feet from the ground with its tail dragging. It just narrowly avoided the massive boulder that came crashing down with a rockslide that threatened to bury it.

I braced my back to the wall of the cliff beneath the ledge, tensing as I was nearly crushed by the rocks. It didn't last long, the dust and dirt mixed with snow raining around me quickly and giving me a momentary shield between me and the beast.

I have to go now. I got up and ran towards the cave while staying by the cliffs, the whistling of arrows and the fierce roars of the Wyvern telling me that the women had begun their diversion. A flash of blue flames from above me struck the Wyvern's side as I reached the cave, Tristan joining in as they attempted to confuse the great beast.

I couldn't spare the time to look back now, focusing on getting into the deep tunnel and working my way to the nest. The roars of the Wyvern echoed after me, but were becoming more and more distant, and were soon only as a rumbling sound as I entered the enormous cavern.

There wasn't much light, just a few stray beams of sun rays shining down through gaps in the walls and ceiling to let me see. My eyes immediately fell upon the enormous dirt and clay nest that took up the central space, the ruined shells of eggs strewn about amidst the shattered bones and skulls of animals and adventurers alike.

Cautiously, I approached the nest, my feet crossing over each other as I kept my sword at the ready and my posture low. Bones cracked under my boots as I walked, my movements slowing as my heart rate picked up. I just had to be careful.

At last, I reached the edge of the nest, freezing as seven wyvern hatchlings raised their heads to look at me. They stared at me with their reptilian gazes, their tongues slithering from between their scaly lips as they crackled curiously up at me. Two of them leaped up from where they had nestled in with their siblings, their wing claws-hooking at the ground as they scrambled aggressively towards me. They paused and arched their necks back, hissing in an attempt to scare me off.

"Nice babies," I tried to coo to them, a little shaken now as I crouched. "Nice babies. Don't call mama. I just need a shell. That's all..."

My sights glimpsed a fairly complete egg not too far from my reach, the side of it broken from where one of the infants had forced their way out. I didn't know precisely how much of the shell would be required, so I figured this was my best option.

Slowly, I lowered myself down, reaching my left hand towards the egg as the hatchlings watched me with predatory stares. One bite could prove devastating, their teeth already sharp enough to take off a finger if they felt so inclined to.

"Easy... easy..." I murmured, watching them out of the corner of my eye, my fingers grazing the shell of the egg.

One of the hatchlings snapped at me, but didn't attack, my hand tensing as I thought to draw back. I managed not to and snagged the egg, pulling away swiftly as the hatchlings all leaped at me, trying to bite me at once. The shredding of fabric caused me to yelp as something sharp ripped into my wrist and I smelled my own blood. It was just a nip from the small creature's teeth, but it was enough to hurt.

Dragging myself to my feet, I swiftly stashed the egg in my satchel and turned from the nest, running back down the tunnel to the exit of the cave. I made it out in less than a minute, skidding as the enormous shape of the hatchlings' mother blocked my path. The Wyvern reared up and swung her tail as she saw me, no longer distracted now that she had seen me.

"Oh, shit!" I jumped out of the way just as the massive tail smashed the ground where I stood, dust and snow flying up all around.

I didn't hesitate, throwing myself up and running, the others already on the move to join me. The wyvern roared furiously and turned after us.

"Run!" I shouted to the others. "Go!"

None of us halted, casting ourselves into a desperate sprint through the maze of high rocks that led to the cave, our goal on reaching the hill that stood several yards away. But just as it looked like we would make it, we heard the beating of large wings. The Wyvern flew over us with a powerful roar. She landed on the hill and blocked us, snarling as her eyes glowed brighter and her throat flared with the light of the flames she was preparing to launch.

"Well, that's it," Tristan staggered, backing up with the women and I, "we're about to be dinner..."

There wasn't time for us to do anything, the four of us seconds away from being burned to a crisp. But fortune favoured us as anther loud roar tore the sky.

Feldspar appeared, his enormous red wings beating the air as he swooped out of nowhere, aiming straight for the wyvern. The dragon unleashed a blast of flames right across the wyvern's back, gaining her attention and drawing her away from us. The wyvern roared back at him in rage and jumped up into the air to chase the silver and red dragon, the two of them now dipping and flapping their wings as they fought.

"Carden!" Syrena appeared at the hill with Caedmon. "Come on!"

"Go!" I ordered the others, making sure they got up the hill before dragging myself to safety.

Syrena had her hand around the pendant at her neck, the glow of crimson energy extending between her fingers. She had her golden eyes set on Feldspar's red and silver shape as he fought the Wyvern, urging him to win silently.

After a few moments, Feldspar gained the upper hand and forced the Wyvern away, making her roar in protest. The enormous dragon roared back as if to end the argument and the Wyvern turned on the wind, returning to her cave. Feldspar made his way back to where we now stood, landing with the thump of his large feet on the ground.

Syrena let her hand drop from the Pendant as its light faded away. She moved forward as her dragon lowered his head to her.

"Good work, Feldspar," she smiled up at him, stroking his face.

"See?" Tristan spoke up breathlessly. "We could have gotten the Dragon to help."

Ellora and Tallinn just shook their heads as I ignored him, Caedmon handing each of us our cloaks now that we were out of danger.

"You have great timing, sister," I told Syrena as I managed to calm my rushing lungs. "Another minute and you'd be scraping up our ashes."

"I'd never let my brother be turned to ash," she smiled, turning from the Dragon. "So, did you get it?"

I nodded. "Got it."

"That just leaves the Phoenix tears then," she noted, folding her arms before her armoured chest. "Let's head back to the castle and see if the offering we placed has drawn one yet."

I nodded, pulling my cloak on and following her.

Hopefully we'll have the tears soon. Then I can get you back, Leander...

* * * * *

"*Four* days! It's been *four* days since we got the eggshells from the Wyvern's nest and still there's no sign of a phoenix!" I slumped where I sat with the others in the dining room, my head hanging dejectedly. "We desperately need those tears or else this is all for nothing!"

"Now, Prince Carden, you know that summoning a phoenix is not a simple thing," Ranzel said evenly, sitting back in his chair opposite me, his meal finished before him. "Phoenixes are rarities in the world as it is and are not birds that come simply by being called like a parrot or a falcon."

"Very true," Fawkner agreed, feeding Farsight on his arm. "You cannot train a phoenix in falconry."

I sighed, folding my arms as I sat back, my fine black shirt folding at the shoulders with the movement. I just shook my head as I regarded the two men grimly.

"We have *one* day left," I reminded them. "Just *one* day before the Dark Moons. If we haven't got the tears by then the Doorway won't open and we will *never* be able to save Leander," I sighed, staring at the table before me. "The darkness from Ragnarok's storms is starting to take over the southern reaches of Valloran even now and it is robbing us of all second chances. We *have* to succeed *this* time, or we're finished... *She's* finished..."

"Do not worry so much, laddie," Dolin advised me from where he and Holger sat at the table, smoking his pipe while his brother still ate. "We will save the lassie. I promise you."

I nodded grimly. "If only such promises could be guaranteed, Dolin. But even now our chance of saving her slips further and further from our grasp with each passing moment."

"But Danika foresaw our success," Tallinn reminded me, sitting back as she held her cup of water in hand, her blonde hair hanging free across her bared shoulders. "That's right isn't it?" she looked to the Witch across from her and beside Ranzel. "That is why you stated that Tristan, Ellora and I going with Carden to gather the tribute would lead to such successes? Is it not?"

I turned my hard green gaze towards the Witch, studying her across the ebony table, my arms tightening their folded hold. She looked as calm as she ever did, minus our encounter with her at her cave. Part of me truly began to believe that the woman never showed any emotion unless it was related directly to her.

"That *is* what you said, Danika," I reminded the woman with a calm, but stern tone. "*You* said we *would* succeed."

"In gathering the tribute, yes, I foresaw your success," she agreed, taking a mouthful of wine from her goblet before setting it down.

"And that we would save Leander," I added firmly.

"Never did you ask if I foresaw her resurrection," she replied nonchalantly.

"You were the one who told us to come here," Ellora pointed out, seeing that I was growing angry, though I managed to more or less keep it controlled. "That means that you have seen success."

"No, that is not what it means," the Witch responded curtly. "My telling you to come to Valloran was only to give you the *chance* to restore her. None of you asked if she *will* be restored."

"Okay," I nodded coldly, leaning forward and resting my arms on the table, trying hard to keep myself from exploding. "Then tell me: do you foresee us succeeding in reaching Lord Azmerath, asking for his aid, gaining it and Leander being resurrected?"

"I see a very long life for the Princess," Danika responded, seemingly dodging the question. "I also see a final confrontation between her and the Shadow Lord before the world meets its fate. Does that satisfy you, Prince?"

"Hardly," I responded, standing up from the table. "You have not answered my question in the most simple of terms, but conjured misdirection around it. *Does the Princess come back to life? Yes* or *no*?"

"Yes," she scowled and rolled her eyes. "Does *that* satisfy you, *Prince*?" she hissed the question in repeat at me.

I sighed and shook my head. "I'm sorry, Danika. I do not mean to be terse. It is just frustrating to be so close and be running so short on time."

"You suffer a terrible affliction, Prince," she said, seeming determined to emphasise my title. "The ailment known as love plays such havoc on the mind and soul."

"I'm not sure I'd call it an ailment," I said softly, meeting her gaze, "but it certainly plays great havoc on me."

"Things will work out, laddie," Dolin said with certainty, puffing at his pipe. "We'll not have come this far to fail now."

"I hope you're right," I turned and started towards the door.

"Where are you going?" Tallinn asked, concern in her otherwise calm voice.

"To sit with her," I answered simply, continuing out of the dining room and into the castle's dully lit stone hallways.

"I'll come with you," she got up with the scraping of her chair, her hurried footsteps slowing down as she caught up to me.

Despite the Witch's words and the encouragement of our allies, I felt deeply despondent. It was all well and good to say that what I hoped for would come true, but it wasn't as easy as all that. To say it would be and to see it actually come to be are very different things, and right at that moment I wasn't so certain of our success, though I continued to hope.

"I feel like I'm out of line," I confessed to my sister of the Guardians, walking slowly down the hallway. "I fear that I am becoming more like my father now that I am here; brooding and demanding, even unreasonable."

"You are just desperate," she said evenly, walking beside me with her eyes ahead of us. "The end of this lies so close ahead, yet this one final encounter stands between us and success, seemingly mocking us. Is it any wonder that you grow impatient? I do too. We all do."

"It isn't the same thing," I sighed, turning down the corridor that led to the rooms where our guests were staying, my room in the opposite wing.

"No, it isn't," she agreed with a shake of her head, glancing up at me as we passed two human guardsmen. "The rest of us seek success in this task for the survival of our world, but you do not. Your focus is the Princess; on restoring her to life and getting her back," she shook her head, looking to the floor as we drew nearer the end of the hall. "You no longer think with your head when it comes to her, but with your heart. That is the way with lovers, I believe."

"You believe?" I raised one thick eyebrow at her.

She shrugged, smiling mildly at me. "I've never known the touch of such emotions, nor do I believe I ever will. I can only imagine what it is that you feel."

I shook my head, trying to be encouraging as I spoke: "Come now, Tallinn. Don't speak like that. You're a beautiful young woman who I am certain any man would be proud to name as his beloved."

"Maybe so, but my place is in the Order," she said with finality and certainty as we reached the door where Joran stood like a statue. "The Oath is my husband. I am no domestic, nor will I ever be, and too many seek just that from women."

"An unfair perception," I nodded as I paused by the door, turning to look down at her. "I believe women are as capable as men, and often more so. It is through you and your gender that life flows while me and mine simply add our seed. I do not see women as the doting wives and housekeepers of their husbands as if they are owned by them, but each one a queen in her own right that we men have the privilege of bonding with as partners in life. I also do not see why men cannot love men, nor why women cannot love women. All people should be permitted their values and their heart's desires without cruelty or discrimination."

"You are a very progressive prince, Carden," Tallinn smiled thoughtfully. "But then, you have seen a good many oddities and rarities in the world now, your experience an overflowing font. Remember the flesh-crafter we met in the Rural Mountains of Vorhalaas?"

"Of course," I nodded, recalling the encounter some nine years earlier. "The people feared what he was doing and that he was a man corrupting and torturing the innocent. Instead, we found that he was trying to aid those whose bodies did not suit their souls."

"Making men into women and women into men," Tallinn nodded thoughtfully. "A strange craft for a sorcerer, though it was not done so against his clients' wills. Gods, I didn't know what to think when I saw that they were paying him to give them the genders they desired."

"That is why we helped him go where he would not be persecuted," I said, folding my arms as I leaned against the doorframe. "I can't see what is wrong with a man or a woman wanting to be healed in such a way, even if being flesh-crafted into the opposite gender is an extreme curative for their ailment. They have as much right as anyone else and it is no different than healing someone of a debilitating disease or injury."

"We faced some unusual things," Tallinn mused, folding her own arms as she looked up at me through her long blonde locks, "and we helped a good many people. You truly did some real good as a Guardian, Carden."

I sighed, nodding as I looked into the room, seeing Leander lying still and silent. "I didn't do her any good, though. If anything, I made it easier for them to get to her..."

"Don't say that" Tallinn touched my shoulder, gaining my gaze back to hers. "You have done so much to help her ever since the day we met her. Though we have all fought to protect and help her, none of us have been as dedicated as you. Even now, you are the one willing to sacrifice so much just to get her back."

"I am willing to do more than you know," I sighed and turned back to where the dead girl lay, studying her soft white features in the candlelight. "I love her so much that I was going to leave the Order anyway, though for a different reason."

"What reason?" Tallinn frowned.

A sad smile tugged at my lips. "I was going to ask her to marry me."

"You were?" she gasped in shock and quiet excitement. "So, when you mentioned this in Silvervale, you actually meant it?"

I nodded, reaching into my belt and removing a silver ring with an amethyst and two small sapphires set into the delicate Elven designs. I had been keeping it wrapped in the silvery pouch the High Elven jeweller had given it to me in. It hadn't been cheap, costing me a great deal of gold, but I didn't care. It would compliment her perfectly and declare my heart's most secret and earnest desires.

"I bought her this in Silvervale with the intention that I would give it to her when the time was right," I explained in a soft voice, allowing Tallinn to see it. "I wanted... I wanted to ask for her hand the night Tristan..."

"The night he made his lusts known," she finished for me in a soft, low voice.

I nodded, feeling my tears falling on my cheeks. I slowly made my way into the room and approached the bed where my intended lay. I crouched and took her cold hand in my warm palm, holding her gently as I still cradled the ring in my other hand.

"My intentions fell away when I saw him kiss her and I flew into a rage," I admitted guiltily, watching Leander's still features with sadness. "Instead of proposing, I accused her of being unfaithful, and unwittingly set her up for the Witches to abduct her."

"That is why you fight so hard now," Tallinn realised.

I nodded and sighed sadly, setting the ring back into its pouch and stashing it into my belt again before I looked upon the girl's permanently sleeping features. I took her right hand in both of mine and held it to my lips, studying her with a heavier heart than before.

"It seems now that my intentions were all for nothing," I murmured. "With less than twenty-four hours left to us, I cannot see how we can hope to gain the last tribute and free her from her deathly state."

I shook my head as I felt Tallinn place her hands on my shoulders. Normally, I would be comforted by such a touch, but right now I felt only grief as the skies were darkening and the moons were nearing the end of their wanning cycle.

Tears slipped down my cheeks as I locked my eyes on Leander's closed ones, feeling that I had to face her in all honesty now. She looked so stunningly beautiful in the dark greens of the bed, her white gown lying around her making her look like an angel in the gloom of my ancestral home. She could have been glowing from how bright she looked now, but it was only the candles illuminating her pallid flesh and pure clothes.

I ran one hand across her cheek, once again feeling the chilled and lifeless skin of her face, longing for her warmth to return.

"I am so sorry, Leander," I whispered to her, letting my tears fall. "I have fought for you to the last and still do, but..." I sucked in a shaky breath to compose myself, focusing on her face, "but we're out of time. The portal can only be opened at the dark moons, and we are nearly there. We won't have another chance."

I shook my head, just wishing she would open her eyes and say something, anything. But as always, she lay dead, and I was left with only her silence.

"I've failed you, Leander," I murmured, shaking my head. "I have failed you again and I am so sorry. I'm so sorry, my love."

I stood up and leaned over her, stroking her head softly with one broad hand. I tried to will her eyes open, but still they lay shut as my own tears fell to her cheeks.

"If I can't restore you then I'll make sure you rest in peace, my princess," I told her softly, drawing nearer to her and kissing her forehead. "I will never leave you. Never, my love."

A strange glow began to fill the room, growing brighter and brighter with each passing moment. A warmth flooded the space, and I squinted as Tallinn gasped behind me, the two of us turning our gazes towards the side of the bed nearer the window.

There was a golden light standing there upon the covers, the heat of flames enwrapping it. The glow grew so bright that I had to shield my eyes, dropping to my knees as it began to take on the form of a beautiful glowing eagle-like bird wreathed in flames of golden-orange. It outstretched its wings majestically, the embers floating from its feathers seemingly keeping themselves from setting fire to the bedclothes and furniture. It lifted its head, a great mane of purple and gold fire streaking from its crown down its back to match its immensely long tail feathers.

"Is... is that a phoenix?" Tallinn murmured in awed disbelief.

I nodded, unable to find words as the phoenix turned its glowing white flame eyes towards us with a powerful reverence I could never have imagined.

Once again, Danika is right...

I didn't know what to say as the phoenix turned its glowing eyes towards Leander's still body, the room illuminated as if there were a star sitting within its dark confines. The mystical bird just seemed to study her face, drawing closer to her with curiosity. It was a wonder to behold such a creature, but one that I couldn't bask in.

"Tallinn," I managed to croak as I regained my composure. "Do you have a spare phial?"

"I'll get one," she swiftly left the room, gone only for a few moments before returning from her quarters across the hallway.

She handed me the small glass phial and I turned back to the glowing phoenix as it lifted its attention to us. It seemed to be waiting for us to do something

"I... I'm not sure what I'm supposed to do," I confessed to the incredible bird. "I don't know if there is some spell to be spoken or some ritual required, but I know what I must ask." I turned my gaze to Leander, feeling the phoenix do the same. "She was murdered cruelly, her life stolen by the monster that tries now to destroy the world," I shook my head sadly, touching her hand again. "I will not try to even pretend to convince you to help me by suggesting such things as we have before about this being your world or anything like that. I simply state the truth," I took in a slow breath, feeling my tears strengthen and my voice wobble. "I love her, and I wish to bring her back. She is innocent and pure, her heart filled with only good."

I looked to the phoenix as it turned its glowing eyes to me, sympathy seeming to appear within them, if that were at all possible for a bird to present.

I let out a shaking breath and made my plea: "Will you show your compassion to us? Will you help me to restore this innocent girl to life and heal her so that she may be given a second chance? She deserves so much more than she's been granted. And more than I have given..."

The phoenix stepped closer, turning its head towards Leander again. It lowered its face to hers and I watched on as the flames of its eyes seemed to release liquefied glowing white tears down its cheeks. They fell from its face and pooled upon Leander's heart as it studied the horrible wound in her chest, the tears seeping into it. They didn't close it but were absorbed into the ruins of her dead heart, sinking into her flesh and leaving a momentary glow there.

I offered the phial forward hopefully, the phoenix turning its tearful gaze to my hand. It then tilted its head and let its tears fall, filling the phial easily with the white glowing liquid fire. It then lifted its head and watched me as I sat back, closing the stopper on the phial. My heart warmed in my chest.

I nodded to the phoenix and smiled gratefully. "Thank you."

The phoenix bowed its head before turning towards the open window. It stretched its wings and took flight, exploding into a stream of white, gold, orange and purple fire that streaked through the opening and out into the cold night. The room dulled again, and we were left with only the illumination of the candles and the glow of the phial of tears.

I couldn't believe it. We had actually done it. We had gotten the phoenix tears and could now prepare for the ritual to save her.

"Tallinn," I stood up slowly, my voice soft despite my internal shouts of joy. "Go and tell the others. We're ready."

Without another word, she rushed from the room, and I heard Joran move, the giant obviously having been watching on.

I smiled and bent to Leander, kissing her lips. "You'll be back with us soon, my love. Just hold on a little longer."

I turned and hurried from the room with a new sense of purpose, entering my own rooms in the royal wing without even realising I had travelled the halls until I was there. Immediately, I set to work getting everything together, setting the phial of tears on the desk with the wyvern eggshell and the gryphon feathers before seeking a bag to carry them in. As I found one, I paused by the desk, seeing Leander's pendant glistening in the light of the candles.

I took it in my hand, feeling a strange warmth in it. *Maybe it knows she's coming back. Maybe it's getting ready to be reunited with her and maybe when it is it will call Amethyst back to us as well.* Once again, my hand plunged into my belt and I withdrew the engagement ring, studying it in my palm next to her pendant. *I'll ask her once she's well enough. I can't imagine she'll be awake immediately, or that she will be well enough to speak for long. But once she is able to stand on her own again and speak with me, I will make her my wife.*

"I *will* marry her," I confirmed aloud in a smiling whisper. "I'll tell her everything and I'll ask her to be my bride."

At that moment, I felt a chill rush through the room, pausing as a frown pulled over my face. I turned slowly as I sensed a presence, the ring and pendant still in my hand.

"Carden," Leander looked at me with a worried expression, standing with her back to the door in the middle of the room, her clothes more like what I had always seen her wearing.

"We've done it," I smiled at her spirit form. "We've got the tributes for Azmerath."

She shook her head sadly. "Carden, no. I told you that I'm dead and I can't come back."

"I thought you would be happy," I said with a frown, staring down at her. "Do you not want us to be together again?"

"But this isn't the way," she pleaded softly, tears on her cheeks. "You're risking your life needlessly just for a chance to bring me back that won't work. Please, Carden, just let this go. Please..."

My frown deepened at the desperateness in her words. They sounded strange and foreign in her voice, her very demeanour and presence not feeling right. For the first time since we had started this whole ordeal, I felt clearer and could sense that something was wrong.

"I don't understand," I spoke slowly and carefully, watching her with a critical eye now that I had never thought to use before. "You speak as if you don't want to live again. We have all that we need to give you back your life and you just talk as if doing so would be more painful than dying."

"My death *was* traumatic!" she insisted desperately. "Do you really want to make me suffer again?! Because that's what you'll do if you bring me back! I want to be with you, but this isn't the way!" she softened her voice, looking up at me with longing and sadness. "I told you that we will be together again, but not like this. After you have passed from your physical body, you will be with me."

She smiled at me, imitating stroking my cheek with one delicate hand, though she didn't touch me, the strange tingling of her energy making my nerves shudder.

"Then we'll be happy forever," she whispered, her smile haunting me.

I narrowed my eyes at her, feeling my jaw tense as realisation filled me.

"You're not Leander," I growled lowly.

She frowned, confused. "Yes, I am. Can't you tell, Carden?"

I shook my head. "Leander - the *real* Leander - would not try to stop me from saving her, nor would she try to convince me that dying is the only way for us to be together."

She took a step back as her chest heaved in a very good imitation of fear, but I wasn't fooled. Not anymore. I knew what it was that I faced now, having seen it four years ago.

"You're *not* Leander," I growled lowly, glaring into her steel blue eyes. "You're the Darkest Shadow."

Leander's face hardened and her fear twisted into a sinister smile as her irises glowed the evil green of Gorth'lakian flame: "So, you finally figured it out, Guardian..."

Chapter Twenty-One
Death's Exchange in a Kiss

Leander's expression darkened as her eyes glowed green, her face seeming more arrogant and sinister than it should have. I watched then as her clothes turned to black misty shadows, warping and changing around her slender frame and curved hips. Her blue velvet gown became a black dress with a sheer black over robe on top. She looked paler and more evil, the Darkest Shadow revealing itself to me the way it had chosen to be the day I had seen it in the depths of Grishk'kinnar.

"I was beginning to think you would never learn the truth," the Darkest Shadow said, speaking in an evil version of Leander's sweet voice, striding slowly towards me with its black dress and robe trailing behind it. "Part of me wishes you hadn't so that I could keep toying with you. Too bad."

"All this time," I realised, suppressing my rage with the knowledge that I couldn't do anything against the evil ethereal monster, "every visitation of her, every dream that became a nightmare... they were all *you*."

It gave me a cold sneer, nodding as it started to move to my left, slowly walking towards the windows. It was bewildering and terrifying to see the Daemon imitating Leander, her innocence and its evil direct contrasts that should never have combined or mixed in any way. To see her eyes glowing with dark fire and her body wrapped in those shadowy robes only made me feel sick in my heart, but the rage was helping me to overcome that.

"Broken hearted young men are so easy to manipulate," the Darkest Shadow remarked as it studied the tribute on the desk, thankfully unable to touch any of it. "All they need is the right visions to turn them into mewling, helpless wretches, leaving them broken and at my mercy."

"I am hardly at your mercy, daemon," I growled, balling my empty fist and clutching the Pendant and ring in the other as if to protect them.

"No. You're not," it turned back to me, staring over its shoulder with Leander's face. "I thought for certain after the dreams I made you have that you would have become inconsolable. Apparently, I was wrong."

"Those dreams..." I scowled, shaking my head, keeping my glaring eyes locked on its face. "They were inappropriate, corrupting something innocent and pure."

"Innocent and pure?" it turned to me, laughing coldly and twisting that beautiful face into a cruel sneer. "Is that what you think sex is? The way you mortals mash up against each other with a fury rivalled only by brutal violence? How you men thrust painfully into a woman's intimacy and rend her open for your desires to fill her like some vessel to hold your wretched little spawn? You call *that* innocent and pure?"

"Daemons like you have no concept of love or passion," I hissed back, keeping my calm as she approached me with a confident and slow stride. "It doesn't surprise me that you can't understand the purity of acts of these natures."

"I understand more than you think, Carden," she leaned close to me, her breath touching my ear as she started to whisper. "I have seen into your mind, witnessed the perverted fantasies and lusts you have for the Princess. I have viewed the images you have of your so-called love and passion..."

I glanced at her, noting her evil smirk, but held still.

"Then, I also saw your... hm..." she laughed softly through closed lips, "more deviant desires. Be honest, *Prince*. You have thought about taking her many times and indulging your baser natures. Every time you saw her wrists bound and her body helpless, you yearned to add to her desperation, to make her *moan* as you lay claim to her..."

"Enough," I growled, pulling away and moving to the desk, setting the Pendant and ring back into my belt pouch as I did.

"You have your own dark desires for her," she turned after me. "You cannot deny the desires you have towards binding her to a bed, unclothed, and just having your way, despite her protests. Such thoughts engorge you even now..."

"I said enough," I snapped, pressing my hands to the table.

She snorted a laugh. "Please... as if you are so virtuous as to not be aroused by my words. No human can resist their want of another, especially one as innocent as the Princess."

"Is this your new tactic?" I demanded, turning to stare her down. "Hm? You are found out, so now you attempt to use my dark impulses to guilt me? Is that it?"

She shrugged her shoulders, the over robe's sheer black fabric allowing me to glimpse her exposed skin where the dress didn't reach. Everything about the daemon seemed as if it were simply attempting to play on my hidden needs and lusts now rather than my grief.

"I will use any tactic I deem fit to achieve my goals," she replied coldly, smirking. "You didn't seem to complain when I entered your dreams and allowed you to *fuck* me..."

I snorted and shook my head. "Your attempts at seduction are crass and ineffective, Daemon. You are a violator, and that is precisely what you did to me in those nightmares."

"Oh, poor little prince," she mocked, her glowing eyes filled with delight at seeing my unease. "Afraid that I'm going to steal your virtue?"

"Not even if I had virtue to steal," I responded coldly, folding my arms in front of my chest as she drew near to me. "There is only one thing you seek: to prevent that which you are afraid of happening."

"And what is that?" she tried to act as if she were seductive.

I managed to push away the thoughts of Leander, reminding myself that this being was the Darkest Shadow and that no matter what, it was just a ghastly horror to overcome.

I will not succumb to its willpower...

I allowed myself a cold smirk as I stared into her green, glowing eyes, just waiting to watch them change.

"You fear that I will succeed, which means only one thing," my smirk broadened. "I *can* succeed. I *can* bring Leander back from the dead."

Her brow furrowed and her smile vanished.

"You didn't expect me to realise it, did you?" I asked with a sense of victory. "You've known all along that *I* am the one to restore her to life, and so you have been trying to stop me ever since we first returned to Lorveren."

The Darkest Shadow backed away slowly, her expression less confident now. It was clear to me that she hadn't thought I would realise the truth about my chances, her confidence having been purely born from keeping me in the dark. But now my world had been illuminated and I could see the truth before me that she had been trying to hide.

I shook my head, striding forward and making her back away further still: "That is why you sent the force of Scourge to Seaguard when we embarked on the *Black Asp*. That is why you had Keilantra send her ships to attack us as we made the Ortagaad crossing to Valloran. That is why you sent the Lost to kill me disguised as Leander... and that is why you have been appearing to me pretending to be her ghost," I smirked confidently, glaring down at the Daemon hiding behind my lover's face. "You want to make sure Leander stays dead so that she can't stop Morod. In order to do that you have to kill me. But you've failed."

"You think I desire that?" she hissed venomously up at me, trying to overpower me with her words. "You think that I *care* about this *pathetic* physical realm?"

"If you didn't you wouldn't have empowered the Shadow Lords," I responded.

I pulled away and moved back to the desk, sensing the Darkest Shadow's rage building. It was satisfying to know that I had gotten under its skin, even if it was just an ethereal being of the Void. After what I had seen it and Morod do in Grishk'kinnar, it felt good to finally be winning against at least one of them.

"I should destroy you!" she sounded like she was close to screaming. "I should reduce you to ash where you stand!"

I turned around and held my arms out to my sides, inviting her to make a move: "Go on then. Do it. Set a fire inside me and burn me to ashes. It's the only way you're going to stop me now. You're supposed to be some great and powerful Daemon God. So go ahead. Kill me and stop me."

I watched the Darkest Shadow as it stood there, tensing in Leander's shape. Her hands were clenching and flinching wildly at her hips, her eyes blazing with green flames as she gritted her teeth. It was all too clear what was happening, and I allowed her to dwell for a few moments before lowering my arms to my sides, shaking my head.

"You can't, can you?" I asked harshly, knowing I was right as she turned her gaze to mine. "That's why you've sent others to do your dirty work and when that failed you tried to coerce me with your words and visions. You can't do a thing."

"That's the problem with the Prophecies," she scowled in anger, slouching her shoulders as her eyes flared. "They prevent me from acting when something I do not wish to see come to pass is close at hand. They were created to nullify my powers, as well as those of all the other Daemon Gods in the Void. Even now, *you* are protected from my powers, Prince. I can do *nothing*."

"Then leave," I told her firmly, folding my arms before me again. "There is no point in either of us continuing this, so just go back to the Void and stay there."

"You really think you can win?" she seethed.

"I know I can win, because you have made sure of it," I replied in a calm, even voice, noting her confused frown. "You have thrown the world into darkness, slaughtered too many innocent people, even murdered the girl I love. But you made *one vital* error."

"Which is?" she raised one slender eyebrow.

"You chose to make yourself look like *her*," I answered coldly, glaring fiercely at her. "Using her to manipulate me and making her your villainous form was the last straw. I will make sure now that Leander not only comes back from the dead and ends your servant's reign, but I will also ensure that you are wiped from existence, Daemon."

"You better hurry then, Prince Carden," the Darkest Shadow stepped back, smirking coldly at me. "Your princess is in danger even now. The Void is hungry, and her soul is slipping from Azmerath's grasp. Soon she will be mine and I will make her suffer for all eternity."

"Leave!" I nearly roared at the Daemon, my body tensing as I felt my predator growing stronger.

She half laughed, standing by the door. "Very well. But be warned: things are *not* going to work out how you want. The Divines are not all that different from us, Guardian. There *will* be a cost for her salvation, and you will be apart, no matter your intentions."

"Get out, Daemon," I scowled.

"So be it," she smirked. "Give my regards to Azmerath *and* the Princess..."

With that, the Darkest Shadow started to disappear, the dark visage of Leander evaporating into shadowy wisps that receded into the darkness of the room. Only the glowing green eyes lingered in the bank of blackness before going out and disappearing all together, leaving me feeling shaken, but convicted.

* * * * *

Night fell and the dark moons rose into a clear sky, the stars shining down on the land like a million twinkling eyes watching what was destined to be. The air was chilled, and the wind blew through the towers with a faint whistle. The castle had been put into lockdown, every Blood Knight and guardsmen on alert now that we were ready. My father wasn't going to take any chances with us opening Azmerath's Doorway.

Syrena led us out of the tower keep to an ancient black stone section of the castle accessible via a bridge. It was built into the rocky cliffs of Death's Shadow Peak, snow wafting down from the night sky to coat all the surfaces in icy powder. There was a wide porch and balcony where the bridge joined the structure, ten guards in heavy black armour always watching over the entrance at any time. Twin braziers stood on either side of the large stone doors, the orange flames illuminating the undercover entryway and large double doors.

Father stepped forward and placed his hands to the doors, pushing them open with a resounding groan of ancient hinges. The doors were far too heavy for any human to ever manage to shift. He cleared the way and led us down the steep stairs, torches along the walls lighting our way as we traversed the craggy cavern tunnel towards the bottom.

I shifted beneath my armour, my hand clutching the hilt of my sword nervously. My gaze drifted to Joran beside me. He carried Leander's limp, white clad form in his arms, her head lolling against his broad chest, her dark hair shielding her face.

Not much longer, I thought. *Tonight, she will be restored to life and free of the pain Morod forced on her. Then I'll ask for her hand and protect her so that she can fulfil her destiny. Maybe then we can live happily ever after...*

We reached the bottom of the stairs, and my family led us into an enormous cavern chamber with a rounded stone dome-ceiling carved into the rocks. The room was lit with braziers all around, columns holding up blue flame torches as a gigantic statue of Azmerath stood at the far end overlooking the circular space.

I couldn't help but look up at the statue, studying its features. It was carved of obsidian and stood about twenty feet tall with angelic wings outstretched from its back, its body clad in sculpted armour. The face was hidden beneath a hood, the sculptor having not seen fit to chisel any features for the God. In one hand the statue held a staff topped with the symbol for Immortality known as the Ankh, the other hand outstretched with a goblet held aloft. At its feet stood an obsidian archway with a solid wall of smooth stone covering the side facing the monument. It was about nine feet tall and carved with ancient vampiric runes all along the archway, the Ankh once again the symbol set at its top. It seemed fairly unremarkable at first glance, sitting on a low set of wide steps that rounded out from its base. It was flanked by two nine-foot-tall angelic statues in armour, both holding halberds, their faces hidden beneath their ornate helms. They looked as if they would come to life and attack anyone who meant the Doorway harm, but for the moment remained dormant.

"Incredible," Ranzel said in awe as he moved up beside me with his staff in hand, his voice echoing around the vastly high chamber. "Never had I thought to ever stand in a monument such as this."

"I do not think any of us thought to," Ellora commented, moving forward to join me where I had stopped before the Doorway.

My eyes drifted up to the ceiling where I glimpsed an opening shielded with perfect glass, the place where the dark moons looked down on the land visible. I couldn't see them, but their shadowy shapes left a void in the stars where they should have been.

"It is time," Father spoke solemnly, moving to the small stone slab that stood before the archway, a ceremonial dagger resting on a stand there. "Gather around."

Our companions all surrounded us, Tallinn, Tristan and Ellora flanking me where I remained beside Joran. Ranzel and Danika stood side-by-side, the two magic wielders the calmest of all of us. Fawkner and the Dwarves remained on Joran's opposite side; their demeanours reminiscent of the reverence shown at a funeral. Lastly, Syrena stood at my side as Caedmon stayed by hers, both of them in their finery rather than their armour.

"By entering Azmerath's Doorway you are putting your very lives and souls in jeopardy," my father explained grimly, locking his eyes on my sister and I. "Lord Azmerath has taken those who are unworthy after stepping through the arch into his realm, so if you have any doubts, now is the time to abandon this venture."

I looked to Tallinn, Tristan and Ellora, the three of them resolute. *I am glad to have such allies willing to stand with me in this. Even Tristan no longer seems the wretch he was.*

I turned back to my father. "We will not turn away."

He sighed, shaking his head disapprovingly. "Very well, my son."

He took the dagger and faced the arch, running the blade along his palm. He didn't even flinch as it cut through his durable flesh and loosed his blood, pain so beyond him at his age. It wasn't something I looked forward to.

Father moved forward slowly, holding his palm up as he locked his eyes on the archway, his gaze drifting to the hooded face of the statue. "My Lord

Azmerath, I beseech thee to open the way into your kingdom so that the living may set foot in the realm of the dead," he summoned calmly, almost as if he had practiced this many times before. "With the dark moons on high and the tributes gathered, these pilgrims have proven themselves worthy to pass by us, the Sentinels of the Doorway, to seek your audience and your favour. Open the Doorway, my lord, and grant them passage to your great throne room. So mote it be."

With that prayer ended, he flicked his wrist at the arch, his blood spattering out in stray droplets. They hit thin air and strange purplish light began to open holes where the blood had passed the arch. We watched on in awe as the rips in reality extended and filled the archway, a black portal mixed with swirling purple shimmering there before us where there had only been an empty alcove before.

Father turned to us and nodded. "He has heard my summons and opened the way for you. Do not anger him or he will not allow you to leave his realm."

"We won't," I assured him.

He held out his hand to stay our feet: "Leave your weapons behind, for you will not need them. Nor will they do you any good."

"Very well," I removed my sword, throwing knives and steel dagger, handing them to Fawkner.

The others set down their bows, swords and other weapons, the Axton twins taking them for safekeeping as Syrena moved to the archway. I turned to Joran and looked up at him, holding out my arms for Leander.

"I should be accompanying her, Prince Carden," he stated in his rumbling voice.

"I know. But I *will* take care of her, Joran," I said softly. "I will *always* take care of her."

He bowed his head and lowered the girl's slender body into my arms, allowing me to wrap one of her limp arms around my shoulders and rest her head to my chest. I nodded to the others, nothing left to be said as I carried her past my father and to the archway.

I turned my eyes to Syrena as she said: "You first, brother."

I took in a slow breath, gazing down at Leander's silent face one more time, then stepped into the portal.

I had expected to feel something more than I did, but the experience was... well, as normal as stepping between two rooms. The thought that passing into Death's realm could be so simple and easy was a little unsettling, yet also comforting in a way.

Leander and I were suddenly in a place that didn't seem to have any real surroundings, only a deep darkness filled with mists and purple shimmers, the stones of the transparent floor coloured in deep violet. It was disorientating, but I didn't bother to contemplate it as the others came through behind me.

"What in the...?" Tristan trailed off as he saw the strange twisting world of shadows, mists and purple light that we had come to find ourselves in.

"This is the Ethereal World," Syrena explained, moving to my side with her red and black dress trailing behind her. "It is where we come to dream and sits right on the edge of the Netherworlds and the Nightmare Holds."

"I have never seen anything like this," Tallinn said, her awe overwhelming.

"We have crossed dimensions and realities when we entered the Doorway," Syrena went on. "Time has a different meaning here. A week in this realm can be a few minutes in the living world."

"Then Leander's soul has been here for years?" I asked, the prospect leaving me with a panicked heart.

Syrena nodded. "Most likely. Come. We do not have time to linger. Just remember to be succinct when speaking to Lord Azmerath. He already knows your reasons, so he doesn't need explanation. This whole thing should be fairly brief."

I nodded and allowed her to lead, keeping Leander's body held tight in my arms as the others followed close at my back.

The path from the Doorway was disorientating, the misty shadows seeming to give way as the world built itself around us. We were walking through halls of transparent purplish stone lit with electric-blue flame torches which ignited as soon as we approached. It felt like we had walked forever when we at last entered through a set of doors into a vast throne room. The floors were tinted with that violet energy, but looked like black marble, an altar of the same design resting before the foot of a throne where shadows were gathering.

At first, I felt myself tense, the forming of shadows reminding me of the Darkest Shadow and of Morod, but they were different. Golden light gathered with the shadows and formed a tall figure clad in ebony robes and glowing golden armour. He looked just like his statue, sitting there upon his throne with his Ankh topped staff in his hand. The difference was that we could see a glimpse of his face. It was simply a skull wreathed in shadows around the eye sockets, but deep in their voids lingered the shimmer of violet light the same shade as all the torches that illuminated the room.

None of us could deny our awe and fear at beholding the God of Death in real living colour, each of us burdened with our own feelings about what our encounters with him would be. For myself, I was hesitant, not really knowing how to begin a conversation with him. After all, how does one commune with Death himself?

"Speak," Azmerath commanded in a deep and powerful voice, his skeleton jaws strangely remaining shut as if he wore a mask.

Syrena looked to me and nodded.

I steeled myself and stepped forward, holding Leander a little firmer. My eyes locked with the pinpoint dots of violet light glowing in the God's eye sockets, my heart racing now that I was here.

Be strong. Do it for her.

"My Lord Azmerath," I started, trying to be as direct as I could. "I have come before you with my sister and companions to plead for the life of Princess Leander Aldrich the Second."

"Have you brought the tributes?" he questioned calmly, his voice unnerving to hear.

I nodded. "Yes. We have."

"Then place them at my feet," he directed.

Ellora moved forward first, taking the gryphon feathers from her belt. She knelt before the God and bowed her head, perhaps the calmest of my three companions.

"My Lord, I offer you the feathers of a gryphon to represent Grace," she said as she set them on the step, then moved back.

Tallinn came forward and replicated Ellora's gesture, holding out the wyvern eggshells. "My Lord, I offer you the eggshells of a wyvern to represent Protection," she set it down and moved back.

Last of all, Tristan set the phial before the God, and bowed his head. "My Lord, I offer you the tears of a phoenix to represent Compassion," he then retreated behind me, and I nodded my thanks to him before facing Azmerath again.

"The offerings are accepted," Azmerath said evenly as he stood from his throne, looking to me. "You have your witnesses, Carden Valerian. Now you must pledge your vow."

"My vow?" I frowned.

He nodded his hooded skull. "The vow that brought you here. The one you made as your lover died in your arms."

I looked down at Leander, letting out a soft breath as I felt like I would cry. All this time I had never once let go of that last vow, even as my others faded into nothingness around me.

"I swore that I would find a way to bring her back from the dead," I said certainly, looking up at him. "No matter the cost."

Azmerath nodded. "Then lay her upon the altar."

I did as he instructed, settling Leander on the altar, her head resting on a silvery pillow that sat at one end, her hands by her sides. I turned my eyes to him as he stood before me. The God took up a golden goblet as if from out of thin air, conjuring it into his hand of bones the way he had conjured himself.

"This is the last chance you have, Carden Valerian," he told me. "If you so choose, you may leave this realm, but by doing so you forfeit her life. If not, I will conjure Ankorect's Flame and create the Elixir of Resurrection to restore her. But it comes at a cost."

"What cost?" I asked softly, my hands upon the altar beside Leander's body.

"Your life," he responded simply.

"What?!" I heard Tallinn exclaim, looking over my shoulder as Ellora grabbed her arm. "Carden, no! You can't!"

Azmerath went on as I faced him again, his deep voice so calming and yet so frightening all at the same time: "In order for the Elixir to restore her, the life force of another must be absorbed into her body. That of he who is made of the same flame as she. That energy shall replace what was taken from her, but it means your life will end."

I felt myself tense, a breath sharply entering my lungs as I considered his words.

The choice had been offered to me, the decision mine alone. As I stood before the ancient being cloaked in the darkness of everlasting death, I felt the difficulty of my decision yet to be made.

I turned my eyes down to her, seeing her beautiful, pale features; her chest as unmoving as I had known it to be in all these months now past. Remarkable that she could be so untouched by time's passage in her death when all others would decay and fade.

Of course you would stay beautiful, my sweet, wonderful girl. You were always the purest of us.

I considered the choice before me, fearing what it would mean. She would live, but I would have to give up my life for her to do so; a thought that left my heart aching.

She will be without me as I have been without her. The Daemon was right. No matter what, we will still be apart. But at least she'll have a chance to live a normal life. How can I deny her that?

A sigh slid free as I came to my decision. For Leander I would give anything at all - my life, my body, my soul - just so she would live once again. I could never deny my soul mate, especially now that there was a chance to save her.

"I accept," I said softly, keeping my eyes on her face as I felt tears fill them again.

"Carden... you can't..." Tallinn pleaded with me.

I looked to her solemnly. "This is how it has to be, Tallinn."

"Are you certain, Carden?" Ellora asked of me, fighting her own sorrow at my choice.

I nodded, turning back to Leander as tears filled my eyes. "Leander has a destiny and a long life ahead of her, but no one said that I would be with her for that life. The least I can do after all the times I failed her is give her this chance."

"You're... you're a brave man, lad," Tristan murmured, shaking his head. "A better man than I."

I turned to Azmerath. The God seemed to be waiting for me to confirm.

"I give my life freely," I pledged, my voice a hoarse whisper. "Just bring her back."

"Very well," he raised the goblet and cast his staff up, ankh to the sky.

He simply nodded to Syrena, and she came forward to assist him, not saying a word as she took the eggshell and crushed it into dust before mashing the feathers into the goblet along with it. She then uncorked the phial and poured the phoenix tears into the concoction, looking up at him.

"Do you gift your immortal blood to the elixir, vampire?" he asked her.

"I do, my Lord," she agreed with a nod.

He offered the goblet forward and I watched as Syrena bared her fangs then bit into her wrist. She held there for a moment before unhooking her mouth and letting her blood flow from the twin puncture wounds into the goblet. Once she had given enough, she licked the wounds and stepped aside as Azmerath lowered his face to the goblet. The skull opened its jaws, and he breathed out a misty violet the same colour as his glowing stare. The contents of the goblet transmuted then into a luminous violet liquid.

Azmerath moved towards the altar then, pausing opposite me with Leander between us. He offered the goblet to me, waiting until I took it in my hands. I honestly didn't know what I should do, looking to Death for the answers.

"Drink," he told me, "Then give the rest to her; an equal portion to bind you both to the transference, as you are bound in the flame of your twin soul."

I nodded and took in a slow breath as I felt my tears begin to slip free. I swallowed back half of the elixir swiftly in one gulp, my body tensing at the unusually sweet taste of the glowing liquid. Then, I lifted Leander's shoulders in the crook of one arm and tilted the goblet to her lips, pushing them open and filling her mouth. Then I influenced her to swallow. Finally, it was done, and I lay her back carefully, stroking her dark hair out of her eyes as Syrena handed the goblet back to Azmerath.

"What now?" I asked, glancing at him.

"Kiss her," Azmerath answered.

"Kiss her?" I frowned, staring at him.

He nodded his hooded skull. "The exchange will be made through a kiss of true love."

I half laughed as I looked back to Leander. "A kiss of true love to bring a princess back to life. Just like in a fairy tale. She would like that."

I stroked Leander's hair, pausing only to take in her beautiful features one more time. I realised that this would be the last time I would ever see her, feeling my tears flow more freely as I imagined her living without me.

Slowly, I leaned my face close to hers as I placed my arms around her, one to her cheek as our foreheads touched for the last time.

"Forgive me, Leander. It's the only way," I whispered and closed my eyes. "I love you, my darling girl. Now and forever."

With that, I placed my lips upon hers and willed all the love I had into it. I felt my tears fall from my cheeks, knowing that they would land on her skin as my lips caressed hers in this final embrace. I felt something then, the glimpse of a glowing energy beneath my sights as I kissed her.

Goodbye, my love....

I let go as I felt my breath steal away, staggering from her. I slumped to my knee, Syrena immediately grabbing my arm. I could feel my body weakening, the life leaving it as I held onto my sister and the side of the altar, my chest heaving as I struggled to draw breath. My green gaze lifted to Leander's silent form. There was a bluish white energy floating above her lips briefly before disappearing into her mouth. A tense moment passed as I tried to hold on, desperate to know that my sacrifice was worth it.

Her lips parted and her chest raised as she drew in a breath with a soft gasp, her fingers beginning to flex at her sides. She began to breathe again, and her heart started to beat after nearly seven months of silence. The glow of that blue light she had absorbed shone up through the wound in her chest, changing into a bright white light as the tears of the phoenix closed the hideous injury and all the others on her body that she had taken.

At last, the light faded, and she was breathing once more, her life restored. Tears were slipping from her still closed eyes to wet her cheeks with each intake of air that painfully entered her healing body. Maybe she knew.

Thank the gods... She's alive...

I groaned and slumped to the floor, resting my head on my arms as I heard the others rush to my side. I coughed and choked, grasping at my throat as pain flooded my senses.

"It is done," Azmerath said, drawing my struggling gaze. "She is restored..."

At least I don't die in vain, I thought sadly, staring at Leander as the pain grew worse and my throat burned with an unnatural, torturous thirst...

Chapter Twenty-Two
Breath of Life

~ Leander ~

I t was raining, the drops falling against the windows of the great hall in a relentless downpour that only heightened the chill in the air. The sound of water pattering on the castle windows filled the room with the only noise other than the crackling of the logs in the large hearth.

I sat in one of the armchairs, laying back with my knees up, hugging them through my dress as I watched the rain. I had been sitting like that all day, just as I had become accustomed to doing every day now that I couldn't read anymore. All the books in the library had become garbled, every single word I read looking like strange runes and gibberish. My mind was slipping, and I found myself getting so tired within an hour of waking up each morning. Some days I didn't even bother getting out of bed, lying there just lost in my thoughtless stares.

A cough ripped from my chest relentlessly as my body retched and heaved violently. My eyes fell shut, tears bleeding from beneath my eyelashes as I covered my mouth with both hands in some attempt to save myself from spraying spit everywhere. After a few minutes, the cough began to subside and I lay my head into the back of the chair, my skull throbbing with the pain of the hard fit.

My gaze drifted back to the large windows opposite me, and I once again resigned myself to watching the rain. My chest was hurting so much worse than it had in all the time since I had first arrived in that twilight world.

My chest is getting worse... I feel like I'm so sick that I'm going to die... Again...

The glimmering golden shape of an angelic came into my view, the enormous being passing by the window without even acknowledging me as it patrolled the castle grounds. It didn't seem at all bothered by the rain that was drenching its body and wings, just continuing to go about its business as it would on a sunny day.

Sunny days... There haven't been any of those in a long time...

As footsteps approached me, I started to cough again, falling into another fit as I buried my face into my sleeve, the blanket around my shoulders slipping with my hard, jerking movements. I had to close my eyes, the intensity of my sickness making me feel as if they would break free of my skull if I didn't. Once more, the coughs faded, and I looked up as the footsteps paused right beside my chair.

Mithras had concern all over his aged face, a tray in hand with some steaming hot soup in a bowl next to a cup of water.

"Your cough seems to have worsened, child," he said, setting the tray down on the table between the chair I sat in and the stool he had set there an hour ago. "You have even broken into a feverish sweat."

I nodded, my breaths wheezing as I tried to speak without coughing, though it wasn't easy. "I think... I have a fever."

He touched the back of his hand to my forehead, frowning and nodding grimly. "Yes, you do. You have been growing more poorly with each passing day."

I lay my head back, sighing wheezily. "The years haven't been kind to me in this place."

"I scarce think spending such a long time trapped in a castle could be good for anyone," he commented, stirring the soup before taking up a red bottle he had on the table. "Here, take this."

"What is it?" I asked softly, trying to read the label, though it just looked like scribbles.

"A medicine that should settle your cough," the old knight told me, uncorking the bottle and offering it to me. "Here."

I took it in my shaking hand, but I couldn't hold it. He grasped my hand swiftly and helped me lift the bottle to my lips. He'd had to start helping me more and more over the past several years, my body seeming to fail at the slightest breeze and in the most inappropriate moments.

"Yuck!" I wanted to spit, but stopped myself, scrunching up my face as he took the bottle away. "That tastes awful!"

"I know, but it will help," he offered me some water and let me drink before he set the cup down.

"I'm sorry I've become so weak, Mithras," I apologised to him, feeling ashamed. "You shouldn't have to be doing so much to look after me."

"A knight always looks after a princess, my girl," he smiled as he dipped the spoon into the soup. "It is my duty and my pleasure."

"But not to this extent," I groaned as the pain in my chest flared. "You shouldn't have to feed me and bathe me like you have been. It's not right... and it's humiliating."

"I know," he said, offering me the spoon. "But it is what it is. You cannot help the failing of your body."

I opened my mouth and ate the soup, swallowing as he took the spoon back to the bowl. It tasted like chicken soup.

"Is this normal?" I asked softly, turning my tired eyes to the old knight's face. "Do souls get sick like this in the Netherworlds all the time?"

"No..." he shook his head, considering his words, though he didn't decide to keep the truth from me. "No, this is what happens when a soul has not passed on for several centuries in the living realm."

"How long have I been here?" I wondered, taking the next spoonful and swallowing back before turning my eyes to the rain on the windows again.

"In this world it has been ten years," he said with a nod, stirring the soup again before making me eat. "But in the living world it has been a matter of months. You haven't been here long enough for you to be suffering this illness naturally."

I swallowed back the soup and locked my eyes on his, feeling as if I could fall asleep. "Then why am I sick?"

Mithras sighed and set the spoon down, resting his elbows on his knees and pressing his palms together in thought. He was weighing the options he had in his mind - this much I could tell after spending most of my life and all of my death with him - trying to decide whether to tell me the truth or not. Fortunately, Mithras was not so inclined to lie to me and I knew I would get the truth from him.

"It's the portal to the Void," he explained grimly, turning his eyes to mine, gauging my reaction. "All I can assume is that the Daemon Gods have been feeding on you ever since it opened, which is why you have lost the ability to read and why you are now infirmed."

It made as much sense as any other theory. My wheezing breath drew another coughing fit that doubled me over with pain. Tears flooded from my eyes as I braced my hands to the chair, trying to hold myself steady.

Mithras reached forward and grasped my arms gently, his expression one of pained sympathy. He wanted to make it all better, but he knew as well as I did that he just couldn't. All he could do was rub my back and try to calm me enough that I could breathe freely again.

The coughing eased and I lay back in the chair with my eyes shut, sucking in deep, wheezing breaths.

"How long do you think I have left?" I asked hoarsely, looking up at him weakly as he brushed my hair out of my eyes.

He shook his head solemnly. "It's difficult to say. Each soul falls to becoming a demented spirit differently. The Void seems to be really working at tormenting you, almost as if one of the Daemon Gods is trying to accelerate the process."

"Like the Darkest Shadow?" I suggested.

He frowned, surprised by my words. "Possibly. Do you have a feeling about it, or have you had visions telling you such?"

I shook my head, looking into the fireplace, my chest heaving beneath the tight bodice of my dress. I had been tightening it since I felt like I was getting thinner, and my clothes hadn't been sitting as firmly as they should have been.

"I just think that's the one who would be after me," I confessed, resting my eyes. "It wanted me to join it and Morod when I was alive, so I think it would still want me now that I'm dead. It just makes sense."

"I will not let it take you," he set his hands to my knees, drawing my gaze back to him. "Nor will the angelic sentinels."

I felt a tear slip from my eyes at his words, knowing that he meant it, but also fearing that he wouldn't succeed. I reached my right hand up and grasped his left one, feeling the warmth of his rough, older skin against my softer, youthful palm.

"You can't protect me from it forever, Mithras," I murmured sadly, feeling like I just had to accept it. "Eventually, I'm going to succumb, no matter how hard we both fight. My soul is being torn apart piece by piece and I'm dying all over again," I started to sob, my chest thrusting with my heavy breaths and the pain in my ruined heart. "How much longer... can I keep this up?"

"Do not give up, Leander," he urged me, reaching with his other hand to touch my cheek and brush my tears away with his thumb. "There is still hope and you are so near salvation."

"What are you talking about?" I mumbled, closing my eyes and laying my head against his hand, feeling comforted by his touch.

"Carden and the others have found the answer," he told me.

"Who?" I frowned, looking up at him.

Mithras seemed shocked at my question. "Carden... Carden Highever..."

I shook my head and shrugged. "I don't know who you're talking about..."

"Carden Highever," he insisted. "The young man who came as a Guardian to this castle while you lived. The man you have fallen in love with..."

I shook my head, the name sounding unfamiliar.

His eyes widened. "You were but seventeen winters when you met him, girl. You are scarcely any older now."

I met his gaze incredulously. "Mithras, I must be an old woman by now, not a teenage girl. How else could I feel so feeble?"

"Illness," he reminded me. "You have the body of a teenager, but the sickness of the Void has been poisoning you, making you feel old. We only just had this discussion two minutes ago."

I frowned as I took in his words and tried to sort them into an order in my mind that made sense. There was a haze that shouldn't have been there, and I bit my bottom lip as I tried to discern what it was that was missing. Suddenly, clarity came to me, and I looked up at him, horrified.

"Oh, Mithras... I keep forgetting," I held my hand to my head, running my fingers through my dark hair as I tried to ease the pain that lingered there. "My mind... is a haze... confusing and... and dark."

"I know," he stroked my head with both hands, trying to help ease my pain. "It is the drain the Void is putting on you as it feeds. You have forgotten so much in such a short time that you shouldn't have."

"I only remember you because you're always here with me," I confessed sadly, tears falling again. "Names... faces... they're all just a blur to me now. I know what I feel, but I can't remember what goes with each feeling, which person makes those emotions come to me."

"Do you feel a love in your heart for a man who you would spend your life with?" he asked me gently, resting his hands on my shoulders. "A man who you want to be with forever?"

I frowned and looked inside myself, staring at my hands where they rested in my lap. The feelings he spoke of were there, but I couldn't comprehend the person he had mentioned. When I looked towards my memories for where that person existed, I couldn't see anything more than a shadowy figure.

"There *is* a man in my memories," I told him in a tiny murmur, "but I can't see him. It's as if my memory of him has been... water brushed away and all that I have left is... is a smudged image in my mind."

"How does he make you feel?" he prodded softly, his eyes studying my face as he tried to analyse me.

I thought about it, feeling a rising warmth in my heart. A smile tugged at my lips weakly and I let out a soft sigh of longing.

"Like I belong with him," I replied. "Like no matter what I should be with him. But..." I frowned again, "but I feel a sadness, as if I never will be..."

Mithras nodded grimly, once again wiping away my tears. "*That* is Carden. Strangely, though he seems but a blur in your memory now, he remains more firmly there with you than anyone else. You have forgotten all others, including your family."

I sighed sadly, slumping my shoulders back and hugging my arms around my midriff. "I haven't seen any memories of them in the halls for years now. I know I had a family, but there's just emptiness where their memories should be."

"It will be all right, girl," he assured me.

"I think I need to rest," I said, laying my head back in the seat. "I'm so tired."

"I'll be here," he promised, gently stroking my head as I fell asleep.

I began to dream, though only for a few minutes, the walls of my mind opening up once again as strange voices came to me. There was someone pleading, a man by the sounds of it, his hands touching my arm, then a strange taste passed my lips, and I was suddenly blinded by a bright blue glow. I closed my eyes in the dream, startled then by the staring face of a pale man with black hair and inhuman red eyes. But that didn't last long, and my mind went blank, leaving me resting for a moment in a beautiful field.

I felt the warm sun on my skin, opening my eyes as I found myself lying amongst spring flowers of gold, blue and violet. There were butterflies flapping their wings over the sound of waterfalls. Trees waved as a gentle breeze pushed through them and the scent of honey touched the air, wafting from the beehives in the branches.

Slowly, I sat up, looking around the verdant meadow. I was wearing a simple long white dress, the sleeves closed over my wrists. I smiled softly as I took in the scents of it all, the sound of something moving drawing my gaze. There was a dragon by the waters of the great pool where the waterfall fed its flow, her scales of violet, mauve, deeper purple, silver and blue, her wings like the most vibrant magenta pink.

A shadow fell over me and I looked up from watching the dragon to see a tall, broad shouldered and athletically built man standing over me. He wore a black shirt and pants, his hand outstretched towards me as he smiled.

I know him... I thought, taking his hand and letting him lift me from the ground. He pulled me into his embrace and, without a single word, kissed me with so much passionate love...

"Carden?" I murmured.

The dream had ended as I opened my eyes to the cold surrounds of the castle and the crackling of the fire. Mithras was still there, tending to the hearth, his hands feeding kindling into the hungry flames carefully as he stoked the embers. To my disappointment there was no sign of the man who had kissed me, or the dragon I had seen in the distance. They had faded away as quickly as my dream had.

Mithras turned over his shoulder and looked to me with a surprised expression. "Leander? Are you alright?"

"Where's Carden?" I murmured, confused. "And Amethyst? Where are they?"

"You remember," he got up and moved towards me, frowning as he touched my forehead again. "Your fever is broken. How do you feel?"

I tensed my body, sitting up straighter in the chair, testing myself out. "Better... Much better. I... I don't feel... sick or..." I gasped as I clutched my chest. "The pain... It's gone!"

"You've been healed," Mithras was astounded. "I cannot explain it. Unless..."

"They did it?" I looked at him hopefully and with excitement. "My friends... Ellora, Fawkner, Holger, Dolin, Tallinn, Joran..."

"Your memories return!" he smiled warmly. "Oh, this is wonderful news!"

At that moment there came a loud knocking on the doors to the keep. Both Mithras and I frowned at each other.

"The main doors?" I asked him.

He nodded. "Come, carefully."

I nodded my understanding and got up, following him from the Great Hall to the main staircase, my dress flowing behind me as I walked. I held the blanket around me as the old knight took a hold of one of the handles on the door and pulled it open to reveal the courtyard of the castle. It was now covered in snow as flakes drifted from the sky in place of the rain that had been drizzling before, everything looking so peaceful. But that wasn't what I focused on. My eyes set on the figure of Azmerath standing there before us, his black angel wings in a resting hold, his staff in his skeletal hand, snowflakes on his hood. I gasped involuntarily.

"My Lord Azmerath," Mithras bowed. "This is an honour."

"I have come for her," the God said in his deep voice, pointing one bony finger at me, resembling every haunting image of Death I had ever seen.

"Come for me?" I asked nervously, hugging my arms around myself tightly. "Why?"

"Your lover has completed the ritual to restore you," he told me. "Even now he is in the throes of bringing you back to life."

"I'm... I'm going to live again?" I was stunned.

"Yes," the God of Death nodded briefly, then beckoned with that same finger. "Come."

"It's all right," Mithras smiled at me, taking my hand in his.

Azmerath turned with the swish of his wings, his black robes flowing around him. He made his way down the steps to the snowy ground as Mithras and I followed, the air feeling somewhat warmer despite the ice and snow. I felt as if I could breathe again, my chest clearer than it had been in all the years I had spent in that castle. I could actually feel my life returning to me, my heart healing slowly from the wound that had killed me.

He's done it... He's saved me. Oh gods, Carden... Oh, I love you so much! I can't wait to see you!

I turned my eyes then to the gates, seeing that the way was clear, and the portcullis was open. The Void portal was gone, leaving only the path across the bridge to Arvon, the angelics watching over the way from where they stood guard.

"It is time, Leander," Azmerath informed me, looking down at me from beneath his cowl and holding his free hand towards me.

"Mithras?" I looked to the old knight uncertainly.

"Carden waits for you, Leander," he told me, brushing my hair from my eyes. "You cannot stay here now. It is time to go back."

I looked down at my hands, then out at the gates where the bridge lay as Azmerath waited for me. I was so uncertain and afraid, not really knowing what I would be going back to. It was something that I hadn't thought I would ever get to do. But now that it was happening, I didn't know how to feel, my mind awash with thoughts and feelings I had long ago thought I'd lost.

To enter the Realm of Death is no easy thing when it is not your time, but harder still when love is blooming in your life. I realised then as I stood in those snows that this was truer than any other truth I had ever known in my life. Besides that of my everlasting heart.

Because of him my life was returning, my breath my own again and my wounds closed. And though my heart ached at leaving behind all those I had loved and lost to Azmerath's watchful care, I couldn't deny my desire to return to my love's arms.

This is right. I know it is. Carden is my soul mate, my true love... I belong with him in the Living World. That is what I want most.

I looked to my old friend, smiling softly as he gave me the same in return.

"Go to him, my girl," he said, his rough voice strangely gentle, his dark eyes softening. "You belong not in this kingdom, but in the one you should rule with him."

"I'm scared," I confessed, looking up at him and feeling a tremble fill me.

"Returning to Life's Light is always frightening," he replied gently. "Yet, you return to his embrace. Do not be afraid, Leander."

I hugged him abruptly, closing my eyes and burying my face into his shoulder. I was so afraid that I was never going to see him again, my heart thudding in my chest with a new strength that hadn't been there for so long. It ached now, but not from my wound.

"I'm going to miss you, Mithras," I murmured into his neck.

"And I will miss you, Leander," he smiled as he pulled me from his arms. "Now, you cannot linger. Go on. Go."

I nodded, wiping away my tears. "Goodbye, Mithras..."

"Goodbye," he said softly, remaining on the stairs, "Princess Leander."

Reluctantly, I took my eyes from him and followed Azmerath, my hand in his, to the gates of the castle.

I felt the world I had known for so long disappearing around me as everything faded into darkness, my body becoming heavier as I passed back into the living world. A gasp of air filled my lungs and I really felt again, the cold air around me shocking me out of my deathly state. My mind didn't return yet, instead leaving me lost in a dreamless sleep as I felt someone holding me, my heartbeat matching theirs as they carried me through dark and cold echoing halls. After that I felt nothing for a while, my body resting soundly as I tried to come back to the Waking World.

At last, I could feel fully again, my fingers curling around the softness of warm sheets and blankets as my head and shoulders lay amidst a deep set of plump pillows. I could smell candles burning and the scent of smoking herbs as the wind rattled against a windowpane and light footed movements made scuffing sounds against the stone floor.

A groan escaped my lips as my aching back started to work again and my limbs stretched as I came to. I felt as if I had been asleep for months, my eyelids so heavy that they hurt to even try to open. But I managed to make them, blinking as my vision cleared and I took in the dark stone walls, green glass windows and the forest green curtains that surrounded the bed I lay in. None of it looked familiar. The sky outside was dark with clouds parting to show me three crescent moons glowing white against the starry blue and black that hung over the world.

I blinked away sleep and turned my head to my right, seeing two familiar figures there. Ellora was pacing distractedly, moving to stand against the wall next to the closed-over door as Ranzel sat in the chair beside the bed, his pipe in hand. The Wizard looked thoughtful, one arm held around his midriff, the other clutching his pipe lightly as he puffed rings of grey smoke casually from the corner of his mouth.

I moved my parched lips, my throat feeling so dry as I tried to make my voice work. Like my eyes, my vocal cords were sore from being unused for so long, an itch in my throat making me cough softly before I could manage to utter a single syllable.

"Ellora? Ranzel?" I croaked hoarsely, gaining their attention.

"Princess?!" Ellora rushed to my side, relief clear in her turquoise eyes as a smile brightened her face. "By Gaya, you are awake at last!"

"How are you feeling, my dear?" Ranzel asked softly, setting his hand on my arm as he lowered his pipe from his lips.

"My body hurts," I admitted, trying to wriggle the pain away. "Everything's... ugh... stiff... and my throat's dry. It... it hurts to talk..."

"I'll get you some water," Ellora said, moving to the sideboard where a clay pitcher stood with some cups. She swiftly poured clear, fresh water into one of the cups.

"It is hardly surprising that you feel stiff and sore," Ranzel stated, lifting his hand back to his midriff and creasing his brown and green robes with his palm. "You've not moved or spoken for a very long time, my dear girl."

"Here," Ellora drew my gaze as she leaned over the bed with the cup of water. "Take it slowly."

"Thank you," I murmured, taking the cup in my hands carefully.

I felt so feeble as I lifted it to my lips, my arms aching from lack of use. It was unbearable, my body almost useless. The cool water washed down my throat, soothing the aching burn that had lingered there with ashen severity, my body relaxing as I finished the whole cup. It was so good to drink again, though I didn't remember never being able to. I handed the cup back to Ellora and she moved to get me some more.

"How long have I been asleep?" I asked, looking to Ranzel.

"Almost eight months," he said solemnly, putting out his pipe.

I raised an eyebrow at him. "Eight months?"

He frowned as I took more water from Ellora, his brow knitting as he once again analysed me. "Princess... what do you remember before awakening here?"

I swallowed down some of the water, lowering the cup from my lips as I licked them, thinking about his words. I went to answer straight away but paused as I frowned. The question shouldn't have stumped me as it did. It would have been such a simple and easily answered request normally. I started to chew my bottom lip as I thought, trying to figure out which memories I had were of this world and which were from the one I had just left. Part of me, however, thought I had dreamed the second one.

What do I remember? Huh... That's so strange...

I shook my head at last, answering honestly: "I'm... I'm not sure. My mind is full of... of images. Dreams, maybe."

"Dreams?" he questioned softly.

I nodded. "Uh-huh... I... I can't figure out what I dreamed..."

"Think carefully," he urged me, lowering his head so that I locked my gaze with his. "What do you remember *before* you closed your eyes?"

I took some more water as I thought about that, drinking down the last of the cupful as I let my mind wander. Then I felt a pinch in my chest, reaching my hand to it as Ellora took the cup from me. My fingers instinctively started searching the smooth skin between my breasts beneath my dress. My index and middle fingers caressed down my sternum and I tensed at the slightly raised flesh that I felt where there hadn't been any before. My heart started to race and hurt as I traced my fingers along the length of the thin, curving line that followed the lower internal edge of my left breast, pausing just before my ribs. I felt tight in the chest as a memory of pain hit me, my eyes flicking down to see the perfectly neat and healed remains of a dagger wound that was now an ugly scar.

Tears swelled in my eyes, and I felt my breathing hitch as I yanked my hand away and pressed my palm into the bed. I could see the Shadow Lord standing over me in my mind, his hand bringing the horrible dagger down as I squirmed against chains holding me to a cold altar.

"I... I was tied to an altar," I murmured, trembling as tears began to fall down my cheeks. "The Shadow Lord was standing over me... with... with a dagger. He... he..." I swallowed hard, starting to sob, "he killed me... Morod killed me... Oh, Gods..."

"I am afraid so, Princess," Ranzel nodded gravely, touching my arm in an attempt to reassure me.

I looked up at him through my tears as my chest started heaving more rapidly, my panic taking hold. "I've... I've been *dead* for *eight* months?"

"Yes, but we brought you back," Ellora tried to be comforting as she came to sit on the edge of the bed, her hand touching my shoulder.

I closed my eyes, trying to prop myself up, my left hand grabbing her right arm wildly until I could get a good grip on her wrist. My chest was moving so fast now that it felt like I would break my sternum, the feeling of where the dagger had pierced suddenly agonisingly obvious to my nerves.

"Princess?" Ranzel asked with concern, standing up as I opened my eyes. "What's wrong? Are you alright?"

"I... I..." I was choking, my throat burning now from too much air instead of too little, panic attacking me like a rabid beast. "I can't... I can't breathe!"

"Shh, shh," Ellora tried to calm me, grabbing my arms with both hands as I gasped and wheezed. "It's all right. Calm yourself, Princess..."

"I... I can't... breathe," I gasped in panic, grasping my fingers onto Ranzel's wide, thick cotton sleeve as he reached out to hold me. "I... I need a-air... Please... I need air..."

"I can open a window," Ellora offered.

I shook my head. "No... N-no... Out-outside..."

"To the balcony," Ranzel suggested, Ellora nodding her confirmation before he started to pull away the sheets that covered me. "Come along, girl. Just hold onto me and we'll get you outside."

I nodded frantically, struggling to draw in an easy breath. I felt like I was being strangled as I shifted my bare legs from the bed and set my feet to the floor. I tried to stand, but my legs gave out, weak and thin from being unused for so long. That only made me feel worse as the Wizard held me tightly to his side, one arm around my back as the other hand took my right wrist carefully.

Ellora rushed from the other side of the bed, grabbing the Wizard's heavy cloak and wrapping it over my shoulders as I managed to drop the hem of my white gown to cover my ankles. She then moved to open the door, allowing Ranzel to awkwardly and carefully guide me out into the hallway of the unfamiliar and frighteningly dark castle. I couldn't help but stare at it all in fear, making this terrible pain worse

"Sarissi?" a deep voice gained my blue gaze, Joran bowing his head as he stood guard at the door to the room.

I wanted to greet him, but I couldn't form the words, grasping at my chest with one hand as Ranzel led me from the room. I felt the familiar cool silver of my Dragon Pendant hanging against my collarbones and instantly wrapped my fingers around it. It was a small comfort, but at least it was something and I was glad that it was no longer absent from my neck.

Joran and Ellora followed along behind Ranzel and me as he took me through the hallways and down a set of large stairs to a grand sitting area where great hearths were lit against the chill. My eyes briefly took in the figures sitting around on the wine-red sofas as we hurried towards the huge archway set with heavy wooden doors. Fawkner, Tristan, Holger and Dolin looked up at me from where they sat, surprise plastering their faces as Tallinn got to her feet quickly. I was stunned to see Danika with them, though I didn't vocalise it or even stop to acknowledge any of them. I couldn't if I'd wanted to.

"She's awake," I heard Tallinn say, the sound of movement telling me that the others were up and following us.

"Open the doors," Ranzel commanded of the two black armoured and masked guardsmen that stood by the doors, the men swiftly doing as ordered.

As the Wizard took me out onto an enormous balcony, I felt the cooling effects of the wind. Immediately, I began to feel better, turning my eyes to the view as I breathed in deep, my chest beginning to slow its rapid heaving. I was feeling calmer slowly.

We came to stand not far from the doors, snow powdering the stone floor of the balcony as the chilled wind tugged at our clothes and hair. I let my gaze rove across the view before me as I took in the mountains, forests and vast horizon, the glow of the moons feeling so good on my skin. I could sense my companions all standing behind me now, but I still didn't have the awareness to start talking to them yet.

Slowly, I freed myself from Ranzel's hold and made my feet work, forcing my legs to keep me standing. I wavered a little as I slid away from his cloak and staggered forward, my hands dropping to my sides to lightly grip the white fabric of my gown as my shoulders slightly bared themselves to the air.

"Princess..." Ellora reached for me but paused when Ranzel grasped her shoulder.

"No. Let her be," he urged her.

I moved out onto the balcony's open space, feeling the chill of the snowflakes on my feet. I let my eyes drop to look at my toes. A smile pulled at my lips as I was able to feel again, my heart leaping in my chest at how exciting something so simple as this could be.

Slowly, I lifted my head to look out at the view of the strange foreign land before me. I had no idea at all about where I was, but I only cared that I was alive. Everything was so vivid and real; my life having seemed so faint and dark for what had felt like years.

A small giggle escaped my lips as I closed my eyes and just basked in the cold air, letting it revitalise me.

At that moment, I felt a familiar warmth spreading from my collar. I opened my eyes to see the Pendant's stone glowing as tendrils of coiling purple energy reached out in a flowering shape before me. It shone brightly and flashed into the air as a roar echoed across the mountains. The great beating of magenta wings made me smile wider as Amethyst rose up from beneath the balcony, her purple, blue and silver scales shimmering in the moonlight. She stretched her wings wide, then lowered herself to stand before me.

"Amethyst," I smiled, taking a few steps forward as the glowing light of my pendant faded.

My dragon looked down at me with joyful molten orange eyes. She growled her happiness at seeing me, murmuring my name in her tongue. I could understand her as clearly as I ever had, moving to stand before her as she lowered her head to me.

I stroked her cheek and lay my face against her smoothly scaled nose, hugging into her in what small way I could. I had missed her so much, just as I knew she had missed me.

She spoke softly, lifting her head to look into my eyes.

"It's good to see you too, Amethyst," I replied, still stroking her face gently.

She lifted her head from me and arched her back as she pulled in a deep breath and let loose a triumphant roar towards the skies as she announced to the world that she was complete. I felt exactly the same as I stood there before the Dragon, watching her stand tall and proud as her call rocked the walls of the castle and echoed across the land below.

Chapter Twenty Three
Bonds Once Strong

I held onto Ranzel as he led me back to my room, my hands grasping at the folds of his rough robes to support myself. I felt calmer now that I had seen Amethyst and had taken in some air, but I didn't feel stronger. My body was still weak from spending so many months lying dead and I wasn't sure exactly how long it would take to recover. Just walking through the hallway from the sitting room and balcony was exhausting, and I found myself forcing my breath to pull into my lungs slowly just so I could keep from choking.

The others followed closely behind us, all of them wearing looks of both concern and wonder at the same time. It was clear to me that a lot had happened since I had died, but right at that moment I just had to focus on walking.

I hate this. I feel so feeble. I should just be able to get up and walk normally. This is horrible.

The Wizard brought me back to the room I had woken up in, my feet stinging from the icy chill that still stuck to them after standing on the snowy balcony. I was shivering as I only wore the white dress I had been put into, though I wasn't sure how long I had been wearing it.

Ellora moved swiftly around the bed to make sure the covers were pulled back before she helped Ranzel get me in. Exhausted and wincing at the pain that filled my now burning limbs, I lay down and groaned, resting my head and shoulders back into the large gathering of pillows. A huff of breath escaped my lips, and I closed my eyes for a moment as I felt my legs get heavy with fatigue.

"You look exhausted, Princess," the Elven woman noted as she started to tuck me back into the warmth of the sheets and blankets.

I nodded, still keeping my eyes shut as I drew in slow breaths. "I am. I never would have thought walking such a short distance would be so tiring."

"An unfortunate side effect of your previous state," Ranzel explained as he returned to his seat by my side. "It will take time for your body to remember how to move after so long lying still."

I just nodded again, resting back into the pillows. "All right. I guess I'll just have to surrender and let people take care of me until I'm strong enough."

"Not something you're all that comfortable with, is it, girl?" Fawkner smiled as he approached.

"Fawkner," I smiled back, reaching out to hug him as he leaned down to me.

"It is good to see you with us again, Leander," he said warmly, holding me in a tight hug before laying me back.

"It's good to see you too," I turned my eyes to everyone else who were now gathering at the foot of the bed. "It's good to see all of you."

"To see you breathing again," Dolin smiled through his beard, his hands on his belt as he studied me where I lay, "is a blessing in itself, lassie."

"Aye," Holger agreed, blinking rapidly as tears appeared on his cheeks. "We thought we had lost you, girl."

"Holger?" I raised an eyebrow at him. "Are you... crying?"

"Ah... No!" he shook his head as he tried to become hardened again, his voice still wobbling. "No... eh... I just... um... have something in my eye."

Ellora moved to his side and placed a hand on his shoulder as she gazed down at him. "Who knew? You have a heart after all, toadstool."

"Heh... I suppose so," Holger replied gently, nodding up at her.

I couldn't help the smile that forced its way onto my face as I saw the Elf and the Dwarf getting along. It was good to see, though I could tell that my friends had been through so much while I had been unaware.

My eyes drifted to Tallinn as she moved to sit on the edge of the bed, her smile sad despite her happiness at seeing me. *I wonder why she's so sad. Maybe... maybe because Aldwyn couldn't be brought back...*

"I am so glad that our quest to restore you was a success, Princess," she said with a soft, honest voice, gazing at me from behind her blonde hair.

"So am I," I replied gently, touching her wrist with my left hand before looking to the others standing over me. "So... you *all* stayed with me? Even though I was dead?"

"Aye, lass," Tristan nodded as he moved forward into my view, his arms folded in front of him and his coat swaying around him. "That we did."

"But... but you could have done anything," I pointed out, feeling bewildered and touched at the same time, my blue eyes flicking between each of their faces as I spoke. "You could have left and gone back to your families and your homes. I... I can't imagine what you've been through to get me to this moment."

"We will not say that it has been easy," Tallinn said with a tired sigh, keeping her eyes on mine. "But it was not something we could allow to go undone."

"I am sure you have many questions, my dear," Ranzel commented as he leaned back in his chair and began to relight his pipe.

"I can hardly decide where to start," I admitted with a shrug, my dress slipping to reveal my shoulders. "I suppose I should ask first, where are we? I don't recognise this land at all."

"We are in the far north," the Wizard explained calmly as he puffed on his pipe, shaking out the match he had used to light it. "We have crossed the Ortagaad Sea and now stand in the heart of the country of Valloran."

"Valloran?" I frowned with curiosity, trying to recall my geography lessons from when I was a child. "That's... that's outside of High-Realm, isn't it?"

"That is correct, your Highness," the old man confirmed with a vague nod. "And, to save you some effort of asking, we are currently staying as guests in Castle Valkirak, home of the King of Valloran: Tiernan Valerian, High-Lord of the Vampires."

"The... the vampires?!" I couldn't help my shocked exclamation any more than my wide-eyed expression.

"It is all right, Leander," Fawkner moved to the other side of the bed where he sat down and reached his hand to touch my shoulder, his expression gentle and comforting. "We are here under a banner of peaceful diplomacy. I have men from Eilath here with us sent under the command of my cousin, King Haral. King Tiernan has been very gracious in helping us and is now calling a lands meet to discuss the situation with the Lords of Valloran."

"What situation?" I frowned, feeling a new dread growing inside me.

I could tell by the hesitance of my companions that it couldn't be good, their expressions like open books to their fears and concerns. Even Joran looked unnerved as he stood guard by the door, his stoic and emotionally monotonous presence suddenly seeming more expressive than I was used to.

At last, it was Danika who spoke and broke the silence, the Witch leaning on her staff as she stood with a confidence the others suddenly lacked.

"The End of All Things, of course," she stated in her casually calm manner. "Lord Morod has begun the Apocalypse and is launching his attacks on all of Therras. Even now, Ragnarok, the Great Dragon of the End Times, lays waste to the lands as his four brothers of War, Pestilence, Famine and Death strike against the world with all of their fury. In their wake the Undead Legions, the Scourge and the Shadow Forces all spread across High-Realm under a stormy sky of darkness to destroy everything for their dread master."

"Yes... Thank you, Danika, for that rather... *blunt* explanation," Ranzel didn't sound too impressed with her as he turned his hazel gaze back to me.

"So... he won?" I murmured, feeling as if I could start to cry, though I managed not to. "Morod won?

"He *hasn't* won," Tallinn said firmly, grasping my wrist in hers and making me look into her eyes. "We *will* stop him. That is one of the reasons why we came to Valloran to bring you back."

"What do you mean?" I asked, frowning. "And... and how *did* you bring me back? I thought the only way to do that was through necromancy."

"The most common way is," Danika confirmed. "However, if we had resorted to such a method, you would not be sitting here asking these questions, but instead attempting to attack us."

"Necromancy doesn't restore a person, Princess," Tristan told me calmly, tensing his folded arms. "It just reanimates a dead body to shamble around and do as commanded by the necromancer controlling it."

"Okay, so then how did *you* do it?" I questioned them with a deepening frown.

"That is perhaps something to discuss when you are stronger," Ranzel stated, putting an end to the conversation. "As it is, the hour grows late and you, Princess, must rest."

"I feel that I have rested so much," I sighed, laying my head back into the pillows. "I don't want to just lie here and be useless."

"You must recover your strength," Fawkner advised me gently. "Do not worry, though. We will not leave you."

I nodded, my lips tugging into a small smile at his words. "Thank you. I'm so glad to have all of you as my friends. I don't... I don't even know what to say. Thank you for saving me doesn't even seem like enough."

"Leander, you need not worry about it," Fawkner smiled as he patted my hand. "We would all do it again. We're a family now, and family cares for one another."

Those words caused my heart to grow warmer inside me and I felt so loved.

I had spent so long grieving my parents and family's deaths, thinking that I was alone as an Aldrich. But I wasn't. My companions had become my friends and now, after all of this, they were my new family.

I nodded softly, taking in all of their faces. "We are. You're right, Fawkner. I couldn't ask to have met more wonderful people than all of you. I am so proud to be part of this... strange little family of ours," I half laughed, drawing the chuckles and smiles of the others.

"We will let you rest then, lass," Tristan patted my foot through the covers, then started for the door.

As they began to move, I studied each of them, suddenly frowning as I noted that there was one person missing.

"Wait... where's Carden?" I asked, looking around at the others uncertainly.

The apprehension that greeted me from my companions made my heart sink.

"He's in his room," an unfamiliar voice answered, drawing all of us to look to the door behind Joran's mammoth muscular shape.

A woman was standing there with long black hair as dark as coal that gently curled as it fell to the small of her back, her skin whiter than my already snowy complexion. She wore a fine dress of crimson and black with the bodice laced in silver cords, her style so similar to my own, though she seemed more curvy and certainly much bustier than me. She wore a circlet of gold around her head with a blood red ruby set into the front, her gown flowing as she moved into the room. But what stood out the most for me about her were the fangs I glimpsed between her full lips and her predatory, yet beautiful topaz-amber eyes.

She's a vampire. She must be.

The vampire woman smiled at me, then glanced to the others briefly: "I see our youngest guest is finally awake. It is about time."

"Princess Leander Aldrich," Ranzel nodded to the woman as he spoke, indicating her to me, "allow me to introduce Princess Syrena Valerian, daughter of King Tiernan and the most gracious of our hosts."

"It is a pleasure, Princess Leander," Syrena smiled at me warmly.

"The pleasure's all mine, Princess Syrena," I responded tiredly, though politely as I tried to hold the same decorum I had been taught to have when meeting foreign royals.

Syrena smiled at me. "There is no need to concern yourself with niceties, Princess. You are in need of rest and food. I will arrange something to be brought to you from the kitchens, if you'd like."

"Um... yes. Thank you," I said gratefully, though I felt overwhelmed.

"I shall also tell my brother that you are awake," she turned for the door, her gowns swishing around her as she did.

"Your brother?" I frowned, confused.

She turned back to me and nodded. "Carden."

"Carden's your brother?!" I exclaimed in shock, looking to the others. "That means..."

"That he's a vampire, yes," Syrena nodded.

"No... I... I mean, that he's... a prince?" I couldn't believe it.

But he told me he was orphaned in Gorvenna. That he grew up on the streets of Nargilith. He never said anything about being from a royal bloodline.

"Don't feel too slighted by my brother's deceptions," Syrena spoke calmly as she turned back to me, holding her hands together before her waist. "We both found it necessary to craft falsehoods about our pasts when living in High-Realm in order to protect ourselves."

I had nothing to say to that, simply nodding as I felt like my whole world had changed so drastically while I had been dead.

"I will arrange your food," the other princess said and left the room, a glimmer of red and gold at her neck making me stare.

That's a Dragon Pendant! She's a holder, just like me! Wow... Now I really don't know what to think...

"Are you all right, lassie?" Dolin asked lowly.

I nodded. " Yes... Um... My head is just hurting. This is all so much to take in."

"Rest," Ranzel urged me. "There will be time enough to talk later."

The others started to leave, but I grasped Fawkner's arm as he stood, holding tightly to his sleeve. He paused and looked down at me with a raised eyebrow, Tallinn halting where she stood across from him.

"Stay with me, Fawkner," I pleaded, then looked to her. "You too, Tallinn. Please?" I shook my head, feeling like a child. "I... I don't want to be alone."

"Of course," Fawkner nodded, taking the seat Ranzel had just vacated as I released my hold on his sleeve.

"I will just feel better having Guardians with me," I confessed as I lay back, my eyes getting heavy, though I resisted letting them drop.

"Then we'll be glad to stay," Tallinn bowed her head slightly, getting another chair from across the room.

I took in a slow breath as they sat with me, Joran closing the door over once all of the others had left the room. I chewed on my bottom lip for a moment, then looked up at the two Guardians with certainty and conviction.

"Tell me everything," I insisted in a soft voice, my throat beginning to feel dry again as my focus became as clear as any ruler's should be.

* * * * *

A week passed by in the castle, my body slowly beginning to heal as I rested. I took to using the magic of my pendant to speed up my recovery, only able to hold the energy for a few minutes at a time before needing to rest. But I didn't care. I was determined to walk freely again and be able to spend more than a couple of hours awake at a time. It just seemed that I was as weak then as I had been in the Netherworlds when the illness from the Void had been afflicting me, and I didn't like it.

Thankfully, Ranzel and Danika had been working on ways to help me heal more rapidly without causing me greater harm. They said that the problem was that lying dormant for so long had caused my body to lose much of its strength despite the fact that I hadn't suffered any atrophy.

Tallinn and Fawkner had confessed the full truth to me, though it had taken some serious convincing to get them to do so. I actually had to use my station as princess to order them into answering me - something I really didn't like to do - but I had stubbornly decided that I needed to know everything. It was my own fault that I ended up regretting the decision once they explained it all to me. I had tried not to think about all of it after that, but it was hard. The idea that I had been taken to the ethereal plains where Azmerath resided in order for my friends to restore me was difficult enough. Especially after hearing all about what had happened at Safferan and Silvervale. But it was what Carden had done that really plagued me. Suddenly, his illness that he had so carefully hidden made much more sense and I remembered how Aldwyn had been warning him about being around me.

So many feelings churned inside me as I thought about the fact that Tallinn and Aldwyn had known the truth about him, especially once Tallinn made her confessions that night to me. She had lied to cover Carden's identity all this time since they had first met in Nargilith, the only part of the story he had told me in Arvon that actually seemed to be true.

What sense of betrayal I felt disappeared quickly, though, and I just started to wonder when he would come to see me as I lay in that bed, trying to recover.

Princess Syrena was visiting daily to see if I needed anything, though she didn't stay long, admitting freely that my scent was enticing her hunger. That was a little unsettling, but I didn't think for a moment that she would actually prove to be dangerous to me. All the same, I was glad that Fawkner had four Lorveren soldiers stationed outside my room with Joran to keep watch over me.

I rarely rested alone, one of my friends always staying with me in case I needed anything. They were even helping me to eat, which at first proved to be rather difficult where it should have been simple. Thankfully, my strength was returning. And though my friends were willing to, I didn't feel the need to talk every time, just liking to have someone with me. From what they told me it seemed that I had always had company while I lay trapped in my death, Carden usually the one to come and sit with me.

Why hasn't he come to see me? I wondered as I lay there, studying my hands on the bedspread. *I thought he would have been the first person I would have seen when I woke up. I hope he's all right. I'm really worried about him.*

These thoughts felt like they repeated with each passing day that he didn't come to me, my heart aching at his absence. I just wanted to see him, to talk to him about everything and embrace him like I had spent so long dreaming of doing.

At last, I had strength enough to stand and take care of most things by myself nearly nine days after my resurrection. I bathed, feeling as if I had carried the dirt of half the world with me when I soaped my skin and rinsed it down. That was when I didn't want anyone to help me, though Ellora remained by the door of the bathroom just in case. But she did have to help me step out of the bath, wrapping a towel around me for modesty's sake before leading me back to the bedroom.

She had laid out my clothes for me after I had told her that I wanted to get dressed and leave the bedroom for once. I was glad that she had just done so without argument, though I frowned now as I studied the blue velvet and purple silk dress before me. It was the same one I had worn the night the Witches abducted me from Silvervale. Strangely, it was a comfort to have it returned to me. They had even brought all of my other dresses too, which surprised me.

I thanked Ellora as she left me to dress and started to dry myself before putting on my underwear. With my slip pulled on I then slid into the long-sleeved lilac under dress, then tugged on the royal blue velvet over dress. Tying the dark coloured cord at the bodice, I studied myself in the mirror, my black leggings covering my legs and my boots on my feet to shield against the cold.

I sighed with relief: *There. Now I look more like myself again.*

Running my hands through my hair, I took in the sight of me. My hair looked as if it had actually grown, hanging just past my shoulder blades to be visible behind my arms, the dark auburn locks shimmering with red and gold as the sunlight shone through the window behind me.

It feels good to actually dress like the princess that I am again. It's been so long since I stood before a mirror with any sort of pride in my appearance. I hope I look presentable enough. Maybe...

"Ellora?" I called to the door.

"Yes, Princess?" she returned, having been waiting for me.

I looked over to her as she entered. "Could you help me apply my makeup, please? My hands are still shaky."

"Of course," she moved to the table and started gathering the items needed. "Would this have anything to do with Carden?"

I blushed and nodded. "You know me too well."

She simply smiled and started to help me, naturally powdering my face before applying a mild shadow to my eyelids. When she was done, I looked as natural as I could, my paled skin now appearing a little healthier. I didn't want to look like a sick woman when I went to see my lover.

I thanked Ellora, then left the room, my boots scraping the floor as my dress flowed with my easier movements.

It feels good to be able to walk without staggering again. I'm in no way recovered yet, but at least I'm not collapsing from exhaustion.

The corridors were so unfamiliar, and I found myself lost for a few moments. I had to be brave and ask one of the guardsmen for directions, seeing the gleaming golden eyes and the pointed fangs the second I looked at him. The second guard with him was staring at me, the pair of them seeming inexorably drawn to me the way a mountain lion is drawn to a young doe. I cringed back my unease and followed the directions they had given me, entering the corridor that led into the royal quarters.

I was startled as I came face-to-face with the towering and impressive vampire king while I turned the corner, his eyes locking onto me the instant we crossed paths.

"Princess Leander," he smiled, flashing his fangs at me. "At last, we meet. I am King Tiernan. It is a pleasure."

"Oh... uh... your Majesty," I gripped the sides of my dress and immediately curtseyed, knowing how meek I must have appeared to the great King. "Thank you for your hospitality. I can't express my gratitude for all you've done strongly enough."

"I assume that your companions have explained everything to you, Princess," he spoke calmly, his dominance making me nervous as I straightened up with my arms by my sides.

I nodded softly, falling into the old habits of my royal deportment training. "They have, your Majesty."

He smiled coldly, that same predatory stare filling his eyes. I wanted to wrap my hands around my neck, if only to shield it from his gaze, but I knew two things that would come with such a move. Firstly, it would likely insult my host and incur his anger, and secondly, it would do no good since he was at least twenty times the strength of an able-bodied man, let alone a heavily weakened teenage girl. I had no knowledge beyond the legends and stories I had heard as a child regarding how to defend myself, but I noticed that the herb known as vervain seemed to be purposefully absent from the castle.

"Do you seek my son?" he asked of me, lifting his golden eyes from my exposed neckline to meet my steel blue gaze again.

"Yes, your Majesty. I do," I confirmed, trying to keep my voice even. "We have a great many things to talk about, he and I."

"I am sure you do," he said contemplatively, still studying my soft, young features and skin. "I should warn you, however, that he is *not* in a fair mood, nor has he been since he carried you back from Azmerath's Doorway. You would do well to tread carefully around him, Princess. Humans do not often do well in the presence of the newly initiated."

I pressed my lips together and nodded as I tilted my head up to look at the towering six-foot five king. His mere presence was intimidating, even without his words: "I understand, your Majesty. I will be careful."

He smiled and cupped my cheek briefly in one icy cold hand, a shiver involuntarily running through my body. He regarded me for a moment.

"Such a beautiful and respectful girl," he mused, taking his hand back before striding past me in a sweeping flurry of red and black robes. "I would certainly hate to find that he has lost control and spilled your blood across the floors."

His last words were unsettling to say the least. I tensed as he spoke them, left standing there trying to figure out if he was saying that he didn't want me dead, or if he didn't want to have his floors ruined. Either way, the concept was disturbing and nearly made me turn away. But I didn't.

Pushing myself to keep going with the reminder of who it was that I was going to speak to, I walked the last few steps to the end of the hall and tentatively knocked on the heavy wooden door. My heart was racing as I waited to be permitted to enter, my chest heaving beneath my bodice despite all of my attempts to calm myself down.

I wonder how different he is. Does he still dress as he did or is he now wearing the finery of a prince? And what about his eyes? Are they still green? I loved his green eyes...

"Come," the familiar deep tenor called from within, startling me out of my thoughts.

Carefully, I grasped the latch on the door and lifted it, pushing it open with both hands as I entered. I was instantly struck with the heavy colouring of red and black that filled the room, the sun streaming through the window seeming to strangely make the space darker rather than brighter. My eyes took in the details of the room with a curious stare, noting the large bookshelves to my left and the ebony desk opposite where I stood. The centre of the room was occupied by a king size four poster bed, dressed in blood red sheets and guarded by deep crimson drapes. I nearly jumped as I glanced to my right and momentarily thought there was a guard in the room. But I quickly relaxed when I saw that it was just a mannequin dressed in a suit of armour identical to the ones I had seen the castle's knights wearing.

My attention swiftly turned from the mannequin to the figure standing in front of the desk, his back to me, his black hair neat. He wore a fine long doublet of deep crimson that reached to his shins, the shoulders and most of the upper torso coloured in midnight onyx. Every trim and detailing running through the garment was silvery and catching the gleam of the sunlight. I glimpsed the tell-tale black of his shirt underneath, the high collar done up around his throat. It seemed that he wore only black beneath the doublet, his pants and boots identical to his shirt, though they had a more brownish tinge to them. Around his waist was a black leather belt with golden circles set into it all along the length, part of it tucked up and under the front to allow it to hang before him.

I took a sharp intake of breath as I saw him, his height seeming so much more than I remembered. The edge of his cheekbone, forehead and jaw were only visible as he made sure to face away from me. He had his large hands braced to the top of the table, his shoulders slouched slightly as he glanced towards me without turning, the sunlight from the window silhouetting him.

I twisted my hands together before my midriff uncertainly, trying to figure out what to say first. I hadn't actually planned anything specific, and now that I stood before him, I found myself lost for words. At last, I just let myself speak, not really sure what was coming out until I heard it, my voice a soft murmur.

"May I come in, Carden?" as I said the sentence it suddenly seemed like the most obvious thing I could have chosen.

He seemed to tense at my voice, which I found odd. He had never been so unnerved by me speaking, his hands flattened to the table. He simply nodded, but didn't speak, keeping his back to me as I entered the room and closed the door.

I studied him uncertainly as I moved further into the room, keeping my hands together lightly, my fingers grasping each other absentmindedly. I had never felt so awkward with him in all the time I knew him. Maybe it was just the fact that he hadn't been there when I had woken up, or the fact that he looked so different now. But then again, maybe it was the fact that in the past he had been the one to speak first in most of our conversations, his confidence now replaced instead with a strange apathy. At least, I hoped it was apathy.

I wet my lips as I felt my throat grow dry, turning my blue eyes to his face - or what I could see of it - as I tried to form the next sentence that came from my mouth. But there were no words, my mind a blank as I tried to figure out what I should say. Finally, as I was about to speak, he lifted his head, keeping his face hidden from me as he let out a sigh.

"Do you intend to just stand there and stare at me all day?" he asked, his tone so unlike himself in its strange harshness.

I shook my head, looking up at his words in surprise. "No... Of course not. I... I wanted to see you."

"Did you?" he responded lowly, still not turning to me.

I bit my bottom lip and frowned, my shoulders shifting beneath the open neck of my dress in time with my breaths, my chest heaving slightly.

"The others tell me that... that you saved me," I said softly, trying to get some idea as to what he was thinking. "Were it not for you, I wouldn't be standing here. But..." the words paused as I bit my lip again, pulling in a shaky breath, "but they say that bringing me back came at a high cost for you."

"It did," he confirmed with a nod. "As it did for you too."

I raised an eyebrow curiously. "What cost have I paid?"

"One that was too high," he replied solemnly.

I knitted my brow as I looked at him, studying the way he moved. He was not himself, this much too clear to me. I carefully edged closer, reaching out one hand towards him.

"Carden..." I lay my palm to his shoulder.

"Don't touch me!" he jerked his shoulder forward and turned swiftly around behind me, making sure to hide his face.

I followed him with my gaze, turning to face him again, so confused by his strange behaviour.

"What's wrong, Carden?" I asked, stepping after him.

"Don't move," he snarled, making me pause. "Just stay still."

"Carden, please. Just... just look at me," I urged him gently. "Please."

"No..."

"The others told me what happened," I said gently, holding my hands together again, my long flowing sleeves dropping down from my elbows. "What you... what you had to become to save me."

"Yet, you still stand there," he remarked with dark amusement in his voice.

I kept my eyes locked on his back, nodding faintly in response to his words. "Is there a reason why I shouldn't?"

Slowly, deliberately, Carden turned around to face me, his new appearance revealed. I opened my mouth to say something as I saw his alabaster skin, his pointed fangs and his golden eyes, but I couldn't find the words. He looked like the man I knew, just paler and with a stranger eye colour than I had thought, but he was no different otherwise.

"There is an abundance of reasons why you shouldn't," he told me coldly. "Chief among them would be the mere fact of *what* I am."

I shrugged one shoulder at him lightly, shaking my head. "I don't care about that."

"Yet, your heart quickens at my approach," he observed the physical reactions of my body so clearly that it was as if he were right beside me instead of several feet away. "Your breath hitches and you tremble at the sight of me."

I couldn't deny that I was nervous, but it wasn't because of what he had become.

"Admit it, Leander," he said, moving to stand over me, forcing me to angle my neck up so that I could look into his eyes. "You're afraid of me."

I shook my head. "No... No, I'm... I'm not afraid of you..."

"You're lying," he uttered confidently.

"The way you're speaking and acting," I murmured, closing my eyes for a moment to compose myself before looking up at him again, "makes me nervous."

"You should be nervous," he responded coldly. "You stand in a room alone with a predator."

I shook my head fervently. "I don't believe that."

"Of course not," he scoffed, passing me by and moving back to the window. "You're in love."

"I am," I agreed, turning around to face him again, this back and forth through the room starting to make me a little dizzy. "I have been in love with you since the day we met...

"And now you're blinded to the truth," he grumbled, studying the view of the forests and foothills below the keep's windows.

"What truth?"

"The truth that I am a dangerous monster," he said harshly, turning to stare me down. "The truth that I could tear your throat out and feast on your virgin blood quicker than you can utter a scream."

"You won't do that," I moved closer to him, demonstrating my trust. "I know you..."

"No, you don't, Leander," he said grimly, grasping my wrists in his cold hands before I could touch his chest, a gasp escaping my lips at how chilled his skin had now become. "You know the man I was, the Guardian who pledged his heart to you. You do not know the prince who stands before you."

"They are the same man," I insisted, his hold on my wrists both comforting and disconcerting. "You *are* the *same* man."

"And you are an adolescent girl with a clinging infatuation for an immortal," he snarled down at me.

"From what Tallinn and Fawkner tell me," I said carefully, keeping my eyes locked with his, "it sounds like that's something we share in common now."

He nodded. "It is."

"So what they told me is true?" I asked with a thrill of fear. "Azmerath really did banish us from his realm?"

"As part of the cost of bringing you back from the dead," he confirmed slowly, "I had to give up my life for you and die in your place. But such a simple exchange only works for *normal* humans, not beings cursed like us. Instead, I was made a full vampire, and you and I were made Deathless, never again to pass into Azmerath's Kingdom of Death."

"Deathless?" I felt my heart sink and my skin pale at his words.

"Neither of us can *ever* die again," he explained coldly, staring me down. "We are both doomed to forever exist as un-aging, unending, eternal reminders of that sacrifice and covenant with Death himself," his gaze darkened. "Which is why it is time for you to go."

"Go?" I frowned, confused by his words. "What do you mean "go"? I don't understand."

"What isn't there to understand?" he asked me softly, but harshly. "You need to go. Now. You have a kingdom to retake and to rule, as well as a world to save from destruction. I merely played my part in the prophecies, but now it is your turn to play yours."

"You're... you're telling me to leave?" I could hardly say the words, choking on them in my throat, tears threatening my eyes. "Why?"

He released my hands and stepped back, staring at me with a hard expression, but sorrowful eyes: "Because you must and because you are no longer safe with me."

"That's not true," I murmured.

He sighed. "You stubborn little human girl..."

"It's not true!" I insisted louder, keeping my eyes locked on his as I briefly shook my head before going on. "You are the *one* person who has risked everything for me, the *one* person I share this new deathless existence with, and the *one* person I am willing to abdicate my throne for!"

His eyes widened as I said this, clearly never having thought about me ever doing that.

"Can't you see, Carden?" I edged closer to him, biting my lip as I tried not to cry. "I am so in love with you that I held on to you in the Netherworlds longer than anyone else. When all of my memories were fading from me and I was about to be stolen into the Void to suffer for eternity, the thought of *you* pulled me back from the brink. Just as you brought me back from the dead in this world," I pressed my hands to his chest, feeling his heartbeat for a few moments before looking up into his eyes, pleading for him to see the truth. "Tallinn told me what you did before Azmerath. True love's kiss..." he looked so broken as I said those words. "That's how you achieved it. Through true love," a small smile tugged at my lips as I felt a tear slip down my cheek. "You kissed me and brought me back to life... just like in a fairy tale. Can't you see what that means?"

He was frowning, his expression dark as I reached up to touch his cheek with one hand, gently trying to soothe him. His pain was so clear and all I wanted was to take it away, to make him feel happiness again.

"Please, Carden," I pleaded in a whisper, meaning to kiss him as I edged closer. "I love you and I know that you love me..."

"Maybe so," he uttered, turning his golden eyes to my steel blue ones as he grasped my hand and held it, lowering it from his face. "But the truth that you have to accept is that not all fairy tales have happy endings, Leander. Such is the fate of ours."

I frowned desperately, shaking my head. "That's not true..." my voice was a hoarse whisper, my heart hurting, my scar burning.

"You have to leave now," he urged me quietly. "Please. Before I lose control and cause you harm."

"You won't!" I insisted firmly. "You won't! You're not a monster, Carden! You're not!"

There was a sudden rush and I screamed in shock, feeling my back and shoulders slam hard against the stone wall. Before I had a chance to move, my hands were suddenly seized and forced above my head, my arms straining and my feet barely touching the floor. Tears blurred my vision as my breasts heaved beneath my dress. His body was pressed up against mine, his fangs bared and his eyes like blood instead of gold. A whimper escaped my lips as I tried to pull myself free, but it was useless. His grasp was like iron, so much stronger than it had ever been before. I could do nothing but hang there, staring up at him with terrified and heartbroken eyes. And as he lowered his lips to my neck and bared his fangs, I closed my eyes and turned my face away, a weak sob slipping from my lips before I could stop it.

"I told you that I am not like other men," he growled lowly, holding me firmly. "Do you now see that I *am* dangerous, girl?"

I nodded sadly, crying softly through closed lips as I felt his hold tighten a little more. I didn't want to admit it, desperate to prove that he was the same man I loved, but I was struggling to do more than sob at that moment.

"The man you love is dead," he murmured into my ear with sadness. "Carden Highever would never have harmed you, but Prince Carden Valerian is dangerous. The only reason I won't kill you is because you're the one who can end Morod's blight once and for all. Do you understand?"

I nodded quickly, trembling as my arms strained more and I began to fear that he had dislocated them from my shoulders.

"Good," he released me, gaining my teary gaze as he threw open the door. "Goodbye, Princess."

I rushed from the room, throwing myself out of the door all while trying not to let him see my tears. There was no way he couldn't have seen them, but it was clear that he didn't care as he slammed the door shut behind me, finalising our horrible and painful confrontation.

I ran down the hall, sobbing as I went, my heart hurting as the pain of where I had been stabbed seemed heightened all of a sudden. There was no escaping that pain, the wound now emotional rather than physical.

What felt like only moments later, I pushed through the door to the room I had been staying in and slumped to the floor by the bed, bursting into tears. I could only lie there and cry, burying my face into my arms against the mattress as my mournful sobs made me struggle for breath. It felt like it didn't matter that my heart had been healed from Morod's strike. Carden's blow had been far more devastating than the Shadow Lord's ever could have been.

I wish he'd left me dead! He shouldn't have brought me back! If he hates me so much, then he should have just let me stay dead! Oh, Gods... Please... Why?! Why is he doing this to me?!

I felt a large hand against my shoulders, lifting my head to see Joran crouching over me. There was no need to say anything, the Storvari's eyes showing his understanding at my pain. He just pulled me to his chest as he sat cross legged on the floor, letting me cling to him as I wept hopelessly.

He remained silent. After all, what good would there be in speaking about what I had just suffered at the hands of the man I loved?

Chapter Twenty-Four
Absent Heart

It was early morning when our company were preparing to depart, Amethyst and Gaspeite having come to the main courtyard to await us. Feldspar, Syrena's red dragon, was sitting by the main gates, watching on in silence. The Lorveren soldiers that had come with my friends to bring me back were double checking the packs that King Tiernan's people had provided us, ensuring that everything was secure before hefting the bags over their green cloaked backs.

I walked slowly down the steps of the castle with a black cloak draped over my frame. Syrena had given it to me, the black velvet and cotton cloak thick to the touch and warm inside its subtly detailed folds. For the moment, I let the hood hang down my shoulders, my long hair pulled back from my face with a clasp to keep it from blinding me in the snowy winds. As I reached the snow-covered courtyard, I couldn't help wondering how I must have looked to my friends gathered there.

I must look like a sad and broken girl, my mood as blue as the dress I wear.

Ellora and the Dwarves were at the bottom of the steps waiting as Joran followed at my back, the four of them solemnly protective of me. They had such strong looks of sympathy on their faces. But my mind was shying from the pity that each held as they watched me. I had no desire to be pitied any more than I desired to remain in Castle Valkirak now that the *prince* had made his feelings known.

They're false feelings. You know that. He still loves you, no matter how you feel... I suppressed the thoughts, joining Fawkner, Ranzel, Tallinn, Tristan and Danika as they stood with King Tiernan, Syrena and her husband.

"Are you certain that you will stay no longer, Lord Fawkner?" King Tiernan asked quietly, though his tone seemed very harsh. "The Lords will be attending the lands meet soon and it would be most helpful to our cause if they were to meet with yourself and the Princess."

"I understand your position, your Majesty," Fawkner said solemnly, looking to me briefly as I approached, "but the Princess has made her desire to return to High-Realm very clear. As the highest titled of our company, she is the one whose will must be obeyed."

"Especially given the destiny that lies ahead of her," Ranzel added quietly, his words making me suppress a cringe.

"No matter the outcome of the lands meet, my friends," the King assured us calmly, "you will have the armies of House Valerian at your side in the final battle against the Shadow Lord."

"Our thanks, your Majesty," Fawkner bowed his head, the others following suit.

King Tiernan turned his golden eyes to me, his expression softer than I had expected. He almost seemed sorry for what his son had made me feel, though I wasn't sure he truly was. I couldn't imagine that someone as old as my friends had said he was could ever feel true sympathy for a broken-hearted human.

"Princess," he addressed me gently, "I do wish that I could convince you to stay."

"There is little reason for me to stay, your Majesty," I said honestly, trying not to be too outwardly sad. "Besides, I have a kingdom of my own to liberate and rule. I *must* return to Aldegaad and free my people from my uncle's oppressive tyranny."

"Then, I wish you luck, your Highness," he said in earnest. "I am certain that you will make a great and beautiful queen."

I nodded softly. "Thank you for your hospitality, your Majesty. And for helping my friends to resurrect me. I will do all I can to repay the debt I owe you all."

King Tiernan simply bowed his head as I did the same in return, the two of us separating as I turned my gaze to his daughter.

Syrena took my hands in her alabaster ones, squeezing them gently as she looked into my eyes apologetically. "I wish things had been different, Princess Leander," she said with regret in her voice. "Please, do not think too harshly of my brother. I truly believe that he *does* love you."

"I know. I believe so too," I murmured, trying to hold back my tears. "But he has chosen to turn away from me, and I... I can't push him to do what he doesn't wish to. That would be selfish of me."

She nodded. "I understand. Just know, Princess, that you have a friend in me. After all, we are both holders of Dragon Pendants."

"We are," I agreed, fighting my heartbreak. "Take care, Syrena."

"And you, Leander," she replied gently, trying to smile at me.

I withdrew my hands and joined the others as Ranzel placed his palm to my shoulder, leading me towards Amethyst. It was decided that I would ride her, given that I still wasn't strong enough yet to walk the far distance we would need to travel to reach the *Black Asp*. I wasn't about to argue, feeling a sense of comfort as I climbed onto my dragon's back.

With nothing more to say, we started towards the gates and the bridge of the castle, Gaspeite taking to the air so as to keep a watchful eye on us from the sky with Fawkner's falcon. The soldiers surrounded us as Ranzel took the lead, snowflakes coating his hat as he walked forward, staff in hand.

I felt a need to look back as Amethyst carried me to the gates, gazing over my shoulder towards the tower keep behind me.

The obvious red of his clothes stood out against the black stone walls and the white snows where he stayed on a low balcony watching us, his black hair tussled by the winds. Carden looked so sad, his arms crossed before his broad chest, his golden eyes seeming dulled as he let his gaze linger on my slender shape. He was as unmoving as the stone gargoyles mounted on the ledge surrounding him.

I wanted to drop from the Dragon's back and run to him, images of the two of us rushing to embrace in the falling snow in a sorrowful reunion playing through my mind. But I didn't move from my place any more than he shifted from his overlooking the courtyard.

Letting my eyes linger on him for a few moments more as Amethyst took me through the gates, I felt a sense of loss deeper than any death. I drew my black hood to hide my tears, grasping the Dragon's scales as I let my cheeks get wet and turned away from him.

The man I love was really like someone from a fairy tale. He was even a prince... But now he's gone, and my heart is as broken as it was when Morod put his dagger through it. I will never love another as deeply... And I don't want to...

* * * * *

Our road headed to the east, winding its way through the craggy foothills of the valley at the base of the great peak Castle Valkirak stood upon. Ranzel had chosen to take us along the paved roads that avoided the marshes the map he carried warned us of, heading directly into the mountain range he explained was called the Fog-Strewn Mountains. It seemed like an unimaginative name to me, but I had no desire to voice my opinion on the subject any more than I had the right to.

The road became steep and treacherous, our group taking its time to climb the paths as the ground grew slick with ice and snow. I could only hold on tightly to Amethyst's neck and scales so that I wouldn't fall, glancing to my left at the ever-deepening drop from the narrow path.

Amethyst spoke gently, looking up at me with one glowing orange eye.

I met her gaze from beneath my hood, knowing that my look of fear made my words seem less than convincing: "I know you won't let me fall, Amethyst."

She asked a question.

I nodded, letting out a shaky breath as I clung to her tighter. "Yes. I trust you. I am glad that we're not flying though."

She turned back to the road ahead, making a snide and joking comment.

"I could so handle it," I replied, though I knew that wasn't true.

She made a cackling noise that sounded so much like laughter.

I just sighed and conceded: "Fine. You're right. I'm too afraid of heights to fly."

* * * * *

As the sun set after a few more hours, we came upon an abandoned inn; the doors broken, and the walls snapped open in a few places. Fawkner sent several soldiers in to check the place out and see if it was suitable for us to make camp, the men soon returning with good news.

In no time the soldiers had erected tents around the building while my friends had made the inn sheltered enough for us to rest in. They had even set up one of the old rooms for me to lie in so that I could sleep without disturbance.

I tried to rest for a while, but I just found that I couldn't, not with the absence of my friend and true love still burning hard in my heart.

I got to my feet from the old bed and shrugged back into my black cloak, stepping out into the main room of the ruined inn. A fire had been set in the central pit, wood crackling and burning as the others were gathered around. They were eating and trying to get some rest along with some of the soldiers that accompanied us.

As I passed through the room I overheard the conversation between Ranzel, Danika and Tallinn. The two magic users were speaking to her as the most senior Guardian there was left to us. Fawkner was sitting not far from them, Farsight perched on his arm as he petted her feathers.

"If we hold to this road, we will be in the eastern port in three days' time," Ranzel explained, pointing his finger to the path on the map. "My correspondence with Captain Karrer shows that the *Black Asp* is moored there and will await our arrival."

"And have we determined what we will do when we return to High-Realm?" Tallinn asked sternly, her demeanour more that of a focused leader than the gentle woman she was with me.

"Return to Eilath," the Wizard stated evenly, leaning back in his chair with his pipe to his lips. "We will then gather our strength and prepare for the battles to come."

"I hope you have a plan for such actions, Ranzel," Danika commented casually, pacing with her staff across her back and her arms folded before her chest, her robes swaying with her movements.

"We will devise them with our allies," the old man responded. "For the time being, our priority must be the Princess' safety..."

I tuned out once they started talking about me, making my way to the door and the porch of the inn. I had no desire to hear whatever it was they were planning to do that involved me, though I knew now that they had resurrected me because of the words in some old scroll.

Nothing has really changed, I thought as I sat down on the steps, looking out at the mountains surrounding us and gazing past them to the valley below. *My companions are still my protectors, and I am still under guard for my own safety.* I half laughed, half grimaced. *Some hope for the world I'm supposed to be...*

My eyes drifted in my deep despondence towards the faint glow of Castle Valkirak's fires in the far distance. My heart ached, feeling a profound absence within it now that he was no longer with me.

Carden's words were so wrong. He wasn't speaking at all like the man I've known these past few years. I can't even begin to understand why he would speak like that to me. He isn't cruel and harsh... It's just not like him...

My tears fell freely again, and I cuddled into my black cloak sadly, letting my gaze drift now to my feet. I just wanted to close my eyes and forget everything, but it was worse when I did that. After all, I *had* asked Tallinn and Fawkner to tell me everything. I started to think of Azmerath's banishment of me from his realm. I didn't really know what that meant.

What am I supposed to do? I can't be what they need me to be. I'm not some warrior or heroine. I'm not even a skilled royal. I'm just a frightened girl facing the end of the world... without my true love...

I sighed as I heard floorboards creak behind me, hugging my knees tightly and blinking away my tears against the cold and bitter winds. I hadn't even thought to turn to whoever it was that stood at my back, my mind too preoccupied with my sadness.

"What are you doing out here, girl?" Fawkner's voice startled me, causing me to turn to where he stood by the doorway.

I sniffed back my quiet sobs and wiped away my tears, trying to appear strong. "Nothing... Just... just sitting. Thinking."

"Oh," he nodded thoughtfully, drawing his fur topped cloak further around his shoulders. "May I join you?"

"Of course, Fawkner," I replied, trying to smile, though I knew how sad I must have looked to him.

He moved to my left and sat down beside me on the steps, drawing a few glances from the men that patrolled the area to keep us safe. He studied the way ahead as I drew my hood against the chilled winds, my shivers starting to become a little too much to bear.

I could feel his stare move to me as I let mine turn back to the castle and its overshadowing mountain peak in the distance. I was glad that the fabric of my cowl blocked me from seeing his gaze. At that moment the last thing I needed was to endure the sympathetic glances of my companions, especially after all that had happened to bring us to this point.

"You truly seem more than vexed, Leander," he stated softly, keeping his gaze on my hooded shape. "Understandable, of course, though I am concerned for your well-being."

"My well-being," I uttered softly, musing on that single subject ironically. "It seems that my well-being has been the cause of all this pain and loss; the singular focus that brought us to stand here in these mountains now as High-Realm falls to Morod's evil."

He made a soft intake at my words, his expression of incredulousness obvious to me, even though I didn't look at him: "You speak as if our caring for you has been damaging in some unreasonable way."

"Hasn't it?" I asked, turning my head to look at him, my hood covering the left side of my face as the icy winds plucked at my auburn locks beneath the black fabric. "Has my survival and welfare not brought down the wrath of so many enemies upon us? Has my very existence not been plagued with danger and destruction that harms others?"

"Do not say such things," he murmured. "You are a good, kind, generous person, Leander. A woman of conviction and deepest love."

"I am not a woman," I retorted softly, turning my gaze to my feet as I rubbed my hands together before me in an attempt to warm them. "I can never be a woman. Morod stole my life from me and ensured that I be young forever; trapped always on the cusp between adolescence and womanhood," that thought had never stopped hurting, though at that moment I felt it even stronger than I ever had before. "And now, from what you, Tallinn and Carden have told me, I am cursed twice again by Lord Azmerath himself; banished from ever entering his kingdom and doomed to live an eternal existence. Do you even know what that means for me? Because I don't."

He shook his head solemnly. "No... No, I...I don't. I'm not sure any of us can understand. Except perhaps Ranzel, Danika and Ellora, given their naturally long life spans."

I nodded, pressing my lips together into a grim line. "And Carden... Carden understands. He understands as he suffers the same fate as me. Yet, he has turned me away with harsh words that sound poisonous and wrong when spoken in his velvety voice."

"His words to you were unfair and untrue," Fawkner nodded glumly, resting his forearms on his knees, his brown hair catching in the breeze to flick against his bearded jaw. "One does not carry the corpse of their soul mate across half the world to resurrect them, only to then cast them aside as if they are nothing more than a frivolous plaything whose usefulness has come to its end. It is not the truth of love."

"Love..." I sniffed, feeling my tears flow down my cheeks again. "I can't be more certain than I am now that I have felt love's touch. Because if I didn't then I wouldn't still feel as if I have a knife through my heart."

"I know," he said softly, placing his hand to my back.

"Maybe things would have been better if I had never been rescued from Averet," I sighed through my tears. "Maybe, if you had just given me to Morod that night, or if the Guardians had arrived only a few minutes later, things would have been better than they are now."

"How can you even utter such falsehoods?" he questioned with a hard frown.

"It's true," I insisted sadly, biting my bottom lip and shaking my head as I gazed at the snowy earth before us. "If Morod had succeeded in taking me that night, then none of you would have had to suffer through all that you have. Or... or maybe it would have been better if he and Manth had taken me when I was a child."

"When you were a child?" his frowned deepened with puzzlement. "What do you mean?"

I shrugged my shoulders in a heavy slump, hugging my aching midriff with my arms as if to keep my insides from falling out, settling instead for my tears.

"When I was maybe only seven winters old, I wandered away from my sister while we were in the fields of Arvon," I explained in a soft, meagre voice, keeping my eyes on the snow as I recalled the memory that had returned to me after my death. "I got lost and ended up wandering towards the river. That was where I met a woman in black robes and a man cowled in shadows whose face I never saw. Even as a little girl, the Shadow Lord hunted me, his dark deeds planned to be carried out on me strong in intent even then."

"Have you told the others?" he asked softly, concern in his voice.

I shook my head. "No. You're the only one I've told this to," I exhaled slowly, my breath shuddering and my chest hurting as I made myself push on. "I feel that if... that if Mithras and my father hadn't interrupted them that day... if Aislinn hadn't found me so quickly, that I would have been taken and all of this pain would have been avoided. Carden would still be human, you would still have all of your children, and there would not have been the devastation that has come from my well-being and survival being so dogmatically focused on."

"That... is the single *stupidest* thing I have *ever* heard tumble out of your mouth, girl," he scowled with disgust, instantly drawing my gaze. "That you could *ever* think anything so horrid is bewildering, let alone the *idiocy* of even uttering such thoughts aloud."

I frowned, pulling back a little as he leaned over me. I felt like I was being scolded by an enraged parent, though Fawkner's tone was even and at a normal speaking level. He didn't shout at me, which was actually much more frightening than if he had.

"But... but it's true..." I started only to be cut off.

"You stupid little girl!" he snapped at me, abhorrence colouring his face as he narrowed his angry eyes at me. "Do you *truly* think so little of yourself?! Hm?! Is that what you *really* believe while we have all followed you and protected you?! Is that why Mithras and Aldwyn died?! Because you think that you are a blight upon our lives and the reason we have all suffered at that bastard Shadow Lord's hands?! Are you truly so selfish?!"

I was sniffing back tears as I braced my hands behind me, the Guardian and Lord leaning towards me with a scowling face and burning eyes. I had never seen him so angry before and it scared me.

He went on fervently: "Let me explain something to you, *Princess*. Whether you had been taken as a child, at Averet, or when you actually were by Lord Morod, it would have made *little* difference to the way things have played out. You may never have known us, nor felt what true love is in Carden's embrace, and you would not have left a mark on our lives, but that does not mean that we would live without Morod's wrath!" his voice grew a little in volume as he glared me down hard, his jaw set firmly as he spoke. "The *only* real difference for us beyond having never met you would have been that we would not have been there to unravel his foul plots and make the attempts that we did to prevent them! Do you understand me, girl?! That we have met you and guard you against him is not such a curse as *you* seem to think, but more a lasting hope that good may triumph against his evil!"

I let my face drop, sobbing softly as my eyes blurred at his words. I felt ashamed, my behaviour and self-doubt worse than being just wrong about things.

Fawkner drew in a calming breath, easing his voice back to a softer tone: "I know that you take the pains of others onto yourself, absorbing them into your soul, but you do not need to carry the blame for that hurt as your own," he touched my chin with his fingertips, making me look up through my tears at him. "You are just an innocent girl pulled into the middle of an aeons old war because of your bloodline and heritage. Stop carrying the weight of what others think and feel upon your shoulders, for you carry a burden that is already heavy enough without all of that. Your heart is broken, yes. So let it be broken and feel your *own* feelings rather than regret that you survive while others do not. You are *not* to blame, and I will no longer tolerate you harming yourself with such thoughts and words, Leander. Not after all that was done to bring you back."

"I'm sorry," I whispered through my sobs, trembling at his hold. "I'm so sorry. I... I shouldn't be so hopeless or so hard on myself. I just don't see how bringing me back will do anything to stop all of this, any more than I can see how to live on without... without him..." I broke down, closing my eyes.

Very gently and with the care of a father, Fawkner pulled me into his arms and cradled me close. I felt his hand rubbing my back as he held me to his armoured chest, his chin pressing to my hooded head as he kept me wrapped in his arms.

"Do not worry about that now," he urged me. "All you have to do is continue to regain your strength as you heal. The Shadow Lord and the Prophecies will be attended to once you are well enough and with the strength of each of us standing with you."

"And my absent heart?" I sniffed in a murmur, laying my head to his chest.

"Your heart isn't absent," he said softly. "Broken hearts often feel as if they are absent. Do not try to deny what you feel, but simply let it be felt. Even if that means crying."

"I really... I really am sorry for my behaviour, Fawkner," I apologised again, my voice shaking. "I... I didn't mean to be so stupid."

"We can all be stupid, Leander," he remarked, offering me a gentle smile and a caring shoulder to cry on. "Especially with a broken heart."

I said nothing else, simply closing my eyes and cuddling into his broad chest, huddling with him under the warmth of our cloaks as the icy winds howled ever more fiercely over us.

I thought on all that he had said as my tears started to slow their terrible pace, my heart easing its frantic race inside my chest. *I am stupid for thinking like that. I am not to blame for my parents' deaths, or for the deaths of everyone else who has been lost since this all began. And I am definitely not to blame for Carden's choice, even though it feels like I am. I have to stop giving into such blames and just try to be strong in this. Fawkner's right, after all. I am allowed to cry and have feelings that are my own. Even if these prophecies say what they do about me, I am not defined by them, and I don't carry the weight of the world on my shoulders. I shouldn't have to...*

"Come," Fawkner's voice drew my gaze. "It is getting colder and quite late. We must get indoors and to bed. We have a long journey before us in the morning."

I nodded and let him help me to my feet, quietly following him back into the old inn to lay down and rest away my hurts. At least in my dreams I could escape a little, even if it wasn't for very long.

Seeking solitude and trying to avoid the gazes of the others - as they had clearly heard our raised voices, despite the mountain winds - I went to the room I had been set up in, dropping down onto the creaking bed with a heavy sigh. As I closed my eyes, I let myself wipe all thoughts from my mind, though my heart still ached and would for a long time.

True Love can never be gotten over. It just can't be...

My body relaxed and I fell asleep, though it felt like only a few moments before I was waking up again, exhaustion clinging to me like the cold air around me. I shivered as I blinked against the icy grey light that streamed through the gaps in the walls, yawning with my return to consciousness. I didn't have time to really come to though, the sounds of rushed movement and shouts snapping me fully back to awareness.

The door flew open, and Tallinn stood before me with a look of concern, her black and silver cloak swaying as her chest heaved beneath her black armour and shirt, her bow in hand. I didn't need to ask anything of her to understand what was happening, the sudden heat in my pendant as it flashed warningly telling me enough.

"Princess, get up!" she hurried me with an urgent tone. "We have to get you out of here now!"

I just nodded, throwing myself from the bed and rushing behind her to the inn doors.

The two of us hurried out into an early morning of deep fogs, harsh grey light and the clashing of swords in battle...

Chapter Twenty-Five
A Difficult Choice

With frantic, wide eyes, I took in the scene before me, the thick fogs that choked the mountains making everything more ghostly and frightening than I thought it could be. The Lorveren soldiers were swinging with swords, maces and axes, their shields clashing against the weapons of their attackers as men's shouts and monsters' roars echoed across the mountaintops in a deadly chorus.

Gathlorks! Those are Gathlorks attacking us! Oh my gods! How did they get here?!
"This way, Princess!" Tallinn moved quickly down the steps, her cloak flashing around her as she strung arrows swiftly and released them, spinning to strike as the Gathlorks rushed at us. "Hurry!"

I did as she commanded and ran after her, grasping the hems of my dress to keep myself from falling. All I could do was try to stay with the Guardian as she defended me amidst the terrible onslaught of monsters as Hurgarks and Orcs begun to appear out of the heavy fogs to attack our escorts.

We ran through the mists to where green flashes signalled across the murky air, the shapes of Ranzel and Danika coming into view a few moments later. They were busy fighting off the attacking Scourge with magical blasts, Ranzel extending the auric field of his pendant to cast away large groups as Gaspeite roared and landed amidst a sizable number of beasts. The dragon immediately lashed out with fire and claws, snapping the Scourge creatures into the air fiercely before leaping into a short flight as he attempted to hold back the seemingly endless onslaught.

Arrows whistled from atop a seven-foot cliff, Ellora stringing them rapidly to her elegant Elven bow, her red hair streaming past her shoulders in the dull winds. She was the single archer we had with the farthest range of sight, her Elf eyes easily detecting creatures that the rest of us couldn't. With every shot her arrows disappeared into the mists only to announce their kills with the grunts of their targets.

Dolin and Holger were in the thick of the battle, fighting side-by-side with Tristan, the three men swinging sword, war-hammer and battle-axe into the horde that was violently trying to crush down on our position. Fawkner and his steward were behind them, their hair flashing around their shoulders as they twirled their swords to carve down enemies amidst the green cloaked and scale armoured Lorveren soldiers.

"Ranzel!" Tallinn shouted as she ushered me towards the others, her back to me as she fired three more arrows expertly into the Hurgarks and Orcs.

I rushed to where the Wizard stood, breathing hard as I looked around frantically. I had no sword or bow, completely helpless to defend against this onslaught.

"Stay behind us, Princess!" the old man commanded of me, stamping his staff against the ground and creating a shockwave of invisible energy that cracked the earth beneath the stone to cast several enemies from their feet.

"How did they find us?!" I exclaimed, staying at his shoulder as he swung his sword, shrieking a brief scream as I narrowly avoided the four-foot Hurgark that he smote before me.

"I do not know, Princess!" he responded, aiming the crystal of his staff towards three large Gathlorks and throwing them back with a bolt of green light that impacted them with a hard thud. "The Shadow Lord should not have been able to ascertain our location! Our Dragon Pendants should have safeguarded us from his sights!"

The crushing of earth caused me to turn around, my heart sinking as a massive, hairy Erk lumbered towards us from the slopes at the back of our group. It narrowed its beady black eyes at me and gnashed its heavy jaws, its upward pointing tusks gleaming with drool as it punched its boulder-like fists to the ground. Leather wrapped Gymphs scurried out from behind it, their dagger-handed limbs slashing as they shrieked and hissed. Their red eyes locked on me as I staggered backwards towards the Wizard.

Before they could reach me, I heard the familiar roar of Joran as he leaped from the cliffs above, his twin curved blades tainted with blackish-green blood. He landed with a heavy thump to the ground, snowy powder being thrown up by the impact of his massive feet. In one fluid movement he started to cut down the screaming Gymphs as he set his eight-foot-tall hulking body between them and me.

In the same instant, a jet of flame struck out of the mists at the Erk, catching its furry shoulders and making it howl in frantic agony. Purple and deep blue scales flashed through the fog as Amethyst roared out her battle cry, her claws burying deep into the monster's hide. She easily beat her wings as she dragged the beast's seven-foot, muscular shape from the ground, hurling it away from me and back towards the inn. She released her hold and a moment later the sound of wood splintering tore the air as the Erk landed through the walls of the already derelict building.

Amethyst can breathe fire now?! I couldn't believe my eyes as my fierce dragon beat her wings and sent another jet of flames down upon the Scourge that rushed us from our ruined camp.

"We will not last long against this onslaught!" Ellora shouted, firing her arrows swiftly and with the precision of some kind of automated machine. "They must have opened a portal somewhere!"

"Which means they guard a Shadow Acolyte!" Danika agreed, stabbing the bladed tip of her staff sideways into the midriff of an Orc before ripping it free and spinning it to connect with two more of the creatures and a large Gathlork. "If we are to have any hope of stopping this tide of enemies, we must slay him!"

"Not while the Princess is in danger!" Tallinn shouted sternly, dropping another Hurgark with an arrow before stabbing an Orc with the head of a second and firing it into a Gathlork that rushed us.

"Get her out of here then!" Tristan shouted, casting magic from his hand to imbue his sword with blue fire, easily slicing the armour of a Gathlork captain as it rushed him.

"No!" I shouted, looking at my friends with wide and terrified eyes at such a suggestion. "We all stay together!"

"Not this time, lassie!" Dolin called to me, swinging his axe to uppercut an Orc and drop him backwards before turning on a pair of Hurgarks, downing them as he sliced their heads from their shoulders. "You've got to run!"

"No!" I insisted in panic.

"Princess, you must!" Ranzel stated firmly, slamming his staff into the faces of a group of Hurgarks and slashing them with his sword, before looking over his shoulder to me. "If you die so too does any hope of stopping Lord Morod! You *must* go!"

"Tallinn!" Fawkner stabbed a Gathlork and shoved him back, rushing towards me and seizing my arm firmly. "We will take her from here!"

"Yes! You're right!" the blonde-haired Guardian agreed, slinging another arrow from her bow before turning and running towards the open pass behind her. "This way! Hurry!"

"Joran, Amethyst! Come on!" Fawkner called to the Storvari and the Dragon.

"We will buy you all the time we can!" Ellora called as she leaped from her perch and landed on the snowy ground behind us, her arrows whistling relentlessly.

I struggled in Fawkner's hard grasp, trying to keep up with him as he rushed me after Tallinn. Joran was thundering behind us with his twin blades swinging to carve down two more Gathlorks. I didn't want to run from the battle and leave the others, my heart racing as the very thought of abandoning them left me with a hard lump in my throat and frantic thoughts in my head. But my protectors weren't giving me a choice.

"This way! Hurry!" Tallinn was rushing on ahead, her bow ready with an arrow, her hazel eyes searching the mists as we climbed the rocky paths farther up the mountain.

"Stop! Stop!" I shouted, trying to make Fawkner slow down as he forced me after her, my free hand clawing at his fingers in a vain attempt to prise them from my arm. "Don't do this!"

"We have to move, Leander!" he told me sternly, dragging me beside him with the same urgency as he had the night he had taken me from Arvon.

"We can't just leave the others behind!" I insisted frantically as he paused to look down at me. "Please! We can't!"

"We must!" he responded sternly, but with sorrow in his eyes.

"Fawkner's right, Princess!" Tallinn agreed with a haunted expression, though she managed to stay stoic as always. "Our duty as Guardians is to protect *you*! So, do not delay any longer with your protests and move it! Now!"

Her forcefulness made it all too clear that I had no say in the matter, Fawkner continuing to hurry us up the slippery, icy slopes as Joran stomped up the rocks at my back. The continuous flash of silvery and purple scales in the air told me that Amethyst was circling us as we fled, her diligent gaze all but guaranteeing my protection.

The sounds of roars from below drew our attention, the four of us looking back down towards the paths we had climbed. We had already reached a good height more than I had expected in such a short time, the flashes of flames and green energy in the mists far below telling me that at least Ranzel and Gaspeite were still alive. But their fate was suddenly not a priority as a sizable force of leather armoured Gathlorks were scrambling up the rocks after us.

"Run! Now!" Tallinn shouted, turning on her heel and sprinting up the path.

I didn't argue anymore, grabbing my dress hems in bunches and running as fast as my legs could carry me. My cloak and gown were like blue and black fire dancing with my desperate sprinting. I reached the smoother path Tallinn had found at the same time as Fawkner, just as another two Erks leaped out at us. My scream of panic echoed across the peaks as I staggered away from them. My dragon heard me.

Amethyst roared and swooped, her jaws snapping at the two seven-foot beasts ferociously as she clutched onto them with her talons. She flapped her wings to keep herself aloft as she whipped them with her tail, struggling to keep them back as Joran swung his blade to topple the first of the Gathlorks that was too near to us.

"Go! Go!" Fawkner pushed me forward towards where Tallinn had gone, running beside me with his sword at the ready.

I didn't hesitate, my need to survive now taking over everything else. In moments I had caught up to Tallinn thanks to my longer stride, despite my skirts, my boots pounding footprints into the snow with my desperate race to escape.

The four of us weaved through a narrow path and came to a cliff edge. I skidded and let out a shriek of panic as I just barely stopped before the edge,

Fawkner and Tallinn both grabbing onto me a moment later. There was an old rickety rope and plank bridge across the drop that led to a ledge on the other side. The thick fogs that obscured the mountains around us left us no way of knowing how far a fall from it would be.

We turned over our shoulders as we heard the howling of the Gathlorks drawing nearer, their footsteps like thunder on the snow as they were already rushing up the narrow path between the cliffs. Joran had his back to me now and was readying his blades for a fight.

"The bridge is our only option," Fawkner stated quickly, breathing hard as he held me close to him.

"We won't make it across before they reach us," Tallinn noted.

Nodding at her observation, Fawkner released his grasp on me and snatched his dagger from his belt. "Here," he offered the weapon to me, "take this. You'll need it in case there are more enemies on the other side."

I took it without argument as he pushed me onto the bridge. I staggered a little as the bridge wobbled at my footsteps, looking to him uncertainly.

"Go!" he urged me. "Get across now! Hurry!"

I steeled myself against my fear of heights and moved as quickly as I could, the dagger in one hand as I gripped onto the coarse ropes of the bridge with the other. I didn't think about what I was doing, just trying to reach the other side.

"I'll cut the ropes once she's across," I heard Tallinn say. "At least that will buy her some time."

"What?!" I shrieked in panic, turning over my shoulder to look back at them. "No! You can't!"

"You have to keep moving, Princess!" Tallinn shouted to me as she dropped her bow and drew her gleaming sword.

"I'm not leaving you!" I argued.

"You must!" she retorted fervently. "Keep going and find a place to hide! We will re-join you once we're done with these beasts!"

"Don't worry, Leander!" Fawkner called to me. "We will find another way across!"

"But I-" I started.

"No arguing, Princess!" Tallinn cut me off sternly. "*You must* survive this or everything we've done has been for nothing! Now go!"

My eyes burning with tears of guilt and fear, I turned with a pained frown and pushed myself to the other end of the bridge, struggling not to fall as it swayed violently with my movements. I didn't want to do this, but I knew I had no choice, afraid that I wouldn't see them again.

I stepped from the bridge and onto the other side of the cliffs with the crunching of snow beneath my boots. The roars of Gathlorks and the clangs of swords made me turn around just in time to see Fawkner and Joran fighting against the creatures as they bottlenecked in the narrow cliff passage. I could do nothing as Tallinn swung her sword and cut the first rope, the bridge bowing and shaking as it snapped. She turned swiftly and broke its other mooring with a quick swipe of her blade and the wooden planks broke apart as they fell to the cliffs below. She joined the fight again as the collapse separated them from me and blocked my pursuers' path.

Tears wetting my cheeks and guilt crushing my heart, I grasped the hems of my dress again and ran from the battle, trying not to think about what could happen to my friends. All I could do was keep moving and hope that I could find a place to hide and wait for them to find me.

* * * * *

After what felt like ages, I found my way to the top of a plateau where the ruins of an old stone structure stood. I couldn't hear the battles anymore, my heart heavy with the fear that they were now over with my friends having fallen. Though I also held the hope that I was just too far away to hear them.

My boots crunched the snow as my body tired and I slowed my pace, moving towards the centre of the ruins where the frosty powder was at its thinnest. My legs gave out and I collapsed to my knees, breathing hard as I braced my hands to the floor. Tears blinded me as I tried to fight back the sobs that were relentlessly pulling their way out of my heaving chest.

Why did they make me run?! Why?! Why would they do that?! I didn't want to leave them! Oh gods! Oh gods, please, don't let them be dead! Please!

My shoulders shuddered as I closed my eyes and lowered my face to my arms, clutching at my sleeves in desperate panic. I had never felt so helpless as I did then, not even when I had been sacrificed on that altar to free Ragnarok. All of my training with a sword and bow, all of my conviction, was useless now and I had no way of knowing whether my friends would survive the battle or not. Worst of all, I could do nothing to help them.

How can they just give up their lives to protect me?! That's insane! It's stupid! Oh gods... what do I do?! Please, tell me... what do I do?!

After a few more minutes crouching there in the permafrost, I managed to calm my racing panic and slow my breathing to an easier rate. I sat up slowly, keeping my eyes shut as I breathed in deep, the frosty mountain air refreshing my burning lungs and throat while also chilling my nose. I sniffed away my sobs and felt myself relax. But that relief was short lived.

The crunch of boots on snow made my eyes fly open and my fingers strangle the hilt of the dagger at my side. I scraped the blade back towards me across the stony ground, my body sensing the gathering of figures that were now approaching me without looking.

"Well, well, well," a coldly cruel female voice jeered lowly, "look what we have here. A helpless little human girl... all *alone* in the snow."

I swallowed hard and gathered myself to my feet, my blue and black clothes falling around me to straighten out as I lifted myself from the ground. Clutching the dagger at my right side, I turned slowly around, the wind casting thick strands of my dark auburn hair across my eyes.

Adriana stood there before me, clad in her black and crimson dress. Her heaving, bountiful chest was lifting with her intensely eager breaths, her crimson eyes locking on me from her perfect white face. Her dark hair hung around her cheeks, pulled back by a clasp and left long while also tied into a loose braid, her fangs displayed as she smiled at me. Two vampire men in black armour stood with her, their hungry stares locked on me as their hands hung at their hips, itching to snatch up their weapons.

The three vampires were terrifying enough to behold, but it was their escorts that drove my fear to my knees and made them shake. Black clad Shadow Knights surrounded them, at least eight of them, their cloaks swirling behind their spiked pauldrons, their gauntleted hands calmly resting by their sides. They stared at me with pale white eyes from beneath their hideous helms, the shadows within the masks looking as thick as pitch and seeming alive now that I could see them in clearer sunlight, even if it was masked by the fog that surrounded the ruins.

I took a staggering step backwards as Adriana began to move forward. My chest was heaving under my bodice, my heart pounding so hard I could feel the beat in my neck.

"So," the vampire woman mused, "the rumours are true. You have come back from the dead, girl."

"A-Adriana," I murmured her name, taking another step back.

"Oh, you remember me," she smiled coldly, mocking me with her false kindness. "How wonderful. I had hoped that I had made an impression, Princess. However, it is odd to find you here, all alone and unprotected."

I couldn't bring myself to speak, another haltering step nearly spilling me to the ground, but I managed to save myself. I kept my eyes locked on the vampire's face as she paused, standing a good twelve feet away from me.

"It's not like my son to just abandon you," she mused thoughtfully, her tone still mockingly casual as she studied me with her crimson eyes. "If nothing else, he is a man of great commitment and loyalty."

"Unlike his mother," I mouthed off before I could stop myself. Though it was only a murmur, it certainly gained a reaction.

"You *dare* to assume to know me, girl?" she hissed, her expression severe as she took another purposeful step towards me.

"I know enough," I replied, staggering backwards two more steps, throwing a quick glance over my shoulder to make sure I still had room before locking my stare on her again. "I've met your family..."

"Ah... Have you?" she smirked, her voice hissing the words at the edge of an icy chuckle. "Did Tiernan make me out to be the treacherous vampire queen to you? He so likes to do that."

I shook my head. "No. In fact, we never even discussed you."

"Really?" she pretended to be hurt. "That's upsetting. I had thought I left a mark," she locked her predatory stare on me more firmly. "So, why does my boy not stand at his lover's side?"

I felt as if I could cry, but I managed to hold it back, shaking my head. "We're not lovers... Not anymore."

"Well now, that is a pity," she sighed. "I really wanted to see his expression when I kill you. Again."

My sharp intake of breath made her smirk widen and I shuddered through another step as she drew closer. She was slowly lessening the space between us and the distance I had to the edge of the plateau.

"Yes, Princess," she confirmed. "That *is* why we are here. Lord Morod was most displeased to learn of your resurrection from the Darkest Shadow. Just as It was displeased to be unable to prevent it."

I raised the dagger's point towards her, trying to remain steady, though the shivering of my cold nerves and my terror didn't seem to help me.

"Stay away from me!" I warned her, the fear in my voice making me cringe.

She won't take me seriously if that's how I sound.

Adriana chuckled as she eyed me off. "Oh, come now, girl. You would never use that little blade."

"*Yes, I will,*" I forced myself to sound stronger, trying to hold my conviction.

"You cannot kill," she mewed at me, casting aside her cloak to reveal the two sinister black daggers that she carried on her hips. "You haven't got the stomach for it. You're just a frightened little girl facing a pack of hungry predators."

I felt my whole body tense up at the sight of the gleaming blades, the thought of her taking them up from their sheaths to slash through my skin screaming through my head. I managed to keep my blade steady, tears welling up in my eyes as I looked back to her face.

"And even if you *did* try to use that dagger and *could* kill," she mocked me, letting her hands drop to her sides, "it would do you no good. I could snatch it out of your hand and *shatter* your wrist before you could even inch your arm towards me."

I took another step back, blinking against tears of fear. My hand shook a little as I levelled the blade at her smirking face. My body was trembling relentlessly as she stepped closer again.

"Don't!" I shouted, starting to lose my conviction.

"Let's see how well you do," she mewed, then bared her fangs in a snarl.

I tensed and got ready to fight her, knowing in the back of my mind exactly how this would turn out. Before I could do anything, she became a blur of colour and I was suddenly bent painfully backwards, her right hand around my neck and her left crushing my wrist. I cried out in shock, then in pain as she twisted my arm and eased my body into a deeper incline, my spine feeling like it would snap at any moment. The pain became too much, and my fingers lost their hold on the dagger, dropping it harmlessly to the snowy earth beneath me.

Whimpering, I looked up into her callous red eyes as she stared me down with her fangs showing and hunger on her lips. I tried to struggle, but it hurt so much. She added to the pain with another minor tense of her fingers. I screamed, ceasing my movements, if only to save myself from the pain. She was holding me with the strength of stone, relentlessly stretching my arm out from my body as she squeezed my throat. I grasped at her right wrist with my free hand, futilely trying to pry her hold away from my throat with my fingers.

"See? What did I tell you, girl?" she gloated. "You cannot hope to best a vampire. Not even the largest and strongest of men can. So how could a frightened little slip of a girl like you stand a chance?"

I gasped as she squeezed my throat tighter, tears bleeding from my eyes. "No... Please... Please, don't..."

"The only reason you survived before was because Lord Morod wanted you to," she whispered to me, leaning her face towards mine, "because he had a use for you. Now he just wants you *dead*."

I stared up at her through my tears, trying to move again and crying out as she reminded me of her strength.

"If you think your death before was painful," she hissed down at me, studying my frightened features with her inhuman eyes, "then you cannot begin to fathom what you are about to go through," she smiled evilly at me. "While virgin blood is certainly sweeter than any other, I think I'll just let my boys over there bite and rape you to death. We'll see if you come back from that, though I doubt you'd want to."

I tried to shake my head, tears pouring frantically down my cheeks. "No... No, please..."

"But first," she bared her fangs, sizing up my throat, "I will taste you for myself as I've wanted to since the first day I saw you cowering behind that Wanderer. Oh, and a little warning, Princess..."

I couldn't do anything but meet her gaze as she leaned over me, staring deep into my eyes. The suspense of her threats and her imminent acts of violence was making me feel like I would pass out.

A sinister smirk broke across her lips. "...I'm *really* going to make this hurt."

I closed my eyes as she prepared to bite me, tensing up and waiting for the pain to begin...

"Stop!" a deep tenor voice commanded.

Before I could react, I was suddenly standing upright on my feet, my back now against Adriana's chest as she used me as a human shield. She pinned my right wrist behind my lower back and clutched at my throat with her long, spidery fingers, tilting my head awkwardly so that she could easily bite me. Though the position and sudden movement left me in pain and disoriented, I now found myself facing the speaker with wide eyes.

The Shadow Knights and two vampire men stepped aside as Carden strode into view. He was wearing his deep crimson princely doublet with its wide collar underneath a swirling black pulled across his broad shoulders. He had his belt of throwing daggers around his waist and his sword at his side, though all of the weapons were now the designs of the vampires rather than men.

With great focus in his golden eyes, the Vampire Prince stepped forward, his movements slow and perfectly graceful. He came to a stop about ten feet from where Adriana threatened me, his gaze narrowing as he took in our position.

"Carden," Adriana smirked as she held me tightly before her. "So nice to see you, my boy. And I see that you have finally embraced your vampire blood."

"I have," Carden agreed darkly, glaring at her.

"I suppose you want me to stop throttling your little human?" she asked, squeezing my throat and forcing my arm up my back, drawing out my gasp of pain to illustrate her menace.

"Yes. I do," he growled.

She scoffed. "Do not think for a *moment* that you can prevent me killing her."

"You misunderstand, mother," he turned his eyes towards me, a predatory stare locking onto my fragile and vulnerable shape. "I do not come to stop you from killing her. I come to do it *myself.*"

"What?!" I gasped, then yelped as she throttled me hard against her to shut me up.

"I think I deserve to be the one to rip her open. Don't you?" he questioned his wicked mother coldly, a sinister sneer edging his lips. "I mean, I *am* the one who has suffered the most because of this wretched little girl. I think I have the right to have her for myself."

I glanced between the two of them frantically, my heart racing so hard I thought for sure I would die. I just couldn't believe that he was siding with her, never having imagined that the man I loved and trusted with every part of my being could ever do this to me.

It can't be true! It can't! He can't be doing this! Please, he can't! my thoughts screamed where my voice couldn't as my tears grew cold.

"Well... now *that* would be a *painful* end for her," she sounded so wickedly amused by the idea. "You *do* plan to take your time? Don't you, Carden?"

He smirked as he let his eyes wander the length of my body. "Oh yes. I am going to take her in every intimately painful way I can before I tear her throat out."

"Carden, no..." I shook my head desperately, tears blinding me from seeing his sinister snarl.

"Shut up, girl!" Adriana hissed at me, throttling me briefly again. "It's time for you to die screaming!"

She shoved me towards him, his fingers instantly closing in tight on my arms as I braced my hands against his chest. I was crying now as I imagined the intimate pain he was going to inflict on me, my mind still a screaming mess that insisted none of this was real. *It's a nightmare! It has to be! It has to be, please!*

Carden pulled me close to him, making me feel the strength of his hold and the new hardness of his torso. I looked up at him, sobbing in fear, my chest rushing with frantic breaths of panic.

"Please... please, Carden," I begged him in a sobbing whisper. "Please, don't do this..."

"I am going to enjoy this," he snarled, pulling me right up against his chest and slipping his arm under my left shoulder, his hand clutching my cloak to my back.

Tears kept running from my eyes as my sobs grew more desperate, my chin up on his shoulder as he bared my neck to him. I felt his hot breath as he kissed my throat, squirming just a little before he tightened his hold on me. I whimpered loudly and sobbed in panic as his fangs grazed my soft skin, my fingers crushing around the fabric of his doublet in anticipation of his delving bite. There was no point in begging now, his dark passion against my skin making me certain that he was going to go through with this.

He's going to kill me. The man I love is going to kill me...

"Hm," he sniffed in my scent. "*Beautiful*. I can't tell you how long I've been longing to taste your blood, Leander. I can hardly contain myself now."

I squeezed my eyes shut and tightened my fingers' hold on his clothing as he kissed my throat and leaned his face to my ear.

His whispered words vibrated against my flesh: "Get behind me."

I opened my eyes, frowning in stunned disbelief. But before I could even question the statement he made and the strange change in his voice, there came the whistling of crossbow bolts.

The silver bolts cut through the air and dropped the two vampires who had stood with Adriana, the Shadow Knights drawing their swords as she staggered backwards in shock.

In one fluid movement, Carden unhooked me from his body and pushed me behind him as black armoured and masked Blood Knights suddenly appeared as if they had burst out of thin air. There were only a few of them, maybe four that now surrounded us, but they were not alone. Syrena and Caedmon were suddenly flanking us, both wearing the same armour, their swords at the ready as King Tiernan strode forward to join them. He wore the same armoured chest piece and pauldrons but was otherwise dressed in his kingly crimson robes and cloak, a silver sword in hand.

"You treacherous bastard, Carden!" Adriana seethed, anger in her eyes as she snarled at him.

"There is but *one* traitor here, Adriana," Tiernan declared, standing ahead of us with his sword ready and his golden eyes narrowed on her. "You turned from me and from our vows as eternal mates all to side with the Shadow Lord. That is *unforgiveable*, my beloved."

"Oh, yes," she hissed at him, drawing her twin blades from her sides. "The old guilt trip so artfully wielded by my husband. You are weak, Tiernan. You *and* our children."

"*You're* the weak one!" Syrena was ready to fight, her sword held up in both hands, her raven hair flying behind her shoulders in the winds. "Any mother who turns her daughter and lets men force themselves on her, or who tries to force her son to murder his beloved is not strong enough to be a mother!"

Adriana snarled. "Why do you continue to deny your true natures?!"

"No, mother," Carden shook his head at her as he clutched me close to him. "It is you who denies your true nature."

"I am the only one to embrace it," she insisted.

He scoffed at her. "Then why do you not embrace your elven side? Hm? Or the fiery heritage of your dragon's nature?"

I frowned up at Carden. *Elven side? Dragon's Nature? He makes her - and him and his sister - sound like hybrids...*

"You were only turned by Father," he went on. "He gifted you the legacy of the Vampires, but that is no reason to deny the legacies of your own bloodlines."

"Be silent, whelp!" she snarled viciously, but made no move to attack. "If you are so proud of the dragon blood that mixes with that of the vampire within you, then why not use it? Or do you fear that you will rip her apart if you do?" she made a point to glare at me.

Carden said nothing, his golden eyes intense as he stared her down. I clung to him a little tighter, my heart racing and hurting as I was reminded of the scar that cleaved it.

"I will give you *one* chance, Adriana," Tiernan stated, never blinking as he drew her focus from us. "Surrender now and you need not die for the Shadow Lord's treachery."

"No, Tiernan," she retorted fiercely. "I will not surrender and be your vacuous little queen. Not again. I will instead kill you and both of our children in the name of Lord Morod. But you and that pathetic little human girl that clings to you, my son," she pointed her blade at Carden and I viciously, "I will enjoy making you suffer before killing you both."

Carden pushed me further back, his right hand crossing his hip to his sheathed sword as he got ready to fight.

"Adriana, don't!" Tiernan warned fiercely, flashing his fangs and raising his sword.

"Shadow Knights!" Adriana commanded furiously. "Kill the King and his loyalists! Kill them all! But leave my son and the girl for me!"

The Shadow Knights immediately began striding forward with their swords and shields raised. The vampires launched themselves into battle with superior speed. Metal clanged and slashed as they started fighting, Adriana's two vampires - who had recovered from the silver bolts - running with their swords drawn towards King Tiernan. He engaged them with ease, moving faster than both of them as they started their speeding fight.

"Leander, go!" Carden readied his sword and pushed me towards the ruined archways. "Run!"

I did as he told me, running towards the archways as he leaped between Adriana and me. Their blades clanged and slashed violently, the ferocity of the two vampires battling before me so much faster and aggressive than anything I had seen from human combatants.

"She's not going anywhere!" the woman roared as she fought her son.

I reached the archway and went to pass through only to scream in terror as grasping hands struck out at me from the shadows. A Shade Seeker emerged from the gloom of the arch, its black robed ethereal body floating before me as it turned its glowing blue eyes on me. It shrieked with an elongated jaw, forcing me to try to run in another direction as six more of the ghostly monsters appeared. They were blocking the archways and preventing me from escaping the fight, the way behind me blocked by the vampires and Shadow Knights currently battling to the death across the mountain top. The only thing that saved me from the Shade Seekers was the sunlight, which, though it was streaming through deep mists, seemed enough to deter the ghastly wraiths from leaving the archways.

I pulled myself away from them and looked back to the scene before me as Carden and Adriana flashed from place to place as if by magic. They were moving too swiftly for me to really see them, and I wasn't certain which of them was gaining the upper hand.

Adriana slammed Carden into the ruined wall of the old structure, dropping him momentarily to the ground before turning her gaze to me. She snarled and rushed at me, making me stagger quickly backwards before she was suddenly stopped. Carden had recovered and threw her down to the snowy ground, placing himself between me and her.

"Stay behind me!" he commanded as his mother flashed at inhuman speed to strike at him again, her clothing swirling around her as she twirled her blades.

I got too close to one of the Shade Seekers, its hand grasping at my cloak. I struggled and screamed, trying to get free as it started to drag me towards it. I suddenly remembered how I had beaten them back in Hecturn. *My Pendant!*

I turned myself towards it and allowed the Pendant's stone to face it. As it had before, the Pendant shone bright with purple energy and pushed the Shade Seeker back, burning its skin until it released me. As it shrieked and howled, I recovered from where I had dropped to the ground and ran back to the open space of the plateau. Carden and Adriana were still staying close, both fighting for possession of me.

My foot slipped and I jerked myself away from the cliff's edge in panic, staring at the drop below me. There was nowhere left for me to run now as the vampires were getting the upper hand against the Shadow Knights all around us. I moved away from the edge and watched as Carden fought to protect me, desperately trying to figure out how to help him. Adriana seemed to be overpowering him.

I frantically looked for something to use, spotting the dagger I had dropped lying on the other side of their fight. Without thinking, I threw myself forward and reached for it just as Adriana threw Carden to the ground, my movement gaining her attention.

Just as I grasped the dagger, I felt her grab the back of my neck and drag me up from where I stooped with a violent snarl: "You're not going anywhere, Princess!"

I stabbed at her across my body, managing to get her in the left shoulder. She howled and threw me down, hammering me to the ground painfully. I slowly recovered with a cough, propping myself up on my elbows as she withdrew the dagger with a seethe of anger and pain.

I told her I would use it... the small satisfaction I felt at that thought swiftly vanished as she snarled and turned on me, forcing me to try to drag myself backwards through the snow.

"Leander! No!" I heard Carden shout as his mother stalked me down, glimpsing him turning over from his hard impact with panic in his eyes.

I could only stare at Adriana as she towered over me, bringing her blades up ready to kill me. Then I heard a call on the wind and felt an urging coming from my pendant.

Okay... I can do that... Just hurry! I answered in my mind.

"Time to die, Princess!" Adriana scowled as a shape emerged from the mists.

I put both hands up as I had when I had fought the Revenant, my pendant curling its protective purple energy from its core. It gathered as she swung her blades, and I willed it to thrust forward. The glowing light hit the vampire woman mid-swing, throwing her away from me. She didn't fall, but was cast back from me, her feet skidding in the snow. It was just room enough for what was coming, but I only had a few moments. Adriana recovered and snarled down at me. I stared at her with wide eyes as Carden rushed to his feet.

"Carden, get back!" I shouted, making the woman look towards him.

Carden skidded to a halt, then quickly leaped back as he saw the magenta wings and purple body break through the mists.

Amethyst's roar rocked the plateau as Adriana turned towards her in terror. The Dragon swept over her and opened her jaws wide, her throat coursing brightly with purple and golden flames. I shielded my face with my arm as the jet of fire plunged from Amethyst's roaring maw and engulfed Adriana, the heat erupting through the cold. The woman screamed in terrified agony, dropping her blades and thrashing wildly as my dragon ceased her attack.

Carden moved swiftly then and rushed towards her, his sword cutting up through the misty cold air faster than I could see. There was a sickening slicing crack and Adriana dropped to the snow, her burning head separating from her body with a resounding snap and a dull thud...

Epilogue
A Prince's Proposition

Carden turned from the flames that consumed Adriana, his golden eyes looking haunted, yet also relieved. I couldn't begin to imagine what thoughts were going through his head as I watched him from where I still lay, only knowing that the decision he had made couldn't have been easy. He sheathed his sword as the fighting started to die down. Amethyst had turned on the Shade Seekers with her flames and forced them to disappear back into the shadows of the archways, freeing us from their attacks. He came to me as the Dragon ended the fight and crouched down, drawing my tense expression as I slid back a little farther.

"Are you okay, Leander?" he asked with genuine concern. "She didn't hurt you too badly, did she?"

I shook my head, breathing in slow, deep breaths. "N-no... No, she didn't."

He reached forward and pulled me to his chest, holding me close to him. He was on the verge of tears. I could feel his heart racing inside him.

"I'm sorry!" he apologised furiously, cradling me to him. "Oh, Leander, I am so, so sorry! I didn't mean the things that I said to you! I didn't!"

"You didn't?" I asked in a murmur, my heart thudding heavily as he looked down at me.

He shook his head. "No. I was just afraid I would hurt you. I was a fool to do that. Even my father says so. That's why I came after you. But when I saw what was happening here, I had to act."

"I really thought you were going to kill me," I admitted, trembling as my tears slid down my cheeks.

"I'm sorry," he sighed, wiping my tears away with his thumb. "It was the only thing I could think to do to get you away from her."

I just hugged into him, burying my face into his neck. "I'm so glad you came for me, Carden. I really am."

He cuddled me for a few moments, the two of us sobbing. All the shared hurt was obvious now and I could see how much it had tortured him to send me away. It must have been agony for him to do it, but at least it was good to know that he truly still loved me.

"Can you stand?" he asked me after a few moments, looking into my eyes with his topaz stare.

I nodded. "Yes. Yes, I can."

"Come on," he lifted me to my feet, steadying me, snow and dirt sticking to my cloak from my fall. "We need to get you back to the castle."

"What about the others?" I asked, afraid of what the answer would be.

"Your companions live," King Tiernan said as he approached us, sheathing his sword at his side. "My forces arrived to aid them shortly before we found you, Princess."

I nodded, glad to hear it. But before I could say anything, I caught a flash of movement coming up a path opposite the one I had followed to reach the plateau. Fawkner, Tallinn and Joran jogged into view, their eyes taking in the scene before them as the vampires stood victorious over the Shadow Knights, whose bodies were now turning to ash as they faded away.

"Leander!" Fawkner called, both he and Tallinn rushing to where I stood with the Valerian men.

"Fawkner, Tallinn!" I couldn't contain my relief, hugging them both in turn. "I'm so glad you're alive!"

"We're glad you are too," Tallinn agreed, hugging me, then looking to Carden. "Carden...?"

"Hello, Tallinn," he said quietly, a sheepish expression on his face.

She smirked and shook her head. "I knew you wouldn't really leave her."

He just smiled and nodded, pulling his arm around my shoulders as I rested my hands on his chest. My eyes were now on the King as he stood over the burning remains of his wife, his daughter joining him.

"King Tiernan," I murmured with sympathy and regret, "I'm so sorry about Adriana."

"Do not be, child," he responded grimly, looking towards me solemnly out of the corner of his eye. "My wife died a long time ago at the hands of the Shadow Lord when he corrupted her with his dark essence. This," he gestured with one hand to the flames, "is a kindness for her compared to that."

"It really is," Syrena agreed as Caedmon came to her side, wrapping his arms around her.

"Come," Tiernan said, tearing himself away from the flames. "Let us return to Castle Valkirak. It seems that we have much to discuss now that the Shadow Dominion has made such an obvious incursion upon our domain."

"As you command, Sire," Fawkner nodded, starting after him.

I looked up at Carden, gaining his soft, but hurting smile. The two of us spent a moment longer to pay our respects to his mother as Amethyst moved to join us. We left the plateau then with the others surrounding us, making our way back down the sloping paths to where the main battle had occurred, and where the rest of my companions were, thankfully, still alive.

* * * * *

I was sore from having fought with Adriana, but the next few days proved to be helpful as I rested and recovered within the safety of Castle Valkirak. Two days of sleep had done me good, and I had spent the third day with my friends trying to relax now that we had a safe place to stay.

The sun was setting as I went to the balcony of natural stone that overlooked the castle's gardens and allowed access to where the Dragons were staying in the caves. Though the balcony was stark and grey with snowy tints powdering its structure, I still found it a peaceful place. It was basically just a courtyard full of nightshade, death-bells, belladonnas and blood roses, but it was very well kept and as beautiful as any of the gardens in Castle Arvon.

I sat down on the wooden bench before the ornate barrier, my hands in my lap as I watched the sunset with a distant stare. I didn't feel the cold there, the balcony well-guarded from the chill by large braziers. I had chosen not to wear my cloak given that I had only stepped out there to take a break from the lengthy discussions going on within the keep. The thought of returning to High-Realm was admittedly difficult for me at that moment, especially knowing that the second I set foot on the shore of any of the seven nations I would have assassins after me. Morod seemed to want me dead even more now that I had been resurrected from his first murder; something that stung me like the scar that tainted my otherwise unblemished sternum.

Just thinking about it made the scar ache and my left hand pressed to my bodice where it lay hidden beneath my clothes. *It's something else I'll always have to live with now because of him. I just hope it won't always hurt.*

I heard the door open behind me, turning as footsteps approached. My heart warmed at seeing Carden, his body clad in a knee length, short sleeved crimson doublet with silver details, a black shirt worn under it. He had left the collars open just like he always did when dressed as a Guardian in the past, exposing his athletic chest just a little.

"I had a feeling I'd find you sitting out here," he said, joining me as Amethyst lifted her head from where she lay in the gardens, watching us with her glowing orange eyes.

I shrugged, turning my gaze back to the sunset. "I just wanted to get away from all the war plans and tactical discussions going on in there."

He sighed painfully and sat down on the bench beside me, leaning his elbows on his knees as he clasped his hands together. "Yes... Ranzel, Fawkner and my father certainly seem determined to devise some kind of a strategy for confronting Morod."

I nodded softly, looking down at my hands in my lap. "I just couldn't sit there listening to them talk about it anymore. Especially since it's all about how I'm supposed to be the one to defeat Morod."

I noted his frown as he watched me, feeling my nerves heighten as a cold wind caught on my skin.

"I've spent my whole life trying to avoid being like the Great Heroine of legend," I mused glumly, studying the nuances of my hands, "but it turns out all this time that I *am* the Great Heroine, *not* her descendant," I shook my head in bewilderment. "I can't even find the words to describe how that feels."

"I don't think you have to," Carden said softly, my eyes lifting to his as he spoke. "I think you should just take all of this one day at a time and worry about what *you* need for the moment rather than what the world requires of you."

"You make it sound so simple," I observed with a mild chuckle.

"I know it isn't," he admitted, turning his eyes out towards the sunset again, "but sometimes what you need is to just be human."

"Good advice," I murmured, watching him.

He turned and smiled at me, that same handsomely roguish grin that I adored returning. "I speak from experience."

We were quiet for a moment, then the question I longed to ask pushed its way out of my mind. "Why didn't you tell me the truth about who you are when we first met?" I looked down at my hands for a moment before turning my gaze back to his alabaster face.

He let out a slow sigh, staring at the floor at his feet as he considered my question. He nodded subtly as he mused, the wind flicking lightly at his black hair while it pushed my free-flowing sternum length auburn locks away from my face.

"I spent much of my life running from who and what I am, Leander," he explained evenly, "living with the knowledge that my adulthood meant becoming a full-fledged blood kindred. People fear the Vampire Lords of Valloran after what happened during the War of the Shadow. I have seen that fear everywhere in people whenever the mere mention of vampirism is heard while I travelled. And so, I joined the Guardians in the hope that maybe I could do some good."

"That's a noble sentiment," I said softly, keeping my eyes on his.

"Well, I had to do something worthwhile in my life," he responded gently, staring now at the golden and orange hues of the sunset. "You saw what became of my mother. I swore that I would never be as bad as her and that I wouldn't be as domineering as my father," he half laughed thoughtfully. "Funny. Since my return, he seems like the man he was in my youth. It is good to see."

I nodded, looking back to my knees as I twisted my hands together uncertainly. I had a question to ask, but I was afraid to upset him, not because he was a vampire and could easily snap me in two, but because I didn't want him to leave again. His absence had been too hard to endure for me to have to face it a second time.

I drew in a shaking breath and asked: "So... you lied about who you were because you were afraid?"

He nodded, looking to me. "At first I was afraid of what people would do if they knew that a vampire was trying to help them. There aren't many humans who like the idea of our kind wandering close to their homes, let alone being the defenders of the innocent."

"Yet, that seems to be what your family does here in Valloran," I pointed out, still looking at my dress.

"That's true and it's also why the Guardians accept vampires into their order," he explained. He touched two cold fingers to my chin and lifted my face to look into my eyes, his golden ones full of longing and desperate hope. "But when I met you, the thought that you would be afraid of me was no longer my greatest fear. Somehow, I knew you wouldn't be."

"Then what were you afraid of?" I asked softly.

He stroked my cheek, brushing my hair from my eyes lovingly. "That I would never be allowed to know you or be by your side."

"You thought being a vampire would deny you that?" I half smiled at the silliness of the idea. "Really?"

"No. Not being a vampire," he replied.

"Then what?" I frowned.

"Being a prince," he answered honestly.

I felt my eyebrows raise as he said that; the words surprising me. "You think I wouldn't have wanted to know you as a prince?"

He shrugged lightly. "I know it was a foolish thing to think. But I saw how you reacted to men like Tibain Seward, and I heard you say how you don't like someone who thinks he can do whatever he pleases because of his title," he stood and moved to the barrier, placing his hands there as he gazed out at the view before us. "I thought about telling you the truth so many times, especially after we shared our first kiss in the Ivory Leaf Grove. I wanted to alleviate your fears about us being kept apart because of our stations in society, to let you know that there wouldn't be any problems because of all of that."

"Why didn't you then?" I asked softly.

He sighed and shook his head. "Because it was at that moment that being a vampire would have been worse than being a noble."

I chewed my bottom lip in thought, getting to my feet and moving to stand by his side. I reached out one hand and touched his cheek, feeling the freshly shaved stubble against my fingertips as I made him look at me. I had to tilt my head up or I would have been staring into his throat. His height seemed to have grown since he had changed, though I thought it was more likely about my body still recovering from being dead. Or perhaps I'd shrunk.

"None of that would have mattered to me," I told him honestly, drawing a breath and exhaling it slowly as I felt my heart yearn me on. "Being with you is all I want, and I am so glad that I found you at all. To me, you're not a Prince, a

Vampire, or a Guardian. To me, you're Carden Valerian, the man I love, the man I want to spend the rest of my life with," I let my eyes and hand drop as I thought about that confession and of what had been done to me since my eighteenth year had started. "Considering that the rest of my life is now eternal, I think that says a lot."

Carden thought about my words for a few moments, his hand going to his pants' pocket beneath the folds of his long doublet. He wore an expression of deep consideration, like he was trying to decide whether to do something or not. Finally, he turned his golden eyes towards me with a serious and hopeful light to them.

"Do you really mean that?" he asked.

I lifted my eyes to him, nodding softly. "Yes. I want to be with you forever. I'm in love with you."

He nodded, looking down as he withdrew something from his pocket, holding it in his hands for a few moments.

"If that is what you want," he said as he considered the thing that he held hidden in his fingers, "what you *truly* want, then it should be done right."

Done right? I frowned, studying him in confused curiosity. *What is he talking about?*

"All right," I said carefully, raising an eyebrow at him.

"I... I have a proposition to make," he said solemnly, locking his gaze on mine, his velvety voice tugging at my curiosity even more with each word he spoke. "A proposition I have been considering making ever since we were reunited in Silvervale."

"What kind of proposition?" I asked in a small voice, holding my hands together against my midriff and fingering the cord lacing my bodice.

My heart began to race as he lowered himself to one knee, my chest heaving slightly as I stared at him. I didn't know what he was doing, my mind suddenly blank to all reasoning. I could only watch him as he gazed at his hands one more time, then looked back to me. He lifted his left hand with a small box held out, a silvery Elvish ring set into the velvet folds within.

My right hand lifted to my lips as I gasped, my mind numb as I saw the ring, knowing without conscious thought what it was. A tremble started to work its way through my body, and I felt my knees weaken, afraid that I would collapse and ruin the moment. I managed not to, my body forcing me to stay standing under the command of my heart.

"Leander Idona Aldrich," he proposed with all the deepest sincerity I had ever heard leave his lips, his eyes set on mine, "will you do me the great honour of sharing our eternal lives together as companions and soul mates?" then he added with an even deeper yearning: "Will you marry me?"

I felt my heart flutter as tears pushed their way into my eyes with happiness and surprise for the first time in ages.

"Yes, Carden," I whispered, smiling softly and nodding. "Yes, I *will* marry you."

He smiled, carefully lifted the ring from the box and took my left hand as I tried not to lose myself in the joy. He delicately slid the ring onto my third finger, trying to touch it as little as he could, setting its jewels perfectly upwards and the arrow shape aiming towards my fingertip. He then held my hand in his and kissed it before getting back to his feet and pulling me close.

I let him hold me as I looked down at the ring on my hand, a feeling of complete and perfect happiness I had never known filling me. I was betrothed to my Guardian... my Prince... no, my Soul Mate. This was the first meaningful moment of life as a normal girl that had been given back to me after all the terrible things I had suffered over the last four years.

Carden tilted my head with two fingers to my chin, smiling lovingly down at me. I felt my heart grow warmer and skip a beat as I looked into his eyes, knowing that this was right.

"I love you, Leander," he said softly.

"I love you too," I replied, smiling. "Always and forever."

He nodded and smiled: "Always and forever."

And in the fading light of the sunset as he leaned his face down to mine, I didn't feel afraid or worried about the darkness that had overtaken the world. As he pulled me close with his hands to my hips and mine to his chest, I didn't think about what was still to come. I didn't think of what had been lost, of the Shadow Lord and the dark dragons terrorising High-Realm, or the knowledge that I would have to return to Aldegaad to free my beleaguered people from my treasonous uncle. At that moment there was only one thing that mattered to me. And as our eyes fell shut with the gentle caressing of our first betrothed kiss, I could feel the strength of the love in our hearts growing stronger.

I reached my arms up around Carden's shoulders as he let one hand brace to my shoulder blades, deepening this kiss in the glorious sunset. Nothing else existed in that moment of pure bliss except us.

No matter how brief these moments would be I would embrace them and hold them as close to my heart just as I held my intended to my body in that kiss. Our future together and our destiny was set. And no matter what challenges came our way, we would endure them together, our love the power that gave us the strength we would always need...

The Story Continues in Book 5...

Pendant of Dragons
Defenders of Therras

Excerpt from Defenders of Therras

Something caught my eye as I lifted my gaze. It was a flicker of silvery-green in the water. I frowned, wondering what it was. It was probably just some plant drifting by. But a familiar, oceanic feeling came over me and a tugging like a mental undertow filled my mind.

The thing moved again, and I glimpsed fins breaking the water. A mermaid! I don't really remember much from the moment I saw her in the waters to the seconds that led to me opening the northern cliff door and making my way down to the castle dock. I was soon standing at the water's edge with no light to see by. So I focused, held my hands to my neck and conjured the purple glow of my pendant's stone. The purple light gave an eerie sort of appearance to the riverside and the castle base in that thick as pitch darkness. Everything seemed surreal and a little frightening, which was only enhanced when I caught movement in the waters.

At first it was the eyes I saw, their colours forgotten in the purple illumination, the whites standing out and reflecting back at me. Then, I took in the rest of her face as the figure lifted up to float in the waters, the surface just hiding her breasts.

"Queen Aegaea," I was stunned, but glad to see her. I dropped to my knees at the dock's edge as she swam nearer. "What are you doing here? I thought merfolk lived in the seas."

"Some of us do, like we of Merrow blood," she confirmed, her voice so sweet and melodious, her red hair seeming to have a life of its own despite hanging soaked around her shoulders. "But where there is water to swim, we can travel; rivers and estuaries become our roads inland. As for why I am here, I have come to help you find what you seek, Leander."

"You knew I'd need help finding it?" I asked, my palms pressing to the stone dock.

"My dear girl, I am what is known as a sea-witch. A calling I share with humans and sea elves of the same title who hold such a deep magical love of the oceans," she explained. "And my daughter gave you her aquamarine," she indicated the bracelet on my wrist. "She sensed your angst as if it were her own, and I used my magicks to ascertain the cause. Such a strange connection you share with her..."

"Rinnaria isn't with you?" I was half-hoping to see my sea-twin emerge by her mother's side.

Queen Aegaea shook her head. "No. Her father was reluctant to allow me to come up the River Arvon as it was. He worries that we might be set upon by oceanic dangers that rival your land-bound ones, like the Abominations."

"Abominations?" I raised a worrisome eyebrow.

"Twisted creatures," she explained grimly, "resembling merfolk, and yet... monstrous..."

"I see," I bit my lip, nodding. "What help can you offer me, your Majesty?"

"The chamber to the secret of Arvon has two entrances," she explained, bobbing in the water as her tail swept beneath the surface, making her body sway and shift with natural grace. "The entrance by land was blocked when Castle Arvon was attacked and clearing your way through will cost you far too much time. But the entrance by water is yet open and clear to you."

"The entrance by water?" I questioned. "So, there's a secret passage under the castle in the river?" I raised an eyebrow at her. "How is it that you know about this?"

"Because I helped Leander the First construct the chamber and added my magic to hers when we sealed it," she replied.

"How do I get to it?"

"Your pendant can allow you to take on our form, as you did in the open ocean with my daughter," she instructed me. "It was your ancestor's design that only merfolk could enter via the watery passages, but we cannot climb on legs from the waters as we did in days of old. So, only the holder of her pendant possessing the Mer-heritage in her blood could find the way through."

"All right," I nodded. "What do I do?"

"First, undress and enter the waters," Queen Aegaea instructed me, then added: "I promise that you are in no danger. I will protect you as if you were my own daughter. Though, that is easy for me, given your shared likeness."

Standing up, I slipped my boots off, then untied my cloak and bodice. Fabric fell in piles around me until I wore nothing, my body exposed to the air. I slid from the dock into the river, gasping at the chill that pervaded my vulnerable, naked skin. I instantly began treading water and tilted my head up to breathe.

"You are a strong swimmer," the mermaid applauded me softly. "The Blood of the Merrow truly does flow in your veins. Now, concentrate on spreading your pendant's energy around your body and taking on your mer-form."

"This water's freezing," I griped, shivering as I closed my eyes and focused.

"You won't feel it in a minute," she assured me.

Pushing the icy feeling on my skin out of my mind, I focused, imagining that my legs were a tail like that of a fish or a porpoise. I started visualising the mermaids and their movements. My mind presented Rinnaria to me and how she had looked in that first moment when I had seen her. I studied how her tail and hips moved, my own hips beginning to imitate the swaying swishes hers made. I imagined that I was her. Then, I felt warmth fill me, my legs begin to move as one, my toes stretch and thin, and the chill of the water leave me. Opening my eyes and laying back in the water, I examined my new shimmering purple tail. I was in awe that I had actually succeeded.

"This is... I don't have words," I confessed.

Queen Aegaea smiled. "As I said, you carry the Blood of the Merrow within you, Leander. Just as your ancestor did before you. Now, follow me," she dived into the waters, her tail flicking with silvery greens and blues in its scales and fins.

Following her lead and imitating her movements, I leaped up from the water with ease, momentarily exposing my naked body and purple scaled tail before plunging face first into the river again. Amazingly, I could see as if the light of my pendant were illuminating the sky above, not just the riverbed. Then I noticed something odd. A sensation between my eyes that felt like breathing.
Breathing in my forehead? I dabbed my fingers to my brow but felt nothing unusual. Huh... Strange. But this feels amazing and so freeing... so... natural. I could get used to this. I've never felt so graceful and... well... free... Maybe I was born a mermaid in another life... I actually smiled, enjoying how it felt to have fins instead of feet.

"Leander," Queen Aegaea's voice was as clear in the water as it was in the air, but it seemed stronger somehow, amplified by the river. Her perfect red lips moved with each word so naturally in the river's body as they would on land. "I know you're enjoying the experience of being a mermaid, dear, but we must focus."

"Right. Of course," I nodded, still astonished that I could speak underwater. "Which way?"

"Here," Queen Aegaea turned with a sweep of her silvery-blue tail, her red locks trailing behind her. They seemed as if they were swimming with her like extra fins, though more languid than her tail and webbed hands.
She dived towards the riverbed at an angle, her translucent tailfins guiding her like a dolphin's. I swept after her, staying close to her side.

Once again, awe washed over me as I saw the muddy riverbed, the shimmering black and white river stones, and the swaying green plants that streamed up from the soggy earth. There were even little blue periwinkles and minnows swimming about, the tiny fish undisturbed by the presence of a pair of mermaids. The large trout that passed us, however, made them scatter.

A cave came into view as my pendant's light shone over its entrance, its depths darker than the sky above the river. It made me hesitate, but Queen Aegaea simply took me by one wrist and guided me forward. The two of us delved deeper and deeper in moments, the way getting darker. Still, I could see my way, both my pendant and my eyes showing me the path with an ease I'd never find on land.

This is incredible magic, I considered as I followed the Mer-Queen along the narrow, twisting passages of underwater natural rock. My eyes should be hurting, but I can see as well as I do in the air...

A bluish light suddenly appeared before me, but I didn't feel the need to squint. My eyes were perfectly adapted to everything. Queen Aegaea produced a crystal in one hand that glowed a soft ocean blue and illuminated the way, adding to my pendant's own light.

"It gets much harder to see ahead," she warned me, sweeping left into another passage.

Moving with an ease I never imagined I could, I swam after her, my magically constructed tail feeling so limber and flexible compared to my normal legs.

Soon, we came to the heart of Castle Arvon's depths, the two of us bobbing up through the water's surface and into an underground cavern. I ran my hands over my head, smoothing down my drenched auburn hair as I felt the air on my bare skin anew.

"Wow..." I gasped, staring at the chamber we came to find ourselves in.
The cavern was filled with crystals that glittered like a trillion stars in the night, the lights we carried dancing in their sheens like faeries at Litha. I had never seen anything like it.

"This place is incredible," I said as I gazed at it all, settling on a platform in the centre.

The edge of the platform was raised and had a small number of steps that reached up to the central dais. That was where something glimmered gold in the hands of a statue of white stone. Queen Aegaea's hands pressed on my shoulders, and she urged me: "Only you can take your ancestor's treasure. Go on, sweetheart." She was almost motherly.

"Are there any traps?" I asked, looking through my wet auburn locks over my shoulder at her.

She shook her red-haired head, her crown of coral gleaming. "This place was built by the merfolk. We don't make traps. Especially not when the only person who can open the case is the holder of the Amethian Pendant and descendant of she who commissioned this chamber."

"Okay," I let out a long, slow breath, then climbed up onto the stone platform, using my arms to pull me from the water. My pendant released my form back to human with a snap and a hiss of purple magic and returned me my legs in a mere instant.

Aww... I was disappointed to shift from mermaid to human again. I feel as if I'm missing a part of myself now... I pushed that away and focused.

Getting to my feet while feeling the need to cover my nudity with my arms, I started up the steps towards the statue. It was at that moment that I recognised what it depicted. There was a beautiful, bare breasted mermaid with flowing hair and a graceful tail seated on a large stone slab, her hands up before her chest with something held in them. Behind her was an immense dragon with very feminine and stunningly gorgeous features. The dragon was encircling the mermaid, protecting her with her wings. There were other statues surrounding the chamber's walls, as if they were sentinels guarding the treasured secret. The six in total were of what looked like athletic and muscular men whose bodies were covered in scales and plates. Their feet were angled, their hands were clawed, and they sported both a tail as long as their bodies and great dragon wings.

I've never seen such dragon-like men before. Who are they? I wondered as I gazed at them. I turned back to the central statue as I finally drew near enough to see full details.

"Ankorect and Isnari..." I realised, studying the two goddesses' combined statues.

Reverent and not so confident - given my lack of clothing - I approached the statues, wrapping my arms around my now toned waist; four years on the run had some benefits at least. My gaze fell to the object in Isnari's hands, drawing a puzzled frown across my brow. She held a kind of case that looked like crystal, a golden cylinder about thirty centimetres long resting on a cushion of white velvet within. Studying the case for a few moments, I found a kind of keyhole, but it was made of crystal and was so magical that I could feel it humming.

"I wonder..." I slipped my pendant from my neck and pressed it front-ways to the hole. "Open..." I whispered, knowing well enough now how my necklace worked.

The Pendant's stone glowed purple, the shimmering light beaming out of the crystal lock. There was a click and the case opened on its own as the magic holding it released.

Setting my pendant around my neck again, I hesitantly reached out and lifted the golden cylinder in both hands. It was ornate, engrained with carvings of dragons, the strange dragon-men and mermaids. There was a definite theme apparent in my ancestor's designs. A cap was set on one end, which I carefully unscrewed to reveal the contents. I tugged loose a rolled-up scroll of paper, gingerly setting the cylinder down so that I could examine it.

"Oh, my gods..." I smiled softly with quiet excitement as I unfurled the paper, studying the shapes and lines on its rough and tanned skin. "This is it."
"You have your answer," Queen Aegaea called, gaining my quick look over my shoulder.
I nodded, gazing back down at the paper in my hands. "My ancestor's map," I murmured. "This shows us the path to the Valley of Dragons... and the Sword of Light..."

Other titles by K. Isabella Frost

Pendant of Dragons: The Aldrich Legacy (Book 1)
Pendant of Dragons: Custodians of the Past (Book 2)
Pendant of Dragons: The End of All Things (Book 3)

Visit whitelightuniversal.com.au

White Light
PUBLISHING